MW00628987

EMPTY HORIZON

BENJAMIN ASHWOOD BOOK 4

AC COBBLE

Cobble Publishing LLC

EMPTY HORIZON TEXT COPYRIGHT © 2017 AC COBBLE
ALL RIGHTS RESERVED
ISBN: 9781947683037
ASIN: B01MSLXCZZ
Cobble Publishing LLC
Sugar Land, TX

CONTENTS

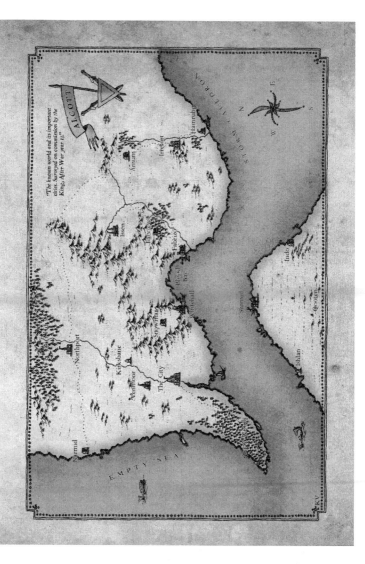

ALCOTT

"The known world and its important cities. Surveyed on commission by the King, After War year 13."

1

INDO

"It's possible we may not all survive this," stated Ben.

"You might not," Corinne snorted. "I certainly intend to."

The huntress was squatting on her haunches, swaying with the gentle motion of the ship. She hovered over their assembled collection of weapons. They'd laid them out to take stock and make the best use of the resources they had available. She laid a finger on the rusty tines of a trident.

"You sure you want to use this?" she asked, looking to Milo.

The young man's loose curls flapped in the sea-breeze as he nodded. "I have the least amount of weapons training. It makes sense that I get the worst of the lot. Besides, we don't have any other options, do we?"

"He's right. We don't have much choice," Rhys reminded Corinne.

She glanced around the companions, scooped up her two hand axes, then paused, as if ready to take her bow as well, but it had been lost in the escape from Hamruhg.

"Sorry, Milo," she offered. "Maybe you won't need to use it."

None of them believed that.

Rhys gathered his longsword. In the bright light of day, the silvery runes were muted like Rhys himself after the battle of Northport. The rogue had regained his sense of humor, but he didn't move with the same lethal aggressiveness he had before. He'd aged a decade and a half in that fight. Not even being long-lived could bring his vigor back.

Rhys toed the vambrace he'd taken off the dead Thin Blade in Irrefort. Ben recalled the tight burst of fireballs the device had shot at Rhys when they were ambushed on the way to the keep. Everything after that had been so crazy he'd forgotten Rhys took the weapon.

"This thing needs a bit of mage training to operate," advised the rogue. He looked between Amelie and Milo.

Milo shook his head.

Amelie knelt and grabbed the vambrace. She strapped it on her arm and grunted. "I can feel the heat."

"Be careful with that," advised Rhys. "Don't forget we're on a ship made entirely out of wood. I'd hate to start swimming because you couldn't wait to try out your new toy."

Amelie rolled her eyes at him.

"It may not be much more useful on land," added the rogue. "Any magic could draw Eldred right to us, and you have a history of giving yourself away with fireballs."

"You think I forgot?" chided Amelie.

She picked up her rapier as well. The mage-wrought dagger she used with it had been lost in Hamruhg, buried in Eldred's stomach. The rapier was serviceable, though, and she slid it into her sheath with confidence that she didn't have when Ben first met her.

Milo took the salt-stained trident they'd purchased off one of the sailors and hefted it, a slight grin lifting the corner of his lips. The only other option had been a club the cook used for braining rats. They all agreed the cook could keep his club.

Ben picked up his longsword last. He tilted it and studied the bright sunlight reflecting along the silver blade. The cross-guard was of the same silver material, forged by a mage to be lighter and stronger than even Venmoor steel. It was shaped like a tree, the branches of the cross-guard growing out from the trunk of the blade. The branches were delicate and beautifully formed, but they were strong enough to stop any conventional blade. Ben had found ample opportunities to test that since he'd acquired the weapon.

The wire-wrapped hilt felt comfortable in his hand, and even in the steamy humidity from the sea, he knew his grip wouldn't slip. Holding it felt natural now, like the mage-wrought steel was an extension of his arm. On the pommel, the longsword was capped with a polished sphere of curiously striated wood. When he'd first found the blade in the Wilds, he hadn't recognized the strange material. Now he knew, it was anima-wood.

"That's a fine weapon," remarked Milo, leaning close to Ben and studying the sword.

"Care to try it?" asked Ben.

Milo shook his head. "I'd be liable to chop my foot off if I handled such a sharp blade. You found it in an abandoned lair of the Purple, did you say?"

Ben shrugged. "We think so. There wasn't much left in the place to identify the owners. There were some writings, though, the stuff Towaal mentioned back at the Hangman's Noose. It seemed like it could have been the Purple's. Did the Librarian tell you anything about the place, an abandoned outpost in the Wilds?"

Milo shook his head. "If you have time this evening, I'd love to hear more about what you found. Maybe I'll recognize something."

"Milo!" interrupted Towaal. She was stalking across the deck, the only one of the companions who hadn't selected a weapon from the pile. She didn't need one. "Show me what you can do."

Milo's gaze dipped to the trident he was holding.

"Not with that," grumbled Towaal. "With your will."

Milo blushed. "I can't really do much with that either. Certainly not combat. The little bit of light I made at the inn is the extent of it."

"Surely, you can do more than that," challenged Towaal. "The Librarian was the most powerful mage I've ever encountered. He must have taught you something you can use. Come. We'll go behind the galley where the sailors can't see us."

The pair vanished around the corner, Towaal practically dragging the timid young man.

"He's not good at much, is he?" asked Amelie, looping an arm under Ben's.

He paused before answering, "He was an apprentice to the last living member of the Purple in Alcott. He somehow made it out of Northport in the heat of the battle with the demons, and he survived Rettor and the council in Irrefort. No one is that lucky."

BEN TOSSED the skin of a bright green fruit into the wake of the merchant sloop and watched it disappear under the churning dark waters. It was the same fruit he'd tried for the first time in the City so long ago. It seemed like a different life then, like he was a different person.

The moonlight sparkled across the choppy water, nature's own fireworks show. Ben tilted the mug in his hands and looked into it. The moonlight didn't reach the bottom of the cup, giving the liquid a sinister aspect.

Behind them, the darkness in the cup was mirrored by a wall of black that was slowly swallowing the stars. A summer storm was quickly gaining on their vessel. Ben couldn't help but think it was a metaphor for the last several months. The battle with the demons in Northport, the flight from Eldred. It seemed no matter what they did, the darkness was always behind them, always threatening to catch up.

He sighed and tried to relax. According to the sailors, they were in for a rough night, but now, the sea was calm and peaceful.

Beside him, Amelie sipped her mug and pulled a face.

"You're certain we need to drink this?" she asked, lips puckered at the sour liquid.

"The sailors say we do," replied Ben.

He took a sip from his mug and winced at the burn. Lime and grog wasn't much of a drink, but apparently, it kept away a certain kind of sickness that sailors were prone to. Something to do with their diet while at sea. He'd doubted them at first, but night after night, they faithfully put down a mug of the foul-tasting concoction.

"The cook told me it gets better after the first one," offered Ben.

Amelie snorted. "That's because he gets drunk after the first one."

She tilted up her mug and gulped it down, evidently deciding that quick and painful was better than slow and painful. She shivered, coughed, and set the mug down on the weather-beaten planks of the deck.

Ben grimaced and followed her lead, quaffing the grog and trying to ignore the sting in his eyes and the burn in his throat.

Amelie laid her head on his shoulder and scooted closer to him.

"Just three more days until we'll make land," she said.

"I'm ready," remarked Ben. "I feel like this boat is getting smaller every day. There's nowhere to stretch out and nowhere to be alone. In the crew quarters, there is always someone. The watch is always on deck. Even in the cargo hold, they've bunked the ship's boys to make room for us."

"And if you had somewhere to be all alone, would you want to be?" asked Amelie, looking up at him. Her eyes sparkled in the moonlight.

Ben grinned down at her. "Well, maybe not completely alone."
He bent to meet her lips.

"Three more days," she mumbled a long time later, face buried
in his neck. "Just three more days, then we can be alone."

THE TOWN of Indo sat peacefully in the late afternoon sun. Steep,
verdant green hills spread out behind it. The town snuggled
below on a wide stretch of sandy beach. A roughly constructed
stone pier jutted from land into the calm waters of the South Sea.

Ben shook and squeezed his hands, trying to lose an incessant
tingling sensation.

Amelie, standing beside him, gripped her hands together too.
"It feels like I've been sitting on my hands and feet for hours," she
complained.

"Your hands have fallen asleep. That is what we called it in
Farview," said Ben.

Amelie's eyebrows knitted. "Because it happens when you fall
asleep?"

Ben shrugged.

"I suppose it's a minor inconvenience, and it should be gone
within a few days," continued Amelie. "At least, that's what
Towaal claimed. If it works, it will be worth it."

"Every day, every bell, every heartbeat we can steal an extra
step on Eldred is worth gold," Ben agreed. "It's worth it."

He glanced at the sky above them, clear blue with a few puffy
white clouds in the distance, leftovers from the storm the
previous night. He couldn't see it, but somehow, one hundred
paces above them, Lady Towaal was altering the spectrum of
light that reflected off their ship and the water. She assured them
that to anyone far-seeing from above her barrier, it would appear
they were just a stretch of empty sea.

They hoped the light shield and the subtle alteration of their blood chemistry that Towaal had conducted during the storm would foul Eldred's attempts to track them. It should work, in theory, but Towaal had never done it herself.

Three weeks prior, when they'd used the thought meld to contact Jasper, he'd given Towaal advice on how to avoid detection. He'd been hiding from the Sanctuary for centuries and had developed a full bag of tricks to stay hidden. By altering their blood, Eldred wouldn't be able to track them using any samples she'd collected in Hamruhg. Shifting the spectrum of light above them would prevent her from using far-seeing to locate them on the open sea.

The problem had been that when they first spoke to Jasper, Eldred already knew their course. Even a novice hunter would be able to extrapolate from it. They'd been headed directly for the port of Shamiil, the largest port in Ooswam. It was the closest major port to Hamruhg and provided the best roads and most direct route to Qooten. It was a natural choice. Almost all travelers to the South Continent berthed there.

Three days out from Shamiil, the storm had brought opportunity. As soon as Towaal saw the thunderclouds bearing down on them, she'd prepared to shift their blood. When it hit, the powerful wind had blown them nearly fifty leagues away. The black clouds and sheeting rain would have obscured any of Eldred's attempts at far-seeing. When the rain stopped and the clouds rolled away, their blood had been chemically altered, and the light shield was in place.

Ben looked to the mage and saw her with her eyes closed, rocking gently on the bridge of the ship, head bobbing with the motion of the vessel. She'd gone a day and a half now with no sleep, remaining vigilant to hold the light shield. Ben hoped she could make it just a few more bells. If she fell asleep, the shield would falter. If Eldred happened to be scanning the area they were in, the dark mage would be back on their trail.

"She'll make it," assured Amelie.

"She looks asleep right now," grumbled Ben.

Amelie grinned. "Have you met a more strong-willed person than Towaal?"

Rhys and Corinne crossed the deck to join them, the rogue holding a hand above his eyes and studying the town of Indo.

"What's that on the hills?" he asked.

"Grapes," responded Corinne. "Can't you tell?"

Rhys grimaced. "I guess my eyesight is fading in my old age."

Ben frowned. His friend hadn't lost his dark humor after Northport, but the wings of white that now graced his temples spoke of a deeper cost.

Every morning, Rhys would work through the sequences of the Ohms, stretching and twisting. His unspoken concern was clear. He wasn't as limber as he used to be.

Each evening, the rogue spent half a bell going through the sword forms with Ben. On the rocking ship, they didn't spar, but Ben knew his friend had lost some of his quickness. Ben guessed that if they did spar, he'd be half a step faster than Rhys. Despite that, he still wouldn't want to face the rogue in a real fight. The man had centuries, probably millennia, of experience, and a deep well of animal cunning. Until the day he died, Ben was certain Rhys would remain deadly.

"Grapes," asked Ben, shaking himself out of his thoughts. "For wine making like they do north of the City?"

His companions shrugged. Rhys, who'd been to the South Continent, told them earlier he'd merely passed through Shamiil on his way to Qooten. Much of Ooswam was as foreign to him as it was to Ben.

"Saala would know," remarked Amelie.

Ben nodded. It would have been good to have the blademaster with them on this journey, but they hadn't seen the man since before they fled the City.

"What do you think he's up to?" wondered Ben.

"Last I heard," answered Rhys, "he'd left the City for White-hall, trying to find you two."

They cut the conversation short as Milo approached. Without discussing it, they all acknowledged there was something strange about the former librarian's apprentice. The timid young man was too quiet, thought Ben. When he'd brought it up to Amelie, she'd laughed at him. Worrying a librarian was too quiet sounded silly, he knew, but it was true. The boy never spoke, and he padded about the ship as silent as a cat.

"If he was here," claimed Rhys, "right about now, he'd be telling us to get packed."

Ben smiled and looked to Indo. A bell, maybe a bell and a half, and they'd drop anchor. Their sloop had too much draft to pull closer, but the captain promised that in the calm waters off the South Continent, it'd be an easy row to the pier. Some of the crew would take them in one of the small boats they kept for fishing and shore exploration.

"Sounds like good advice," responded Corinne. "Come on, Amelie. Let's go pack up our cabin. Rhys, you want to get Towaal's gear? I don't think the mage will be moving until they drop the anchor. Every extra moment she maintains cover is longer that Eldred can't find us."

THE BOAT BUMPED against the stones of the pier, and Ben leapt across the narrow gap of water. He hauled hard on the hemp hawser he was carrying and looped it around a thick iron bollard. His companions scrambled after him.

Ben's knot wasn't up to sailing standards, but the water was calm, and the boat barely moved with the gentle surf. The sailors told them that the waters off the South Continent were usually calm until a storm rolled in from the sea with lashing rain and driving wind.

Rhys was the last off the boat. When the rogue sat foot on the pier, Ben untied the line and cast it to the sailors. They waved a quick goodbye, and oars dipped into the water, propelling them back to the merchant vessel.

The captain had been happy to drop them at Indo when he felt the heft and clink of gold in the purse Towaal offered, but his cargo was for Shamiil. For a sailing man, time was money. He was eager to get going.

Watching the merchant vessel, Towaal stood at the end of the rocky pier. She was anchoring the light shield. By doing so, she thought she would be able to extend it two or three leagues away from the pier. It would be less effective without constant supervision, but since she wasn't having to move it along with the vessel, she could set it in place and leave it.

If Eldred happened to be watching when the sloop suddenly appeared from under the shield, she'd certainly suspect what happened. The odds were in their favor that she wouldn't be watching that small section of the sea, though, and if even she was, they hoped they'd be away long before she reached Indo. As long as they could leave minimal sign of where they went, they would be relatively safe.

Ben hitched his pack on his shoulders and gestured to Indo. "Shall we?"

The ladies led the way down the pier to a collection of stark white stucco houses bordered with black wood trim. It was neat and clean. Everything was in its place. Even the fishing boats pulled up on the beach looked freshly painted and fastidiously organized. The scent of the sea hung over the pier without the stomach-churning smell of rotting fish and offal that was common in other ports they'd been to.

As they drew closer, Ben saw the people wore loose clothing, similar to what Saala wore. It wasn't as fine or as colorful as the blademaster's attire, but the garments made sense in the stifling heat and humidity.

A trio of short-haired dogs burst out from behind a building and charged, barking to scare off the new arrivals. When the party drew close, the dogs turned tail and ran back behind the building.

"They must have smelled you, Ben," jested Rhys. "Enough to make anyone turn tail and flee."

Ben rolled his eyes but didn't respond. It was true. He hadn't bathed in the three weeks on the ship, but neither had the rogue. It wasn't just the ladies this time who were looking forward to a hot bath.

Evidently alerted by the dogs, a portly customs official came bustling out of a small shack at the end of the pier.

"You not docking?" he inquired, glancing hungrily at the sloop anchored offshore.

Rhys shook his head. "We just caught a ride. They'll continue to Shamiil."

The official frowned, licked the tip of an ink-stained quill, and then made a few quick scratches in a small notebook. "I still have to charge you for arrival. Three silvers will cover the group."

Rhys flipped the man the coins.

"Can you recommend a good inn?" asked the rogue.

The customs man nodded. "There are only two, the Merlion and the Salty Dog. For you, I recommend the Merlion. It's where the merchants stay. Classier fare than the Dog. Fewer sailors and fishermen at the Merlion, so you can get rest at night. Head up the street, and you can't miss it. It's the tallest building in town."

The street was hard-packed dirt. Tiled gutters were built along the sides and sloped down to the sea. Further into town, bright green flowering plants grew in large pots next to the buildings. The street was lined with vegetation. Some of the pots held bushes dangling fat, finger-length peppers or larger squashes. Ben saw strange vegetables he couldn't identify. Vines were set in pots beside doorways, and twisting creepers climbed up the sides of the houses. Many of the plants were in bloom, decking the street in spots of purple, red, orange, and yellow. The splashes of color stood in stark contrast to the uniform white walls and black trim of the buildings.

"Pretty," mumbled Amelie.

Corinne added appreciatively. "It's not Northport."

Ben inhaled deeply and smiled. She was right. It wasn't Northport or like anywhere else he'd been. He thought he could grow to like the suffocating heat, as long as it came with the pleasant scent of the flowers.

"There," declared Rhys.

Ahead of them stood a five-story building. In contrast to the rest of the town, the first two floors of this one were encased in stone, possibly a former keep from when the town was even smaller. Flanking the door were two man-high statues. They had heads of lions and bodies of fish. Their eyes were carved into menacing scowls, their mouths open in silent roars.

"Merlions?" wondered Amelie.

"Must be. Maybe the creatures are some sort of local legend."

Ben glanced at Towaal to see if she had a comment, but the mage was stumbling along with her eyes fixed on the ground. She'd been awake for two straight days to maintain focus holding the light shield above them.

They passed between the two statues and ducked through the low door of the inn. Ben blinked in surprise as he walked into a cool wall of air. The low door, lack of windows, and thick stone of the walls had another purpose, he realized.

The first floor of the inn was a broad, open room with thick columns spaced through it supporting the floors above. Wide planks covered the floor, and smooth circular tables sat atop it, each table with eight chairs placed carefully around. In the back, a bar blocked an open kitchen. Ben could see scullions rushing around, sweating over hot grills and tending to flickering fires. In one corner, there was a small stage with a single woman on it. She was strumming a stringed instrument on her lap. Everything was clean, spotless. It was cleaner than any inn Ben had ever stepped foot in, he was sure of that.

"This is a nice change," mumbled Amelie.

Ben was staring around the room when a petite girl bustled up in front of them. Raven black hair was tied in a neat bun behind her head, and a simple, but well-made, dress covered her from neck to foot.

"Hello, travelers. Room and board?" she asked in a lilting accent.

Rhys nodded. "A couple of rooms, cold ales, hot meals, and an even hotter bath."

"Of course," demurred the woman. "Let me show you around the property. You can leave your packs in the rooms and then take your meals or bathe at your leisure. Welcome to the Merlion."

The girl took quick, mincing steps to the stairwell, her feet hidden beneath the hem of her dress. It gave Ben the impression she was floating across the floor. He was slightly disappointed when she led them up the stairs and her knees bent to climb, ruining the effect.

In the room, Ben placed his pack down on one of the three narrow beds. Rhys and Milo were also settling in, dropping packs and sifting through them to find changes of clothing.

Ben sighed. After three weeks at sea, he had been looking forward to sharing a bed with Amelie.

"When you pay, you pick the rooms," said Rhys with a knowing wink. "Come on. Let's go find these baths."

Ben followed his friend down a narrow set of stairs at the back of the inn and they emerged into a quiet courtyard. It was nothing like the muddy stable yard he'd expected. Instead, short, manicured pine trees sprouted from carefully arranged piles of rocks and loam. A creek trickled by and a short foot-bridge crossed it. Behind a head-high embankment on the other side of the creek, they heard splashing.

Rhys led them along a stone path which meandered through waist-high, flowering bushes until they found an open-air, thermal-heated pool. Steam boiled off the surface of the water, and a dozen heads bobbed, hidden underneath a carpet of mist. Low conversation and the gentle lap of water against stone filled the air with sound. A rack of towels and soap stood beside a table with heavy, earthenware pitchers that beaded with condensation.

"Ah." Rhys sighed. "This is what I needed."

The rogue peered inside the pitchers then quickly filled three mugs with wine. He passed one each to Ben and Milo, stripped off his clothes, stuck them in a row of cubbies, and dipped a toe into the water. Heartbeats later, he sat his mug down and jumped into the pool, splashing a wall of water that sent bathers scrambling away from him.

Ben rolled his eyes and walked down a set of carved stone stairs into the pool. The heat immediately soaked into his body, relaxing tense muscles and soothing aches from the weeks at sea.

"Not bad, is it?" asked Rhys, a grin spread across his face. The rogue waded over to the side of the pool and tipped up his wine mug. To Milo, he asked, "If you're not getting in, mind refilling me?"

The former librarian's assistant topped off Rhys' mug then he joined them in the pool.

Ben sipped his mug, enjoying the contrast between the cool white wine and the heat of the water. He felt a sharp finger jab into his shoulder. He turned and nearly spilled his mug when he saw a dark-haired girl floating just behind him.

"It's impolite to be noisy in the bathing pools of Ooswam. I can't imagine I need to tell you this, but splashing the other bathers is also frowned upon," she informed him. "I can see you are foreigners and have no knowledge of our customs, so I am reminding you kindly. This time."

"I, uh, it was my friend," Ben stammered.

The girl swept her long, black hair behind her head with a wet hand. Ben's eyes bulged as her bare arm and shoulder peeked above the dark water of the pool. He swallowed and looked around wildly. The pool, it seemed, was not segregated by gender.

The girl was certainly naked and floating half a pace away from him. His face flushed as it occurred to him that he'd just stripped naked in broad view of everyone in the water.

"You or your friend, I do not care," declared the girl calmly. "You should both follow our rules."

"Ben," called Amelie.

He turned and saw her standing on the side of the pool, a short linen robe pulled tight around her. Corinne and Towaal were by her side.

"Is that you?" she asked. "I can barely see through the steam. I believe this pool is used by both men and women. We did not see a separate one."

Ben coughed. "Yes, it is me. I believe you are right. Both men and women use this pool." He silently wished the girl by his side would discreetly float away.

"It is the custom in Ooswam to bathe together," said Towaal.

Drowsiness clouded her voice, but Ben knew the mage would want to wash away the three weeks of filth from their time at sea before spending the next day in bed. He detected a new lilt to her tone, similar to the serving girl and the one floating beside him.

He nearly leapt out of the water when Towaal calmly discarded her robe and tossed it into one of the cubbies. The mage's body was lean and fit, toned from years on the road. Ben tore his eyes away and found himself staring into the face of the dark-haired girl.

"You should ask your companion about our customs," admonished the girl. "There is no excuse for ignorance when you are traveling with a local."

The girl mercifully shot him one last glare then swam away into the mist.

Ben turned back to his companions and jumped again. Amelie was right beside him.

"Who was she?" Amelie asked sharply.

Ben winced. "I don't know. She just started berating me because Rhys jumped into the water and splashed everyone."

"She was lecturing you, not me," quipped the rogue. "Don't bring me into it."

Corinne splashed a handful of water at Rhys.

"That's what got me in trouble the first time," moaned Ben.

"What she said is true," admitted Towaal, floating over to them. "You should learn the customs of this place and try to follow them. I believe we lost Eldred in the storm, and we can cloak ourselves from magical detection, but she could still locate us through mundane means if we leave a trail. Word of strangers, rumors of magic, all of that could give us away. We should blend in as best we're able."

Ben's face felt flushed. The heat of the pool didn't help, but Amelie, Towaal, and Corinne were all bobbing around him, bare shoulders poking up from the dark water.

Amelie ran a hand across his back. "Are you okay?" she whispered.

He squeaked. "Just tired."

Towaal dunked her head under the water and started scrubbing herself with a slippery bar of soap.

Ben tried to ignore the mage, but he couldn't help feeling Amelie bump against him. The way her body felt in the hot water was very, very interesting. She wasn't trying to avoid contact with him, and he realized the innocent seeming bumps might not be so innocent. He closed his eyes and tried to remain focused on the discussion.

"In the morning," suggested Towaal, "we'll talk about Ooswam and its customs. For now, I must rest. If I'm not up by midday tomorrow, wake me."

The mage dunked herself again to rinse off the soap and then strode out of the pool. Ben couldn't help but watch her, seeing water cascade down her slim figure until Amelie dug an elbow into his side.

"You should be paying attention to me, not her," complained Amelie quietly.

Ben grinned at her. "Sorry. This is all so strange to me. I'm not sure where to look. It's nothing like Alcott."

"Ooswam is not all strange, is it?" asked Amelie, drifting closer to him. "The wine looks the same."

Ben took a sip to steady his nerves. "Yes, that is the same."

"Let's get you another one and then come with me. We're going to have to figure out a way you can bathe on this continent without getting distracted."

"You're the only one who distracts me," claimed Ben.

Amelie snorted.

He refilled his wine from a pitcher Rhys had set on the side of the pool.

Amelie clasped his hand and pulled him deeper into the water and the steam. At the back of the pool, away from their companions and other bathers, she wrapped her arms and legs around him and kissed him deeply. He forgot about everything and everyone else. Even his wine sat untouched and unnoticed beside him. Gentle waves lapped around them as they tangled together in the hot water.

THE NEXT MORNING, Ben sat in the common room with a wide grin plastered across his face. The ladies hadn't appeared yet. Milo was fixated on his breakfast, and Rhys was engrossed in repairing a tear he'd found on his cloak. Ben was sitting, enjoying the relative cool of the morning and sipping at a hot, mint-flavored tea. He missed kaf. Apparently, it was rare in the South Continent.

He'd gone to bed content, but since waking, all he could think about was Amelie and the way her wet body had felt when she pressed it against him, the passion of her kisses, the thrill of being in the pool with the others just out of eyesight in the cloud of mist.

"No more splashing in the bath after I left?" asked a soft voice, jolting him out of his day-dreaming.

Ben coughed, choking on his tea.

He glanced over and saw the small girl from the night before. Jet black hair hung around her shoulders and she wore flowing, bright green trousers and tunic. She was young, about his age, but her eyes looked at him with an elder's disapproval. She reminded him of Towaal after catching him hungover from drinking with Rhys.

He gagged, trying to clear his airway of the minty tea.

The girl rolled her eyes. "Foreigners."

She spun on her heel and glided away with the smooth grace of a dancer.

Two hulking, bald-headed men stalked after her. Each had broad bladed scimitars hanging from their belts. They moved with grace too, the grace of predators.

"Just like Saala," mumbled Rhys.

Ben glanced at him.

Rhys nodded after the departing pair. "Swordsmen, trained just like Saala. Not far from him in skill either if I'm any judge of these things. Paid for by the girl's family. They're most likely top tier merchants or even the lords of these parts. My advice, keep your head down and stop antagonizing her. She'll cut your heart out in the blink of an eye. In Ooswam, if her family is powerful enough, no one will raise a hand to stop her."

"I'm not antagonizing her!" exclaimed Ben. "You were the one who jumped in the pool."

"Who is Saala?" asked Milo.

Ben met Rhys' eyes. He'd forgotten the former librarian's

apprentice was with them. Milo was so silent he seemed to blend into his surroundings. They had told the young man much of their story, but after the first few days with him on the ship, they started holding back. Milo knew all about their struggles against the demons and quest for the Purple. He even knew Towaal's and Rhys' place in the group, but there was something unusual about him, and they decided anything he didn't know yet would remain unspoken.

"A friend," responded Rhys. "One we haven't seen in a long while."

Milo nodded, apparently content with the vague answer.

A quarter bell later, Amelie and Corinne arrived at the table. They ate a hearty breakfast, seemingly glad to be off ship's rations. Then they all went about keeping themselves busy until they could wake Lady Towaal. Ben and Rhys found a quiet place on the grounds of the Merlion to spar while Amelie, Corinne, and Milo went into the town to restock supplies.

Shirtless in the sticky morning heat of the South Continent, Ben and Rhys swarmed back and forth across a small, tree-encircled space. Mage-wrought blades flashed in the sunlight.

Rhys tried his normal tricks, kicking up a clod of dirt toward Ben's face, attempting false tells with his movements and eyes, and shouting in alarm at phantom threats. Ben fell for none of it. After his time with Jasper, he'd learned to stay focused, to concentrate on what was real. He was aware of his surroundings but only in the back of his mind. He knew there was no one sneaking up behind him, so when Rhys pointed at an imagined interloper, Ben struck at the rogue instead of freezing.

Before long, Rhys was on the defensive, stepping back as Ben aggressively pursued him. Ben tried to corner the man against a pile of rocks, but his friend was too wily to be trapped. He slipped away and lashed out with a kick that caught the side of Ben's calf, nearly spilling him on the ground.

Ben recovered, barely in time to defend against Rhys' attack. He parried, and they began a slow circle of the clearing again.

"You're getting good at this," panted Rhys.

"Tricks don't work, so now you try flattery?" replied Ben.

Rhys held up a hand to pause. "Really, Ben. If you find the right opponent, I believe you could earn your blademaster sigil."

Ben blinked. He couldn't tell if his friend was serious or if it was another trick.

Rhys grinned. "We'll talk about it when we're not sparring. You should consider it. A sigil has some downsides like visibility which we don't need right now, but it has some upsides as well, particularly if you want to continue wooing a lady like Amelie."

"How does a sigil help me with Amelie?" asked Ben, certain now Rhys was trying to distract him.

"She's a highborn lady," responded the rogue. "You're common blood. A blademaster is welcome in elevated circles. A brewer is not."

"She doesn't think of herself as a lady anymore," declared Ben. "Her home is in Coalition hands, and her mother betrayed her father and their city. She doesn't want any part of that life now. Besides, we have more important things to focus on."

"It's in her blood. If we're successful, you won't always be battling the demons. What happens then?"

Ben frowned then attacked. They sparred back and forth without speaking for another bell until they were both pouring sweat and stumbling through the forms.

"I want an ale, but I need water," groaned Rhys. "It's impossible to be civilized in this heat."

Ben nodded and sheathed his longsword. He tried to wipe the dripping sweat off his forehead, a vain attempt to keep the stinging moisture from his eyes, but his wet hand just smeared it.

"Do you think they have cold baths in Ooswam?"

"We can ask," answered Rhys.

～

THAT EVENING, they sat around one of the circular tables in the common room and Ben stared apprehensively at a shallow bowl of noodles in front of him. Chunks of meat and peppers dotted the dish. Two slender sticks sat beside it. In the center of the table were other piles of noodles, fried bites, mysterious sauces, and a sliced chicken sitting on a bed of rice. He didn't see a knife, fork, or spoon anywhere in the common room.

"How are we supposed to do this?" he asked again.

Lady Towaal sighed. "As I told you already, like this."

She picked up the two sticks by her bowl and expertly scooped a bite of noodles. She bent over her bowl and slurped them up.

Milo clutched the little sticks like Towaal had and, with some difficulty, snagged a slippery bite. He almost made it to his mouth before the noodles slid off the tip of his sticks.

Rhys, faring slightly better than the others, managed to chomp sloppily down on a clump of noodles.

"I'd forgotten about this," he grumbled around the mouthful of food. "It's like they're not even aware of the advances in utensil science."

"Maybe we should open a business selling forks," joked Ben.

"Enjoy the sticks while you can," responded Rhys. "When we get to Qooten, you'll only use your fingers."

Ben frowned, unsure how serious Rhys was.

"It's true," advised Towaal. "Qooten is the same land it was five hundred years ago, or even a thousand. Exposure to Ooswam or Alcott through trade has not changed it or its people."

"Have you been to Qooten?" asked Corinne.

"Long ago," responded Towaal. "Before I joined the Sanctuary."

"How long ago was that?" quipped Amelie.

"Long ago," answered Towaal.

"That girl was right. You're from Ooswam!" exclaimed Ben.

Towaal eyed him over another bite of noodles. "Where did you think I was from?"

Ben blinked. He'd never really thought about it. Everything he knew about her history was from the Sanctuary, so he'd assumed she was from the City.

"Is your family still here?" asked Corinne.

Towaal smiled sadly. "My family is long departed, girl. If any descendants remain, they would have forgotten me ages ago. Besides, my family is from the western side of Ooswam. We are several hundred leagues east of where I was born."

"How did you end up in the Sanctuary?" inquired Ben.

He finally managed to pin a bite of noodles together with the sticks and brought it to his lips. They were good, a little sweet and a little savory. Then his teeth crunched something, and heat filled his mouth. His eyes began to water and his head swam. Perspiration popped out on his forehead. He exhaled through his nose. It felt like fire was blowing out his nostrils. He coughed and choked, scrambling to grab his ale mug.

Rhys chuckled and sipped at his own ale.

"Try this," suggested Towaal.

She tapped a plate with chunks of some indeterminate stuff floating in a pea green sauce. It looked highly suspicious.

"It will cool your mouth," she explained.

Ben drank his ale and took a bite of the mysterious mix Towaal suggested. She was right. It was like a soothing balm spreading across his tongue. His coughing finally came under control. He glared around the table, piqued that none of his friends warned him about the noodles. He thought it'd be bells or even a day before he could taste anything again.

"You should avoid the little red peppers," advised Rhys. "There will only be a few of them. The rest of the dish has some heat, but those are fire."

Amelie stared at the rogue coldly. Ben saw one of the tiny red peppers in the clutch of her sticks. She'd been heartbeats away from eating it.

"Didn't you think you should warn us before we ate one?" growled Amelie.

Rhys shrugged. "It was funny seeing Ben's face get red."

Ben grunted and dumped a pile of safe-looking chicken and rice onto his plate. After a pause, he added a scoop of the green sauce too. Despite Rhys' assurances that it was the red peppers, he wasn't bold enough to try another bite of noodles yet.

"How did you end up in the Sanctuary?" Corinne asked Towaal, picking up Ben's lost trail of inquiry.

Towaal sat down her sticks. "It's a bit of a long story."

"We're not going anywhere until morning," responded Corinne.

"You came from a wealthy family, didn't you," guessed Amelie. "Were you highborn?"

Towaal smiled. "I did come from a wealthy family, and they were highborn, you could say."

The mage shifted in her seat and ate another bite of noodles while she thought.

"In Alcott," she said after swallowing, "there are three types of power; military, political, and economic. Military power is what the largest cities and most powerful lords control. It's how the lords determine standing amongst themselves. A more powerful lord has the ability to invade and control the weaker lords. Political power is gained through a fortunate birth into a highborn family, ideally, one that happens to control valuable geography. Even a minor lord has some measure of political power because a stronger lord will cater to them to gain loyalty and access to their military might. Powerful lords need allies to provide additional troops in times of need and a buffer against other powerful lords in times of peace. Witness the Alliance and the Coalition." She ate another bite then continued, "In Alcott, economic might is the only form of power available to those born in the common class. It is valuable but tenuous. A wealthy merchant can buy a palace, jewels, whatever they desire, but they are still at the mercy of their lord. The lord has the swords and axes. With those, they could seize the merchant's assets at any time."

"Won't the merchants leave if the lord takes their things?" asked Ben.

Towaal nodded. "Of course, which is why economic might is a legitimate source of power. An intelligent lord knows to feed and support the merchant class instead of starving or abusing them. If one merchant is treated unfairly, then others will see that, and they will leave. The heavier the ruler's hand, the quicker the successful merchants depart. Before long, the lord's tax base has disappeared, and he can no longer afford to feed his army."

"The South Continent isn't the same?" wondered Amelie.

Towaal sipped her wine. "Not exactly. In Ooswam, there is no practical difference between highborn and the very wealthy. Both own land, both can build a city on the land, and both can rule the people living in the city. There is an emperor, but he is largely a figurehead. He spends little time on the squabbling between the elites. He merely ensures it does not get out of hand. His primary concern is the relationships with other lands, which, given how inwardly focused most of those lands are, the emperor has a limited role."

"Merchants can own land, build a city, and rule it?" questioned Amelie.

Towaal nodded. "The only real difference between a successful merchant and a lord in Ooswam is time. Over generations, a successful merchant family will build a business empire and pass it to their successors. They may build cities and then tax the people who move there. The younger generations are born into this wealth and pass it to their children. When the accumulated wealth transfers from generation to generation, they are essentially the equivalent of highborn in Alcott. Formally, many of the merchant families then declare themselves to be an official House, which entitles them to a place in the emperor's court and the title of lord. That requires a substantial payment to the emperor, but many families consider it a business expense. They pay to join the emperor's court, and then they have proximity to him to try and influence trade or laws within the country."

Amelie pushed a strand of hair behind her ear, clearly struggling to understand.

Ben tentatively took another bite of noodles, careful to avoid the tiny red peppers. The bite was hot but not the scalding burn he'd experienced earlier. He quaffed his ale and downed another bite of noodles. He thought he might learn to enjoy the spice if he could avoid the peppers.

"It's not so different in Farview," Ben remarked to the silent table. "We have no lord, so a man's standing in town and on the council is really about what he's been able to build or what his father built before him. If a man creates a successful business, then he's likely to earn the respect of the others. If he fails at his business, then no one wants to hear what he says."

"That's so arbitrary," argued Amelie. "Just because someone is good with commerce doesn't mean they would make a good ruler."

"More arbitrary than birth?" chided Rhys.

Amelie sat back frowning. "I just... I think there could be problems with a system purely driven by accumulating wealth. If that is the case, then the powerful will always be trying to improve their own standing and not that of their people."

"I'm not arguing for it," said Towaal. "I am just stating that is the law of this land. You are right. There are problems. Because the emperor pays little attention to the conflicts among the elites, they are free to play their little games to improve their position. Disputes amongst them are rarely settled in front of the emperor. Assassinations and even open battles among feuding lords can happen here. There is little law outside of the town walls or whatever valuable geography a lord decides to protect. When we see armed bands, we must assume they are hostile. They could be a lord's guard patrolling the area, but they are just as likely to be bandits or raiders."

Towaal glanced around the room and subtly gestured to one table in the corner. Ben saw it was the young girl who kept speaking to him. Her two guardians were dining with her, one eating and one watching the room.

"When we encounter an elite, be careful. On their own lands, they make their own laws with little oversight by the empire. They can be very dangerous. She's taken an interest in you, Ben. Do not encourage it."

"I didn't do anything!" he protested.

"You do have a way of getting in trouble with highborn ladies," mentioned Rhys.

"Highborns are crazy," declared Ben. "I do my best to avoid them."

Lady Towaal, Lady Amelie, and Lady Corinne all stared at him.

Ben swallowed. "Well, you three are different. You're..." he trailed off, at a loss for words.

Rhys leaned close to him. "Sometimes it's best to quit while you're still able."

Ben sighed and sat back in his chair.

Rhys refilled his ale mug, and Ben cradled it in his hands, doing his best to ignore the withering looks from the ladies.

2

BLOOD AND FIRE

BEN DRANK his ale and remained quiet the rest of the evening. He listened closely while Towaal described the culture of Ooswam. He tried to memorize the subtle gestures and remarks which held particular meaning in the country.

"Precise," described Towaal, "that is the word I would use for the social interactions here. Every word, every inflection is studied for meaning. Conversations can feel minimal or even rude because people do not rush to fill the silent spaces. That restraint is probably what makes the people so adept at poetry, painting, and even the sword. They are careful, and when they act, it has significance."

Ben glanced at Amelie and saw her listening seriously. He gripped her hand under the table and she shot him a quick smile. He was glad she hadn't been too offended by the highborn remark earlier. He didn't think of her as a lady anymore. He just thought of her as Amelie. To him, that was a compliment.

Towaal stood and began demonstrating a range of non-verbal greetings, a short bow with hands pressed together or by her side, a nod, a tilt of the head, or nothing. They all communicated different degrees of familiarity and were intended to send a message to the recipient. Ben thought back to the serving girl when they first entered the Merlion. She'd pressed her hands together and given a shallow bow from her waist. It meant welcome and willingness to serve.

Ben was so engrossed with Towaal's lessons that he jumped when he felt a presence at his shoulder. He turned to find the slight, black-haired girl watching them. Her men stood a pace behind her. Again, all three had approached without Ben or even Rhys hearing them.

"Good. I see you've taken my advice," remarked the girl. She looked hard at the companions and then back to Ben. "Do you intend to remain in the prefecture long?"

Ben blinked. "Perfect what?"

"This region," the girl said sharply. "Do you not even know you are in Lord Iyrron's prefecture? Indo, Seawatch, Ayd, and Siind are all part of the lord's domain. Will you remain here or leave?"

Ben forced himself to not roll his eyes. "We leave on the morrow."

"It is good for foreigners to come here and learn our customs, but it is better when they leave." The girl glared around the table one last time, turned, and strode between her guards. No bow, no nod. Ben didn't need Towaal's lessons to interpret that.

They watched the girl stride to the stairs. One of her guards smoothly stepped in front of her and went up first. The other followed behind, keeping an eye on the common room.

Their serving girl appeared at their table.

"More ale?" she asked.

Rhys nodded. "Keep 'em coming."

"Who is she?" asked Towaal, gesturing to the staircase where the girl and her men had just ascended.

"Lady O'ecca Iyrron," answered the girl. "I saw her speaking to you. That is a high honor."

"I don't think she meant to honor us," muttered Ben.

The serving girl's lips twisted wryly. "She has a lot of pressure on her lately. Her father, Lord Iyrron, has suffered bad luck in commerce and at the gaming tables in Shamiil. The house has been weakened. The Lady is strong, though. She will bring House Iyrron to its rightful place in the empire and beat back the sniveling dogs that have been nipping at the edges."

"We will be traveling on the morrow," mentioned Towaal. "Should we be worried about unrest in the region?"

The serving girl shook her head and blushed. "I am not the one to answer that question. There have been bandits near Indo, but there are always bandits. There are always rumors of this House or that House having trouble. Those things are over my head. All I know is that I have lived in Indo my entire life, and I have seen the Lady coming to the Merlion since she was a little girl. She is strong and wise. I trust her and her brothers to keep us safe. We all do."

"Thank you," murmured Towaal. She flipped the girl a silver coin.

The girl offered a quick bow and retreated

"Bribes are frowned upon in Ooswam," said Towaal, continuing her instruction, "but tips are appreciated. If you offer someone coins prior to them performing a service or giving you information, you will be viewed with suspicion, and it's likely they will not do it. If you give them coins after, they will be grateful and be at your service whenever you need them. It is about perceived intent. Paying them implies they shouldn't be doing the act. Tipping them implies thank you for what they provided. As I said, you must be precise in your interactions."

BEN LAY AWAKE in his bedroom, listening to the deep breaths of his friends. The ale left him pleasantly loose but not fuzzy headed. He was awake because he couldn't stop thinking about the differences between Alcott and Ooswam. Both nations had someone who made the rules and the common folk were lucky if they didn't fall afoul of that person. There were little distinctions between the two, but those seemed only important to the elites. They were different paths to the same place, he eventually decided. Neither one was better.

Not that it mattered. He was common, a subject to the ruling class, not a decision maker. No one was ever going to ask his opinion on what form of government was best. He snorted softly. After this adventure was over, he'd probably never see another throne room in his life.

And that was why he was still awake. If they defeated the demons, he didn't know what would come next. Would Amelie return to the hallowed halls of the highborn, or would she be content to be with a simple brewer?

As he lay there, half-drowsing, he noticed something else tugging at the edge of his conscious. A sound, just barely audible above the breathing of his friends. It could be the wind whipping under the eaves of the roof, distant surf, thunder from an approaching storm, or screams.

He sat up in bed, frowning.

Again, he heard it. It was far off, but now that it had his full attention, he knew somewhere outside, someone was screaming. Or maybe it really was thunder, he told himself. Dark clouds had been creeping in from the north all afternoon. The locals agreed a storm would hit sometime in the night and said it would bring plenty of rain and lightning. That's probably what it was, just the storm rolling in.

He slipped out of the bed and padded over to the open shutters. They'd left them that way in hopes of catching a breeze to move the stifling air. Now, the air was cooler. It smelled heavy and damp. Thunder rumbled in the north. He heard it clearly that time. Rain was coming.

Ben moved to close the shutters, then paused. He couldn't see any movement in the streets below, but it wasn't just thunder he heard. It wasn't the music from below either, or a drunk getting rolled in an alley. It was sharp, terrified. He leaned out the window, looking up and down the dark streets. In the distance, he heard the unmistakable clash of steel against steel.

"Rhys, Milo," hissed Ben.

Rhys grumbled and rolled over in his sleep. Milo remained silent. Ben called at them again, louder. By the time Rhys was reluctantly acknowledging him, Ben was already back to his bed. He slipped on his boots and was searching for where he'd put his longsword.

"There are screams outside. Coming closer, I think. Someone's fighting," stated Ben.

Rhys muttered a curse under his breath then pulled his blankets up higher.

A clear, piercing cry ended in a strangled whimper.

Both Rhys and Milo jumped out of bed at the same time.

Rhys looked at Ben appraisingly and saw he was dressed. "Go wake the girls."

Ben nodded and dashed into the hallway. By then, a few doors were opened. Bleary-eyed guests were peeking into the hall. Ben had to bang on the door of the girl's room for several moments before a disgruntled Towaal answered.

"What is it?" she complained.

"Screams."

She blinked and then glanced at her own open window.

"Rhys and Milo?" she demanded.

"Getting dressed, and armed," responded Ben.

"Meet in the common room as soon as they're ready," instructed Towaal tersely.

Behind her, Amelie and Corinne were already shrugging into tunics and picking up their weapons.

Downstairs, the companions gathered in the common room with two dozen other guests. The sounds of battle were drawing closer. It was obvious now that it was no simple disagreement. It was an attack.

A half-dozen armed men came stomping down the stairs then exited into the street without pause.

"Shall we go find out what is happening?" suggested Rhys.

"Better than waiting here and finding out too late we should have fled," agreed Corinne.

Ben nodded and took the lead, following the armed men into the streets of Indo.

Outside, the sounds of battle were clear. Ben flashed back to their panicked flight through Hamruhg. Unlike then, there were no magical explosions, no unnatural blasts of energy. Men and steel were responsible for this clash. He knew that wouldn't make it any better.

Ben jumped at the peal of a thunderclap, and a bolt of lightning illuminated the street in stark black and white. The storm had arrived.

In the brilliance of the lightning flash, Ben saw a woman clutching her abdomen stagger into the street. She was too far away to see the nature of her injury, but it was clear she was hurt. Another thunderclap and the woman's head snapped to look behind her. She started to run.

"We have to help her!" called Ben.

Rhys grunted, but he followed Ben and the girls as they ran to the injured woman.

Thunder, shouts, and clashes of battle alternated in a cacophony of sound. They were a dozen paces from the woman when the skies burst open. A sheet of hard rain swept in from the sea, pelting into Ben's back and sweeping over the woman. She stumbled and fell as the torrent crashed into her.

Amelie and Towaal were by her side in a heartbeat. Amelie tried to shield the woman from the rain while Towaal bent to examine her injuries.

Ben and the others stood watch, peering nervously through the curtains of falling water, looking for signs of the battle.

Behind them, Ben heard a jingle of armor. He turned and saw the slim young girl, Lady O'ecca Iyrron, leading a score of heavily armed men. They carried short spears in their hands and wore broad-bladed scimitars on their hips. The men had bulky armor and large helmets, which Ben saw between flashes of lightning were formed into the shapes of ferocious animals, a snarling tiger, a shark, and a bear. The girl wore the same thick armor but no helmet. In the rain, Ben couldn't see details, but the armor appeared bright green, matching the clothing the girl wore earlier that day. He also noticed she was carrying a strange spear. The haft was the height of the girl. On top of it was a long, curved blade. It was close to the length of his arm. He'd never seen a spear like it.

The girl met Ben's eyes and flicked down to the injured woman Towaal was helping. She nodded at Ben. Then her group passed, the men not sparing a glance for Ben's party.

"I told you to watch out for her," mumbled Rhys.

Towaal stood and shook her head. "She was holding her bowels in with her hand. When she fell, she lost her grip. There was no chance to save her."

Ben swallowed uncomfortably and looked toward the sound of fighting. "There could be more like her."

"It's not our fight," admonished Towaal.

"We could say that about the Veil, Lord Jason, or even the demons," argued Ben. "Our fight is when someone needs us."

"Don't act noble to impress that girl," snapped Amelie.

Ben looked at her. "People are dying, Amelie, people like this woman. What do you want to do? Go and help, or hide in the inn? Your decision."

Amelie winced. She paused, then drew her rapier. "We'll get closer and see if we can help protect the innocents. We do not engage unless we have to."

"Of course," agreed Ben.

He drew his longsword and felt the crash of the storm in his head. It wailed in counterpoint to the fury of the one overhead. Rhys and Corinne drew their weapons as well. Milo hefted his trident.

Ben led them forward, trotting down the street and turning the same way Lady Iyrron and her men had. Ben was sure they were headed to where the fighting was hottest.

"This won't be like fighting demons," called Rhys, speaking loudly to be heard over the pounding rain.

"We've fought men before," reminded Ben.

"Not like this," said Rhys, his voice tense. "This will be different. There will be people like that woman. Children, too. You'll see them, dead or injured. It will be hard, but ignore bystanders if there is an armed man nearby. You can't help the innocents if you turn your back and get yourself killed. Focus on opponents. Once you've dealt with them, there will be time to tend to the injured after the fighting is done."

Ben swallowed and gripped the wire-wrapped hilt of his longsword. He'd faced his share of men and even a few women. He'd never seen an innocent child cut down.

"Remember. Don't engage," added Amelie.

They rounded another corner and stepped back when a billow of flame erupted from the next street over.

"Not a mage," declared Towaal. "Either the lightning or the raiders set something afire. It must have found oil or another accelerant. Hopefully, it was an isolated warehouse. If not, this could turn into an inferno."

Ben shook his head, not understanding what she was saying except that it wasn't a mage.

"There," shouted Corinne, pointing down the street.

A woman and two children were scurrying under the eaves of a building, trying to stay unnoticed. Ben and his companions moved toward them. The woman gripped her children tightly when she saw their party but relaxed as they got close.

"Turn around, you fools!" she shouted. "The Red Lord is here."

"The Red Lord?" wondered Ben.

"He won't stop until every last one of us is butchered. Our only chance is to flee and hope they don't have the town surrounded." The woman eyed their weapons. "We're going to the beach, young man. You can come with us. I'll show you the way out."

Ben shook his head. "No, we're not leaving yet."

The woman didn't respond. She simply grabbed her children and hurried away.

"Who is the Red Lord?" Ben asked his companions.

"A bad guy, it seems," responded Rhys unhelpfully.

Another boom and gout of flame burst up beside the first. The rain would keep the fire from spreading, but whatever was catching there was blowing up big.

"Let's go this way," said Ben, leading the companions away from the fires. The sound of fighting was coming from all sides now, so one direction was as good as another.

Before they made it to the end of the street, another family came running their way, splashing through puddles, panic painting their faces. Behind them, half a dozen warriors poured around the corner. They were armored like O'ecca's men but black instead of green. Short swords waved in their hands as they ran.

"Amelie, you won't get through their armor with your rapier. Aim for the gaps," instructed Rhys. "Ben, you'll cut through that lacquer armor easier than steel, but be careful, it can still foul your blade. They won't have faced many mage-wrought blades down here. Use the surprise."

Ben nodded grimly. Amelie flanked him on one side, Corinne and Rhys on the other. Towaal and Milo hung back. The mage would only use her power if necessary. If she was too obvious with her magic, word could get to Eldred.

The fleeing family saw them and turned toward Ben's friends. Evidently, they decided that any armed party was better than the six blood-thirsty men chasing them.

The armed men drew closer, and Ben saw their armor was jet black with bright red splashes of paint on the chest. The Red Lord's men, he guessed.

He set himself, prepared to meet the charge, then jumped in surprise when Milo's trident flew past his shoulder. The three-pronged weapon caught the leader of the oncoming men in the face. Ten paces away, the man flipped backward from the impact, rusty steel buried in his head.

Ben recovered quickly and took advantage of the surprise. He rushed to meet the attacking men. Rhys, Corinne, and Amelie came beside him.

Ben's first opponent raised a vambrace-covered arm to deflect Ben's apparently wild swing. Once deflected, the man likely assumed Ben would be wide open and unable to defend against a counterattack. Instead, Ben's mage-wrought steel sliced through the armor and severed the man's hand. The man was spun from the force of the blow. Ben left him momentarily to parry the thrust of a second attacker.

He brushed aside a sweeping strike from the man's heavy sword then thrust at the soldier's neck, burying a hands-length of steel in the soft flesh. The warrior dropped his sword and clutched at the gaping hole in his throat before falling back into the rain-soaked street.

Amelie was on the first man, stabbing under a plate in his armor and finding the meat beneath it. He flailed the stub of his arm at her, but life was quickly draining from his body.

Rhys was standing over a headless, armored body. Corinne was kneeling to pull her axe out of the corpse of the fifth warrior. That left one more combatant for Ben to face.

The man's eyes darted around wildly, clearly aware he was now outnumbered and his companions had fallen without wounding Ben's friends. The warrior staggered backward and then hurled his sword at Ben's face.

Ben ducked the blade and watched as the man ran the other way, boots splashing in the rain soaked street.

"Not going to chase him?" asked Rhys.

"Minimal engagement," stated Ben.

Rhys grinned at him.

They cleaned their swords and Milo retrieved his trident.

"You could take one of their weapons," suggested Ben.

Milo hefted the three-pronged spear. "This feels comfortable."

Ben didn't argue. The way the former apprentice had hurled the thing was impressive.

The next street they came to was filled with mayhem. Flames flickered weakly in the deluge of rain. They barely lit struggling fighters, dead bodies, and blood. Every few heartbeats, the scene was sharply illuminated with a fork of lightning followed by a crash of thunder.

Ben swallowed the bile in his throat when he saw that among the carpet of dead were unarmed men, women, and children.

"Focus on the combatants," yelled Rhys over the rumbling thunder.

As they watched, the tide of the battle was turning. One side, outnumbered and injured, were forming a thin line. The other group bunched up at the far end of the street, preparing to charge.

"Oh no!" cried Amelie.

A trio of adults were leading a long line of children out of a burning building. The children were panicked and screaming. Some of them couldn't have been more than two or three years old. They were barely able to walk in the pounding rain. The adults scooped up as many as they were able, but they couldn't carry all of them.

Slowly, they made their way out of the building and into the street. The top of the building was drenched, but through the open doors, Ben could see smoke and fire. They had nowhere to go with the little ones but into the middle of the battle.

At the far end of the street, the warriors had formed into a wedge and were preparing to attack. Black armor with bright red slashes. The Red Lord's men.

"They'll massacre those children," lamented Corinne.

"No," responded Ben forcefully, "not while we're here."

He trotted forward, his companions falling in behind him. There were twice as many of the Red Lord's men, but the defenders had Ben and his companions. He judged it an even fight.

The crescendo of wind was building in Ben's head. He knew he could unleash it and amplify the power of the storm. It'd be enough to send the entire group of attackers tumbling to their backs, but it could also alert Eldred to their presence in Indo. She'd experienced the wrath of his sword. An unexplained blast of wind would be like a brightly painted sign for her, pointing directly to where they'd been. No, Ben knew they'd have to do this the old-fashioned way, with steel and determination.

Ben's friends joined the motley clump of defenders and they all moved in front of the retreating children. There were townspeople brandishing tools, city guards, and what looked like the tattered remains of Lady Iyrron's men. Ben glanced down the line and saw her there as well, black hair plastered to her skull, bladed spear in hand. She was standing boldly in front of her men, waiting on the charge. Only one of her guardians appeared to still be standing. Ben hoped she knew how to use that spear, but he didn't have long to worry about it. With a shout, the Red Lord's men surged forward. Two score of them. Swords and spears waved wildly as they ran.

"Protect the children!" shouted Ben.

The world descended into chaos. In the torrential rain, visibility was cut in half. The dirt streets of Indo were slick with water and blood. Ben settled his feet as best he was able and waited for the attackers.

The first assailant swooped in, swinging a powerful overhand attack, rainwater flying off his blade as he swung down. Ben ducked under it onto one knee and the man slid by, unable to arrest his momentum in the slippery mud.

The next man followed on the heels of the first, apparently believing his companion would barrel over Ben. He caught Ben's longsword in his gut before he could react. Ben surged off his knee and yanked the blade clear, a spray of bright red blood illuminated by a blast of lightning.

A body crashed into his side and Ben stumbled, nearly flopping down. One of the black-armored men was furiously defending an attack from the other direction, his back facing Ben. Ben smashed the hilt of his longsword down on top of the man's head, crunching his helmet and his skull.

Steel split the curtain of rain and a sword punched toward Ben's chest. He twisted at the last moment and scrambled away from the fallen man he'd just brained. He ignored the sting on his ribcage where the tip of the new assailant's sword scored him.

The black-armored warrior fell back, more competent and cautious than Ben's earlier foes.

Ben advanced, probing at the man with a high thrust.

The man stepped back again in time to avoid a fatal blow, but Ben's sword caught his intricate insect-shaped helmet, knocking it askew. The man's head snapped to the side and his free hand immediately shot up to adjust his helmet so he could see.

Ben didn't wait for him to recover. He punched his longsword into the man's breast plate and shoved it through, piercing his heart. The armor was thick, but not as strong a steel. Rhys had called it lacquer. Ben wondered briefly at what it was made of, but he didn't have time to examine it.

He turned and saw the back of a warrior threatening Amelie.

She was defending competently but would have trouble scoring a killing blow through the man's armor.

Mage-wrought steel slid easily into the man's back. A quick check on Amelie showed she was uninjured.

The battle swirled around them, black-armored warriors fighting guards and townspeople. The townspeople were getting the worst of it, but the Red Lord's men and Lady Iyrron's men were fighting to a draw. Without Ben and his friend's help, it would have been over already.

Ben turned and plunged back into the thick of battle. He felt slightly guilty as he stabbed another man in the back, but it was war, and they would have done the same to him. He resolved to remember that. He spared a glance behind to make sure no one was creeping up on him.

Suddenly, Rhys was on his right and Corinne was on his left. They'd sealed the end of the line. They turned as a group, flanking the remaining Red Lord's men.

Battle cries turned into shouts of alarm as Ben and Rhys used their mage-wrought blades to hack through the warrior's thick armor. Side by side, the two friends were deadly. The Red Lord's men were slowed by the weight of their armor, and it didn't protect them against mage-wrought steel. It was like fighting a one-armed man, but Ben didn't hesitate. These men would have killed the children, and still might if they weren't stopped.

Within heartbeats, half a dozen of the black-armored men broke off and began to flee, running down the street the way they'd come. More of them saw their companions retreat and turned to join the route. The rest of the raiders were already engaged or too lost in the heat of battle to see the tide had changed. They were mopped up quickly.

Ben surveyed the remains of the defenders. There were a dozen left. At their center stood Lady Iyrron. She was panting heavily and leaning on her bladed spear. Somehow, she'd gotten the thing bloody, but in the chaos of the fight, Ben hadn't seen her use it.

"Who are you?" she demanded between rasping breaths. "Why are you fighting with us?"

Her surviving men and the town guards turned toward Ben's companions, waiting on a response. The townspeople who'd taken up arms shuffled to the sides of the streets or fell to their knees by fallen friends.

"We saw you were protecting the children," explained Ben. "We thought we would help."

Lady Iyrron stared back at him, evidently unsure how to react.

"There!" bellowed a voice.

Ben turned and saw a huge, red-armored man standing at the head of three score of the raiders. The Red Lord himself, thought Ben. He was large, at least a hand taller than Ben, and thick. His armor made him look like a war-wagon rather than a man. On his shoulder, he rested a huge two-handed sword. It was nearly Ben's height. Ben shuddered, thinking of meeting a blow from the heavy blade.

"We might not survive this," said Lady Iyrron grimly, her voice carrying across the street.

Ben glanced at her.

"If we fall," she continued, raising her voice so all of her men could hear, "The Red Lord and his raiders will rape or kill anyone they find in this town. Men, women, or children. Your families. They will loot what is left and burn it to the ground. They did it to Lord Syvann's prefecture. The only thing stopping them here is us."

Her men gripped weapons tightly and turned to face the new arrivals, five times their number. It was long odds, but they stood ready to fight.

"We'll stand by you," declared Ben loudly.

The girl didn't acknowledge him. Her eyes were fixed ahead.

The Red Lord was booming instructions to his men, exhorting them to a battle fury.

Ben didn't need to look at his friends. They knew the children would only be two or three blocks away at best. If Ben and his companions ran, the Red Lord and his men would finish Lady Iyrron and be on the children long before they could escape Indo. They couldn't let that happen.

"I have an idea," said Towaal. "Be ready."

A battle cry went up followed by an ominous peal of thunder. The black-armored men charged.

Halfway down the street, in the midst of the charging horde of raiders, a brilliant white bolt of energy snapped down. The concussion of thunder filled the street and bodies went flying. A dozen men were tossed into the air like jacks. They crashed down into the mud or were flung against buildings, motionless and sizzling. A dozen more stood in the middle of the street blinking and confused. They appeared blinded and deafened from the lightning.

Ben shook his head, trying to clear the bright streak from the middle of his vision. Towaal had found a way to get involved without giving away her magic, he realized. It barely slowed the charge, though. The Red Lord himself still stood, and he bellowed at his men to continue the advance. There were still three times as many of them as there were defenders.

"Our turn," said Rhys. His sword shimmered in the rain and bright lights of the lightning, but Ben could tell he wasn't drawing on its power. Like Towaal, he didn't want to give away that they had access to magic.

Ben fought the urge to unleash his wind. It would easily tip the battle in their favor, but Eldred would instantly know it was him if she heard about it. Instead, he set his feet as best he was able in the slick mud and gripped his sword tightly. If he had to, he'd unleash the power of the wind, but until then, he'd rely on his steel.

The pack of black-armored men hit them like an avalanche.

Ben had faced groups of charging demons before, but they acted as individuals. These men fought as a coordinated group. Right before they hit Ben's friends and Lady Iyrron's men, the attackers bunched into groups of three. Rather than pausing to set their feet and attack, they smashed through the line, using their armored bodies like battering rams.

Ben tried to duck out of the way, but a group of three men crashed into him like a bull running downhill. He whipped his longsword around and cut deeply into one man's thigh, but the other two bowled over him, tumbling Ben beneath their feet.

He rolled off his back and onto a knee, shaking his hand from where one of the men's heavy boots had stomped it.

Amelie was down as well. Towaal and Corinne had vanished. Both Rhys and Milo somehow kept their footing and were turned to face the attackers. Ben didn't have time to look further. Behind the first wave came a second. These men were tasked with finishing whoever the first bunch knocked over.

One came at Ben, hacking at him with a heavy blade.

Knowing he couldn't get his longsword up in time to defend himself, Ben lurched forward off his knee and caught the man in the mid-section with his shoulder. The man's thick armor would prevent any injury, but Ben wrapped a hand around one of the man's legs and churned forward, knocking the armored man down onto his back with Ben sprawled on top of him. He snatched his hunting knife off his belt and brought it down, stabbing the man in the eye.

Amelie screamed.

Ben jumped off his opponent and spun to find her. His heart sank when he saw she was still down, scrambling back on her elbows and feet, trying to escape two men who were closing quickly.

Ben kicked himself free of the dead man and ran to help her.

Miraculously, Milo swept into view and leapt over Amelie.

The former apprentice thrust with the butt of his trident into the neck of one of the approaching men. Over the thunder and sounds of battle, Ben still heard the sickening crunch as the man's windpipe was crushed.

With one man going down grasping at his ruined throat, Milo stabbed the sharp end of the trident at the other. That man got an arm up in time to block a fatal blow, but two prongs of the trident sank deeply into his forearm.

Milo yanked it back then dropped into a squat, spinning on one foot and kicking out with the other. His foot smashed into the side of the warrior's legs and sent him flailing down into the mud. Milo pounced on him like a cat, stabbing down with his three-pronged spear. This time, he caught the warrior through the slit in his helmet. The former apprentice pushed the tines of the trident deep.

Ben stood still, blinking. Milo had just finished two heavily armored warriors in the space of half a dozen heartbeats.

Amelie scrambled to her feet and met Ben's eyes.

Behind Milo, Ben saw the first wave of armored men coming back. The young man was tugging at his weapon, trying to pull it free from where it must have gotten lodged in bone.

"A little help," he snarled.

Ben nodded and rushed past him, facing off against two of the raiders at once. One went high and one went low.

Ben jumped into the air, leaping over a low slash that would have taken out his legs. Still airborne, he blocked the high strike with his longsword.

The attacker was a big, powerful man. The blow sent Ben flying back. He landed awkwardly in the wet street, slipping and barely maintaining his footing. He slid one foot back, stabilizing himself, mimicking one of the Ohms positions without thought.

The man who'd gone low was spun off balance by the force of his blow and went down on one knee. The second stumbled, following the momentum of his attack.

Ben recovered faster than either and took advantage of his opponents being off balance. He stabbed at the second man's helmet and felt his blade crunch bone. The first man was struggling to his feet in his heavy armor, his head tilted over as he used his sword to push himself up.

Mage-wrought steel flashed down into the back of the man's neck, finding the gap between his helmet and his back plate. The armored head went spinning to the ground.

"Ben!" shouted Rhys.

He turned and saw his friend rushing toward a pack of eight black-armored figures who were chasing after Amelie and Corinne. The girls were brave and skilled, but their light weapons couldn't easily penetrate the heavy armor of the warriors.

Ben shot after them, jumping over bodies and praying he could keep his footing in the slick mud.

Luckily, the girls were unencumbered and were quicker than the men chasing them, but while Ben watched, the men realized this and started to spread out. They'd form a net and trap the girls against the wall of a building. Amelie and Corinne would have nowhere to run.

Ahead of Ben, Rhys picked up speed. To Ben's amazement, when he got close, the rogue jumped into the air, flying at the Red Lord's men, feet first.

His boots smashed into the back of one of the armored men and sent him soaring like he was thrown out of a catapult into two of his companions. All three of them went crashing to the ground, falling in front of a fourth man who tried to hurdle them, but in his heavy armor, he couldn't make the leap and ended up flopping heavily on top of the pile.

Rhys landed hard on his back, and one of the standing attackers spun and charged at the fallen rogue.

Ben snarled a battle cry and arrived just in time, wildly slashing his blade over his friend's body. He caught the attacker on the side of the head. The man's helmet caved in and he issued a gurgled scream as he toppled over. Ben knew he wouldn't be getting back up.

Rhys spun on his back and kicked the feet out from under another man, sending him flopping down beside the rogue. Rhys whipped out a long knife and rolled on top of the man, slamming the blade down.

Corinne and Amelie had another attacker on the defensive. He was scrambling back and trying to bat away both Amelie's rapier and Corinne's hand axes. He wasn't successful for very long.

Rhys yanked his knife out of the fallen man under him and pitched it at the last standing warrior, the blade caught the man in the face and he went down onto his back.

Ben closed on the four men who'd been tumbled by the rogue's initial kick. They were still struggling to disentangle themselves. One was finally rising to his feet. Ben felt a momentary twinge of guilt and then thrust his longsword into the man's side.

The three on the ground gave startled screams. They were quickly cut short when Ben's companions converged on them.

In the momentary calm at the side of the street, Ben eyed his friends. They all had a couple of cuts and scratches that were inevitable in a pitched battle, but none seemed to have suffered serious injury. He glanced around and saw the battle wasn't going well for the other defenders. They'd fallen back halfway down the street, leaving most of their number behind, dead in the mud.

Towaal appeared at their side and Milo shuffled over from where he'd been watching the defenders retreat.

In the center of the churn, the huge Red Lord was swinging his massive two-handed sword like he was scything wheat. Guards and townspeople fell like mowed grass before him. In the mix, Ben couldn't spy any of Lady Iyrron's green-armored men anymore. He hoped it was because of the pouring rain and the chaos of the battle.

"If we all hit them together from behind, the surprise might be enough," started Ben. He trailed off when at the far end of the street, two score more black-armored raiders appeared behind Indo's defenders. Indo's men were surrounded and outnumbered six to one.

"Without magic, you can't win this fight," declared Milo.

Ben grimaced but didn't dispute the young man's statement.

"We've spilled a lot of their blood," added Rhys. "In short fashion, they'll finish that fight and come for us next."

"There's no shame in retreat from a hopeless battle," suggested Corinne. "We can't fight an army. The little ones are gone, Ben. We did what we could."

Snarling, Ben slammed his longsword into his sheath. He couldn't bring himself to say the words, but his friends were right. Even with magic, they might not be able to win the fight. He wouldn't ask them to risk their lives on a hopeless cause.

Sensing Ben's distress, Amelie took the lead. "There isn't anything at the inn we can't live without. I think it's best we leave this town as quickly as possible."

The companions started trotting up the street, away from the battle behind them.

Two dozen paces later, Ben saw a heap of green-armored men. Lady Iyrron's guard. He couldn't help himself. He veered closer to see if the lady herself had fallen.

To his surprise, he saw her. Face down, trapped under the body of one of her men, she was struggling weakly to push the man off her, but with his heavy armor, she couldn't move him.

"Rhys!" called Ben.

The rogue jogged over and looked down.

"I suppose you won't be budged on this?" he muttered.

Ben knelt and grabbed one of the dead man's limbs.

Rhys sighed dramatically and grabbed another. Together, they heaved the body off of the lady.

"We need to hurry," advised Corinne from a dozen paces away.

"Can you walk?" Ben asked Lady Iyrron.

"I can't feel my leg," she answered through clenched teeth. "My men, where are they?"

Ben didn't answer. Instead, he unceremoniously grabbed the girl's arms and nodded for Rhys to take the legs.

"My naginata!" she cried. "I can't leave it."

With a frustrated curse, Corinne dashed back to pick up the bladed-spear while Ben and Rhys scurried away with the limp body of the girl hanging between them.

The companions followed Towaal down the first available side street, trotting quickly and then making two more rapid direction changes before they saw the open gates of the town.

"With any luck," said the mage, "none of the Red Lord's men saw which way we went. In this storm, it will be impossible to track us."

3

THE ROAD

"THE TOUGHEST PART," said Rhys, "is knowing when to pick your battles."

Ben grunted.

For the last bell, Rhys had been trying to convince him that leaving the town of Indo was the only sensible decision. Ben agreed that it was the sensible thing to do, but leaving wasn't the only choice. Just like Amelie's mother back in Irrefort, they had other choices. What they decided to do spoke to their character.

Rhys sighed. "Ben, in life, you cannot win every battle. You must understand that. When you're faced with a fight you cannot win, and you have the option to retreat, you do it. Throwing away your life in a battle you will lose is foolish."

"I thought you'd pledged to follow me," groused Ben.

Rhys snorted. "I choose to follow you and still do because I'm hoping do something good with my life. I don't intend to throw it away. If you want to be a leader, your leadership has to take people somewhere they want to go."

"I didn't ask to be a leader."

"You didn't have to become one," challenged Rhys. "When

Towaal and I pledged to support you, you could have said no. You didn't, though, because you know you need help to accomplish what you want to do. You want to find the Purple. You want to learn how to defeat the demons. I'll help you do that, but I won't follow you to certain death in some random fight in some random town. We have a larger mission to worry about."

Ben dropped the conversation and looked around. They were in a long stand of trees, nestled in the rolling hills south of Indo. They'd made it there the previous night and stopped for rest and healing.

Ben and Rhys were stalking the woods, hoping to find fresh game. They'd left their travel rations with their packs at the Merlion when they fled Indo.

Back at the camp, Lady Iyrron was soundly asleep and Towaal was resting. Towaal had tired herself pouring healing energies into the small girl. The wound on her leg had been deep, to the bone, and the frantic flight had nearly killed her. There wasn't time to stop and properly tend to her wound until they were well away from the town.

After the exhausting night, they all agreed they could spare a day of rest. Ben knew they would need to be on the move when the sun rose the next day, though. The towering smoke from Indo told him that the Red Lord wouldn't be paused for long.

Rhys caught Ben's arm and held a finger to his lips.

Fifteen paces a way, the undergrowth rustled.

Ben raised the trident. He'd borrowed it from Milo and was glad they had it instead of the cook's rat bashing club.

A plump rabbit hopped out of the bushes, slowly bouncing away.

Ben hurled the weapon at it and grinned when he hit his mark.

Rhys hurried forward to collect their prize and tied it next to another one on his belt. "One more and then back to camp?"

THE POP and crackle of sizzling meat woke Lady Towaal from an afternoon nap. She sat up and yawned, jaw cracking.

"What time is it?" she asked, glancing at the thick clouds overhead. The storm had rolled away shortly after dawn, but the skies remained heavy with the promise of more rain.

"Three bells before dusk," responded Rhys.

Towaal glanced at the still-sleeping Lady Iyrron.

"Has she woken?"

"No," answered Amelie. "She's been sleeping peacefully. Breathing is even. Color and pulse are holding steady. She'll have a nasty scar on her leg, but I think she'll be able to walk tomorrow."

"Is she coming with us?" asked Towaal.

Amelie looked to Ben.

He shrugged. "Away from here, at least. Maybe we can deposit her at the next village. I can't imagine she'll want to go further than that, and we won't give her any reason to. She doesn't know anything about us. For all she knows, we're simply a group of travelers unlucky enough to get caught in the middle of a battle. She doesn't know our mission and has no reason to be interested in us."

"She's awake," mentioned Milo.

They all looked at the girl and her eyes flicked open.

"What mission?" she inquired.

Ben groaned.

THE GIRL LEANED on her long-bladed spear with each step, but it didn't seem to slow her down. She kept pace with Ben as they hiked over the rolling green hills of Ooswam. Knee-high grass swished around their legs as they walked.

"You should tell me what you are intending to do in Ooswam," demanded the girl. "Why did you stop in Indo? Why did you fight the Red Lord's men?"

"I told you." Ben sighed. "We are just passing through to Qooten. We had no plans in Indo or anywhere near it. Indo was a stop on the way. We only got involved in the battle because I couldn't stand to see the children butchered."

"Where are you coming from?" pressed the girl. "You are northerners. The shortest route to Qooten from Alcott is not Indo. It is through Shamiil."

Ben glanced at Amelie and Corinne. Amelie arched her eyebrows at him as if to say, 'I told you so'.

He turned back to the girl. "I explained that as well. We were blown off course by a storm and thought to make land at the closest port."

"You are hiding things from me," accused the girl. "I mean to find out what."

"Look, lady," snapped Ben. "We saved your life back in Indo. If I hadn't stopped and dragged you out of that mud, you would've bled to death in the street or worse if they'd found you. Show a little appreciation, and let it drop."

The girl pursed her lips but didn't question him further. Based on the day so far, it was only a temporary reprieve.

The night before, she'd mourned. She'd lost her two guardians as well as her father's arms men. People she'd known for over a decade in the town of Indo were presumed dead. She'd taken it hard when she heard the news. Ben and his friends gave her what little information they could and offered condolences, but they didn't know her, and didn't know the people.

The girl had gone to bed quietly that night, soft sobs emanating from her bedroll, but since daybreak, she'd been pestering Ben. Alternating between questions about their mission and how they'd healed her leg. Thankfully, she'd dropped the inquiry on her leg when he offered to put it back like they'd found it.

The girl wasn't stupid, and while she was barely lucid when they found her, she must know something strange occurred when she was healed. She avoided that topic but pressed him on others. When he got frustrated and stopped answering her, she would change the subject, and a bell later come back to her original questions. She avoided the women in the party, but apparently, Ben was fair game. Evidently, she decided he would spill his guts about their purpose. Nothing he told the pugnacious girl satisfied her.

He hated to admit it, even to himself, but he was impressed with her tenacity. She'd woken up in the middle of a band of armed strangers after her men were slaughtered less than a day before. Her injury had been mysteriously healed, and there was a powerful lord who wanted her dead and was certainly searching for her. Through all of it, she was still focused on uncovering what Ben and his companions were up to.

Three days, he told himself. In three days, they'd pass near her father's hold, and she would leave to give Lord Iyrron the news about the Red Lord sacking Indo.

"You brought her with us so you are responsible for her," declared Amelie.

Thankfully, she'd lost the bitter edge around Lady Iyrron, but she wasn't helping Ben with his plight. The girl was relentless, constantly following him around, constantly probing for more information.

"I just thought, as a fellow female, you could tell her to back off your turf," Ben suggested gently. "I'm with you, Amelie, and she should respect that."

"She's not trying to sleep with you, Ben," Amelie retorted. "She sees you as the leader of our merry little band, so you're the one she's going to pester."

Ben scratched the back of his neck. "We're doing this together, aren't we?"

Amelie smiled at him. "We're finding the Purple together, and we'll fight the demons together. Any foreign conflicts you decide to involve yourself in, any damsels in distress you decide to rescue, we need to talk about first. You're on your own with this one."

"She's right, Ben," agreed Corinne. "You can't involve yourself in some foreign highborn's business and expect unquestioning support. Our mission is too important to get distracted with these little adventures."

"You're a foreign highborn," accused Ben.

The huntress winked at him but didn't respond.

Ben realized he wasn't going to win the argument. He leaned back on his elbows and looked around their campsite. They were perched atop a low hill surrounded by a sea of thick, green grass. In the distance, stands of thin-trunked trees sprouted up, displaying bursts of small leaves.

Lady Iyrron told them that two bells walk to the east was a proper road, but with the Red Lord's men possibly in the area, they'd been avoiding it and any other sign of civilization. Out here, despite the lush summer growth, there were no farms, no people.

There was plenty to forage, though. Animals, unbothered by people, were plentiful under the trees. Brightly covered fruits dotted many of the bushes, and Rhys was able to find several root vegetables they could roast. In the flight from Indo, they'd lost their packs and their cooking supplies, but they had their weapons to hunt with. Towaal and Amelie had no problems starting fires with their magic. The weather was warm and, after the storm, mercifully dry. Sleeping outside was pleasant. The only thing Ben missed was a water skin. Or even better, one full of ale. The terrain hid plenty of small streams, but without means to transport the liquid, they were reliant on finding the next source.

If it wasn't for the panicked flight from Indo, the threat of Eldred, and the seriousness of their quest to locate the Purple and stop the demons, it'd have been a rather enjoyable journey. Ben grimaced and mentally added one more problem to his calculation as he saw Lady Iyrron returning from the stream at the bottom of the hill.

"By midday tomorrow," declared Lady Iyrron when she arrived, "we will come across the village of Ayd. It's not much, to be honest, mostly just a fork in the road, but they will have supplies for you to continue your journey. I will leave you there and go to my father."

"Do you expect there could be trouble from the Red Lord's men?" asked Rhys.

The girl shook her head. "The Red Lord is acting boldly, but I believe Ayd is close enough to my father's hold that we should not worry. My father is strong still. The Red Lord will not risk a direct confrontation. I do not believe he intends to occupy Indo. He will destroy it then leave. My father will lose one of the two ports in his prefecture, which will severely limit the revenue he can raise to support his army. The Red Lord means to frustrate and wound us. In time, he will weaken us to where he can take our lands and rule our people. That will take years, though, maybe decades. After the attack at Indo, he will return to his own lands and see how we react."

"Does the emperor do nothing?" wondered Ben.

Lady Iyrron shook her head. "If we are not strong enough to protect ourselves, why would the emperor bother to protect us?"

"Why do you bother with an emperor then?" challenged Ben.

"That is the way it is," responded the girl coolly. "How is it in

Alcott when the lords make war on each other. Does someone stop them?"

"There is no emperor," answered Amelie. "Alcott is made of many lands, many nations, like how Ooswam and Qooten are different."

Lady Iyrron frowned. "Qooten is not a nation. It is rock and dirt. It is filled with a barbaric people. They live in tents and have no homes. It is not part of Ooswam because the emperor does not wish it to be." She glanced at Towaal. "Why are your friends so ignorant about your home?"

The mage thought briefly before replying, evidently deciding how much to tell the girl. "I was born in Ooswam, but it is no longer my home. It has been a long time since I lived here."

"If you were born here, it is your home," insisted the girl.

"Maybe so," responded Towaal.

"Can you tell us more about Qooten?" Ben asked Lady Iyrron.

The girl eyed him. "Can you tell me more about this mission of yours?"

Ben made a snap decision and told her what they intended. "We're looking for a group of mages."

The girl glanced at her leg where Towaal had healed her. She hadn't pressed them on it, and no one had told her what happened, but it was clear magic must have been involved. She took a deep breath then let it out slowly.

"Mages are bedtime stories in Ooswam," she admitted. "Many in the peasant class do not believe they exist. The noble class knows of the City and the Sanctuary, of course, but even in that enlightened group, mages are thought to be manipulative and power hungry. Never accept help from a mage as you'll certainly find yourself giving more than you got, or so the stories would tell you. Most people in Ooswam who do know mages exist want nothing to do with one."

"Manipulative and power hungry," responded Towaal. "That's a fair assessment of the Sanctuary, but not all mages."

"These mages you seek," asked Lady Iyrron, "you are certain they are in Qooten? There are no mages there that I am aware of. Surely, the emperor would be interested if there were. Why do you seek them?"

"We're not certain they are in Qooten," admitted Ben, "but if they are, we need their help to battle a threat looming over all of Alcott and likely here too. You are familiar with demons?"

The girl nodded. "We have demons in Ooswam. Rarely near cities, though. I've never seen one myself."

"There was a device, something that made the demon threat manageable in Alcott," explained Ben. "It was destroyed. Demons are appearing now in numbers that haven't been seen for millennia. There are swarms of them rampaging across the north of the continent. Hundreds of them are working together. We believe it is only a matter of time before they've grown in power to the point no force can stop them. The mages we seek in Qooten may be able to help."

"Are you from the Sanctuary?" the girl asked Lady Towaal bluntly.

With a shake of her head, Towaal responded, "Not anymore."

The girl seemed to make a decision she had been considering. "I will not oppose you."

Ben blinked. "Uh, thanks."

"When we get to Ayd, I will ensure you are provisioned for your journey into Qooten, but there are some things you should know."

The fire popped and Ben jumped inadvertently. Amelie pinched him and whispered, "Don't worry. I'll protect you."

Ben rolled his eyes at her.

"Qooten," continued the girl, "has no cities, towns, or even villages as you would know them. It is governed by the Dirhadji, a group of men who have dedicated their lives to combat. They're nomadic, and from what I understand, they only stay in one location for a few nights. A few weeks at most. Their women are treated as chattel, the spoils of battle."

She looked around the group. "You must be prepared to protect yourselves, because if you are unable, the women in this party will be taken. The Dirhadji use women like beasts of burden. They are kept as slaves who cook and clean. Powerful warriors keep harems for sex. Do not think I exaggerate when I say your lives will be worse than death."

Ben looked at Rhys. The man had spent time in Qooten. He learned the Ohms there. Surely, he would have mentioned this previously.

Rhys winked at him and whispered, "You thought this was going to be easy? At least it's not the Wilds."

Ben grunted.

"Food and water will be difficult to find," continued the girl, ignoring Ben and Rhys. "Most of Qooten is desert. Rocks, sand, and lizards will be all you see for days. Even if you do find water, it could be surrounded by a tribe of Dirhadji. They are unlikely to share without a fight. When they exhaust the water in an area, the tribes move. Whatever tribe your mages are part of is going to be just like the others, constantly relocating."

Ben frowned. The physical challenges she described would be difficult but not impossible to overcome. Finding a particular group of secretive mages in a nomadic society, though, was going to be a problem.

"We have to do this," declared Amelie. "No matter the difficulty. It's too important to give up. Do you have any suggestions on what we could do?"

Lady Iyrron nodded. "Find a guide. Someone who knows the desert. Someone who knows the culture much better than I do but is no longer a part of it."

THE NEXT MORNING, a bell away from camp and another two or three bells from Ayd, Lady Iyrron fell in beside Ben as they hiked up a gentle hill. She was walking normally now. With the help of Towaal's healing, her leg only displayed a thick scar where she'd been injured.

The bladed spear she carried, a naginata she called it, was balanced on her shoulder. Her thick armor had been left behind at their first camp. The stuff wasn't suitable for a long, cross-country journey, and it had been badly damaged in the battle for Indo.

"I am not interested in cavorting with you," stated the diminutive lady. "You can tell your woman that she has no cause for concern."

Ben coughed and nearly stumbled.

"I do not mean it personally," assured Lady Iyrron. "I come from a very wealthy family. My father would be disappointed if I romped with a peasant."

Ben glanced at her.

"Sorry," she said. "I should say commoner. I understand people in the north are offended when called peasants, even if they are. I'm afraid my father would disapprove of a liaison with a commoner no matter the circumstances. He is from an older generation and is not as enlightened about these things as we are. Still, he is my elder, and I must respect him."

Ben stared straight ahead, his face filling with heat. He wasn't sure how to respond to the lady's cynical assessment of a potential relationship. It came uncomfortably close to what Amelie said to him several months before.

"Your girl," explained Lady Iyrron, "was giving me unpleasant looks this morning out of the side of her eyes. I am certain it is because of my interest in you. Tell her it is not sexual. That simply does not happen between highborn and common."

Finally, Ben gathered himself enough to answer. He swallowed and then replied, "Yes, I believe she thought that once as well. I'll assure her you have no interest."

Lady Iyrron glanced at him uncertainly, contemplating his answer. Then, as highborn do when they didn't understand something, she chose to ignore it.

"Now that we have that settled," she said, "I want to know about the mage."

Ben sighed. He was tempted to tell her that Amelie was a mage in training as well, but seeing the shock on the girl's face wasn't worth leaving another potential clue for Eldred.

He opened his mouth to respond when Rhys, who was leading them, pulled up short and started cursing.

Ben looked in the direction his friend was facing and started to curse as well.

Half a league away, flowing over the verdant green hills, was a black mass.

"Is that what I think it is?" asked Milo nervously. He clutched his hands on his trident and frowned at the approaching shapes.

Rhys looked to Corinne. "You have the best eyes. How many?"

She held a hand over her brow for shade and grimaced. "Twenty, maybe twenty-five?"

"Damn," muttered the rogue.

"These are the demons you spoke of," queried Lady Iyrron, peering curiously at the approaching shapes. "The reason you are seeking the mages?"

"Yes," replied Ben. "This many of them are referred to as a swarm. They're extremely dangerous. Twenty-five of them could easily overrun a village, and they'd be a serious threat to most towns. They are faster and stronger than any human opponent you will have faced. It's best if you stay behind us with Lady Towaal and Milo."

"You are strong enough to stand against these creatures?" asked Lady Iyrron.

"We can try," responded Ben.

Iyrron slung her naginata off her shoulder. "Just because I have never personally seen a demon does not mean I cannot defeat one. If they are as dangerous as you say, then my assistance is needed."

"We need all the help we can get," Corinne said to Ben.

He sighed and joined Rhys at the crest of the hill. Amelie, Corinne, and Lady Iyrron flanked them.

"I wish I hadn't lost my bow," grumbled the huntress.

"Me too," responded Rhys. In a terse voice, he issued instructions. "We'll have to make do with what we have. Ben, you hit them with the wind when they are ten or fifteen paces away. Towaal, do what you can while they're down. Don't worry about subtlety. We can worry about leaving clues for Eldred if we manage to survive this. Focus on the arch-demon first. With good throws with my long knives, I can stop two more of them, but after that, it's blade to claw. Amelie and Lady Iyrron, stay between Ben and I. Stab anything that slips through our line."

The swarm drew closer and nervous tension spread through the group. These demons appeared just like their peers to the north; thick, slobbering, dense muscle, sharp teeth. In the midst of them, an arch-demon kept pace. It was half-again as tall as Ben, and unlike other arch-demons they'd faced, this one wasn't letting its minions run in front. They'd have to deal with the smaller creatures and their leader at the same time.

"What is that?" asked Lady Iyrron in a quivering voice. They'd finally found something that intimidated the feisty girl.

"That's the arch-demon," responded Ben. "Don't get hit by it."

Amelie fell into place behind Ben and Rhys. Lady Iyrron stayed by Ben's side.

He glanced at her, but her eyes were straight ahead. Determination spread across her face. Her knuckles were white on the haft of her naginata, but she'd dropped into a ready stance. Faint tremors shook her body. Ben gave her credit for not backing down.

He shook himself and turned to the demons. Iyrron had faced combat before if not demons. He had to remind himself that he'd seen her stand against the Red Lord's men in Indo. He couldn't let worrying about her distract him from the approaching violence. If he didn't knock the creatures down with his wind, his friends would be overwhelmed in an instant.

The swarm closed, grass and dirt flying behind them as sharp claws dug into the lush turf. Frantic runs became leaping bounds, the creatures covering a dozen paces with each jump. The arch-demon strode forward, easily keeping up with its smaller minions.

The bright yellow sun, clear blue sky, and vivid green grass was a disorienting contrast to the black horrors. They belonged in the cold, grey winter of the Wilds. Not the bright summer.

At a hundred paces, the sound of the wind was wailing through Ben's head, building easily into a crashing gale. He thought about the storm during the battle in Indo and the crescendo in his head soared higher, drowning out the sounds of his companions and even the snarls and shrieks of the demons.

At fifty paces, his eyes began to water, his body straining to release the power that was growing inside of him.

At fifteen paces, he swept his hand forward, willing the storm into a narrow channel. It burst directly into the face of the demons, catching most of them mid-leap.

Ben held his longsword in one hand and the other he kept forward, palm facing the demons. The power continued to flow through him, a torrential blast of force that smashed into the creatures. The smaller demons were blown back, mere leaves in a storm. Even the arch-demon stumbled, staggering away from Ben and his friends. Confusion and anger etched its face. Its jaw opened to roar at the shrieking gale that battered it back.

"Keep your eyes ahead!" shouted Towaal.

From behind Ben, a blaze of pure light exploded and then narrowed, focused on the arch-demon's face. Its dark eyes flashed and Ben saw the steady beam of focused light reflected back at him. The huge creature bellowed an ear-shattering cry of pain and slumped down, its wings pulling forward, covering its eyes.

"It's blinded," yelled Towaal.

"Attack!" screamed Rhys.

They surged forward. Ben was surprised when out of the corner of his eye, he saw Lady Iyrron sprint ahead of him.

As she raced forward, she placed the butt of her spear into the soft turf and used it to vault into the air, spinning on her side like a top. While flying through the air, she whipped her spear around. With incredible velocity, she brought it down onto the head of the first demon. The creature was still scrambling to its feet but never made it upright.

The blade of the naginata smacked into the beast's skull, shearing through it. Half the demon's head flew off to the side while the rest of the body collapsed down to the grass.

Lady Iyrron landed lightly on her feet, naginata held confidently in front of her.

Ben looked away from her as he and his friends waded into the mass of demons. Nearly all of them were still down, struggling to comprehend the force that had sent them flying. They were still dangerous, though, and Ben had to jump over a clawed hand as it lashed out, trying to catch his legs. As he landed, he plunged his blade down into the demon's chest.

Corinne swung a hand axe into a demon's head next to him.

He turned and slashed across the neck of another one. Frantically, he hacked his way deeper into the swarm. They had to kill or disable as many of the creatures as possible before the beasts recovered from the wind. If the demons were all standing, Ben wasn't sure the party could survive facing the entire swarm.

The towering arch-demon had regained its feet and was lashing out blindly. Ben and his friends didn't go anywhere near it, yet.

It didn't know that, though, and it was frantically trying to defend itself. One of the smaller demons stumbled close. Claws the length of Ben's arm smashed into it, tearing the creature's body in two. Purple blood flew like it was tossed from a bucket. The smaller demon's torso bowled into one behind it, knocking the second creature to the ground. The strangled wail of the victim didn't stop the arch-demon from thrashing about, seeking Ben's companions but catching its own minions instead.

Ben snickered and turned to find two of the beasts had made their feet and were closing on him. He stepped to the side, watching as they closed together, fouling each other's attack path. Then he leapt forward. His longsword stabbed into one of their muscled necks. The second demon reached for him, but Ben edged around the dead body of the first, blocking the second with it.

A howl of frustration was cut short, turning into a screeching gurgle as Ben's sword thrust into its open mouth.

"Ben!" shouted Amelie, drawing his attention to Corinne, who was scrambling back, trying to defend against three of the creatures.

The huntress had faced more demons than the rest of them combined, but her hand axes didn't have the reach to provide any real defense. Instead, she relied on quick attacks to finish them before they could strike her. Against three of the demons, she was overmatched. She couldn't land a fatal blow on one of them without opening herself up to attack by the other two.

Ben jumped over the body of a demon's corpse then stopped.

Lady Iyrron's naginata plunged into the back of one of the creatures facing Corinne. She then twisted the haft of her spear and shoved the body of the demon into the path of another.

Corinne saw the opportunity and struck, parrying a clawed hand with one axe and smashing the other axe into the demon's face.

The two ladies were more than sufficient to finish the

remaining demon, so Ben turned to find Rhys crouched, eyeing the arch-demon and eight smaller ones clustered around it. They were communicating somehow and had managed to calm their leader. Its eyes were still squeezed tightly shut, but it was no longer thrashing around wildly.

"Too bad," remarked Rhys. "That thing was taking out more of them than I was."

Ben chuckled mirthlessly. Even blinded, the arch-demon was still deadly. With the eight smaller creatures around it, this wasn't going to be easy.

"You want the big one or the little ones?" asked Rhys.

Ben was about to answer when the eight smaller demons charged forward simultaneously. The arch-demon took a step behind them, advancing as part of a coordinated attack.

There was no time to plan with Rhys, so Ben attacked. If the demons were coordinating, they couldn't allow themselves to be surrounded or stuck dealing with the smaller ones when the arch-demon could reach them.

Ben ducked under the first claw and drew his blade along the demon's abdomen. Lurching to the side, he avoided the falling body, but the next creature crashed into him with a heavily muscled shoulder, sending him flying onto his back. He grimaced in pain as a heavy foot stomped down on his arm. Luckily, the demon was moving too fast to stoop and maul him.

It stumbled by, glaring down at him. Its snarling, tooth-filled mouth hung open in hunger.

Ben watched as Amelie's rapier slid smoothly into that mouth, skewering the beast and sinking steel into its brain.

Beside her, Corinne smashed a hand axe into another demon's neck.

Ben clambered to his feet, grateful the girls had arrived to help, but not wanting to spend any longer than necessary on the ground in the middle of a fight with a demon swarm.

He got up just in time to meet a creature hurtling toward him.

He thrust his sword into its chest and leaned to the side. This time, it didn't have a companion coming close on its heels. He let the creature's momentum carry it safely by him.

Lady Iyrron was battling a demon next to him, swinging her naginata for a decapitating stroke, but the demon got an arm up in time to block the fatal blow. The blade of the spear sunk deep into its arm and an animalistic shriek burst from its throat.

Iyrron reversed the direction of her spear and spun it the other way, the butt of the weapon smashing into the side of the demon's head. Bone cracked as the sturdy wood haft pounded the beast's skull.

It didn't stop it.

The demon snarled at her and lashed out with its good arm, catching the haft of the spear. The force of the blow sent the naginata flying from Iyrron's hands and she stumbled back, falling over, clearly stunned by the demon's strength.

The demon stepped forward, spittle flying from its open mouth, ready to pounce on the defenseless girl.

Ben arrived just in time, hammering his blade into its back.

The tip of the mage-wrought steel punched through thick muscle and slid out the front of the demon. He kicked a foot up and set it on the demon's back, shoving the thing off his blade.

Iyrron looked up at Ben in shock. Then her eyes grew even wider.

Sensing danger, Ben hurled himself forward and felt the swish of a powerful blow sail just behind him.

A bestial roar tore through the air as the arch-demon swung in vain, trying to hit anything other than its own demons.

The companions all scrambled back, forming a loose circle around the monster. All of the smaller demons had been dispatched, and Ben's friends were still standing. So far, so good, thought Ben.

"Any suggestions?" asked Corinne between heavy breaths.

"Bit by bit," said Ben. "It can't see us, but it can hear us."

He stalked closer to the arch-demon and shouted at it. Its head snapped toward him, but he was ready and jumped away as soon as it moved.

Rhys closed behind it and delivered a wicked slash to the back of the demon's leg.

The big creature pivoted, but the rogue was already scampering away.

Ben danced close and sliced a deep laceration on its arm.

The arch-demon was spinning, flailing wildly, trying to catch Ben or Rhys as they darted in to deliver small but damaging strikes.

One of Corinne's hand axes flew end over end to smack into the side of its face. Both clawed hands went up to protect its head. Ben and Rhys sprung forward, one longsword stabbing into its abdomen, the other finding its back.

Purple blood streamed down its sides and the arch-demon wailed in agony. It was slowing, and Ben and Rhys used that to devastating effect, raining blows over and over until the creature was bleeding from two dozen cuts and punctures. It fell to one knee, struggling to rise.

Rhys met Ben's eyes.

Ben charged from behind and plunged his blade into the arch-demon's back, burying the weapon halfway to the hilt. It howled and spun on its knee, ripping Ben's weapon out of his hands. He knelt under its sweeping arm.

Rhys was ready. He strode in and thrust his longsword into the arch-demon's throat, angling the point of the blade up into its skull. He twisted the blade and yanked it out, an eruption of purple blood following his weapon to splash on the green grass.

With an earth-shaking boom, the creature fell forward on its face, motionless.

Gasping, Lady Iyrron asked, "How many of these things did you say are loose in Alcott?"

"Thousands after the battle of Northport," answered Amelie quietly. "More are generating every day."

Iyrron didn't respond. She leaned on her spear with one hand and clutched a gash on her side with the other.

"Do you need healing again, Lady Iyrron?" asked Amelie.

The girl grimaced. "Call me O'ecca."

4

AYD

THEY TOOK a bell to patch up small, superficial wounds and clean their weapons. After that, it was a quick two-bell walk to the town of Ayd. They needed to gather supplies there and send O'ecca on her way.

Ben had to admit he'd been impressed by the tiny girl's prowess fighting the demons. She made up for her diminutive stature with exceptional speed. When she attacked, she committed to it fully. It allowed her to strike with more power than should have been possible with her small frame, but it also opened her up to counters when her initial attack wasn't successful. It was a bold and risky style.

"You've saved my life twice," O'ecca remarked to Ben. She was walking by his side, occasionally decapitating innocent blades of grass with her naginata.

Amelie was on his other side. After the demons, the girls seemed to have dropped any animosity toward each other.

"I was in the right place at the right time," responded Ben.

"With the right skills," added O'ecca. "Where did you learn to fight like that?"

Ben shrugged. "Good teachers and experience, I guess. We've

69

been traveling a lot in the last year. I've picked up a little bit from a lot of people."

"You use forms I've never seen before, but some that are quite familiar," commented O'ecca. "My father has a blademaster in his employ. There are several others that come close. Well, there were several others before Indo. They taught me what I know. You fight like one of Ooswam's blademasters. With an added layer, I would say. An extra viciousness."

Ben kept walking. He was startled at how easily the girl was able to assess his skill. She was right, of course. Saala had been his first tutor. After learning from Saala, Ben had added nasty little tricks from Rhys, Jasper, and even Black Bart.

"Have you trained with a blademaster from Ooswam?" asked the girl directly.

Ben glanced at Amelie out of the corner of his eye. He didn't want to admit he knew Saala.

"She already knows about Towaal," mentioned Amelie. "There's nothing more Eldred or her henchmen need to know to find us."

Ben looked back to O'ecca. "You know by now we are being tracked by someone, someone who knows us well enough to trace any word or even rumor of us."

O'ecca frowned. "I've seen you all fight, and you have a mage with you. You are still afraid of this person?"

Ben nodded.

"Then I must tell my father," stated the slender lady.

"I think its best you do not," suggested Ben. "Our hunter has no interest in the South Continent, only in finding us. I believe if she passes through your lands, she will do so without causing disruption. You will probably never know she was there. If challenged though, she is exceptionally dangerous."

"She is a mage?" queried O'ecca.

"She is," Ben affirmed. "One a great deal more powerful than Lady Towaal. Believe me. You do not want to anger her."

O'ecca frowned. "For now, I will keep your secrets about the mages. No one is likely to believe it anyway, but a blademaster from Ooswam is not part of that. Tell me, who trained you?"

"Saala Ishaam," answered Ben.

The girl stumbled and Ben caught her arm. She stared at him.

"You know Saala Ishaam?" she demanded.

Ben frowned, unsure if that was a good thing or a bad thing.

"I know him," he confirmed. "I take it you do as well?"

"I know of him," answered O'ecca quickly. "I was just a girl when his family disowned him."

Ben looked at Amelie again. Her lips were pursed in thought.

"His family disowned him?" she asked hesitantly.

O'ecca nodded. "Did he not tell you? It was not a secret in Ooswam."

Ben shook his head. "I gathered there was some sort of falling out, but he never told me the details. He's a rather quiet fellow when not giving advice about handling a sword. I never probed too deeply into his past."

"It's best for a student to not question his master," agreed O'ecca. "Saala Ishaam's story is well known here, but I am not sure it is my place to tell it."

"I did save your life twice," chided Ben. "I also told you who trained me in good faith."

"Very well," O'ecca acquiesced. "Some time ago, maybe fifteen years, the trouble started. Saala was the first son of Lord Syo Ishaam, the Ram Lord as some call him."

"Why do they call him that?" wondered Ben.

"He has a helmet with ram horns attached," answered O'ecca.

Ben waited for more, but apparently, that was it.

"Anyway," she continued, "the Ram Lord at the time was the fourth most powerful lord in Ooswam. For years, he had been building on his own father's legacy to grow that power. Their House held nearly unlimited timberland, which was harvested to build an unsurpassed fishing fleet. The other lords called him a fool, as fishing was the work of peasants, but the Ram Lord proved them all wrong. At one point, my history tutor estimated that two thirds of the fish consumed in Ooswam were brought in by the Ram Lord's fleet. He used that revenue to buy beef cattle, pigs, and ostriches. These animals are common here, but many cities became reliant on the scale of the Ram Lord's supplies. He spread wealth and abundance around his lands and the people thrived. They started businesses and brought even more economic activity into the prefecture, which, of course, the lord then earned taxes on. It became apparent that within decades, the House of Ishaam may control nearly as much wealth as the emperor."

Ben thought back to Saala's lectures about politics. He wished he could recall more of the blademaster's words, but he had a new appreciation for Saala's description of a lord's ability to win the trust of the people. O'ecca's tale was starting to sound familiar.

"The neighbors grew jealous," stated O'ecca, "but none would dare make a move. Even with superior military might, they knew they couldn't field an army without food from the Ram Lord. No army will march far on empty bellies, as the war-masters say."

Amelie bumped against Ben and raised an eyebrow when he met her look. Ben knew Saala had come from a wealthy family, but this was beyond what he'd imagined.

Lady Iyrron kept speaking, caught up in her own story. "Saala, from what I'm told, grew up like any child of a powerful lord. He studied poetry, painting, and music, as we all do. The sword is where he excelled. He was a blademaster by his twenty-second summer."

"You know a lot about him," remarked Amelie.

Ben smirked. He knew she was thinking about the years she'd known the man. Ben suspected Saala had told her none of this. Her certainly hadn't told Ben.

O'ecca nodded, oblivious to the subtext of Amelie's comment.

"He became rather notorious for what happened next. Any member of an established House in Ooswam knows the story. These days, it's told as a caution to ambitious younglings."

Ben frowned.

O'ecca shifted her naginata to the other shoulder. "It was expected that by the time leadership of the House of Ishaam passed to Saala, it could be the third most powerful family in Ooswam. They would only be surpassed by the House of Vinn and the emperor. Apparently, that wasn't enough. Saala, perhaps fearful of the neighboring lords' intentions or perhaps simply overly ambitious, started to build his own power base. He sought out the greatest swordsmen in Ooswam and began to bring them under his banner. It wasn't an army in the traditional sense. There weren't more than a dozen at first, but they had the skills to sway a battle."

"One thing you should understand about Ooswam," explained O'ecca. "The lords constantly test each other's boundaries, probing for territory. Border skirmishes are frequent, but pitched battles like you saw in Indo are rare. At least, they used to be. A few arrows may be fired at a passing patrol, a scuffle in a neutral tavern that occasionally ends in a stabbing, an assassin strikes a family member. From time to time, there might be a raid, but only with the intent of setting a few fires and scaring people away. It's incremental jostling for territory and hasn't broken out in open war for over a century."

"At first," she continued, "Saala and his cohort were like any other band of talented lordlings. They protected their family's territory, and no one thought it strange they did so with a little more viciousness than was strictly necessary. After all, some violence between the Houses isn't uncommon. Over time, Saala's men became exceptionally effective, and their brutality grew as well. When they raided, they would seek blood. When they encountered a patrol, they didn't fire an arrow and ride away, they attacked and pursued their opponents until they were dead or captured. Many fell under the swords of Saala's band. On a small scale, his men were ruthless, and no one could compete with them."

"That doesn't sound like Saala," said Ben, defending his friend. "I've never seen him draw his blade when it wasn't strictly necessary."

"He's a good man," agreed Amelie emphatically. "I've never seen him act the way you describe. He was always loyal to us."

O'ecca simply shrugged. "I am telling you what my tutors taught me. Maybe it is inaccurate, or maybe the man has changed over the years. We agree on one thing, though. He was loyal. He would stop at nothing to help his House."

Ben frowned. He was thinking about one of his earliest impressions of Saala, the time Meghan was accosted in Murdoch's Waystation. The blademaster had decimated a merchant's guard in a fight. The man was down on the barroom floor, unable to rise. The bouncers had just arrived. Saala ignored them and brought his boot down. He ruthlessly crushed the man's hand. It likely disabled him permanently.

"Continue," urged Ben, cutting his gaze at Amelie. "Saala has been a friend to us. He wouldn't be our only friend with a checkered past."

From ahead of them, Rhys snorted. The rogue hadn't shown any other sign of it, but he was clearly listening to the conversation.

"Saala and his band, the Red Hand, as they called themselves, began to range further from home. He was no longer simply defending his father's lands or people. He was encroaching into neighboring prefectures. The emperor took notice, and he reprimanded the Ram Lord for letting his son get out of hand. He charged a levy on the fishing fleet and confiscated some of the herds. It was merely a setback for the House of Ishaam, but Saala and the Red Hand did not take it well. They grew bitter at the emperor, convinced he was taking sides in the constant games of position that the lords played. They felt it was a plot against them."

Even Towaal was walking closer, ear cocked toward the conversation, though, she was also pretending not to listen.

"The Red Hand had been operating for about six years, and they'd grown to nearly one hundred men. They were not all blademasters, but they were experienced and deadly. No one was willing to stand against them. They raided at will, taking what they wanted and always growing their power and reputation. They'd grown strong enough that even the emperor was getting nervous. He used the fear of Saala's band to rally the other lords. In truth, at that point, it did grow into a plot against the Red Hand. For the lords, choosing between a benevolently neglectful emperor and an upstart raider was an easy decision. I'm told with little prodding, the lords joined the emperor's plan."

Ben was fascinated with O'ecca's story. To him, Saala had always seemed unflappable and unlike the young man she described, but the actions had echoes of the philosophies he'd taught Ben.

She cleared her throat. "Sorry. I could use a water skin right about now."

"I'm sure we'll find a stream soon," assured Ben.

"Hopefully," she responded. "There isn't much left to the story. The emperor and the lords suspected the Red Hand was ready to take bold action, so they made it easy for them. They staged a winter festival. The main event would be a special hunt for a white bear that had been spotted in the mountains south of the emperor's city of Shamiil. There was an actual bear, apparently, and it was quite large. It had been harassing the peasants who lived in the foothills of the mountains and killed scores of them. While the bear was real, and the need to hunt it was real, the rest was a setup to draw out the Red Hand. The emperor invited all of Ooswam's powerful families and decreed that whoever took the bear's skin would be rewarded. The successful hunter and their party would win a newly commissioned fishing fleet the emperor was building. It was intended to be seen as a direct threat to House Ishaam's prosperity. Each lord was allowed four companions. Even the emperor himself would participate. Just like the others, he would only have four men with him. It was expected that all of the young and powerful in Ooswam would be in the forest with minimal protection, a perfect opportunity for anyone looking to strike a blow against the empire."

"Devious," muttered Amelie.

O'ecca nodded. "The emperor and the lords weren't actually planning to be out there with so few guards, of course. They sent imposters on the hunt and waited for the Red Hand to make their move. When they did, the might of the most powerful lords in Ooswam surrounded the wood and closed the noose. Saala and his men were trapped, but remember, these were the best blades on the continent. They fought fiercely. Some escaped, including Saala, but most were slaughtered. A few, it turned out, had already been working for the emperor. They betrayed their fellows and went on to reap great rewards. The Red Lord was one of those."

Ben glanced at her. "The Red Lord was in Saala's band but betrayed him?"

She nodded. "The emperor hoped that by vanquishing Saala, he would stop the bloody infighting among his lords and return to more congenial times. I think you saw for yourself in Indo how well that worked. The Red Lord is still trading on the credit he earned back then. Any of Ooswam's other lords would have already been called to task by the emperor."

Ben opened his mouth to respond, but at that moment, they topped a hill and looked down on the town of Ayd.

It was full of green-armored figures. To the north of town, a huge pit had been dug. Next to it were stacks of cloth-wrapped tubes.

"That looks like a-a..." stammered Amelie.

"...mass grave," finished Ben.

THEY SAT in the common room of the only inn in town and waited.

O'ecca had disappeared upstairs with the captain of her father's men.

The companions had a lot to discuss. The town of Indo was overrun, and presumably ransacked then burned by the Red Lord. The town of Ayd had been overrun as well, but these people had suffered at the hands of demons.

Grimly, Ben wondered which town had fared better. The thought of being consumed by a demon was awful, but the creatures moved quickly. They couldn't hold a candle to the depths of cruelty that humans were capable of. A sudden spray of life-blood out the neck and a quick death were better than torture, rape, and watching your children be taken for unknown purposes.

They suspected the swarm that swept through Ayd was the one they faced and defeated, but the Red Lord was still out there. Lord Iyrron's resources were rapidly vanishing. His remaining forces had work to do.

"Do you think they'd mind if I got an ale?" asked Rhys.

"The innkeeper is dead," answered Milo darkly. "Surely he wouldn't mind."

"It's not a good impression," chided Corinne. "We're supposed to be waiting patiently for Lady Iyrron to release us. These soldiers may have not lived here, but certainly, some of them had friends or family in this town. Be respectful."

Rhys sighed. "I hate waiting."

Ben turned from his friends and observed the room around them. Serious-looking men bustled in and out, all heavily armored in House Iyrron's green. They carried wide scimitars, spears, and short bows. By now, all of these men would know it was demons that attacked Ayd. Demon attacks were rare, but they happened often enough that some of these men could identify the signs. The soldiers wouldn't know Ben and his companions, along with the lady, had already dealt with the threat.

Grateful for their help, O'ecca had promised to keep their identities and what they were capable of a secret. Eventually, someone would find the site of the battle, and they worried that news could get to Eldred's ears. There was nothing they could do about it now.

"There have to be three hundred of these soldiers," muttered Amelie. "Maybe more that we didn't see."

Ben glanced at her.

"Where were these men when Indo was attacked?" she asked.

"Close to the lord, protecting him," guessed Rhys.

The mood in the room suddenly changed. Ben looked to see Lady Iyrron descending the stairs with her father's captain in tow. He was adamantly arguing a point with her, but from what Ben saw, she'd already made up her mind.

"Good," grumbled Rhys. "Maybe we can finally get out of here. Sitting in a tavern but not drinking is shameful."

Lady Iyrron headed directly to their table.

She began without preamble. "What the Red Lord did in Indo to our people was horrible, inhuman. The rest of our towns must be secured, and the Red Lord must be dealt with. I will write to my father and inform him of what happened there. If the emperor will not act, then we must raise the banners of war and deal with it ourselves. What happened here in Ayd, though, is something beyond the understanding of my people. Those creatures we fought..."

She trailed off, a sick look on her face.

After a deep, steadying breath, she continued, "My father and brothers are in position and capable of raising our militias to meet the Red Lord. During the battle in Indo, it was apparent there is little I can do to assist in that war. I was merely one blade on the line, and that is not what our people need from me. I have thought about this, and there are threats to our people from the Red Lord and these demons. Both should be met head-on by House Iyrron, no matter the personal risk, which is why I will accompany you to Qooten."

"Yes," agreed Ben. Then he paused, blinking uncertainly. "Wait. What did you say at the end?"

Lady Iyrron met his eyes. "I have decided to travel with you."

"I, uh," stammered Ben.

He looked to his companions for help. The girl was impetuous and demanding. He worried that if she was with them, she would try to take over leadership of their little band. The mission was too important to get side tracked.

He stalled for time to think. "You want to travel with us?"

Lady Iyrron waved her hand in the air. "You saw what happened here just as well as I did. This cannot be. I will go with you and will help find a way to stop these awful beasts."

Ben frowned.

"We need to obtain supplies, and there is no one to buy from here," mentioned Towaal. "She could also ease our travel to the border."

"Yes, supplies," responded O'ecca. She turned to the captain. "We require seven fully provisioned travel packs with sufficient food and water to travel through the desert of Qooten."

"Lady, your father…" protested the captain.

"Will have my letter explaining the situation," interjected O'ecca sharply.

"There are a few more things we could use," suggested Rhys slyly. "We lost our packs in Indo after we battled to save the children from the Red Lord."

"Inform the captain. He will find what you need," assured O'ecca. "Now, there is a shop here which I believe will have suitable desert attire for the women. If you'd care to accompany me, we can gather what we need."

As soon as the girls exited the common room, Rhys turned on the captain. "Half a dozen ale skins, a few pints of Ayd's finest spirits…"

Ben snorted at his friend's requests and leaned back in his chair. She was strong-willed and volatile, but they had another recruit to their cause.

THEY SPENT the rest of the day in Ayd, gathering supplies and preparing to venture into unknown territory. As they moved through the town, Ben glanced around the carnage-filled streets. Demons were spawning, and the world was growing to be a dangerous place anywhere you went.

He thought back to the previous year and the threat that a lone demon posed to Farview. That creature had killed several people. It would have killed more if strangers had not arrived and saved them. Now, swarms led by massive arch-demons were roaming the countryside. Small villages like Farview would be overrun in heartbeats, just like Ayd was.

Beside Ben, Milo delicately stepped around a torso of a villager. The legs didn't seem to be anywhere nearby. Ahead of them, Rhys ducked his head into an unmarked storefront. In a town like Ayd or Farview, shopkeepers didn't need signs out front. Everyone knew everyone else. They knew what each merchant sold.

"Tools and other equipment," called Rhys. He gestured to Milo. "Come on. We might have better luck in here than we did the blacksmith."

Milo nodded and disappeared inside.

They were looking for a suitable weapon for the former apprentice. He'd displayed surprising ability with the trident, but the rusty tines were liable to snap the next time he needed to use it.

Ben waited outside with Rhys while Milo poked around inside.

Lord Iyrron's men hadn't cleared the street yet, and its length was littered with bodies of men, women, and children. Most appeared to have been taken down mid-flight. Only a few had weapons lying near them. Ben shook his head. These people had no chance.

"Do you think we caused this?" Ben asked Rhys.

The rogue's eyebrows knit. "How do you mean?"

"Closing the rift, increasing the frequency of demon spawnings," answered Ben. "Are we responsible for these people's deaths?"

Rhys leaned against the side of the building and unhooked a flask from his belt. He took a drink and passed it to Ben. Ben took a swig as well and winced as the liquid burned down his throat.

Finally, Rhys answered, "Destroying the rift had consequences. We knew it might. Had we known how quickly the swarms would form all over the world, how many demons would come pouring out of the Wilds, would we have done it again? I don't know. It's possible we choose poorly and people like these are paying the price. It's also possible our actions saved countless lives in the north and gave us time to figure out a plan to defeat the demons once and for all. Think about it. What if Northport had been completely overrun by that swarm? What if that giant arch-demon and its thousands of minions were turned loose on an unprepared world?"

The rogue swept his hair back from his face and looked up and down the street.

"I don't know if we did the right thing, but I know we did the best we could."

Ben drank again and handed the flask back to Rhys. He didn't have a response to that.

"You can carry the guilt with you," continued Rhys, "but that doesn't help. Trust me. I've got centuries of self-loathing under my belt. That rots you from the inside and only makes things worse. You can't solve a problem with guilt."

Ben turned and surveyed the street around them. He counted a dozen bodies. He gripped the hilt of his longsword in frustration.

"Look," advised Rhys. "The rift is gone. It's done. You have two choices now. You can torment yourself for what happened, or you can acknowledge that we made the right choice at the time with the information we had. If you want, you can sail back to Alcott and hole up in some tavern and waste away while the world burns around you. I don't think that's what you're going to do though, is it? Towaal and I didn't agree to follow you because we thought you'd give up and sulk into oblivion."

Rhys took another swig of his flask then hooked it back on his belt.

Ben's gaze dropped to the flask then back up to his friend.

Milo stepped out of the shop. In his hand, he held an iron sickle-shaped blade. It was a little longer than his forearm and had a utilitarian wooden handle and no cross-guard. Ben suspected it was crafted for agriculture instead of battle.

"It's not perfect," mumbled the former apprentice, "but I guess you just do the best you can."

Ben nodded. "The best you can. That's all you really can do, it seems."

Four days south of Ayd, they approached the border city of Vard. It was technically part of Ooswam, but as Qooten had no permanent settlements, it attracted a lot of desert dwellers for trade. The humidity near the coast had faded, but the heat increased. The landscape was turning to parched red dirt, bare rocks, and scraggly pine trees that hardly cleared Ben's head.

"It reminds me of the Wilds," remarked Ben. "It's hot instead of cold, and there isn't any forest, but this land is unforgiving to people. It's a wonder anyone chooses to live here."

Rhys nodded in assent. "Tough living makes for tough people. The Dirhadji are some of the toughest I have ever encountered. They're unfriendly to outsiders and they're as likely to steer you into trouble as they are away from it. Living in such a difficult environment makes self-sufficiency a critical trait."

"When you were here before, you must have made some friends," stated Ben. "How did you convince them to teach you the Ohms?"

Rhys smirked. "I challenged one of them to a drinking contest."

Ben eyed his friend. He wasn't sure if he was serious.

Rhys continued, "The Dirhadji are nomadic, and they have very few possessions. There is little material wealth out in the desert. Aside from their weapons, they place little value in any object. What they do value are ability and experience. Fighting, drinking, and loving are what they do, usually in that order."

Ben gestured to the empty surroundings. "What are they fighting over?"

"Women," answered O'ecca from behind them. "As I told you, the Dirhadji keep women as chattel. A chieftain or powerful warrior will have many women. A young warrior or an ineffective fighter may have none, though, ineffective fighters who've lasted past their youth are rare."

"They raid each other constantly," agreed Rhys, "with the aim of capturing women."

"The women allow this?" wondered Ben. "They go with whoever takes them?"

"The women of Qooten are not strong," claimed O'ecca. "They

are not taught how to fight and defend themselves. Instead, they survive by attaching themselves to the most powerful warrior they can. If they are in the harem of a chieftain, they know he and his men will be able to obtain food and water. The woman and her children will be protected as part of his household. The chieftain rules a tribe, so that protection will extend to anyone who travels with them. Even with a low-level warrior in the tribe, a woman knows her sons have the opportunity to become powerful warriors. They could even vie to the title of chieftain themselves one day. Her daughters, though, will most likely be taken after their first blood by the chieftain for his own harem or given to one of his favorite warriors."

"The chieftain wouldn't make his sons the next leader?" asked Ben.

O'ecca absentmindedly spun her naginata in front of her while walking. "A chieftain has many sons from many women. His warriors will have many sons as well. The next chieftain will not be decided by which father was strongest. It will be decided by who is the best warrior and who can attract other warriors to support him. Even a weak warrior's son can rule if he proves himself worthy and convinces his peers to follow him."

Ben shifted the heavy pack on his back. He thought it might be helpful to choose a leader based on merit, ability to fight in this case, but the Dirhadji's system of rule seemed to invite constant upheaval and violence. He said as much to Rhys and O'ecca.

"Of course," agreed Rhys. "Why do you think there are no histories about the people in Qooten? Education and writing is worthless in a culture like theirs. When you know you could die with a spear in your gut at any time, you don't spend your time studying. You spend it fighting, drinking, and fucking. Each generation reinforces the ways of the ones before."

"There!" called Corinne from the front of their party.

She was pointing ahead, and Ben saw a collection of stone

buildings rising out of the desolate landscape. At first, he wondered if they were occupied. After a while, he realized there were thin streams of smoke drifting up from some of the structures. The wide, red-dirt road led directly into the formation. From what he could tell, the settlement was the end of the road. To the south, there was nothing.

"Welcome to Vard," muttered O'ecca. "The last bastion of civilization, if you can call it that."

As they drew closer, Ben could see the stone buildings housed inns, homes, and shops. In the middle were a number of tented market stalls. People browsed in the loose, flowing robes and britches of Ooswam. Others wore undyed, light, linen robes and had turbans wrapped around their heads. A few wore dark leather.

"It keeps the heat off," explained Rhys, nodding to one of the turbaned men. "They can also pull the wrap up over their mouth and eyes when there are sandstorms."

"Sandstorms?" wondered Ben.

"There are places deeper in the desert where the sand extends for leagues in all directions. A powerful enough wind can kick it up and blow it around wildly. When we're out there, watch the horizon constantly. If you see a storm building, we must immediately take shelter."

Ben grunted. "There's a lot to know about surviving in the desert."

"It's a good thing you have me with you," said Rhys.

Ben rolled his eyes.

"I have never been to Vard," interjected O'ecca, "but my father and brothers have been many times to trade with the desert folk. I recommend we stay at the Goat Tender's Daughter. It is where they always stay. From there, we can find a guide."

"I thought you were our guide?" questioned Ben.

O'ecca shook her head. "I know of the desert, but I do not know the desert."

"We need to find someone who knows the geography as well as the Dirhadji do," added Rhys.

"They aren't all Dirhadji?" asked Ben.

Rhys shook his head. "The people here live on the outskirts of the desert. Sometimes, they may venture deeper for trade, but they do not follow the ways of the Dirhadji. The Dirhadji rarely come into any town. They live in the deep desert and stay there. If the Purple are looking to stay hidden, that is where they will be. The Dirhadji are the ones we must find."

They stepped into the town and strange smells filled Ben's nostrils; sharp spices, dust, and the pungent odor of animals.

The buildings were comprised of roughly stacked stone, many of them built into the rocks and hills around them. There was no wooden construction. Instead, fabric hung over doorways and windows. It blocked the light, but Ben was certain it did nothing to keep out the sounds or the smells.

Exotic music, oddly accented shouts, and bleats filled the thick, dusty air. As they entered the village proper, a troop of the goats streamed across the road in front of them. Ben and his companions had to stop while two score of the skinny animals were herded past.

"Goats and maybe a few ostriches are the only livestock they'll have," mentioned Rhys. "Nothing else can survive on the scrub brush that grows around here. I hope you like goat milk. Fresh in the morning, cheese at midday, fermented in the evening."

The people seemed friendly enough, but they got a lot of stares. Back in Ayd, they'd changed into the loose tunic and trousers that were common in Ooswam, but they couldn't hide their pale complexions. They were clearly foreigners. Vard was a town built on trade between two distinct cultures, though, so people seemed curious but not concerned.

The Goat Tender's Daughter stood near the center of town,

just off the market. O'ecca and Rhys led them to the door. After one step inside, they both came backpedaling out.

"Maybe another inn," choked O'ecca, bright crimson flooding her cheeks.

Even Rhys whistled through his teeth and mumbled, "Now that was an inn."

Corinne peeked inside then quickly scampered after Rhys.

"There are girls in there that are..." Her face flushed and she trailed off.

Ben's curiosity got the best of him and he stepped toward the door. Amelie caught him and slid her arm through his. She steered him after their friends.

"If it makes Rhys blush, then you don't need to go inside," declared Amelie.

Ben grinned at her. "I'm just trying to take in the sights and experience the culture."

"Sure," she responded, rolling her eyes.

Three buildings down from the Goat Tender's Daughter, they found the Brown Lizard. At least, Ben thought it could be called that. There were no letters, only a rough, painted outline above the door. It was, almost certainly, a lizard. Whether it had originally been red and faded to brown or brown from the beginning, he wasn't sure. Either way, on the red-brown rock, it gave the painting a chameleon-like feel as if the place was trying to remain unnoticed.

At the door, O'ecca hesitated before brushing past the linen curtain and shuffling inside. When she didn't immediately come stumbling back out, they followed her in.

Ben wasn't sure what he thought he'd find inside, but it certainly wasn't this.

All around the room, low couches and thick carpets were scattered haphazardly. Short tables sat in between the couches. Most of the tables held colorful glass vases with thin tubes sprouting from the tops. Richly scented smoke poured out of

AC COBBLE

several of the devices and robed men were huddled around them. They inhaled the smoke, blew it back out in thick clouds, then reclined and sipped at delicate tea cups.

A slim man approached them, his long robes rustling around sandaled feet. Long, oily locks fell around his shoulders. His face was clean shaven except a narrow beard sprouting from his chin. He'd styled it into a sharp point and it glistened with the same oil he'd rubbed into his hair. He ignored the women and focused his attention on Rhys, clearly the oldest man in the party.

The rogue negotiated two rooms for the night and asked what was on the hearth. Ben barely hid his grin when the innkeeper proudly answered, "Roast goat, stewed goat, and a goat cheese with bread."

Before showing them the rooms, the innkeeper offered them mint tea and appeared only slightly offended when Rhys asked for an ale. Towaal interrupted, and they were shown the rooms first.

Rhys, Ben, and Milo returned downstairs quickly after dropping their packs in the room. They picked a spot and reclined on a set of the low couches. Ben eyed the glass device on the table in front of them.

"It's for smoke," explained Rhys. "Like from my pipe, but they flavor it. Herbs, fruits, all kinds of things."

"Is it good?" Milo asked curiously.

Ben was surprised. The former apprentice rarely spoke up.

"Let's find out," responded Rhys with a grin.

A quick wave to one of the serving men and soon they had three mugs of ale, a small bowl full of dried herbs, and a plate of flat bread and some sort of mushy paste.

"Dip the bread into the paste," advised Rhys while he crumbed the herbs into a bowl on the glass vase.

Ben tried what Rhys suggested and was pleasantly surprised. The bread was hot and fresh, and the paste had a rich, earthy flavor. He dipped his bread again and tried the ale. It wasn't good.

88

He sat it back down and watched as Rhys lit the herbs and picked up one of tubes. The rogue sucked on the tube then sat back, a cloud of blue smoke slowly escaping his lips and nose.

Milo picked it up next and also inhaled deeply. He let the smoke pour out of him. His lips curled into a smile and he coughed weakly. "That's not bad."

Ben pursed his lips and tried the smoke as well. He inhaled deeply, the smooth flavor reminding him of the scent of the rogue's pipes but with cinnamon and baked apples. He exhaled slowly, blue smoke billowing up in front of his face. On the way out, he felt his throat tingle, and he involuntarily fell into a fit of coughing.

Rhys passed him his ale and Ben drank gratefully, trying to ignore the taste and let the liquid soothe the burn in his throat.

Around them, men smoked and drank, talking quietly. In the corner, an older woman was slowly strumming an almond-shaped stringed instrument. The room was quiet and peaceful. Ben wondered about the violent descriptions his friends kept giving for Qooten.

He said as much, and Rhys responded, "We're not in Qooten yet. This is still Ooswam. The deeper we go, the more obvious the changes will be. Besides, even here, if you pay attention, you'll see we are right."

Milo nodded, puffing thick rings of smoke from his puckered lips.

"Look around," suggested Rhys. "How many women do you see?"

Ben took the tube from Milo wordlessly and studied the room. Rhys had a point. There were only a few women, and most of them old or clearly with a group of men. Ben blew the smoke out like Milo had, attempting to form the rings. Instead, he only produced misshapen balls that quickly dissipated.

"I'm sure you can do it with practice," consoled Milo, taking another turn and producing more perfectly formed rings.

"Have you smoked from something like this before?" asked Ben, curious if he could get Milo to open up about his past.

The former apprentice shook his head and didn't give any more details.

Ben grunted and sat back on the couch, nursing his ale.

He'd only gotten to his second one when the women appeared. Amelie flopped down next to him on the couch and helped herself to the foamy liquid.

"That's not very good, is it?" she asked, wiping her hand across her lips.

He nodded. "It's terrible. Everyone else seems to be drinking tea."

"We should as well," suggested Towaal. "Drinking heavily is frowned upon in southern Ooswam. It's unusual to see a local consuming alcohol in a place like this. When they do drink, it's in places like the Goat Tender's Daughter. In Qooten, drinking is only done after a raid or during a few auspicious times of the year."

Rhys snorted but didn't comment.

"Mint tea is popular around here. It should be quite good," advised O'ecca.

Towaal leaned forward and brought one of the smoking tubes to her mouth. She drew in a deep breath then relaxed. She puffed out a wide ring of smoke that slowly drifted away from her. Next, she blew a long streamer of smoke which caught up to the ring and passed through the center. She sat back on her couch and winked at Ben.

"You were watching us," he muttered. "How did you do that?"

"I keep telling you. You can do anything in the world if you have the will to make it happen," responded Towaal.

Ben's eyes widened and he glanced around, alarmed someone had seen her. He hissed, "You used magic!"

She raised an eyebrow at him. "Whether I did it with my mind or my lungs, both are efforts to manipulate the smoke. What's the difference?"

Ben eyed her suspiciously.

"She grew up not too far from here," mentioned Rhys. "Probably not her first time smoking from a water pipe. My guess, it's evidence of a misspent youth."

"Really?" wondered Ben. He looked to the mage for confirmation.

"Where, exactly?" asked O'ecca

Towaal sighed heavily. She glanced meaningfully at the girl. "It was long ago."

The diminutive lady seemed confused about Towaal's look, but Ben and the rest of the companions understood. The girl had a difficult enough time coming to terms with the idea that Towaal was a mage. She didn't need to know Towaal was long-lived. Ben suspected when Towaal said long ago, she was talking about centuries.

"As Rhys said, I wasn't always the paragon of pure living," added Towaal. "When I was younger, my friends and I would smuggle water pipes from the men's quarters and smoke until my father's guards found us. My father would be apoplectic. It took me years to realize it wasn't that we were sneaking away and smoking. He was livid at the idea of us being in the men's quarters." Towaal chuckled. "If only he'd known what we were up to with the boys from the University who came to tutor us. He would have had their heads on the block before the sun set."

"Your father's guards?" queried O'ecca. "He is a lord, I presume. Maybe I know him."

Towaal shook her head. "I don't think you will."

"What is your House name?" insisted O'ecca.

"House of Towaal."

The girl frowned. "I am not familiar with that house."

"I didn't think you would be," murmured Towaal. "My family fell on hard times. Our lands were forcefully absorbed by one of our neighbors. Aside from me, I don't believe there is anyone left who claims the name."

"This is why you left for Alcott?" queried O'ecca.

"It is one of the reasons I stayed in Alcott," answered Towaal.

Rhys, clearly sensing the young lady would continue to probe, interrupted to discuss what they should order for dinner, which led into how teas should be paired with the different types of goat, which led to whether goat cheese was really superior to cheese from a cow. By the time he was done, O'ecca had forgotten to ask further about the House of Towaal. Towaal, it seemed, was still thinking about it. Ben caught a far-off look in her eye, one he wasn't used to seeing from the highly focused mage.

When they retired to the rooms, Ben thought to ask Rhys what else he knew about Towaal's past, but as he opened his mouth, he saw Milo shrugging out of his clothes and slipping into his bed. Without knowing why, Ben decided he'd wait until he and Rhys were alone.

THE NEXT DAY, Ben, Rhys, and O'ecca stepped into the dry morning air. It was warm but not yet the blistering heat of full day. Tiny clouds of dust puffed up as they walked down the street.

"Does it ever rain here?" wondered Ben.

"The locals say there is a rainy season," answered O'ecca, "but for those of us near the coast, calling it rainy season is being a bit generous."

Ben kicked at the dry dirt and followed O'ecca. She was taking them to the goat pens where she said they could find someone who knew the desert. If a goat herder knew the watering holes well enough to keep a pack of goats alive, he could do the same for them.

Halfway there, a brawny, black-haired man stumbled drunkenly out of a tavern directly in front of them. The man crashed into O'ecca and she went flailing backward to land on her bottom.

She scowled up at the man and Ben bent to lift her to her feet.

Before he could, the man took a swig from a battered leather drinking horn and snarled, "Watch where you're walking, bitch."

O'ecca's foot lashed out and swept the man's feet from under him. He flopped down on the hard dirt street. A grunt of pain and surprise burst out of his mouth. O'ecca sprang up and kicked the man again, hard in the gut.

"Speak to me like that again, peasant, and I will geld you," she shouted. She raised her naginata menacingly.

The man curled into a ball on his side and coughed weakly. One hand reached out to grasp his now empty drinking horn. The contents were quickly soaking into the dust.

From the door of the tavern, several men burst out laughing.

"Thyr," called one of the men. "How's Lana going to cut off your balls if this girl has already done it?"

The man rolled over onto his stomach and looked longingly at his disappearing ale. He slurred, "The only thing either onna them is gonna do to my balls is lick 'em."

The fallen man's companions wailed with laughter.

O'ecca glared down at the man, her hands shifting dangerously on her weapon.

Ben placed a hand on her shoulder. He knew the lady in her wanted to teach the man a painful lesson, but there was nothing to be gained from it. It was critical they avoid trouble with whatever passed for the authorities in this place.

"You sure about that?" jested one of the man's companions. "Looks to me like you're groveling before this little thing. You're wiggling on your belly like a worm. She made you look like you're a little boy still on your mommy's teat."

The man on the ground snarled. Shockingly fast, he sprang up and snatched O'ecca's naginata away from her. Before she could react, he spun the weapon around, the heavy blade streaking toward her body.

O'ecca stumbled back and the tip of the spear sliced her shoulder, a thin spray of crimson flying from the wound. She cried out and gripped her shoulder, blood immediately welling up around her fingers.

The naginata continued to turn and the man swung it back at her, this time the sharp blade directed at her head.

Ben shoved past and raised a hand. The wooden haft smacked painfully against his palm. He stumbled back, but he stopped the weapon from hitting O'ecca.

The man blinked uncertainly at Ben, the naginata hanging motionless in his hands.

Without thinking, Ben swung a haymaker at him, putting all his weight behind it.

His fist crashed into the side of the man's head with a smack. Ben saw all awareness flicker out of the man's eyes. His body went limp as a wet rag, and the man crumpled into the dirt street.

An angry growl alerted Ben to the man's friends. He turned toward them, dropping a hand to his sword. Rhys had already interceded. He was standing between the men and Ben, his longsword held steadily in his hands.

There were three of them, all dressed like the first with black, braided hair, leather vests studded with bone trinkets, loose trousers, and broad-bladed scimitars hanging from wide belts.

One man dropped his hand to the hilt of his scimitar.

Rhys stopped him.

"Do the Dirhadji no longer allow a man to fight his own battles," snarled the rogue. "You think so little of this man that you will dishonor him?"

The man glared at Rhys. His companions spread out behind him, preparing to fight. "You know nothing of us foreigner. Do not speak of dishonor."

"He injured an unarmed woman," snapped Rhys. "He was trying to kill her. By your code, he should be gutted and left on the rocks to die."

"She was armed with that spear," retorted the man.

"Then he took it from her and attacked," admonished Rhys. "Look at her. She is grievously injured. She may be crippled."

Calling O'ecca unarmed was a tenuous distinction, thought Ben. She really was wounded, though.

He met her eyes and saw she would be okay. A steady trickle of blood made its way down her arm, but the naginata hadn't hit bone or vital organs. As soon as they got back to the inn, Towaal could heal the girl.

The strangers didn't know that, and Rhys was using it.

"That is desert law, and we're not in the desert," growled the man.

Rhys stared at him, not responding. The man shifted uncomfortably and shot a glance at his companions.

"Only a chieftain can administer the code," claimed the black-haired man. "We do not have the authority to do as you say."

"Then I demand you take us to your chieftain," replied Rhys coldly. "Unless you are refusing to follow the code, in which case we'll settle this now."

Rhys tilted his blade and a faint shimmer of silver smoke oozed along the blade.

The two silent Dirhadji, for Ben realized that must be what they were, backed away from their leader nervously. The confidence was leaking out of their stances as more of the silver smoke drifted away from the rogue's blade.

Rhys, evidently sensing their hesitation, pressed harder. "I'll make sure your tribe learns about the dishonor you brought upon them. Injuring a young unarmed girl, refusing to acknowledge the code, getting drunk and fighting foreigners, getting knocked unconscious. I'm sure your chieftain will be glad to hear about this. Your wives will be passed to more honorable warriors and your children will be turned out of the tribe. Your friends will spit on your names."

"This just a misunderstanding. The girl was not seriously harmed," complained the leader. "Thyr is drunk. Let us pay the price in gold. There is no reason for this to go further."

"This girl is the daughter of a powerful lord in Ooswam. She's unspoiled, a virgin." The rogue glanced back at O'ecca and winked. "As you can see, she was quite beautiful before your friend mauled her. We are owed the full price, in blood."

A grimace crawled across the leader's face and his shoulders slumped. "Thyr is meant to take my sister next week. She will become first among his wives. She will be devastated if he does not return. If you think nothing of him or of me, think of her. If she was here, she'd fall at your feet and beg you. Gold, gemstones, anything you desire. My family is very wealthy for Dirhadji. Let me pay you."

Rhys looked down at the unconscious Thyr and drawled, "Take me to her."

The leader blinked.

"Take me to your sister," insisted Rhys. "Let me see what you can offer, and then I will decide if we shall extract the blood price."

The leader's mouth opened then closed.

"You want to go into the desert?" questioned one of his companions incredulously.

"Yes, or we'll settle it here," demanded Rhys. "Since your chieftain is not available, the code instructs the most senior of you to enforce it. Which of you will slit his throat?"

Thyr, still motionless, groaned.

"R-Raim," stammered the companion. "We are to meet Jordi. We have to be there."

The leader, Raim, held up his hand and addressed Rhys. "You are right. I have shamed myself by needing a foreigner to hold me to the code. Ingar is right too. We have a commitment we cannot break."

Rhys tightened his grip on his longsword and didn't back down.

Raim continued, speaking fast to placate Rhys, "There is another solution."

Ben eyed the three Dirhadji. They were tense, but hands had drifted away from weapons. None of them were preparing to strike. Around them on the street, passersby steered wide of the confrontation. No one made any move to interfere, and no guards or watchmen had arrived to intervene.

"Thyr will take you himself," stated Raim.

Rhys turned to look questioningly at Ben and O'ecca.

Ben nodded consent.

He knew what Rhys was at. Enlisting a Dirhadji to take them to find more Dirhadji was a brilliant entry to the desert. They weren't going to get a better guide, assuming the unconscious man was willing.

"He will do this?" questioned Rhys.

"He will," continued Raim. "When he sobers, he will not risk dishonor on himself, his family, and our tribe by refusing this. If he did, he would have to deal with me, but I believe you will find he is a good man."

Rhys stood up straight and sheathed his longsword. "We shall see."

5

ROCK, SAND, LIZARDS

BEN WOKE to see the Dirhadji Thyr squatting on the other side of the camp and staring south. His expression was tight with anger. When the man had come to the day before in Vard, his friends explained what he'd done. His eyes had fallen to his feet and a pressing weight seemed to settle around his shoulders. Surprising Ben, he didn't protest taking the party into the desert to find his tribe and his promised wife. He hadn't made a move to flee either and didn't plead for mercy.

Ben watched him silently. The Dirhadji wore sturdy britches, an open leather vest, and an undyed linen shirt. Around his head, he'd wrapped a turban of the same undyed linen. The material was loose and hung down around his shoulders, covering most of his head and neck. Good for keeping the sun off. On his hip, he carried a broad-bladed scimitar, similar to the ones they'd seen on men in Vard and Ooswam. He also had a utilitarian knife and a sort of half-pack that he carried high on his shoulders. Under the pack he wore a huge water skin. It didn't take an explanation. In the desert, water was a precious commodity. Changes of clothes, cooking implements, they were all nice to have. Without water, you'd die.

The man didn't turn, but he must have sensed a change in Ben's breathing.

"You're wondering if I'll turn on you," suggested the Dirhadji.

"The thought crossed my mind," responded Ben, shifting into a sitting position. "We're on the way to your death sentence."

The man stood and glanced down at Ben. "Life in the desert is fragile. A poisonous snake or lizard bite, drinking tainted water, sandstorms, heat exposure, death in combat, these things can happen to any man, any day. To live in the desert is to accept that death is always waiting for us. It can happen at any time. Those who cannot accept it leave. They move to the fringe towns like Vard. I am of the desert. I am not afraid to die."

"No one wants to die," argued Ben.

Thyr shook his head. "You misunderstand. I do not want to die. I want to live very much. Everyone in the desert wants to live. They have to. Death is easy. Life is difficult. But while I do not want to die, I will accept it when it happens."

Ben grunted.

"Besides," continued the Dirhadji, "if your friend wanted my death, I never would have woken. I do not know what it is you want, but I know you are no more interested in meeting my future wife than I am in introducing you to her. I was drunk and foolish when we first met, but do not assume I am always a fool."

Ben stared at the man, unsure how to respond.

The light scuff of Rhys' boots announced his arrival. He had the latest watch, so Ben guessed he'd either been making rounds outside of the camp or napping. The rogue wasn't the most trustworthy sentry.

"Ben," suggested Rhys, ignoring the Dirhadji. "Should we practice the Ohms?"

Ben shrugged and rose. The girls were still sleeping, and they only had sausage, cheese, and hard biscuits for breakfast. Nothing to prepare and nothing to do until everyone else woke.

Thyr watched suspiciously as the two friends began the

sequences. By the third, a low growl emitted from the back of his throat.

Ben and Rhys paused and glanced at the man.

"My friends told me you know the code," said Thyr. "More than a foreigner should. A foreigner shouldn't know these movements either. Teaching them is a violation of the code. It's punishable by death."

"I spent some time in Qooten years ago," offered Rhys. "The man who taught me is already dead."

"Good," muttered the Dirhadji.

"It's not a death sentence to join us in practicing the movements, is it?" asked Rhys. "As you can see, we already know them. I'm told the Ohms are best when performed as a daily ritual. Some Dirhadji consider the Ohms just as important as breaking fast. Have you done them today?"

Thyr glared at Rhys, considering his choices. Finally, he took a position beside Ben.

The three of them dropped into the start of the fourth Ohm and slowly began rotating through the positions. Ben watched Thyr out of the corner of his eye. The man moved with absolute discipline. Every foot placement, every breath, every turn of his body was perfectly controlled.

The Dirhadji moved slower than Ben was used to, and unconsciously, Ben fell into the man's rhythm. It was difficult, moving so deliberately. After half a bell, Ben's arms and legs were trembling with the effort. It would be so easy to simply set a foot down, but at Thyr's pace, it was a measured, intentional moment when boot touched dirt.

"Move with purpose," said the Dirhadji softly. "Nothing should affect you, and you should only effect what you mean to."

Ben grunted and studied Thyr openly as they moved through more of the sequences. They did a dozen more. When they were dripping with sweat in the early morning desert heat, they stopped for a water break.

Ben opened his mouth to thank Thyr for the instruction, but the man turned away. The Dirhadji squatted on the side of the camp and peered into the distance, ignoring the party.

By then, everyone was awake and preparing for the travel ahead. The girls set out breakfast and Milo folded and packed the few tarps and sleeping mats they'd brought. In the desert, explained Rhys, extra weight could be fatal. Besides, thought Ben, it wasn't like it was going to get cold.

They ate quickly, drank sparingly, then slung packs onto their backs.

Ben glanced around the campsite. It was hard rock and loose dirt. A skilled tracker may be able to tell someone had stayed there, but it would be nearly impossible to know how many or which direction they left in. If Eldred was following them, she'd have a bear of a time keeping up.

"Six more days then I suggest we pause at the village of Frisay," remarked Thyr. "It's the only permanent settlement south of here that we can safely stop at. After Frisay, we'll be at the mercy of the tribes."

"I didn't think there were any towns in the desert," questioned Amelie. "Aren't the Dirhadji nomadic?"

Thyr nodded. "The Dirhadji are nomadic. The people in Frisay are not Dirhadji."

"Who are they?" asked Towaal, suddenly interested.

Thyr shrugged. "Outcasts. Like the Dirhadji, they follow no lord. Unlike us, they are not from the desert and do not follow our code."

"The Dirhadji haven't run them off?" pressed Rhys. "The desert is considered sacred. I'm surprised the chieftains let someone else settle there."

Thyr looked uncomfortable. "When these people first arrived in the desert, they were raided. As you say, the chieftains meant to run them off. Instead, the people dug in and fortified their settlement. They have an unnatural ability to determine when raiders are coming close, and their defense is highly organized. Many Dirhadji were killed before the chieftains decided that particular part of the desert was no longer sacred. Now, the people are allowed to stay there and trade with the tribes. They do not venture deeper into the desert, and my people no longer harass them."

Ben caught Towaal and Rhys sharing a look. The mage was curious about his settlement. Even if it wasn't a natural stop for them, Ben suspected she would have steered that way. Anything out of the ordinary could be a clue.

"If there is nowhere else to get supplies," agreed Towaal, "we should take advantage of it. Thyr, lead us to this place."

BEN BLINKED, trying to clear the grit from his eyes. It was futile. The sand was embedded all over his body like a second layer of skin. In his eyes, in his hair, under his finger nails, it was everywhere. He was being scraped raw by the harsh material.

The beating sun didn't help matters. It felt like one of the fires he used to boil wort at his brewery was constantly blazing down on him, heating his skin like it did his copper kettles.

Amelie shuffled one foot in front of the other ahead of him. She was tired, bone tired. She no longer bothered to lift her feet off the sunbaked rocks. Her hair was piled in a loose bun that Ben definitely wasn't going to mention was similar to O'ecca's. It kept the sun off her neck and allowed the rare stir in the air to cool her sweaty skin. Below the neck, her clothing, recently acquired in Ayd, was coated in the gritty red sand that blew everywhere.

Ben understood why the desert folk didn't bother to dye their clothing now. Before long, it was going to be red regardless of what color the fabric was.

"How much longer did you say?" Ben asked Thyr.

The Dirhadji glanced over his shoulder at Ben. "Four days, though two of them will be across the sand sea. Depending on how the dunes have shifted, we could be delayed there."

Ben grunted.

The sand sea. The Dirhadji seemed to take pleasure in telling them awful tales about the vast, open plain of loose sand. Wind whipped across it, unblocked by rock or hill. Water was nonexistent, and the terrain shifted constantly. Frequently, the sun was obscured by blowing walls of grit. Thyr was certain without his help they'd be hopelessly lost within two bells. He was probably right, but Ben was getting tired of hearing about it.

"If the sand sea is so deadly," questioned Ben, "why is this town of Frisay so close to it?"

Thyr dropped back to walk beside Ben.

Amelie plodded on in front of them. They were headed due south. For that, they didn't need the Dirhadji's guidance.

"It wasn't built there originally," explained Thyr. "Decades ago, when it was first settled, the sand sea was further north. It was here, in fact."

Ben frowned. "It moved?"

Thyr nodded. "I keep telling you, but you do not listen. The sand moves constantly. Thirty years ago, the sea was here. In ten or twenty more years, maybe it covers the town of Frisay."

Ben scratched at his neck, wincing at the feel of sand stuck to his skin. His sweat was like glue for the infuriating red grains.

"Will they move?" asked Ben.

"I don't know," admitted Thyr. "The Dirhadji tend to avoid the people of Frisay. We speak to them as little as possible, only what is necessary to conduct commerce. It wouldn't be wise for them to stay put. You could also argue it's not wise to be there in the first place, yet, there they are. With my own kind, I would not stop at Frisay," continued Thyr, lowering his voice and nodding toward Amelie. "With you, I knew we would need a break. Your women are soft."

"I heard that," called Corinne from behind them.

The Dirhadji turned and eyed her, his face a blank mask.

Ben suspected the man was still adjusting to the armed women in the group. Corinne had her axes, Amelie her rapier, and O'ecca her naginata. Only Lady Towaal was unarmed, though, even the Dirhadji was sensitive enough to understand there was more to the mage than he understood.

Suddenly, startling Ben, an arms-length lizard shot across their path, passing between him and Amelie.

Without breaking his stride, Thyr unsheathed his knife and flung it at the lizard. Twenty paces away, the slender blade skewered the animal. After one violent convulsion, it lay still.

"Dinner," claimed the Dirhadji with a grin.

THREE BELLS LATER, Ben eyed the man queasily as he sunk his teeth into the tough, pale flesh of the lizard. It was neatly flayed, the tough brown skin lying on a rock beside Thyr. That was the only concession the man made toward civilized dining. There was no fuel in the desert, so no fire to cook his meal. The raw meat pulled and stretched before Thyr was able to gnaw off a chunk.

Ben swallowed the bile in his throat and looked away.

"What does one eat in the sand sea?" asked Corinne.

Even though Thyr was rude to her, Ben could tell she was warming to the Dirhadji. Kindred spirits maybe. Before she'd linked up with them, she'd spent her days hunting demons in the unforgiving Wilds. If you ignored the temperature change, it wasn't so different from the desert.

"Whatever you carry with you," mumbled Thyr around a mouthful of lizard. "There is nothing to sustain life there. We'll see some rocks that stick out above the dunes, and there are hollows that the sand has not filled, but nothing can survive long, plant or animal. There is little rain, and the constant wind and blowing grains of sands would shred anything that stood against them for too long. Even the rocks are worn to nubs after a number of years."

"What about us?" asked Corinne. "Aren't we hiking through this thing? Is it safe?"

"No, it is not safe," answered the warrior curtly. "We must cover our skin, or over the course of a few days, it will be scraped raw and bloody. Fortunately, with proper attire, your clothing will take the brunt of the abuse. At night, we'll find an outcropping for shelter or keep walking until we do. There is no other way to sleep comfortably."

"We'd better stock up on lizards," remarked Ben dryly.

The Dirhadji showed his teeth but didn't respond. Ben was realizing the man had a dark, ruthless sense of humor.

THE NEXT DAY, they found the edge of the sand sea.

Their party stood on a rock shelf that overlooked the vast expanse of red grit. Ben hated to admit it, but it looked like everything the Dirhadji said about the place was true. As far as Ben could see, red sand, a few fingers of rock that broke through the surface, and nothing else, extended to the horizon. It was completely empty.

A gust of wind blew around them. Ben watched the red sand swirl away in tiny, knee-high dervishes. Several hundred paces away, the visibility was cut to nothing as the wind picked up the miniscule grains and blew them into the air.

"This isn't going to be pleasant," muttered Ben.

"It's only two days," offered Thyr. "Then, we'll be back in the normal desert. Two days after that, we'll be in Frisay. That's just four days. You can relax in Frisay. There are people like you.

Northerners. Maybe there you will find what you are looking for and let me go."

The Dirhadji watched Ben, but Ben ignored him, pretending to look out into the sands.

Sighing, the Dirhadji turned and began helping the party adjust their turbans and clothing. He tugged at it until no skin showed except their eyes and hands.

"Blink often and cover your hands if the wind picks up," advised the man. "When the grit gets in your eyes, the tears will rinse it out. Don't use the back of your hand to wipe your eyes in any circumstance. You will just make it worse. After a couple of hundred paces, you'll have sand stuck all over you and anything you touch. Breathe through a cloth, or from time to time, you'll accidentally inhale a lungful of the stuff."

"What about our eyes?" asked Corinne. "Surely blinking isn't your only suggestion."

Thyr shrugged. "Hold onto the pack of the person in front of you and close your eyes if the wind picks up too much. It's all you can do. Luckily, there's nothing to bump into out here, and if you fall, you'll land softly. I'll lead the way. All you need to do is keep up."

With that, the man made one final adjustment to his turban and stepped off the rock shelf, his foot sinking into the sand.

Ben leaned close to Amelie and whispered, "Do you think he's planning to lose us somewhere?"

She watched the Dirhadji's back. "He's been trustworthy so far."

"It could have been a ruse to get us somewhere he knew we'd get lost and never return," responded Ben.

Rhys strode by them and stepped into the sand. As he passed, he mentioned, "Worst case, we all die out there."

The rogue marched after Thyr into the empty sand wastes.

"Was that supposed to be encouraging?" wondered Ben.

Amelie chuckled and shook her head. "Who knows. He has a

point, though. A little bit of sand can't be worse than the demons in Alcott, the Wilds, Lord Jason, or Eldred."

She stepped into the sand sea after the others.

Ben took a deep breath then followed her.

Two bells later, he felt like his mouth was as dry and sandy as the ground he was walking across. He tried to spit the grit out, but he couldn't get enough moisture to do it. The water in the skins hanging off his pack was far too precious to waste on rinsing out his mouth.

Thyr promised them they were unlikely to find a source of potable water until they made it to the other side of the sand sea. The constant wind and shifting grains would bury any of the rare springs that might have existed before the sand crept over the area.

Ben plodded along.

The party was strung out in a ragged line behind Thyr. The Dirhadji walked tirelessly across the shifting sand. It was a learned skill, Ben decided. His feet shifted underneath him with every step. He was glad they weren't likely to have to fight someone in the desolate wasteland. He doubted even demons could survive in the sand sea. There was no life there to sustain them.

At the front of their column, Thyr held up a hand. They all paused and slung water skins off their belts. Three mouthfuls, no more, no less. Then they rehung the skins and kept walking.

In the dry heat, they would quickly exhaust themselves without water. Thyr instructed them to immediately let him know if they suffered headaches, dizziness, or cramps. Soon after that, he said, they'd be vomiting up precious liquid they couldn't afford to lose. If they drank too much, though, they wouldn't have sufficient supplies to make the next source of fresh water. It was a thin line they walked.

Ben drank his ration and stoppered his water skin. The Dirhadji was already moving again.

"He's being awfully helpful for someone who is essentially our prisoner," muttered Ben.

"He's curious," suggested Milo.

Ben raised his eyebrow at the former apprentice.

"He knows there is more to our story than we are telling him," explained Milo. "He's not stupid. We aren't following him into the desert simply to settle the score for attacking O'ecca. No, he knows we are after something out here. He wants to find out what. He'll keep us alive until he knows. Then we'll see what his honor is worth."

"You think he'll betray us?" asked Ben.

"I don't know the man any better than you," answered Milo, "but I know we aren't his friends."

BEN SAT CHEWING DOLEFULLY on a hard biscuit. It was bone dry and tasted like the sand that he couldn't get out of his mouth, but it was better than the jerked strip of goat meat Amelie was gnawing on. Across from them, Corinne was poking dubiously at a piece of what could be either dried fruit or vegetable. It had an odd pebbling. Briefly, Ben wondered if it was actually a fungus. Milo had already spit his out. The former librarian's apprentice claimed they could survive for days without food. It was water they really needed, he said.

Ben wasn't sure about that, but he decided he would hold out for more opinions before he tried the dried fruit, or vegetable, or whatever it was.

Behind them, they'd strung three tarps to low stakes. They only came mid-thigh to Ben when he was standing, but they were high enough to sleep under. The tarps were positioned against the wind and would keep most of the blowing sand off of them in the night. Thyr advised they also sleep on their sides, facing away from the direction of the wind.

For three bells prior, they'd looked for a suitable rock to shelter behind, but there was nothing. The wind was light that evening, so Thyr declared it would be safe to sleep under the tarps. They had no fuel for fire, and the temperature would drop quickly in the dry air. The sun was hovering over the horizon, seeming to pause for breath before plunging the sand sea into darkness. When it did, it would get suddenly cold. The one saving grace was that the clothing used to keep sun off during the day would help retain heat at night.

Ben stretched his legs and massaged his calves. In the morning, he was certain they'd be sore from the effort of walking on the sand.

"Try the Ohms," suggested Thyr.

Ben looked at the muscular Dirhadji.

"The stretches are good for you," continued the man. "It increases blood flow through your muscles. You'll feel more rested in the morning. Long term, you'll have fewer aches and pains, and you'll find walking on the sand is easier."

"Is that why the Dirhadji do the Ohms," queried Ben. "It helps you walk on sand?"

Thyr guffawed loudly, shattering the silence of the desert and shocking Ben.

"The Dirhadji do the Ohms," explained the warrior, "because it helps in battle. Speed, strength, stamina, flexibility, and control. Any one of those attributes can help you win a fight. If you do not excel in any of them, it is certain you will lose. That is what is important to a Dirhadji. Battle. I mentioned the walking to you because you are a northerner and soft."

Ben muttered under his breath, but he took the Dirhadji's advice and began working through the first sequences of the Ohms. Before he finished the fifth, the sun had set, and night fell across the desert.

"Control," barked the Dirhadji as Ben transitioned through the poses. "You must maintain absolute control of yourself and your movements. Be aware of your surroundings, but only in the back of your mind. The front of your mind should be focused on what you are doing."

Ben frowned. The control the Dirhadji mentioned sounded suspiciously like the meditation Towaal taught. One involved movement, and the other did not, but the mental focus was identical. Towaal taught the meditation to improve their ability to harden their will.

Lost in thought, Ben stumbled, earning a disgusted snort from Thyr. Sighing, Ben straightened and joined the rest of the group making the last preparations for the night.

They set a watch schedule, and Milo had the first one. The former apprentice was circling their campsite, kicking sand as he walked. It was all he could do. There was nothing else in sight, nowhere to sit. Not even a lone rock had broken the surface of the sand since before midday, and that one had come only waist high.

If the wind hadn't been so low, Thyr claimed he would have forced them to continue marching. Without shelter, lying down, they'd be pounded by the tiny grains of sand all night long. Ben understood the man's concern, but he was so exhausted he didn't think he would have been able to continue for long, shelter or no shelter.

Ben crawled under the tarp beside Amelie and settled himself in the sand. It'd be several baths, he suspected, before he washed all the grit off. He had to admit the sand made for a more comfortable bed than the rocks they had been sleeping on. It definitely made a better bed than the snow and ice in the Wilds.

"I'll be happy when we're rid of that man," mumbled Amelie.

"He's starting to grow on me," remarked Ben. "Once you get past the bluster, he's kind of friendly."

"That's only because you're a man," complained Amelie. "I don't like the way he looks at me or any of the other ladies."

Ben frowned and thought about the Dirhadji's looks as he

drifted to sleep. In the morning, he would say something to the man, but there were only going to be more like him. If they were lucky, they'd soon be in the middle of an entire tribe's worth of Dirhadji.

A DEEP RUMBLE drew Ben from his sleep. Around him, the sand was shifting, and as he blinked sleep and grit from his eyes, he realized the entire ground was shaking. It sounded as if a thousand horses were pounding across the sand sea.

A flash of light lit the tarp, followed heartbeats later by a thunderous boom.

"I thought there wasn't any rain in the desert," complained Corinne, tugging a corner of her bedroll over her head.

"Up, now!" yelled Thyr.

The Dirhadji scrambled out from under the tarp and began frantically stuffing supplies into his bag.

"Hurry, you fools," he shouted.

Ben stood and looked around, confused. He couldn't figure out where the noise was coming from or why the ground would be shaking.

Another flash of light lit the sky, and Ben stared, open mouthed. Several leagues away, the lightning illuminated massive, billowing clouds. They stretched from the floor of the desert far into the sky, soaring out of view.

"What is that?" wondered Ben.

"Sand storm," growled the Dirhadji to the party. "I'll give you two dozen heartbeats to pack your things and then I'm leaving. We have to find shelter, or we die."

They all leapt into action, feverishly stuffing their packs full.

Ben stumbled through the soft sand and started yanking out the stakes they'd used to string up the tarps. Rhys caught his arm.

"We don't have time," declared the rogue. "Leave them."

Ben glanced around and saw Thyr was already striding away into the night. He threw down the tarp and joined his friend, chasing after their guide. Every dozen steps, Ben couldn't help but glance behind and watch the growing storm. One by one, the stars were swallowed. The time between the flashes of lightning and crashes of thunder grew shorter and shorter.

Under her breath, Corinne was counting.

"Three leagues," she estimated loudly.

Thyr grunted and picked up his pace.

Ben gripped Amelie's hand as they struggled to keep up with the panicked desert dweller.

"I've heard these desert storms move fast," declared O'ecca. "We will not make it to cover."

Thyr ignored her.

"Damnit, man," she shouted. "Do not ignore me."

Without turning, he yelled back, "I know we do not have time, woman. These storms move faster than the quickest northlander horse. As I told your friend, just because I am not afraid of death does not mean I welcome it. While there is breath in my body, I will continue."

"Maybe we can go back and hide under the tarps," suggested Ben.

"The storm is too powerful," growled Thyr. "The tarp will be ripped away in heartbeats. If we try to hide in the sand, we could be blown away too, or worse, buried."

"What do we do?" demanded Lady Towaal.

"Keep the wind at our backs and keep moving. If we are lucky, we will stumble across something we can use as shelter. Even then…" the warrior trailed off.

He didn't need to tell them the rest. Even with shelter, the storm carried thousands of wagon-loads of sand, tens of thousands, all blowing faster than the quickest horse could run. Any exposed skin would be shredded. Even behind a sturdy rock, the sand could drop, burying them.

"We'll make it," assured Amelie.

Ben forced a grin in her direction. He wasn't sure she could see it. All of them were shadowy silhouettes in the moonlight, sporadically lit by the flashes of lightning from the storm.

After two hundred paces, they could hear the wail of the wind and the crash of sand growing behind them. It was a brutal pounding noise, millions of fine grains smashing against each other, over and over again.

Stumbling and sliding in the sand, they followed Thyr. With each pace, Ben's heart sank. The lightning flashes were coming faster. All they illuminated in front of them was the empty horizon. He could feel the storm starting to tug at his clothing. Below his knees, sand began to pelt his legs and boots. He could feel thousands of the tiny grains whipping against him. The sound of the storm was building into a crescendo of deafening chaos. The wind was like a thousand waves breaking on a rocky shoreline all at once.

Ben stumbled, losing his grip on Amelie's hand. He kept running and dropped his hand to the hilt of his sword. His mind swirled, and the sound of the wind rose inside his head, a counterpoint to the rapidly closing storm behind them.

A channel, Jasper had called it. He said the sword functioned as a channel for energy which Ben was able to manipulate with his will. Wind was a nearly endless source of energy, Jasper had said.

Still running, Ben awkwardly drew his sword and felt the surge of power coursing through him. Like it did when he anticipated a battle, the sound of the wind grew, crashing and howling with fierce energy.

Rhys, who was running beside him, mouthed something, but Ben couldn't hear him. The rage of the storm behind him and the corresponding force inside his head drowned out everything else. He glanced over his shoulder then slowed his run. He stopped and turned.

Cresting a league above his head, the massive wall of wind and sand billowed closer. It blocked out the stars and the moon, but it wasn't dark. Brilliant flashes of lightning burst like fireworks deep within the storm. With each heartbeat, more flashes and thunder backlit the towering wave of sand. Ben could feel the hairs on his neck stirring with the power of the electrical surges.

He focused on the storm, holding his blade in front of him.

Towaal returned and gripped his arm, but he didn't budge. She pressed her lips against his ear and shouted. He could barely hear her.

"This is too much, Ben. There isn't enough wind within a thousand leagues of here to punch back at that storm. It's too strong. We have to run."

He tightened his grip on the sword.

He didn't need the power she spoke of. He could feel the energy of the storm itself. It pulsed through him, pumping in time with his blood. He felt it like air filling his lungs. It was there, untapped, ready to be used. All he had to do was channel it back into itself. Defeat the power of the storm with its own strength.

Towaal must have read his intentions.

"Ben," she yelled, "you cannot do this. A person's body is only made to handle so much. Manipulating that much energy will destroy you."

She might be right. He didn't know nearly as much about magic as Towaal. He did know what he felt though, and he felt the potential. He looked back and saw Amelie had stopped along with Rhys and Corinne. Thyr and Milo had already vanished into the darkness.

If Ben did nothing, his friends would die. Even if it cost him his life, he would act. The choice was clear, the path obvious. He forced a smile at Amelie. Then he turned to the sand storm. He closed his eyes and opened his senses like Towaal had taught him.

The wind pushed against him, pressing his clothing against his body. Tiny particles of sand blasted his exposed face. He knew that within moments, his flesh would be scoured to the bone.

The wind wasn't constant. It ebbed and flowed. It shifted direction and speed. He listened to the storm outside and the storm inside. In the center, fifteen or sixteen hundred paces to the northeast of him, he felt a calm. The eye of the storm.

He let the energy from the storm flow through him, into his heart, along his veins, down to his arms and legs, and into his sword. The wire-wrapped hilt of the mage-wrought blade felt comfortable in his hand like it was part of him. He could feel the blade, the intricate scrollwork like his own arteries, pulsing in time with his heartbeat, drumming with the fury of the sand storm.

He brought in more. His eyes watered, and pressure built in his head. He didn't hold the power, though, he funneled it down into the weapon, and let it grow there. Let it sing until the blade was humming with trapped energy. Tiny, rapid vibrations rattled his arms.

His teeth were clenched tight and he couldn't relax his jaw. His arms and legs felt both tense and loose at the same time, ice melting to water. He was certain he'd collapse if he moved, but his feet were rooted, his body locked except for the involuntary tremors that rattled through him. He was shivering with cold and burning with heat.

Behind his closed eyelids, he saw the flashes of lightning approaching. There wasn't much time left. Then he knew he'd be consumed by the storm. He couldn't hear it anymore, but he sensed it. He could feel it in his bones. Vast, unimaginable power, rising far above him, ready to sweep him and his friends away.

The hum of the sword and the roar of wind in his mind was reaching its zenith. Within heartbeats, he'd be lost. He knew the power would wreck him, break him down into motes smaller than the sand.

He let go, pouring himself into the blade, extending his will along its steel length. He felt the force of it, the force of the wind, of the sand beneath his feet, the rock below it, and he let it go. Ben channeled everything he had. He was a conduit, pulling from the storm, letting it flow into the sword, and then back out in one gigantic release. One massive pulse of energy. One explosive push. One chance to save his friends.

Ben fell to his knees, then onto his face. His eyes were squeezed tightly shut. There was no will remaining to manipulate his arms and legs, his body was spent.

Around him, he felt the sand. It pressed against his chest, against his back.

It didn't have the force of the wind behind it, though. It had the force of gravity.

Sand was falling on him.

Buckets of it. Wagon loads of it. Hills of it. Maybe mountains. He didn't know. All he knew was that it was burying him.

6

BURIED ALIVE

HE FELT HIMSELF FALL.

It wasn't far, and he landed softly. He still felt half a dozen sharp pricks of pain. His shoulder, his arm, his chest, his face. Warmth leaked down his cheek. Blood, he thought. He wasn't sure why he was bleeding or, for that matter, where he was. The last thing he could recall was sand. Raining sand.

"Damnit," exclaimed a familiar voice. "You dropped him right on his face."

"I've been carrying him half the day in his heat," growled a response. "He's lucky I didn't drop him two bells ago."

"He's bleeding again," worried the first voice.

"Weren't you going to heal him?"

"I did what I could."

He drifted into unconsciousness, floating on the sea of sand.

WHEN HE WOKE AGAIN, his first thought was pain, raw, blistering pain. His face felt like he'd been flayed. His hand rose involuntarily to the skin around his eyes and he immediately jerked it away. His skin felt blistered and raw because it was.

"Hopefully, we can find ointment in Frisay," remarked a voice that Ben slowly identified as Milo.

He opened his eyes and blinked, startled by the bright light around him. Sensation gradually filled his body. All of it was unpleasant.

"Ben," advised Amelie, "move slow."

He tried to answer, but it came out as unintelligible mumbles.

"Here."

Something was pressed against his lips, stinging them. It was worth it when warm water trickled into his mouth. He swallowed and tried to open his eyes again. The world was still bright, but beside him, he could see Amelie kneeling. Other shapes started to come into focus.

A tall structure rose behind Amelie. A rock, Ben thought. Someone leaned against it, probably Milo. Sprawled out between him and Milo was another person. He blinked a couple of times to clear his vision until he could see the prone figure was Lady Towaal.

"Is he up?" asked another voice. O'ecca, he thought. He couldn't see her.

"Barely," responded Amelie.

She tipped the water skin up again and he drank greedily. This time, he had enough control to swish the liquid around his mouth before swallowing it.

His friends kept speaking, planning something, discussing when others would return.

Ben slowly did a mental inventory of his body as his awareness crawled back. He raised his hand. It looked normal except for a strip of fabric wrapped around his forearm. It hurt. A laceration, maybe. How did he get cut by the fine grains of sand? He wasn't sure. He'd ask later.

One by one, he identified other sharp points of pain. Cuts or punctures across his arms and torso. Mysterious. As if he'd been in a sword fight while unconscious. His face was raw and painful. He remembered that at least, the sand blowing with tremendous fury against him, scrapping the skin away. His muscles were sore and weak.

"You'll need to eat," he heard Amelie say.

He turned his head toward her and worked his mouth, slowly getting enough moisture onto his lips and tongue that he could speak. Painfully, he croaked, "What happened?"

Amelie laughed and asked, "You don't remember?"

He shook his head.

"You saved us."

O'ecca squatted next to Amelie. "That is three times you've saved my life."

"How?" rasped Ben.

"The sandstorm was on us," explained Amelie. "There was no shelter in sight, and we had nowhere to run. You drew your sword and stood against it. Do you remember that?"

He nodded.

"Somehow, you pushed back against the storm or did something within it. I could feel the energy flow out, but I couldn't tell exactly what you did. Whatever it was, it blew a hole in the storm. The wind died and the storm collapsed on itself."

"It had already crested above us, though," added O'ecca. "Sand must have hung a league high, blown by the winds. When the wind disappeared, the sand fell."

"It rained sand on us for two bells," said Amelie. "It just kept coming, more and more of it, falling harder and harder."

She shifted the water skin and gave Ben another drink.

"At first," she explained. "We didn't think it would be a problem. Quickly though, we realized if we didn't do something, we'd be buried. In moments, the stuff had gotten to mid-calf on me. Rhys grabbed you and tried to drag you away, but the storm was huge. We ran but couldn't get far. We found Thyr, already stuck up to his waist in fallen sand. It was rising quickly around him. We kept trying to climb it, but it was exhausting. We couldn't keep up."

She gave have him another sip.

"Towaal demanded we stop and circle around her. We did, and she somehow created a force that pushed back up, forming a dome above our heads. I'm still not sure how she did it."

Ben saw the look of concern in Amelie's face. She was looking at the unconscious mage. Whatever the mage had done took a lot out of her.

"The sand fell atop the dome and we were covered. I thought we were going to be trapped under there."

O'ecca shuddered. "It was frightening. The dome started to collapse. The sand dropped a hands-length and we all had to kneel. I thought we were going to be crushed. The mage held as long as she was able, then exploded the sand out, blasting the roof off, so to speak. She fell over and hasn't moved since. The sand was still coming down but not as quickly. We tended to your injuries as best we could and slowly climbed up the shifting slopes of that hole. We kept sliding down, but after two bells, the sun rose, and we finally made it out."

Amelie nodded, clutching the water skin in her hands.

"Seventy, eighty paces of sand had fallen around us," finished O'ecca. "I still can't believe we survived."

"My injuries?" asked Ben. He was looking at his bandaged forearm again. Somehow, he'd missed the part of the story where he got injured.

Amelie swallowed and looked uncomfortably at O'ecca. When Amelie's gaze returned to Ben, he could see she was uncomfortable telling him.

He put his hand on her knee.

Amelie sighed. "Your sword shattered. The energy was too much for the structure of the blade to take, too much for it to stay stable. First, the pommel, the anima-wood, ignited, a brilliant flash of fire that was gone in a heartbeat. Then the blade split with a crack. Pieces blasted outward. You were holding it, so many of them stabbed into you. We counted a dozen or so slivers of the metal, some small, some large. I tried to heal you the best I could while we were hunkered beneath Towaal's dome of sand, but there were so many cuts. Some were deep."

"She exhausted herself," stated O'ecca. "We had to drag the three of you out of that hole."

"Sorry," mumbled Ben.

O'ecca laughed, and Amelie smiled beside her. "Don't take it the wrong way. Any day, I'll drag you out of a sand pit rather than getting shredded by a sandstorm or buried alive. You saved us, and hauling your body for a few bells doesn't make us even."

He grinned, then realized what Amelie had said.

"My sword?" he mumbled, his heart sinking.

Amelie winced and admitted, "It was completely destroyed. There was nothing left to save."

She held his hand, and he allowed his eyes to sag shut.

"I think I'll rest some more."

THE THIRD TIME HE WOKE, he felt like a person, a person who was sore and suffering from a number of puncture wounds but a person all the same. He sat up and breathed deeply. His head swam with dizziness, and his stomach roiled, but he managed to keep down the little bit of water that he'd been able to swallow before.

"Take your time," advised Amelie. "I only partially healed you. Your body was drained and will need time and sustenance to replenish itself before you are back to capacity."

He slowly began stretching his limbs, rolling his head around on his neck and working his jaw. His muscles and ligaments creaked in protest, but it felt good to move again. Like

Thyr said about the Ohms, getting the blood flowing would help him heal.

"Where is everyone else?" he asked, finally becoming coherent enough to realize not all of their party was there.

"Rhys, Corinne, and Thyr went scouting," said Amelie. "That Dirhadji won't admit it, but I'm convinced he got turned around in the storm and is lost. We can use the sun to find south, but that may not help us find Frisay."

Ben grunted. Lost in the sand sea. He hoped she was wrong.

"They left mid-morning," added O'ecca. "It's evening now, and I expect they'll be back before full dark."

"If not..." Amelie started and then trailed off. If they weren't back by dark, it would be impossible to find each other in the flat expanse of the sand sea.

Milo stood from where he was leaning against the rock.

"Regardless, we have to leave in the morning," he stated. The former apprentice jiggled the nearly empty water skin at his belt.

Amelie's gaze fell to Lady Towaal. Then she looked back at Ben. He read the worry in her glance, but he also knew it didn't matter. They hadn't packed enough water to spend an extra day in the baking sun.

A BELL LATER, O'ecca called down from the top of the rock they'd camped next to. "I see them. Far off still but they're coming."

Amelie exhaled slowly.

Ben struggled to his feet. He grew dizzy and nearly flopped over, but he had to be able to move the next day. If he couldn't stand now, how was he going to hike in the morning?

A quarter bell later, the rest of the party made it back.

"Glad to see you up," said Rhys.

Ben smiled at the rogue, then felt his lips turn down. There was a grim undertone in his friend's voice.

"What did you find?" Ben asked.

"More travelers," stated Thyr. "A caravan that must have been on its way to Frisay."

"Maybe they can help us," suggested Amelie.

The Dirhadji shook his head. "They're dead."

"What happened?" queried Ben.

"Buried," replied Thyr. "We saw a flag sticking up behind a ridge of bare rock. Travelers use them out here to find each other in case they get separated. They were likely sheltering from the sand storm there. We investigated the area enough to realize there were at least half a dozen wagons. Could have been more. Buried deep, though, so we couldn't get to the supplies without another half day of digging."

"They were buried by the storm?" wondered Ben.

Thyr met his eyes. "They were buried when it suddenly expended itself and the sand rained down. No way they could have gotten those wagons moving in time to outrun it. Out here, they have broad flat wheels that get them across the sand, but they don't move fast."

Ben grimaced. "You're saying they were buried because of what I did. You're saying I killed those people."

The Dirhadji shrugged. "I'm not saying you meant to. You saved us. If you didn't stop that storm, we'd be the dead ones."

"I killed them," stated Ben, horror creeping down his spine.

"You couldn't have known," exclaimed Amelie.

Ben plopped back down to the sand.

"How many people would be with a six-wagon caravan?" he asked.

Thyr didn't reply immediately.

Ben held his gaze until he answered.

"Getting wagons across the sand is tough. Could have been twenty, maybe twenty-five of them," admitted the Dirhadji.

Ben rubbed a hand across his face and immediately regretted touching the raw skin.

"You stopped the storm Ben," declared Amelie. "You saved us. You had no way of knowing it would harm someone else. It's not your fault."

"It is my fault," mumbled Ben. "If it wasn't for me, they would have lived or at least had a chance."

O'ecca strode up to him.

"You must not think like this," she insisted. "You tried to do the right thing. You acted. Your girl is right. You are not responsible for what happened because of it. It was outside of your control."

"Just because I didn't intend it doesn't mean I am absolved of all responsibility," argued Ben. "When you act, you own the consequences of those actions."

O'ecca shook her head in protest. "Imagine if every lord thought like you are talking, afraid to do anything lest someone be harmed. Nothing would happen. The people would be left to their own devices. The world would be chaos. You have power, and like all powerful people, you are judged on your intentions. Unintended consequences are the unfortunate byproduct of progress. Would you rather you didn't act, and we'd all be dead?"

Ben looked around his companions and saw Rhys staring at him. The rogue's grim look spoke more clearly than words. He knew what Ben was thinking. He'd dealt with his share of unintended consequences.

"There's nothing to be done about it now," Rhys said. "This is a discussion for later, when we're comfortably seated in a tavern and sipping on something cold and foamy. We can talk about it all you want, then. Now, we have something else to deal with."

Thyr cleared his throat. "A spring I thought we may be able to stop at was also buried. There's no telling how deep the sand fell and whether we have the water and strength in our bodies to uncover it."

"We packed enough water for an extra two days, right?" challenged Amelie. "We've spent a day resting, but that should still give us one extra to find fresh water. Frisay isn't much further if we have to push."

Milo coughed discreetly, and the Dirhadji glared at him.

"I, ah, I lost my pack," admitted the former apprentice.

"It wouldn't have mattered," growled the desert warrior. "You weren't sticking to the ration. Your skins were near empty. You thought to hide it, but I saw."

Milo flushed and retreated back to his place by the rock.

Ben sighed in disappointment, but there was nothing they could do about it.

"What do you suggest we do?" Amelie asked Thyr.

"Leave tonight."

"But Ben isn't healthy!" protested Amelie. "Lady Towaal hasn't woken yet."

Thyr shrugged and didn't respond.

"Amelie," interjected Rhys. "We have two days of water left. It's three days to Frisay. Tomorrow, we'll have the heat of the sand sea cooking the moisture out of us even if we rest in the shade. If we don't move now and find a fresh source of water in the desert, we may run out."

Amelie opened her mouth to argue, but Ben stopped her.

"They're right, Amelie. I'm weak as a newborn fawn, but all of us will be weak if we have to hike on a half-day ration of water."

"You're sure this is a good idea?" she worried.

Ben nodded. "Without water, we die."

THE FIRST RAYS of sun were peeking above the horizon when Ben fell face first into a soft bed of sand.

"We'll have shade for another four or five bells," said Thyr. "I recommend everyone take advantage and rest. When the sun hits us, we start walking again."

Corinne grunted and tossed her pack down beside Ben. He didn't move.

"How far do you reckon we made?"

The Dirhadji scratched at the back of his neck. "Four or five leagues. If that's right, we have about the same to make the border of the sand sea and to where I think we can find water. Fifteen more after that to Frisay."

"Could some of us go ahead, get fresh water, and come back?" wondered the huntress.

Thyr shook his head. "There are no roads, no landmarks out here. I can't promise I could come back and find you. If the strongest leave, the weakest may never find solid footing again."

Corinne flopped down and sipped her water.

Beside her, Amelie was kneeling beside Towaal.

"How is she?" croaked Ben.

Amelie grimaced. "She's breathing. She must have pushed herself near her limit."

"Or past it," suggested Rhys grimly. He was sprawled out beside the rest of them. Worn to the bone, Ben suspected. The rogue had been carrying Lady Towaal for most of the night. Thyr had spelled him near midnight, but the rogue took her back three bells later.

"How does it work," asked O'ecca uncertainly, "doing things with your mind?"

Amelie settled down and pursed her lips. "That's a long story."

Thyr handed her his water skin.

"I am more used to this climate than you are," he said. "Drink deeply, then tell your story. I will consider it water well spent. I am curious to learn about what this woman did. We do not have mages amongst the Dirhadji. How does one become one?"

Amelie eyed him then tilted up the water skin.

Ben realized it was the first time Thyr had asked one of the women a question.

"Becoming a mage," started Amelie, "is about acquiring the

necessary will and knowledge. Will to manipulate energy, and the knowledge to know how."

As she continued, Ben thought on what Thyr had said. There were no mages amongst the Dirhadji. Hopefully, the man was wrong.

A JAGGED SPINE of rock tore through the floor of the desert in front of them. Compared to the terrain around Farview, it was nothing, barely even a hill. From the sand sea, it looked like a mountain. The sun rose to the east, red light sparkling along the knife-edged ridge, lighting it like it was on fire or covered in blood.

Ben grunted. In the sand sea, there was no fire, and if they were out there any longer, they'd have no more blood.

He could feel the moisture leaking from his skin, drop by drop. He'd taken to wiping the sweat off his face and licking it from his fingers. Rubbing his face stung, but the salty sweat stung anyway. He hadn't peed in over a day, and he feared the moment when he would stop sweating. Shortly after that, he knew he'd lay down and not be able to get back up.

"Can we drink the last drops?" begged Corinne.

Thyr, marching ahead of them, shook his head. He didn't waste energy on speaking anymore. He barely opened his mouth. It released moisture, he told them earlier.

They each had a mouthful of liquid in their water skins, bouncing by their hips, tormenting them.

Ben knew the water would be hot and taste of the old leather it was stored in, but it would also be the sweetest thing he'd ever put past his lips. Without it, he was dying. Heartbeat by heartbeat, step by step, drop by drop.

He heard a thump behind him and turned to see Rhys sprawled on his hands and knees. Lady Towaal lay in front of him, still unconscious, splayed out on the sand where Rhys dropped her.

Ben staggered back and grabbed Towaal's wrists.

"Ben," rasped Amelie. "You almost died two days ago. You're still too weak."

He didn't answer. If not him, who else would carry the mage? None of them had any more water than Ben. Aside from Thyr, none of them were in much better shape.

The Dirhadji's willingness to help was rapidly fading. He was nice when he was able, but in the desert where their slow speed could kill him, their guide was becoming less interested in what they were seeking. He'd evidently decided it wasn't worth dying to learn.

Ben planted a boot into the soft sand and pushed, dragging Towaal's prostrate body with him.

Corinne helped Rhys to his feet, and the rogue stumbled along, head hung low, his legendary stamina exhausted after carrying Towaal through the desert.

Step by step, Ben half-fell and half-dragged the mage. He told himself, if he could reach the spine of rock, if they could find shade from the brutal morning sun, they could rest. While they were stopped, the stronger members of the party could collect water.

The mage was light, a fraction of her normal weight due to the depravation of the desert. Ben was weak, though, and every step was a struggle.

Dragging Towaal behind him, he walked backward, holding her hands in his. He felt the rays of sun warm his back. He knew that as soon as the brilliant orb in the sky completely cleared the ridgeline, they'd start to bake. One mouthful of water wasn't enough to last very long, even if he wasn't dragging a body behind him.

Thyr led the way, followed by Milo, O'ecca, Amelie, Ben, and Towaal. Rhys and Corinne brought up the rear. The rogue's arm was slung over Corinne's shoulder, and the huntress was supporting his weight as they stumbled along. Ben wished the rogue had said something earlier. Not even Thyr would make it far carrying the big assassin.

Ben watched Rhys and Corinne follow him as he dragged Towaal along. He didn't waste effort watching where he was going. There was nothing but sand until they made the rocks.

Corinne's eyes lifted and she smiled.

"A bird," she stated, nodding toward the horizon. "If there's a bird, there must be water nearby. We're getting close."

Ben didn't spare the energy to look up.

"It's a buzzard," called O'ecca from ahead of them.

Corinne grunted. "Oh."

They trudged onward.

Ben's arms burned with the strain of pulling the mage's body. He looked down at her face, slack and still. She didn't stir as he adjusted his grip, yanking hard on her arms. It would have hurt had she been awake, but there wasn't a glimpse of pain in her blank expression. He would worry about the strain on her body after they got to something resembling shelter and had access to water. There, they'd have time to worry if the mage would recover.

It wasn't the first time they'd had to carry the mage away after she overextended, but they'd never done so in such punishing conditions or for so long.

He wondered what she'd done, how she'd created a dome of force and exploded it upward. Seventy or eighty paces of sand, his friends said. He knew enough to know that much sand could weigh more than a small castle. Nothing the mage told them about using one's will explained how she achieved the feat with the sand. He wondered where she got the energy.

His mind swirled, thinking about conversations he'd over-heard in the past. How they'd used mechanical force to flip their cart back over in the woods before Irrefort, how Towaal had frozen the air to defeat Lady Ingrid, how Amelie gathered heat from the ambient air to form a fireball.

A talented mage could pull energy from any nearby source, the closer, the easier. Ben thought about how in the Wilds, Rhys had taught Amelie how to pull energy from a person.

He looked back down at the mage.

During the storm, he'd been lost in the fury of the wind. He'd rode it like a leaf, blowing where it willed him, but he'd also commanded it like a ship's master, directing it with his will, forcing it to obey him, or so he'd thought.

His recollection of the moment before he collapsed was fuzzy at best, but he distinctly recalled the feeling of releasing the built-up power from his sword, sending it directly into the teeth of the storm. He had assumed his push was what stopped the storm. What if it wasn't? What if that energy was commandeered after he let it go? What if it was used by someone who understood better how to manipulate it than him? There might have been enough to stop the storm and then later save them from being buried alive.

He remembered the unbelievable feeling of power as he gathered the storm's energy. He'd taken as much power as he could and then channeled it to somewhere safe. That hadn't blown the storm back, he suddenly realized with a start. That hadn't shoved the winds away. He'd merely stripped the storm of its energy.

He'd taken the fury out of the storm and directed it into his sword. When he released it, Towaal had taken over. He was sure of it. When the sand fell, she'd used that force to create something that should have been impossible, something that defied his limited understanding of what a mage was capable of. She'd channeled the energy from him and done something exceptional.

The Purple intended to do the same. According to the writings they'd obtained in Alcott, the Purple were attempting to pull power from between the worlds. Unlimited power.

The mage was unconscious, but she was alive. He didn't know

if it was the strain of funneling the incredible force he'd built or if she'd pulled from her own reserves, but they'd stopped a devastating sand storm. She'd moved a thousand tons of sand with a thought. A caravan of innocent traders was killed in the process.

The storm was massively powerful, but it was limited by the rules of physics. With unlimited power from outside the world, mages could control the weather, flatten armies, rule unchallenged. There would be unintended consequences, but would they care? They could become drunk with their own power, their ability to wreak devastation with a weapon that couldn't be challenged by mortal men.

Ben, facing backward and dragging Towaal behind him, smacked into a solid wall and flopped down. He looked up to see Thyr standing above him.

"We made it to shelter," the man said. "Stay here. I'll come back with water."

The warrior bent beside Ben and collected his water skins.

Around Ben, his companions slumped down, dehydrated and exhausted. None of them were strong enough to continue with the Dirhadji. If he chose, he could leave them there. Ben knew they would die where they lay. He was certain Thyr knew it too.

Before he left, Thyr turned to Ben.

"Whatever you seek must be important. It must be worth more than your lives. I think that is interesting."

Ben didn't have the energy to respond.

7

FRISAY

FRISAY ROSE like an arrogant affront to the desert around it. Broken rock and scree surrounded the place for half a league, but the city itself was one solid block of red sandstone. At least ten man-heights tall, Ben estimated, it towered over the surroundings. He couldn't tell if it had been assembled or carved from existing rock. Neither one made sense. The scale was simply too large.

Not as large as Hamruhg, Northport, or even Fabrizo, but in such a desolate location, it was a powerful testament to man's refusal to bow to nature or common sense.

"Why would they build that here?" wondered Amelie.

Thyr glanced back at her. "You'll have to ask them. When you get an answer, let me know. My people have been wondering the same thing for two generations."

"Did they build that or hollow it out?" questioned Rhys.

Again, Thyr had no answer. "I wasn't alive then, of course, but from what I'm told, it just appeared. It may have been many months between times the Dirhadji passed through here, but as you can imagine, they were rather surprised when they saw it.

They approached slowly at first, the lore tells us, but when they realized it was occupied by foreigners, they attacked. The attack was repelled, and many more tried over the next several years. Before I was born, they gave up. My people do not know of structures like this. We have no art to make war against them."

Rhys was eying the city with intense suspicion. Ben felt it as well, but they had to go in. Towaal was still unconscious, and instinctively he knew, if they did not give her time to rest, she may never wake. Water and the bits of healing Amelie was now able to trickle into her were insufficient to keep her alive for long.

"Still, it's the best place to kick your feet up that I've seen in a week," muttered Corinne.

There was no arguing with that.

Rhys chuckled and asked Thyr, "Do they sell ale in Frisay?"

Thyr stared back at him. "My people rarely drink alcohol."

"Could have fooled me," called O'ecca from behind.

Ben wasn't sure if it was sun on the man's skin, but he thought he might have detected a flush in the warrior's face.

"We don't drink in the desert except after a raid," Thyr clarified.

"Do the people in that place drink?" pressed Rhys.

Thyr didn't answer.

"Let's go find out," Ben suggested.

They hiked toward Frisay, stepping over sharp stones, skirting around scraggly bushes. The town was situated at the center of a wide, shallow basin.

"How often does it rain here?" wondered Ben.

Thyr glanced back. "Several times a year. Why do you ask?"

Ben pointed to the town. "There could be tens of thousands of people living in there, right?"

Thyr shrugged. "Ten thousand sounds like too many. It is not crowded like your northern cities, but there are many of them."

"Where do they get water for so many people?"

Thyr frowned.

"Your people move from water source to water source constantly," continued Ben. "If there was enough water here to sustain that many people, wouldn't this area have been settled ages ago?"

"There could be an underground river they found," speculated Rhys.

"I suspect there is underground storage, some salt caverns, or even a river like you say. I bet they fill it from this basin. Look," said Ben, gesturing around the flat, wide open space. "This is a shallow bowl, a league wide. Any rainfall will run fast over the rock and sand. If I'm right, it will all collect there."

Ben pointed at the towering city of Frisay before them.

Rhys whistled softly.

Thyr grunted, clearly disturbed by the idea that these strangers may have found a way to collect and store water in the desert. Water was like gold to Thyr.

Ben hoped the man wouldn't make trouble when they got inside.

The closer they got, the more confident Ben was about his theory. When they were close enough to make out details of the base of the structure, he grinned when he saw thick iron grates spaced along the exterior. They looked like sewer drains if it was a conventional town. He knew this place would be far from conventional.

"There's something else," said Corinne. "Look at the wall. It's smooth, entirely flat. The Dirhadji said this place sprung up in a matter of months."

"It's like the wall of the Sanctuary," remarked Ben. "Remember, Amelie, how smooth that wall was?"

"Yes, I remember."

"We need to be careful in there," advised Rhys.

Ben reached down to clear the hilt of his sword, just in case.

He cringed when he remembered the blade was gone. His ability to call the wind, the ease with which the mage-wrought steel stood against inferior blades, it was all gone. His heart sunk.

At the base of the towering wall around Frisay, they paused outside two tall iron doors. Not iron-banded like Ben was used to seeing in other cities, these were solid iron. Hanging in the center of each door was a huge copper face. One was an old man, his face lined with age. A neat beard covered his chin. The other door had the face of a young man, a few years younger than Ben. By any measure, the faces were incredible works of art. The details were exquisite. The faces were staring out at the desert stoically.

A sinking sensation was settling in Ben's stomach.

"I recognize these," whispered Amelie.

"We should not go here," replied Rhys, shifting Lady Towaal in his arms.

"It could be coincidence," murmured Milo uncomfortably. "Many people travel through the City. Many people have seen the faces of the First Mages. These could be copies."

Ben shot a glance at the former apprentice.

"These are not copies," hissed Rhys, fear seeping into his voice. "No mundane craftsman formed these. We should go."

"I see you're admiring our gates," called a friendly voice.

The companions turned to see a robed and turbaned man emerging from a narrow passageway set beside the iron doors. It was hidden discreetly in the stone. They hadn't noticed it with the huge copper faces in front of them.

"They're, ah, impressive," responded Amelie.

The man nodded. Then a look of concern crossed his face when he saw Towaal. "You have an injured companion?"

"We crossed the sand sea," replied Ben quickly. "We ran out of water. I'm afraid she did not fare well. Is there a place we can recover here?"

"We can find help for your friend. There are healers inside

who are experts at treating heat and dehydration-related illnesses. I'm afraid I must ask, though. Do you have coin or barter to offer in exchange?"

Amelie shook her belt pouch, and the man smiled.

"I apologize for being so callous, but the desert is a difficult place to survive. We are unable to offer assistance for those who cannot compensate us, but we are open to all kinds of commerce, even from a group as strange and diverse as yourselves. Come. Follow me."

The man turned and disappeared back into the passageway.

The companions shared a look and followed him inside. They'd have to watch their backs while in Frisay, but with limited supplies and Towaal still unconscious, they had no other option.

The passageway was a tunnel formed of solid rock, lit only by the light behind them. Above, Ben spied narrow openings in the roof of the tunnel. Places that hot oil or arrows could be rained down on attackers, he suspected. A dozen paces into the tunnel, the passageway turned, and beyond the bend, a stout iron door stood open. This one was normal sized but was as thick as Ben's leg. In the narrow confines of the twisting passageway, no battering ram or serious force could be mustered to bust through it. This place was designed for a siege.

Through the stout door, the passageway opened into a brightly lit courtyard hemmed by tall stone walls, a mustering yard for soldiers or a killing field for enemies. A road zig-zagged away from the courtyard. Fifty paces later, they found themselves in a vast, open plaza.

The robed man turned to them and explained, "Most foreigners stay on this square and conduct their business here. You are welcome to proceed deeper into our city, but you will not find any inns. There are some shops which may be open for outsiders." He turned to Thyr. "Have you been here before?"

The Dirhadji nodded.

"Then," finished the man, "I will leave your companions in your hands."

He disappeared back down the road he'd brought them in on.

The companions turned and surveyed the plaza. It was sparsely populated, with only a handful of small groups walking around together. The square could house ten times the number of stalls that littered its expanse. Ben spied half a dozen small inns and two taverns. There were several open shops selling iron goods, and a few that sold food for travel. There were places that offered clothing, leather wares, and other small items that must have been useful to the desert dwellers who would come here to trade.

The tents and stands in the plaza were set up haphazardly. There weren't enough to make competition for space necessary. They appeared to be manned by outsiders and were selling to robed townspeople. It was quiet compared to any of the other market squares Ben had seen. It looked safe and well-maintained.

"I've stayed at that place before," advised Thyr, gesturing to a non-descript building at one end of the plaza. "Many Dirhadji stay there. It is clean, and there is no drunkenness."

Ben eyed a pair of drunken revelers stumbling out of another place nearby. Cheerful music chased them out the door.

"Let's try that one first," he suggested.

Thyr grunted and Rhys winked.

The building was a hulking chunk of stone. Narrow windows flanked an animal hide that substituted for a door. The hide didn't look very secure, but Ben supposed attackers weren't getting over the thick stone walls around the town so they didn't need secure fortifications at an inn. The sound of music and laughter drifted out to greet them. The sign above had two crossed swords and painted letters beneath.

"The Fisherman's Plow," read Rhys.

"That doesn't even make sense," muttered Corinne.

"I like it already," declared Rhys. He strode to the building and pushed aside the hide door.

The inside was cooler than outside, and Ben instantly appreciated the small windows. In the dim light, they saw rows of tables braced by sturdy benches. Men sat around them, hoisting mugs of ale and talking loudly over earthenware plates heaped with food. Most of the clientele appeared to be fringe desert dwellers like the people of Vard. There were a few that looked to be from Ooswam and even a trio of Dirhadji in the back.

A pleasantly portly innkeeper bustled up and offered, "Rooms, board?"

Ben smiled. It felt like they were back in Alcott.

"Both," he answered. "Also, we have a companion who is suffering from heat sickness. Is there a healer you recommend who could check on her?"

The innkeeper nodded and snapped his fingers, summoning a thin boy who was instructed to show them rooms and then fetch Mother Snell.

"Is the ale any good?" inquired Rhys, thirstily eying three heavy barrels lined against the back wall.

The innkeeper huffed in offense. "Sir, I do not exaggerate when I say it is the best ale in Qooten."

"Perfect," exclaimed Rhys.

Rhys collected a mug of the suds, then they followed the boy upstairs.

After they were settled in their rooms, Amelie told Ben, "Go downstairs with Corinne and Rhys. Someone needs to watch that scoundrel. I'll wait with Towaal until this Mother Snell arrives. Even if none of the ministrations she tries help, it will be good for everyone to think we needed her assistance. In this place, I am certain no one thinks twice about a northerner who couldn't take the heat."

Ben nodded. "Fitting in, I suppose. Just like we planned."

Amelie laughed. "If this was your plan, you need to sit down and rethink things."

Ben grinned at her and then exited into the hallway. He headed for the stairs, certain the rogue was already ensconced near the ale barrels below.

Their mission was nowhere near completed, but they'd survived the sandstorm, and they had made it through the sand sea. They had a chance to rest and recover. Hopefully, with Thyr's help, they could locate some of the Dirhadji in town and learn if there was any indication of the Purple in the deep desert.

As he stomped down the stone stairs, Ben tried to not think about the man's insistence that there were no mages in Qooten. Someone had built this town from nothing, and someone had placed those copper faces on the gate. It may not have been the Purple, and whoever did it could be long gone, but sometime in the past, someone had practiced magic in Frisay.

Rhys and Milo were hunched over two full ale mugs when Ben got back down to the common room. Milo was running a hand through his curly mop of hair, listening intently to Rhys.

From across the room, Ben thought his friend looked worn. The rogue's vigor was drained. The journey into the desert had taken a toll on him. Ben knew he didn't have the same well of stamina that he used to. The effects of the battle in Northport were still catching up, and if Rhys wasn't careful, he'd push himself too hard.

When Ben got closer, he heard Rhys pressing the former apprentice. "You said 'First Mages'. I heard you!"

Milo shrugged uncomfortably. "I told you. It must have been something I read in the library in Northport."

"There is nothing about the First Mages there. I know," growled Rhys.

Ben sat on a bench across from Rhys. The rogue barely spared him a glance.

"You know more than you're letting on," accused Rhys.

Milo leaned back and sipped his ale. "I wasn't even thinking about what I was saying. It just slipped out."

"What are the First Mages?" queried Ben.

Rhys kept glaring at Milo and didn't answer.

Ben turned to the former apprentice.

"I don't know!" exclaimed Milo, throwing up his hands. "Rhys, you seem to know a lot more than you are saying. Maybe you can tell us. I certainly can't share anything else."

"Not here," said Rhys after a long pause.

Ben eyed his friend curiously and then flagged down a server to order another round of ales. Rhys and Milo stared at each other frostily.

When Thyr arrived, Ben was surprised that he was glad. They needed a distraction, even if it came in the form of the Dirhadji.

"Drink?" Ben asked him.

The warrior shook his head.

"I don't blame you," jested Ben. "After the last time I saw you drink, I'd give it up for a little bit too."

"Yes," agreed Thyr. "After the last time when you and your friends sentenced me to death, I decided I would not drink for a little while. Two weeks, maybe three. How long do you think I should wait?"

Ben swallowed. "I, ah…"

Thyr smirked at him. "Do not worry. I know you have no intention of following through on your threat. You used our code to coerce me into bringing you into the desert but not because you felt any sense of injustice. You could have slit my throat in Vard if you wanted to or any time I was sleeping on this journey. No, I believe you are looking for something."

"We, uh, we needed…" Ben stuttered.

"We did coerce you," admitted Rhys, "and you're right, we don't intend to kill you for attacking O'ecca. She was unharmed, and we've been through a lot together since then. I have a feeling that we no longer need to hold the threat over your head. You'll help us anyway."

Thyr glanced suspiciously around the table. "Why do you think that?"

"You're curious," explained Rhys. "You want to know what we're doing."

Thyr sat back in his chair. "I am curious, but I also want to get back to my family. I had no desire to continue with Raim on his foolish endeavor. I only went with him because I am taking his sister. Guiding you was going to get me home and satisfy my curiosity. Before we get to my tribe, though, I need to know what your intentions are. I will not risk my family for your foolish insistence on following the code." Thyr crossed his arms and looked around the table. "Will you tell me what you are intending?"

"We can't," stated Ben. "Not yet."

"Then I cannot take you further," declared the Dirhadji. "Kill me if you must."

"Very well," responded Rhys, sighing dramatically. "We no longer hold you to the code. You are released. You are free to go as you please. You can go back to your wives. We'll continue our mission without you."

Ben raised his mug to Thyr. "Thank you for taking us this far."

Rhys took a long sip of ale and turned to Ben. "I'm not sure if it's the best in Qooten, but it's not bad."

Ben nodded. "Best we've had since Indo. What do you think, Milo?"

The former apprentice grunted but didn't respond to Ben.

Rhys pushed the ale pitcher toward Thyr. "I'm buying for anyone who's traveling with us."

"Just give up, Thyr," said Milo with a heavy sigh. "I didn't want to join them at first either. Eventually, the curiosity will burn a hole in you. You want to know what they're doing, and there's only one way to find out. I can promise you this. Helping them may eventually help your people as well."

The Dirhadji glared at them then finally relented. "Maybe I will have one ale."

Rhys leaned over and slapped the man on the back. "Glad to have you with us!"

Rubbing his shoulder, Thyr muttered, "I hope this is not a mistake."

THE NEXT MORNING, they clustered back in the common room. Upstairs, Corinne was taking her shift watching Towaal. The rest of them needed to strategize.

"You wanted to know more about our mission?" Ben asked Thyr.

The warrior nodded.

"Since you agreed to come with us of your own free will, I think it's important we show a bit of trust and tell you what we're doing," acknowledged Ben. He drew a deep breath before explaining. "We're looking for mages."

The Dirhadji looked at him blankly.

"A group called the Purple," added Amelie. "We believe they fled Alcott and are hiding out here. We need their help. All of Alcott could be overrun by demons without it."

"Demons," responded Thyr, a bitter frown twisting his lips. "I know of demons. We come across them from time to time, but there are no mages in the desert."

Ben smiled at him. "Who built this city then? You have to admit the walls of this city were not built by mundane means in the space of a few months."

Thyr winced. "Let me rephrase then. I do not know of any mages currently in the desert."

"What about strangers?" asked Ben. "Aside from this place, are there other locations with strangers, others who are not Dirhadji?"

Thyr mumbled under his breath and dropped his head into his hands.

Ben waited patiently.

"There is one place," admitted Thyr through crossed fingers. "Some of the Dirhadji do business with them. They sell them things that cannot be obtained from northern merchants. My companion from Vard, Raim, he is going there. I have never been, but I have heard stories. If these are the people you seek, I do not believe they will help you. They are bad men, these strangers."

"Can you take us to where they are?" asked Ben.

"I do not know where the place is," replied Thyr.

Ben opened this mouth to speak, but the Dirhadji held up his hand.

"That doesn't mean I cannot help," continued the desert warrior. "The Dirhadji in this town will not speak to you, but they may talk to me. I will ask around, and I will find where these strangers live. Understand, though, I will not go with you."

"Fair enough," agreed Ben.

WHILE THYR WAS TRYING to connect with the other Dirhadji in Frisay, Ben and Rhys ventured out to purchase herbs for Lady Towaal and a sword for Ben. He'd grown so used to the mage-wrought blade that he wasn't sure how he'd adjust to a lesser sword, but it would be foolish to continue without some sort of weapon.

Mother Snell, who had tended to Towaal, referred them to a

street away from the market square where they could find a specialty healer.

"Maybe she'll know what you're looking for, because I certainly don't," she had offered with a sniff and up-turned nose. With a skeptical glare, she'd muttered, "Northerners. Always thinking you know best."

Mother Snell had recommended rest and water. She seemed offended they were asking about additional herbs. They couldn't tell her it was because she'd misdiagnosed the nature of the problem. The healer had no way of knowing that Towaal was actually suffering from extending too much of her will. Fortunately, that presented many of the same symptoms as heat sickness, so they only had to put up with Mother Snell's frosty attitude. They weren't worried that stories would get around.

Rhys knew of some herbs that could boost Towaal's ability to recover. He wasn't sure they could find them in a desert herbalist's shop, but after so many days, they were willing to try anything.

Rhys and Ben walked through the near empty streets of Frisay, looking for a bright red door. There was hardly any color in the town, and where they did see it, it was usually faded by the sun. They were assured they couldn't miss the red door.

"What did Mother Snell say was the healer's name?" asked Ben.

"Mistress Albie or something like that," responded Rhys absentmindedly.

Ben nodded and kept peering down alleys and cross-streets. At the end of the street they were on, he spied a shop with bright metal hanging out front. Weapons and tools, he guessed.

"Should we stop there first?" he suggested.

"Looks like they have what you need," agreed Rhys.

As they approached, Ben saw most of the blades were the scimitars favored by the southerners. Inside the open windows and door, he spied short spears, and rows of practical-looking knives. There was no armor, but in the boiling desert climate, maybe it wasn't worth it.

"What can I help you with?" called a short, bald-headed man. He sat on a stool in the shade and wore a simple leather vest that left his scar-covered arms bare.

"I'm looking for a sword," replied Ben.

The man stared at him. "Not from around here, are you?"

Ben shrugged. "Do you not sell swords to foreigners?"

"I'll sell to anyone with yellow gold," responded the man. He lurched off his stool and strode over to the rows of hanging swords. "Most of my wares are stuff the locals prefer. Scimitars, daggers, and spears. Won't do you much good facing a man in plate armor, but no one wears that in this heat."

"You're not from here either?" inquired Rhys.

The man grinned mirthlessly. "Only the Dirhadji are from here. Do I look like one of them to you?"

"Where are you from?" wondered Ben.

The man shrugged. "Here and there, boy. You going to buy a sword or not?"

Ben perused the man's wares, hefting a few to check the weight and balance. The scimitars the man carried would be awkward with Ben's fighting style, and the long daggers wouldn't give him the reach he was used to. There were a few cleaver-like axes that Ben thought looked impressive, but those weapons were built for brutality, not the versatile bladesmanship he preferred.

The man watched him silently, not commenting when Ben picked up a sword or when he sat it back down.

Rhys ducked inside and glanced over the armaments in there.

Ben asked for the prices on several blades. While the man's prices seemed fair in such a remote outpost of civilization, the weapons didn't feel right in Ben's hands.

"Do you have anything long with a straight blade?" Ben asked finally.

The shopkeeper nodded then disappeared into the back. When he returned, he held a cloth-wrapped bundle.

"I've been saving this for the last six months, but I suspect the chap I'm saving it for won't return."

Ben took the package and unwrapped it.

It was a dark steel longsword. The pommel was a plain steel ball. The hilt was well-worn wood, stained from use and age. The cross-guard was straight and sturdy. The edge of the blade was sharpened to a razor's edge. When Ben tilted it, he saw subtle waves where nicks and chips had been smoothed over. It was a simple weapon that had seen extensive use. A relief of a lone tower was delicately etched into the blade.

Ben glanced at Rhys, eyebrow raised.

"That sword has been through a lot," offered Rhys. "You don't get nicks like that sliding it into the sheath. It's been proven in battle."

"Venmoor steel," added the shopkeeper. "Best steel you can find."

Ben glanced at it again. The steel was dark, smoky, unlike the bright silver blades forged elsewhere. Ben stepped outside of the shop and spun the longsword in his hands, feeling the wood of the hilt slide across his palms. It was slightly longer than his previous weapon, but the balance felt right. The blacksmith had paid attention to the details when forging this blade. Ben wondered how many battles the sword had seen, how many opponents had clashed against it.

"How much?" asked Ben.

"Twelve gold," stated the man.

Ben grimaced. "That's a lot for a sword. Ten times what you're selling the scimitars for."

The man shrugged. "You can buy one of those if you like. They're a good value. I can see you know what you're doing, though, and I suspect it won't be long before you find occasion to use that blade. When the time comes, you can't put a price on having the right weapon."

Ben hefted the blade, thinking about it.

"Take it," advised Rhys. "It's better to trust in a weapon you know can get the job done instead of untested steel. An old blade is a good blade."

"You would say that," jested Ben.

Rhys shrugged.

Ben's gaze dipped down to the rogue's coin purse.

"You want me to pay?" grumbled his friend.

Ben grinned. "I don't have any money."

Rhys tilted his head, sighed dramatically, then finally opened his coin purse. He shook out twelve gold coins.

The shopkeeper eyed them suspiciously, but after closely examining the coins, he nodded at them both and retreated back inside his shop.

Ben strapped on the battered leather scabbard that had been wrapped with the sword and hung it from his belt. He slid the weapon home and smiled at the sound.

"Feels good?" queried Rhys.

Ben nodded. "Let's go find this healer."

At the end of a dusty, stone street, they finally found the healer's abode. A freshly painted bright red door marked the entrance. Flowers stood in planters beside the door and narrow windows pierced the sides of the building.

"Flowers," mumbled Rhys. "How is she growing flowers in the desert?"

Ben shrugged. "We're hoping she can grow herbs too, right?"

They banged on the door and waited as a muffled voice called out that she was on the way.

When the door swung open, Ben blinked in surprise.

"M-Mistress Albie," he stammered.

An older woman stared back at him. "Yes?"

"I know you," Ben stated.

The woman frowned.

"Damn," muttered Rhys. "Mistress Albie. Now that I think about it, that did sound familiar."

The woman's gaze dipped down to their swords then back up at their faces. "My eyes aren't what they used to be, dears. How do we know each other?"

"Free State," answered Ben. "In the Wilds, in Alcott."

"Ah," responded the woman. She paused. "I do recognize you now. How are your friends? Did they make it?"

"Most of them," Ben answered

Mistress Albie brushed her white hair behind her ears then stepped back from the door. "Come inside. I will make tea. I see you have questions."

"How is it that you are here?" wondered Ben. "We saw Free State. Demons attacked. Everyone was slaughtered."

Mistress Albie bustled about the kitchen, pouring water, shaking out tea, humming to herself.

"I went north to help," she explained. "I'm from the north, originally, and I knew they would need me. Those fools had no idea what they were getting into. I thought with my advice and my healing I could save some of them. I didn't know the swarms would be so bad. It was far worse than I recalled."

Mistress Ablie's head dropped to her chest. "There were so many of them. They hit our little wooden wall and smashed through it like it wasn't there. No one had a chance."

Rhys stated the obvious, "You are still alive."

"I made it out just in time," the healer murmured.

"How?" questioned Ben.

Mistress Albie poured their tea and handed them two earthenware mugs.

"I didn't get to be an old woman by being stupid," she remarked. "I already had a bag packed, everything I would need to make Skarston. As soon as the wall was breached, I fled."

"Before the demons completely overran the town?" pressed Rhys.

"Clearly," responded the woman.

Ben was impressed his friend managed to be polite enough to refrain from pointing out that Mistress Albie was a rather old woman. If she fled a battle as quickly as she made tea, it was a difficult story to believe.

"How about yourselves?" asked Mistress Albie, turning tables. "What did you see in the Wilds? If a swarm that size hit Free State, then certainly you ran into demons as well. Shortly after Free State fell, I'm told Skarston was next to go. I understand even Northport was attacked. People said the battle could have gone either way."

"We saw demons," agreed Ben with a shudder. "More than I ever wanted to see."

The three of them stared at each other across Mistress Albie's rickety wooden table. Ben sipped at his tea, curious to learn what the woman was hiding, but unsure of how to get her to talk.

"We came here for some herbs," said Rhys.

Albie smiled. "You came to the right place then."

Rhys started listing the items he wanted, taking his time and watching Albie's reaction with each new addition. At first, she simply nodded and murmured she could fill their order. By the time Rhys got to the fifth item, her eyes had grown wide.

"I know how you were able to escape," mentioned Rhys.

Mistress Albie frowned. "The woman who was with you, she was from the Sanctuary, wasn't she?"

Rhys nodded.

The healer stood. "I'll get what you need, and one or two other items I keep for myself."

She went out the back, and Ben watched through a narrow window as she knelt by a small garden and clipped herbs. She then disappeared into a stone shed and reemerged holding a linen pouch.

"Make a tea with this and give it to her twice a day," instructed the healer when she came back inside.

"Thank you," murmured Ben.

"Why were you in Free State?" questioned Rhys.

"I told you that. I wanted to help people," insisted Albie.

"You can help people anywhere," challenged Rhys. "Why were you in Free State?"

Mistress Albie snorted. "The same reason everyone else is. I was tired of living under the thumbs of others. Lords, ladies, the Sanctuary. I have no interest in serving those tyrants. In Free State, I have the chance to do what I think is right, help who I think needs it. There isn't some over-confident witch pointing her finger and expecting me to jump."

"You fell out of the Veil's grace?" guessed Rhys.

"She fell out of mine," corrected Albie.

"I understand." Rhys sat back, pushed back his cloak, and tapped one of his long knives. "I used to march to her tune as well. No longer."

Mistress Albie eyed Ben and Rhys. "You went north from Free State into the Wilds, and now, you are here. I answered your question. I'll ask you the same one, why are you here?"

"Same reason we were in the Wilds," said Ben. "We're looking for an answer."

Albie's eyes narrowed. "You think you'll find that answer in Free State?"

Ben blinked. "Free State?"

Albie stared at him. He met her gaze, uncomprehending.

She snorted. "You don't know, do you?"

"Maybe we should save ourselves some time and put all of our cards on the table," suggested Rhys. "What Ben says is true. We went into the Wilds to confront the demon threat. We thought there was a permanent solution. There wasn't, at least not in that place. It may have actually made things worse. We are still searching for an answer, and to correct our mistake. We have reason to believe there are people here, somewhere in Qooten, who can help us. Male mages. Part of a group called the Purple. After Northport, there are thousands of demons roaming the north in Alcott. If we can't find the Purple and gain access to the tools they have to combat the demons, the entire continent could be lost."

"I've never heard of a group called the Purple," responded Albie slowly, "but I might be able to help. There is someone. I can bring him to you. Maybe he can send you in the right direction. He is far wiser than I, and if there is a group of mages in Qooten, he would know."

Ben sat forward. "We'll take any help we can get. You know better than most, the demon threat is real. As you said, the battle of Northport could have gone either way, and they were prepared. Next time, it could be a lot worse."

"I understand, young man. I saw it. I must warn you," cautioned Albie, "the man I am speaking about guards his privacy closely. I will not lie to him, and he will not appreciate a mage of the Sanctuary being here. He may be upset about it."

"If he is the one to speak to about mages in Qooten then we must see him," responded Ben.

Albie held up a hand. "If he agrees to speak with you, you must be honest with him. If not, I fear the consequences. He is known to have a temper. Even if you are honest, it's possible he may not let you leave."

Rhys raised an eyebrow. "May not let us?"

Ben interjected, worried his friend would start unnecessary

trouble. "We'd like to meet him if he'll see us. We're at the Fisherman's Plow."

∽

LATER THAT EVENING, Ben sat in the common room of the inn with his companions, nervously eyeing the other patrons.

Rhys sat across from him, steadily emptying tankards of ale. Milo watched the rogue in awe. O'ecca and Corinne sat huddled close together, discussing something that they didn't want to share with the group. Amelie sat beside Ben, and on the other side of her was Lady Towaal.

At midday, they'd given the mage the tea made from Mistress Albie's herbs. They poured it down her throat and it quickly helped. Two bells after drinking it, the mage awoke. She was weak and barely able to move, but she insisted she needed to eat. They helped her downstairs and had been there since. They eyed the room, and watched Towaal slowly shovel food and water into her mouth. She'd taken another dose of tea and was showing significant improvement from when her eyes had first peeled open.

"I wish she'd told us when this man would come by," grumbled Ben.

"She didn't tell you anything at all about him?" questioned Amelie.

They'd already been over it, but Ben responded anyway, "No, she only implied he was dangerous, which I believed. She's a mage. Weak mages don't survive long outside of the Sanctuary. Whoever this man is, she was afraid of him. She thought we should be too."

"He must be a mage," declared Rhys. "It's the only thing that makes sense."

Ben glanced at Towaal, but she appeared focused on her food.

"Well, no one in here looks like a mage," said Amelie.

Ben agreed. The common room was full of diverse groups of travelers like themselves. Hard-worn adventurers, intrepid merchants, caravan guards, and even the rare townsman who was looking for news from outside of the desert. They were past the fringes of true civilization, and these people looked like they belonged there.

Ben perked up when a slender, hooded man floated into the room. He nudged Amelie and made eye contact with Rhys.

They all watched as the hooded man made his way across the room. Patrons fell quiet as he passed, and several people stumbled out of the way when he drew close. Slowly, the figure approached a far corner of the room and sat, back facing the wall. Quietly, he observed the room. Deep shadows hid his face, but Ben could feel the man's eyes on him as the hood turned and surveyed the patrons.

"Is he just going to sit there, or will he come over?" hissed Amelie.

"Maybe he wanted to watch us first," suggested Ben.

"Maybe we should stop staring at him then," recommended Rhys.

Ben couldn't help himself. His eyes kept snapping back to the newcomer, wondering if he would sit there all evening. Ben started to think they should approach the man and get it over with.

"I was told there was one mage."

All of the companions spun around in their chairs and saw a huge man standing by their table. They'd been so focused on the cloaked figure that no one heard this man approach.

He wore one of the leather vests that were common in the region, but his was twice the size of any others Ben had seen. Tree-trunk sized arms sprouted out from his shoulders, and no clothing could hide the heavy slabs of muscle that covered his chest and abdomen. On a wide belt hung a huge war-hammer. As impressive as the man was, Ben couldn't take his eyes off the weapon. Traces of red seemed to glow in swirling patterns within the heavy black head of the hammer. The metal was solid, and there was no artistry to its shape, but it exuded a sense of power that Ben felt as a physical sensation. He was certain that beside him, Towaal and Amelie's eyes must have been bulging out of the sockets.

Rhys cleared his throat. "And who might you be?"

The massive man glared down at them.

The innkeeper came hurtling across the room to their table, frantically waving his arms.

"Please, please, no fighting in the inn."

Ben stood, his hand dropping to his sword.

"We don't even know this man," protested Amelie.

The innkeeper clutched his hands in front of himself nervously, eyeing the giant.

"I'm here to talk," rumbled the man.

The innkeeper looked around the party and offered, "Would you care to speak in private? In the back room perhaps? Ale is on the house."

They stood and followed the innkeeper out of the common room, passing the darkly robed figure in the back corner. Ben's nose wrinkled at the smell of him. Foul, rotten.

"You going to have my vests done on time?" growled the big man, dropping a hand to his war-hammer and staring at the hooded figure. "You were two days late with the last batch, even after I paid for your expedited service."

"Of course, of course. I was just on my way to finish them!" exclaimed the hooded man.

He stood and scampered toward the entrance of the inn.

"That damn tanner is a drunk," complained the big man. "If you don't keep an eye on him, he'll never finish. Walks around Frisay all the time in that ridiculous hood because he thinks no one knows it's him. Like we couldn't tell from the stench. He's the only one in town who can find a solid piece of leather big enough to fit me, though, so I've got to work with him."

Ben nodded uncertainly at the big man.

Huge knuckles cracked, and the man watched as the tanner disappeared out the door. He turned and gestured for the innkeeper to continue to the back room. When they got there, the innkeeper hurriedly bustled about, asking if they wanted anything.

The big man ignored him and took a seat at the far side of the room. He laid his hammer down on the table, causing it to creak alarmingly under the weight. Ben's breath caught in expectation that the table would collapse. He thought the hammer must weigh as much as he did.

Lady Towaal sat gingerly across from the man.

He eyed her and remarked, "Mistress Albie told me you overextended yourself. Foolish. You must tend to your anima, not burn it."

"It felt necessary at the time," mumbled Towaal.

He shook his head sadly. "The Veil sharpens you once then lets you rust to waste. She should know better. Just like any weapon, your skill must be given care and attention. Stress it too far, and it will break."

Towaal frowned at the man.

Suddenly, the man's gaze shifted to Ben. "How often do you oil your sword?"

Ben blinked. "Ah, every week or so, and after I use it, of course."

The man nodded, apparently satisfied his point was made.

"I do not work for the Veil," claimed Towaal.

The man snorted disbelievingly. "You have her stink all over you. The three of you do."

Amelie blushed, and Milo shifted uncomfortably.

"I was Sanctuary trained, but I left that group. How can you tell?" asked Towaal.

On the surface, she was calm as a winter pond, but Ben had been with her enough to hear the distress in her voice. This man was frightening her.

The innkeeper temporarily saved the man from responding when he bustled in carrying four large pitchers of ale. One of his serving men scampered in behind with mugs. They sat three of the pitchers and the mugs in the center of the table and one of the pitchers in front of the big man. The serving man also sat down a bowl of thick-shelled nuts.

Ben picked up a nut to give himself something to do while they waited for the staff to clear out, but he couldn't figure out how to open the shell. He pinched it, pried at it, and then finally just held it in his hand so as to not embarrass himself.

As soon as the innkeeper turned his back, the big man scooped up the pitcher and drank directly from it.

Rhys whistled softly in appreciation.

"You fancy yourself a drinker, assassin?" asked the man.

Rhys handled the man's abruptness slightly better than Towaal did, though Ben didn't miss the tension growing in his posture. "I do enjoy a drink."

The man eyed them, seeming to peer into each of their souls.

"What are you doing in my town?" he demanded.

Rhys filled his own ale mug, surprising Ben by not following the big man's lead and drinking directly from the pitcher.

"You seem to know a great deal about us," said Rhys, "but we know nothing about you. Maybe we should start our discussion there."

"I'm not barging around your town looking for people."

"Mistress Albie sent you to us. You know why we are here," stated Ben. "We are looking for an organization called the Purple. We're trying to fight the demons."

The man snorted and took another deep pull from the ale pitcher.

"The Purple isn't in Frisay," barked the man, wiping foam

from his mouth with the back of his hand. "I wouldn't let those fools come near here."

Ben blinked. "You know of the Purple?"

The man sat back, the sturdy wooden chair threatening to collapse under his weight. "I know of the Purple. What I don't know is why I should help you find them."

"The demons are a threat to all mankind," started Ben.

"The same could be said for the Purple," guffawed the man, amused at his own joke.

"You are Gunther," interjected Amelie.

Ben blinked in surprise. Gunther, the legendary mage Jasper had spoken of. He glanced down at the hammer on the table. The Librarian had referred to Gunther's hammer in his letter to the council in Irrefort. Ben's gaze rose to the man. He realized Amelie was right.

The big man smiled mirthlessly at her. "So, one of you knows a little something. Yes, I am Gunther."

"The Librarian of Northport reached out to you. He asked for your help," continued Amelie. "He wanted you to use your hammer to battle back the demons so that the Purple did not use a weapon they've been developing here."

A wry smile twisted Gunther's face. "See, you know a lot more about me than you thought. You know I am not beholden to the shrill commands of others. I'm not going to go running every time someone cries for help. That child the Librarian didn't know what he was talking about. His colleagues have spent millennia banging their heads against the wall."

Gunther paused to quaff more ale.

"It's good you know that about me. Hopefully, you understand a little bit about what I'm capable of. Here's the issue. The only things I know about you I don't like. People I don't like aren't welcome in Frisay. In fact, if you continue this foolish quest to find the Purple, I may have to say you're not welcome in the South Continent. Maybe it's best if you go home now, you

AC COBBLE

understand? I don't want to have that kind of unpleasantness. Do you want to have unpleasantness?"

Amelie sat back, uncertainty clouding her face.

"We know your friend Jasper," said Ben quietly. He pulled out the healing disc that Jasper had made for him. "He gave me this and many other things. He believed in our quest."

Gunther frowned.

Amelie took Ben's lead and placed the pouch Jasper had given her on the table.

"He spent weeks instructing me while we traveled together," she said. "He did it because he saw the demon threat with his own eyes. His friends, his home, were all overrun by the creatures. He knew if someone didn't act, Alcott, and maybe the world, would follow. Jasper knew we were looking for the Purple. He was helping us do it."

"I haven't seen Jasper in ages," muttered the big man.

"You still trust his judgement, though, don't you?" asked Ben.

He knew he was taking a risk, making a rather large assumption about Jasper's and Gunther's relationship, but he also knew it was all he had to go on.

The big mage tilted up his ale pitcher and drained it in three great gulps. He looked around the companions, studying each of them.

"What do you plan to do when you find the Purple?" he asked.

Ben took in a deep breath. "We believe they have developed a weapon, something with incredible power, something that we could use to blunt the threat of the demons once and for all."

"Give me that nut," said Gunther.

Ben looked down at the nut in his hand, then flicked it across the table to Gunther.

The mage drew his belt-knife and inserted the point into a split in the shell. With a quick twist of his wrist, he snapped the shell open and dumped out the soft nut. He placed the belt-knife on the table next to his hammer.

"I could have used either one of these tools to open that shell. Why do you think I chose the knife?"

"I get it," answered Ben. "The hammer would be more force than you needed."

The mage sat forward. "Do you really understand? My hammer could easily crack open that shell, but as you say, it would be excessive. It would be so excessive that it would certainly crush the soft fruit inside the shell. It would also smash this table to kindling. If I wasn't careful, I could bring down the entire building. In my hands, this hammer is powerful and dangerous. If I wanted to, I could destroy this city with it. No one could stop me. Even after many, many years, I find the hammer difficult to control. I only use it when I must."

"You're worried we won't be able to control the Purple's weapon," acknowledged Ben. "You think if we were able to access the power between the worlds, we'd use it indiscriminately."

The mage snorted. "I'm talking about the quest for more power in general. The Purple doesn't even know what they've got. They weren't the creators of the staff, and they haven't figured out how to use it. Those fools can't even activate the thing. You wouldn't be able to activate it either. This quest for ever more power is a fool's errand. You should come up with another plan."

"They have the weapon, but they can't use it," mumbled Amelie. "What are they doing then? Why are they still hiding in the desert?"

Gunther shifted uncomfortably in the seat. "As I said, the quest for ever more power is a fool's errand."

"They're working on something else," guessed Ben.

"What is it?" demanded Towaal.

"I don't know," admitted the big man. "For ages, I could feel them tinkering, trying to reach beyond our world. I don't feel it anymore. They haven't accessed the power they were striving for outside of our world, and I would know if they were able to use the staff they stole. Maybe they are trying something else."

Ben's eyebrows rose. The mage gave the impression he knew everything.

"We're here for the same reason the Librarian asked for your help," interjected Corinne. "We're here to find tools to battle the demons. As you say, they're dangerous. If you don't think we're trustworthy, then you do it! You take up the Purple's weapon and help us stop the demons."

Gunther shook his head.

"Then we'll have to find someone else," remarked Amelie. "If not you, then maybe Jasper. Or we could go to the Veil. Surely she'd want to help us stop the demons."

Gunther's hand smacked down on the table, the wood shuddering alarmingly from the force of the blow.

"The Veil must not be allowed access to the staff. That power was taken from the Sanctuary long ago and with good reason! That woman cannot be trusted with that kind of weapon. She'd use it to rule over all of us. The abuses of the lords and ladies would be like a gentle tap compared to the crush of her steel boot."

Ben looked to Towaal and Rhys, unsure how to convince Gunther of their plight. The man seemed unmoved by the terror of the demons and even an appeal involving his old friend Jasper.

"Why haven't you destroyed this weapon. A staff you said?" questioned O'ecca.

Gunther frowned at her.

"You think that kind of power may be needed one day," surmised Amelie. "You won't destroy it because it's worth the risk that it could fall into the Veil's hands."

"Anyone's hands," grumbled the mage. "No one should have that kind of power, not even me. If I don't trust myself with that kind of might, why do you think I'd help you obtain it?"

"If not us, not you, and not the Veil, who would you trust to use it?" asked Ben.

Gunther glared at Ben but did not respond.

"You trust Jasper, right?" asked Ben. "Help us obtain the weapon from the Purple, and we'll deliver it to Jasper. He can decide if it is appropriate to use it or not."

Towaal finally raised her head and met Gunther's eyes. "There are thousands of demons loose in the north. The Sanctuary may have the strength to face them, but you know as well as I that the Veil will not risk all of her resources on that gamble. The lords are focused on their own petty battles. Even if they combined forces, I'm not sure they'd be sufficient. If you do not help us, hundreds of thousands will be consumed by those creatures. By then, they will be unstoppable, even by you. If we do nothing, if you do nothing, this world will be overrun."

"How do I know you speak the truth?" mumbled Gunther, dropping his gaze to his hammer.

Amelie pulled out the thought meld they'd used to communicate with Jasper. "This is linked to Jasper. We can reach him with it, and you can ask him if we are trustworthy."

"I can reach him without that," admitted Gunther.

They sat in silence, watching the big mage think. By sheer luck, they'd found someone who knew details about the Purple and their weapon, but was unwilling to help. Ben clenched his fists in frustration.

The man seemed genuinely concerned about what would happen if the Purple's weapon was used. What could be so terrible that it was worse than the demons? The man seemed willing to risk everything to prevent the Veil from getting her hands on it.

A grim smile twisted Ben's lips.

"There's another problem you should know about," he mentioned.

Gunther, gaze still on his hammer, reluctantly asked, "What problem?"

"There is a mage who is following us," explained Ben, "one who works for the Sanctuary. She is very powerful, nearly unstoppable. We believe she is here and that she may know about the Purple's weapon."

"She is using death magic," added Towaal. "Secrets from long ago."

"Society of the Burning Hand," added Ben.

"She's following you?" asked Gunther, looking up to meet their eyes. "She is here, on the South Continent?"

They all nodded.

"That is not good," mumbled Gunther.

The huge mage stood and collected his hammer.

"I must think about this. I will find you tomorrow. Do not leave."

THE NEXT MORNING, Gunther was waiting in the common room when they got downstairs.

His hammer leaned against the table beside him, and empty plate sat in front of him. He was pouring a mug full of ale.

At least he was using a mug this time, thought Ben.

"A little early, isn't it?" chided O'ecca.

"Late," rumbled the mage. "I was up all night, walking around town, thinking."

Ben and his companions sat across from the man.

"I do not trust you with the staff the Purple stole."

Ben's heart sank, but he listened as the mage continued.

"But with an agent of the Veil on the continent using death magic, I cannot allow the Purple to hold the staff either. They may have the strength to defeat her, but they may not. It is too much of a risk."

"What do you plan to do?" asked Towaal.

"I will go with you. Together, we will collect the staff. I will be the one who carries it, and I will be the one who decides what is to be done. If I decide to destroy it, you will not interfere."

Towaal looked to Ben and Amelie. They were stuck without his help. If Gunther went with them, they had time to convince the man to bring the staff to Alcott and use it against the demons. Even if he didn't agree to use the weapon, they could recruit him to their cause. The Librarian thought he was up to the task. A man like him would make a difference.

"We agree," said Ben, holding out his hand to the burly mage.

Gunther's massive paw gripped Ben's hand and he shook it once.

"There is one problem," mentioned the big mage.

"What is that?" asked Ben.

The man sighed. "Your original plan to ask the Purple for help will not work. They are not good men. They will not allow us to take the staff willingly. We need to steal it."

Ben groaned.

"They do not have the knowledge to use the staff," continued Gunther, "but that does not mean they are weak. Getting into their stronghold and taking it will be difficult. I have monitored their behavior for years, and I have thought long about whether I should take the staff myself, either through stealth or force. One reason I have not is that I worry what else they have discovered. While they are content to sit in their mountain fortress, I have been content to let them. If we are forced to confront them, I am not sure what will happen."

The big man rolled his shoulders and settled back in his chair, raising his ale mug to his lips.

"You want us to fight them?" asked Corinne doubtfully.

"I hope we can avoid that," replied Gunther. He gestured to his massive body. "I am not a very stealthy person, but I believe some of you may be. We will plan to sneak in and steal the staff without them noticing us. If that does not work, we will have to do it the other way."

"Very well," said Amelie. "When do we leave?"

~

THAT EVENING, Ben and Amelie strolled around the plaza outside of the inn. At night, it was lit only by the light that poured out of the surrounding buildings. The downside of a town without a government, thought Ben, was that no one paid for lanterns.

"You've been quiet," murmured Amelie.

"We seem to be going further and further down a hole, and I'm starting to wonder if there is any bottom. What if when we find the Purple and somehow manage to steal this staff of theirs, we still do not have an answer to the demons? Gunther claims we don't have the knowledge to use the staff, and he says he may not be willing. What if this entire trip to the South Continent is a waste of time? The demons are in Alcott. The people there are under attack. We are down here, not helping anyone. Amelie, what if we're deluding ourselves about what we're doing? Irrefort, Qooten, everything?"

Amelie tightened her grip on his arm. "What are you suggesting we do? Turn back?"

"I want to be doing something," declared Ben. "Something I can see. Something I know is helpful. I want to face the demons and fight. We should be protecting people."

"Anyone can swing a sword," argued Amelie. "There are hunters in Northport, Jasper and whoever he recruited, countless towns along the north. Even Lord Jason said he would fight the demons. I'm not saying we would be useless on the front lines, but the world doesn't need another strong arm and a sword. The world needs someone to be creative, to do something dramatic that really changes things. That's what we should strive for. Whether it's the Purple and their weapon or another quest after this one, we can't stop until we have a solution. We could kill hundreds of demons with our blades and it wouldn't change the course of what is happening. The demons will not quit until someone figures out how to stop them from coming. I know it feels like we aren't doing anything, but we are doing everything!"

They walked on in silence for a long time, circling the plaza, enjoying the cool evening air.

"What if it doesn't work?" asked Ben.

"Then we can go swing our swords," replied Amelie.

Ben smiled down at her. "You always know what to say to encourage me, don't you?"

"I've been training my entire life to know what to say to people. My father, my tutors, even the Sanctuary. They all wanted me to be a leader."

"You're good at it," complimented Ben.

"You're getting pretty good at it too," mentioned Amelie.

Ben chuckled. "I'm not sure about that. I trained to be a brewer and then a swordsman. I don't know much about leadership or how to talk to people."

"You know more than you think," replied Amelie. "You connect to people, Ben. You connect in a way I don't know how to. You're authentic. You could study a thousand great speeches, learn the art of speaking from the best stage actors, understand how to logically persuade the most intelligent critics, but it doesn't do you any good if you can't find people's hearts. People trust you, and they know that you'll do your best to follow through on what you say. There's a goodness in you, Ben, and people see that. They want to be part of it."

"I don't know, Amelie," mumbled Ben.

"That night in the Sanctuary," reminded Amelie, "I had to choose to go with you or to stay. Between a life that moments before seemed safe and secure or a life of constant danger. You convinced me, Ben. That moment, I wanted to follow you. Wherever you were going."

"Everyone gets lucky once." Ben chuckled. "I spoke fast and got you out of there before you had time to think about it."

"I don't think luck had anything to do with it," insisted Amelie. She stopped and wrapped her arms around Ben, pulling him close. "You're a very persuasive character. In fact, there's a few other unsavory things you've talked me into since then."

He bent down to kiss her, forgetting everything he'd been worried about.

8
_____

THE HAMMER

THEY LEFT Frisay the same way they came in, through the narrow passageway in the wall.

"Gunther," asked Corinne, "I am curious. How was this wall built so quickly? It's as thick and sturdy as any fortification I've seen. The Dirhadji said it was raised in a matter of months."

The big man filled the passageway in front of them, his shoulders nearly brushing against the walls as they walked.

"I needed a place to stay," he rumbled as they exited into the bright, desert sun.

"What do you mean you needed a place to stay?" pressed Corinne.

"What does it sound like I meant?" growled the mage.

Ben was quickly realizing that the big man was not a morning person.

"I was concerned the Purple were on the verge of a breakthrough, and I wanted to keep an eye on them in case I needed to intercede. I got tired of the lords and uppity merchants in Ooswam pestering me, so I came out to the desert. I'm not a savage. I didn't plan to spend the next couple of decades in a tent."

AC COBBLE

Thyr coughed.

"Sorry I called you a savage," said Gunther, "but you have to admit, your people do eschew the modern comforts, things like walls, roofs, a place to shit without having to dig a hole first. Once you enjoy those amenities, it's hard to go back. I built this place so I could have all of those nice things and so people could come live near me. With proper infrastructure, we were able to form a functioning society. You should try it."

"Are you saying you built this place in a couple of months?" questioned Thyr disbelievingly. "Built an entire city in a few short months?"

"Not all at once," responded Gunther. "I built about a quarter of this in a few months. I've been adding to it over the years since then."

Ben looked back and saw Towaal's tight face. Behind her, the fused stone of Frisay rose straight up into the cloudless sky. It was clear from Towaal's look she was having difficulty understanding the power required to raise a city from rock and sand. A mage with that kind of power was a force to be reckoned with.

"What are the faces on the gates for?" asked Ben.

"Warnings," snapped Gunther.

The big mage's strides lengthened, and Ben and his companions took the signal that he did not want to discuss it further. They scampered behind the man, walking across the broken rock and sand that surrounded Frisay.

Gunther had been close-lipped about where he was taking them, but Ben knew they were headed west, skirting the line between the deep desert and civilization.

After a couple of leagues, Thyr broke away and turned south. The Dirhadji had wives waiting for him, and with Gunther's guidance, they no longer needed his assistance.

Earlier that morning, Ben had asked the man if he'd located the place they could find the strangers. If it didn't work out with Gunther, Ben wanted a backup.

The desert warrior had merely stated, "West."

Under his breath, he'd also muttered something about Raim. Ben recalled that his friend Raim was going to do business with the strangers. Ben asked about it, but Thyr merely shook his head and changed the subject.

As he watched Thyr's back disappear into the harsh landscape, Ben pondered whether the strangers and the Purple were one in the same. If so, what kind of business were the Dirhadji doing with them that they would be so closed-lipped about?

"He turned out to be a good man," remarked Amelie to Ben.

Ben frowned. Thyr had helped them but not for their sakes. The Dirhadji had his own motivations. They weren't the only ones keeping secrets.

O'ecca snorted. She'd never forgiven the man for his initial drunken attack.

Milo caught up to them and they all turned his way. It was rare that the shy apprentice did not hide at the back of the party.

"Do you see his hammer?" he whispered, cutting his gaze toward Gunther.

Ben glanced at Gunther then back at Milo. Of course he'd seen the hammer. It was the size of a small person.

The giant mage had the huge black-iron weapon resting on his shoulder. Flickers of red and orange curled across it like slow-moving tongues of flame.

"There's more light on it today," murmured O'ecca. "I do not understand magic. What does it mean?"

Amelie shrugged. "I am no expert on magical devices."

"It's gathering energy," claimed Milo.

Ben looked at the timid young man. "How do you know?"

Milo shook his loose mop of curls. "I can feel it. A growing sense of... potential. It's not coming from him, though. He's somehow tapped another source of energy, something stronger than anything I've felt before."

"The void between the worlds?" wondered Amelie. "That is what the Purple were after."

Milo adjusted his pack and kept his gaze fixed on Gunther. "I don't know. Keep an eye on him, and let me know what you sense. Maybe you're right, and there is a reason he knows so much about the Purple's weapon."

The former apprentice fell back to his customary position at the tail of their group.

Amelie met Ben's gaze and raised an eyebrow.

He shrugged.

O'ecca adjusted the turban she'd wrapped around her head and complained, "Frisay did not have the comforts of home, but in a short time, I'd gotten used to being out of this sand and heat."

"It hasn't been easy, has it?" agreed Ben.

"This better be worth it," grumbled the lady. "If not, I will hold you responsible. There is much I could be doing at home to help my father."

Ben sighed and kept walking.

THAT EVENING, they erected a handful of tarps to create a rough wind-break. They sat around their sparse campsite, watching the sun fall below the horizon.

There was no wood for fire so no hot meal. Nothing to prepare except to fiddle with the tarps and spread out their bed rolls. They'd restocked in Frisay, and had an ample supply of travel rations. Ben chewed morosely at a tough piece of ostrich jerky. An ample supply of the stuff may not be a good thing, he thought.

He jumped when Gunther settled down next to him and Amelie.

"Mistress Albie told me she'd seen you before in the north."

Ben nodded slowly, swallowing a half-chewed wad of meat.

"Tell me what happened there," instructed the mage.

Ben glanced at Amelie before answering. "We passed through Free State on the way to the Wilds. We were up there looking for a rift, which the Purple created to meter the flow of demons into our world. We thought we could shut it off and help protect Northport."

"I'm familiar with the Rift," responded Gunther. "Tell me about the people in Free State. What happened to them?"

"They died," Ben stated simply.

"I was worried about that," rumbled Gunther. "The Wilds is no place for a colony. By the time I heard they'd left for there, it was too late. The younger generations are overly eager sometimes. They do not think things through. There is no point running away from the lords if you head directly into peril. I wish I could have stopped them."

"Stop them?" asked Ben.

The mage nodded.

"Would they have listened to you?" queried Amelie.

"I would have made them listen," declared Gunther softly. "I can be very persuasive when I want to be."

"I thought the point of Free State was that they made their own decisions," remarked Ben.

A bitter smirk crawled across Gunther's face. "That is true. Maybe you are right. Maybe they wouldn't have listened, even to me."

"Did they know who you are?" asked Amelie.

Gunther shook his head in the negative.

"In my experience," added Ben, "the people of Free State are highly independent. If anyone told them what to do, they'd be more likely to do the opposite."

"Your experience with Free State?" questioned Gunther. "Mistress Albie told me you spent one night there."

"We stopped in a Free State outside of the City too," stated Ben. "It was also just one night, but we spent most of the time speaking to a man named Myland. He seemed to the be the leader, though, he wouldn't let anyone call him that. He explained the philosophy of Free State to us."

"Myland," murmured Gunther. "I haven't seen him for years, not since he went off to start his colony. That fool loved the idea of building it in the shadow of the City. That's what I'm talking about. Directly into peril."

"You know Myland?" asked Amelie.

Gunther chuckled. "I'm the one who gave him that name. You don't think his parents did that, did you?"

Ben sat back, thinking.

"How is he doing?" wondered Gunther.

Amelie shrugged. "He seemed pretty content to me. The people there respected and listened to him, despite his assurances that they did not. The community appeared to be thriving, though, it was pretty rough. Logs, thatch, and mud mortar. They're far enough into the wilderness that I don't think they'll have problems with the Sanctuary. They had plenty to eat, but if we see Myland again, I'd rather drink lantern oil than the foul spirits he's distilling."

A broad grin split Gunther's face. "That's the Myland I know."

"You founded Free State, didn't you?" guessed Ben.

Gunther winked. "I founded a Free State, the first one. Each of the colonies you found were formed by their members. I have very little to do with establishing new colonies these days. When it started, I had no desire to continue living within the power structure that the leaders of this world have thrown across us. Everywhere I went, I had to hide who I was for fear that the locals would try to conscript me into whatever petty cause they had. I didn't want to fight their pointless wars."

Amelie gestured to Gunther's hammer. "Certainly, they couldn't force you to do something you didn't want to do."

Gunther picked up the massive weapon and cradled it in his lap. "No one, not even the Veil, has the strength to force me to do something. A cruel enough person can always find leverage, though. They could damage my property, harm the ones I love. They could harm ones I don't know but am too good of a person to let suffer. There is a lot someone can do to influence you if they are willing to go far enough. You can ask your friend the assassin about that. Sometimes, it would take years, but always, someone would decide to manipulate me. Usually, they didn't understand who I am. They saw me merely as a very large man with a mage-wrought hammer. I was able to hide what I'm really capable of, and that just made it worse."

Ben ignored the jibe at Rhys. "You left to get away from that?"

The huge mage nodded. "I left. I looked for the most remote place I could find, and I lived there. I lived there for years by myself. It was terrible. Almost as bad as being under some lord's boot. People are not meant to be ruled and treated like peasants, but they aren't meant to be alone, either. I returned to the edges of civilization and built a small village. I traded with those near me. Over time, more and more of them came to join me. After enough years, they realized I wasn't aging. They suddenly wanted something from me too, more than I was willing to give. So again, I left."

He turned the hammer in his hands, his fingers drifting over the swirling patterns of yellow, red, and orange.

"That time, I didn't go into isolation, but I didn't stray too close to the seats of power either. I found another area on the fringe, and I started another community. Every decade or so, I did the same. These days, there are enough communities that when it's time, I return to places I've been. Only a few members of the communities know the truth about me. Mistress Albie and Myland, those like them who I can trust. To most, I'm merely the biggest, meanest, strongest, and fastest worker. That's more than enough to gain respect. When necessary, I protect the communities, but they're so spread out now it's become difficult. I regret I couldn't be there to help the people in the Wilds."

"Why do you do it?" wondered Amelie.

"To give people a place to go. There are so many who are oppressed but have nowhere to turn. This is my solution."

"You have the strength to build a real city, a place with rules that make it fair to everyone. You could lead it, and set the example for your people," challenged Ben. "You could turn it into a new land, one where people are treated fairly, and no one is artificially elevated over the others."

Gunther shook his head. "No, if I tried that, I am certain I would end up just like the others. King Argren in Whitehall, Lord Jason in Irrefort, Lady Coatney in the Sanctuary."

"Lady Coatney?" queried Ben.

Gunther nodded. "The Veil."

"I haven't known you long," stated Amelie, "but I think I already know you well enough to understand you wouldn't seek power like them. You are a good man. You could do so much for the world. If you were in Alcott standing against the demons, standing against the wars of man, think how many people you could save!"

Gunther set his hammer on the ground beside him. "None of those leaders started out thinking they would do evil. They all thought they would do good for their people. Maybe even for Alcott and the world. That's not the way it worked out, though, is it?"

Ben frowned.

"Good intentions do not always lead to good actions," continued the mage. "The more powerful someone is, the easier it is to slide down the slippery slope into darkness. Compromises to advance your vision seem worth it, and only too late does one realize how far they've fallen. Remember that as you continue your quest. Remember that both Argren and Jason meant to do good when they started, and I'd gamble they still believe they are on the side of right. What difference does it make for most people, though?

Countless lives will be crushed when those two sides come together."

"We know people will die!" exclaimed Ben. "That's what we're saying."

Gunther held up a hand to stall Ben. "Whether it is those rulers or me, it doesn't matter. Whoever is involved in the conflict, it doesn't matter. The best intentions do not justify war. Nothing does. Those lords would march to battle against me, just like they will against each other."

"Someone has to stand up for what is right," argued Amelie.

"Who decides what is right?" retorted Gunther. "As I said earlier, Argren, Jason, even Coatney all believed at one point they were there to do good. Are we so confident that we can say with absolute certainty, they are wrong?"

Ben and Amelie frowned at the mage, at a loss for words.

"Look at it this way," added the man. "Are the Alliance and Coalition any different? Does it matter to the common man who wins that battle? They say they are different. They have slightly different laws they impose on their populations, though, most people would have difficulty telling you which ones. At the end of the day, to the majority of the population, they are the same. The words even mean the same thing! A coalition is an alliance."

Ben blinked, his mind swirling.

"It's just two sides of the same coin," rumbled Gunther. "You can flip the coin to either side and it looks different to someone who isn't paying attention. Front or back, coalition or alliance, ass or elephant, it's the same damn coin!"

The huge mage stood, dragging his hammer up with him.

"No, I don't trust myself to be a leader. I've been alive too long. I've seen people make too many errors. I can't believe I'm better than all of the leaders who've come before. It's the conceit of man to think that he is wiser than all other men. That's why I've continued to promote Free State. A man does not need someone else to give him permission to live. No one should stand in judgement of another man's choices, to tell him what is right and wrong."

The mage retreated to the other side of their camp and busied himself by shaking out his bed roll. While he'd spoken, the sun had fallen below the horizon, and the warm desert air was rapidly cooling.

Rhys settled down beside them, taking Gunther's place. He passed a wine skin to Amelie who drank deeply, a pensive look etched on her face.

"He's right, you know," stated Rhys. "Too much power inevitably leads to darkness. I've seen it more times than I care to recall."

Ben raised an eyebrow. "What do you suggest then?"

Rhys drew his longsword and placed it on his knees, just like Gunther had held his hammer.

"Draw your sword, Ben," requested the rogue.

Eyebrows knit in confusion, Ben drew his weapon and placed it on his knees.

Rhys slid a finger down the length of his blade. Silvery runes sparkled beneath his touch. A wisp of silver smoke drifted off the blade, barely visible in the low light of the moon.

"In the past, when I disagreed with someone, I killed them," stated Rhys bluntly. "I used either this sword or my long knives. I considered it a simple, even elegant solution. Because of that, I got my way most of the time. I did what I wanted, and it was pretty rare someone was able to oppose me."

Ben and Amelie watched their friend silently.

"Over the years, I got even better at it," continued the rogue. "Killing people grew easy, and I loved the power it gave me. I found myself finding reasons to eliminate someone. For the most part, I think they actually were bad people. Gunther was right, though. Who am I to judge? How could I call someone else bad when I was an assassin? I have no moral right and no ground to stand on. I didn't know how to stop, though. When you have a sword, it's easy to use. I joined the Sanctuary, thinking I could make sense of things, thinking that in her years, the Veil had improved. It seemed the Sanctuary was doing good in the world again. I found out, though, the Veil had just gotten better at keeping secrets. She was up to the same machinations as her predecessors."

"You're trying," said Amelie. "That counts for something."

Rhys shrugged. "I'm not sure it does."

He stared down at his sword, fingers following the etchings in the blade.

"Something changed when I met you two. You don't fight your battles because of what you think you will gain, or because they are easy, or because you're certain you can win. You fight because you believe it's necessary. Whether you will win or lose is a secondary concern, and I've grown to respect that."

Amelie passed the wine skin to Ben and he took a sip.

"Back in Indo, Ben," continued Rhys, "you wanted to stay and fight the Red Lord, to help protect the people there. We talked you out of it, but should we have? Maybe we would have failed. Maybe we would have been successful. I don't know. I do know that had we tried, it would have been the honorable thing. You asked what I suggest you do, and my answer is that you don't give up. You continue to fight the battles you think are necessary."

Rhys pointed to Ben's sword.

"You no longer have a mage-wrought blade. You can't call the wind at will. That wasn't your strength, though. Your strength is your conviction. You don't need a magical sword or the ability to manipulate energy with your mind. The true power you possess, Ben, isn't in your arm. It's in your heart. Do not seek power. Seek to do what is right."

The rogue stood and held out a hand for his wine skin.

Ben passed it back quietly and watched his friend walk away from camp into the dark night. Corinne stood and followed him.

Towaal leaned against her pack, eyes open, staring at the stars above them. Milo appeared to be asleep.

Across camp, Ben saw Gunther lying on his side, the flickering light from his hammer subtly illuminating his face. His eyes were open, watching them.

~

THE NEXT MORNING, the first rays of sunlight beamed down on them, heating the dry air and burning the moisture from the parched land.

Ben stood and stretched, glancing around the blasted landscape. They were away from the sand sea and hadn't ventured into the deep desert, but the terrain wasn't any more forgiving than what they'd seen on the way to Frisay. With cracked rocks, red sand, and only a few scraggly trees poking up in the distance, it was a harsh land they would travel.

The mage Gunther followed Ben's gaze. "We should be there in a week."

Ben looked at the man, their guide, and wondered whether he would help them or not when it came time to decide. He thought about the conversations the night before and decided Amelie was right. Rhys was right. They had to fight the battle because it was necessary. They couldn't be one more sword in the army if they wanted to permanently stop the demons. Even if no one else saw it, Ben knew the hordes of life-draining creatures were the biggest threat facing the world. He wouldn't stand by idly while they ravaged unchecked.

"You're looking fresh and energized," remarked Gunther.

Ben grunted. "As fresh as I can be after spending the night rolling from one rock to the other. Will it get any better as we go west?"

The big mage scratched at his head, shaking a shower of loose sand from his hair. "No, not really."

Ben groaned.

"Take half a bell to stretch out before we start hiking," advised Gunther. "Your body will thank you later."

"The Ohms?" Amelie asked Ben.

He nodded.

Rhys joined them and they dropped into the first stance. As they moved through the positions, O'ecca approached.

"Can you teach me?"

"Sure," replied Ben. He stood and resumed the starting pose, showing her how to do it.

"If the Dirhadji see you doing that, they won't like it," warned Gunther.

"Thyr saw us, and we talked him into joining," responded Ben.

"The Sanctuary mages won't like it either," declared Gunther.

Ben blinked at him.

"Control," said the big mage, glancing in Towaal's direction. "Control over yourself is the first step in hardening your will. The Dirhadji have been refining the technique for centuries. Why do you think no mages live in the desert? Towaal is the first Sanctuary mage who's come here in centuries. They're afraid their power won't give them an advantage. They won't meet a man blade to blade, hammer to hammer. It's why the Purple came here, because they knew no other mage would follow."

Towaal met the larger mage's look impassively.

Ben looked between them. Suddenly, the reason the Ohms felt so similar to Towaal's meditation exercises clicked into place. They felt the same because, at the core, they were the same.

"It's good exercise," advised Rhys with a wink.

"You knew!" accused Ben.

"Most people won't meditate," said the rogue. "It's boring. When you are thinking about how they will help your swordsmanship, the Ohms are exciting."

"Why didn't you tell us?" wondered Ben.

Rhys shrugged. "It never came up, I guess. I didn't plan to

AC COBBLE

teach you to harden your will. It started as something to kill time. Towaal asked me to teach you to fight with your hands, remember? Figured it'd be good for both of us. Once we were in the City, it seemed like hardening your will was a skill you were going to need."

Ben grunted and narrowed his eyes at his friend. The man kept secrets as naturally as he breathed. Even after all of their time together, Ben was certain there were still treasures buried under the surface.

"Well, that's even more reason we should do them," declared Amelie. "Stretching for the day, learning to harden our will, I don't think anyone will argue either one is bad for us."

Gunther turned and tended to his bedroll, folding the thin blanket and stuffing it in his pack.

Ben looked between Amelie and O'ecca and then assumed the starting position again.

O'ecca was a natural at the poses, shifting from form to form with effortless grace. Ben recalled the speed and flexibility she'd displayed when they faced the demons. In the right circumstances, the diminutive lady wasn't someone he'd care to face in combat. She was lithe and quick.

The tip of Amelie's boot caught his backside and Ben stumbled forward.

He spun to her in surprise, ready to admonish her for kicking him, then saw her glare. He flushed as he realized just how closely he'd been watching O'ecca's movements.

Amelie raised an eyebrow, waiting for him to object.

Instead, Ben offered her a short bow as apology.

"If you two are done fooling around," growled Rhys, "let's pack up and get going. It's too hot to stand here doing nothing."

Ben scooped up a small rock and tossed it at the rogue.

"There's only a couple of days' worth of wine in the skins Gunther brought. We have to get moving!" encouraged Rhys.

"There's plenty of wine in the skins I brought, for me," rumbled the big mage.

Rhys effected a hurt expression, and they all busied themselves packing up. Rhys was right. It was foolish to stand around in the heat doing nothing. They should be looking for shade or moving.

～

THE DAYS PASSED IN A HOT, sweaty blur.

They wrapped turbans around their heads, but it did little to blunt the force of the pounding sun. At night, it grew cool. The dry air couldn't retain the heat of the day, and they huddled together for warmth when they slept. There was no wood for fire, and they would have been reluctant to set one anyway. The Dirhadji lived south of them. Gunther advised it wouldn't be prudent to attract their notice. It was a distraction they didn't need. They'd packed plenty of rations, but the dry food held little flavor, and eating it was almost more work than it was worth.

Fortunately, they were able to find ample sources of water. Gunther seemed to have a nose for finding the hidden pools or bubbling springs that quickly vanished in the desert sun. It wasn't until Amelie informed him several days into the journey that Ben realized the man was delving for the liquid.

"He extends his will almost as an afterthought," mused Amelie. "It's as natural as breathing to him."

Ben eyed the big man as he hauled himself up a rock shelf and into a short cave where he claimed a small spring was hiding.

"I believe he may be the most powerful mage alive," said Amelie quietly.

"Stronger than the Veil or Jasper?" Ben asked.

"He is stronger than the Veil," assured Towaal, who'd approached silently from behind them. "Significantly so. If that man chose to do it, he could level cities with that hammer of his. He could face an army and be the only one standing afterward. I'd guess it would take at least a third of the mature mages in the Sanctuary to stand against him, though, with those kind of fireworks, anything could happen."

Ben watched Gunther's tree trunk-sized legs wiggle as he crawled into the cave. He'd fill his water skin and then the rest of them would pass theirs up.

"If he has that kind of power," wondered Ben, "what does the Purple have that even he is cautious?"

Towaal's eyes narrowed. "We'll find out. I believe we should heed his caution. If that man is afraid, we should be doubly so."

THE MOMENT they finally saw Gunther in action was on them before Ben realized what was happening. They were passing through a narrow canyon. Striated red and yellow stone walls rose three man-heights above their heads. The bottom of the canyon was filled with soft, red sand. Ben listlessly kicked rocks ahead of him as he walked, wondering how long it had been since there was enough running water in the desert to carve the canyon out of the landscape.

A low-pitched growl sounded above them.

Ben glanced up and saw a dark shape blocking out the blue sky. Suddenly, he was thrown to the side and bounced hard against one of the rock walls.

Gunther was standing in his place. The huge man swung an arm up to catch a thrashing, green-pebble-skinned creature. Gunther gripped it with one big hand.

The thing clawed wildly at the giant mage, leaving bloody lacerations in his skin. It snapped at him with finger-length curved teeth.

Calmly, Gunther dropped his hammer and wrapped his

second hand around the thing's neck. Its body contorted, clawed-feet scrambling against the hard muscle of his torso.

With a crack, Gunther twisted its neck. Its head lolled to one side, and Gunther tossed the carcass down on the sand.

Laid out, unmoving, Ben saw it was a lizard. A big one. It stretched half again as long as he was tall. Speckles of blood stained its talons where it had gouged Gunther's flesh.

Ben looked at the mage and his eyes grew wide. The bloody gashes were knitting themselves back together.

"H-How…" stammered Ben.

Towaal interrupted him. "You're healing yourself!"

The big mage looked at her blankly. "Of course I am. Infection can be deadly out here."

"How did you do that?" pressed Towaal, momentarily forgetting her caution around Gunther. "I've never heard of a mage being able to heal themselves. It defies everything I've been taught. No one understands the body well enough to risk manipulating those energies. Doing anything other than simply boosting the body's natural ability is, well, dangerous."

"You're long-lived," stated Gunther.

Towaal nodded slowly.

"That is self-healing. Repairing aging cells in your body, replacing them with new, constantly refreshing yourself." Gunther pointed to his abdomen where the last signs of a deep cut were fading into smooth skin. "That is all that I am doing right now, refreshing myself and speeding the natural process."

Towaal looked at him uncertainly.

"Just because you do not have the knowledge does not mean it doesn't exist," added Gunther. "The Sanctuary forgets that too often."

"What if you make a mistake?" asked Towaal. "You could easily harm yourself."

The big mage eyed her curiously. "We're talking about healing, right? The implication is that you've already been harmed."

Towaal frowned at him but didn't have a response.

Corinne was squatting next to the giant lizard.

"What is this thing?"

"Sand dragon," answered Gunther.

"Dragon? Like a wyvern!" exclaimed Ben. "There are real wyverns?"

Gunther shrugged. "I've never seen a wyvern like in the stories. These things are bad enough. The big ones have been known to surprise and eat entire caravans."

Corinne stared at him. "This isn't a big one?"

Gunther grinned. "Don't worry. Those live in the deep desert. The ones here don't get more than seven or eight-paces long. They tend to nest together, though, so keep an eye out."

Ben looked down at the lizard and shuddered.

"Why didn't you use your hammer?" inquired O'ecca. "Surely that would have been easier. You didn't need to let it scratch you up. It's not the nut thing, is it? There are no tables out here to destroy."

She was looking at the long rips in Gunther's leather vest. The flesh below was already healed.

"Every tool has a purpose," responded the mage. "The purpose of my hammer isn't to pulverize lizards."

O'ecca shifted her naginata on her shoulder. "What is the purpose of it then?"

"Maybe you'll see when we find the Purple."

9

HOUSE ON A HILL

BEN WASN'T sure where he expected an ancient, secretive cabal of mages to live. He supposed a mountain fortress, secluded from civilization, and surrounded by an impenetrable-looking oasis was as good a place as any.

"The trees will provide some cover," mused Corinne, studying the layout.

"Will we need to climb the side of the mountain?" wondered O'ecca.

"I don't think we can just walk in the front door," answered Corinne.

"Have you been here before?" Rhys asked Gunther.

The big man shook his head. "Not this close. I've evaluated their defenses with far-seeing and delved what I could of the interior. I'm afraid it's not much detail to plan an assault with. The top of the mountain is ringed by their fortress with a large open space in the middle for gardens. Underneath the fortress, the mountain is honeycombed with passages and tunnels. There are giant caverns inside which may be natural, or they may have been dug by the Purple."

"How many people?" queried Rhys.

AC COBBLE

"Three hundred, maybe more," replied the mage. "Deep in the mountain, it's difficult to tell without letting the mages detect my sensing."

"Look!" hissed Amelie.

She pointed to a slowly moving dust cloud that approached the fortress. Now that Ben saw it, he could see it followed a barely discernable road.

"Traders," speculated Corinne. "They must have some contact with the outside world then."

"Food and supplies," remarked Rhys. "They don't have enough space on that mountain to grow sufficient food to sustain three hundred people."

"The wagon is coming from the south," observed Ben.

"Good point," acknowledge Gunther, pinching his chin, lost in thought as he studied the dust cloud.

"What does it mean?" asked Amelie.

"They're trading with the Dirhadji," answered Gunther, "though, that doesn't make sense. The desert tribes don't have excess fresh produce and meat. They have hardly any industry aside from war."

The party watched the caravan draw closer.

"It's some sort of large boxes," remarked Corinne. "About man high, perforated along the top. They could be for livestock. They have a lot of guards, though. Half a dozen per wagon. Maybe they're nervous around the Purple and they bring a lot of men. There are chains too, I think. Long ones piled on top of the boxes."

"It's not livestock. It's slaves," growled Rhys.

Gunther's knuckles cracked, and Ben shot a look at the big mage. He was staring hard at the caravan and standing slowly.

"Now is not the time," stated Ben.

The mage looked down at him.

"You said it yourself," pleaded Ben. "The Purple is powerful. If we ambush this caravan on their doorstep, they'll

186

know we are here. We'll lose the opportunity to sneak inside."

"This isn't right," rumbled Gunther.

"It isn't the right time, either," challenged Ben. "Good intentions do not always lead to good actions. You told me that. We have to think about what we're doing. We have to plan. When we act, we need to be certain."

"Throwing my words back at me, boy?" snarled Gunther.

Ben met the big man's look and didn't back down.

"They are your words," agreed Ben after a long pause. "Did you mean them?"

Slowly, the mage's shoulders slumped, and he settled back down to kneel.

"What is your plan then?" Gunther asked.

THEY SCURRIED across the moonlit landscape, hugging the ground as they moved, nervous the Purple had watchers on the walls.

"There is no way they can see anything this far away at night," muttered Corinne.

"You can't see that far," reminded Rhys, "but these are mages."

"Watch the foliage when we get under the trees," stated Gunther. "At night, under the canopy, mundane traps will be almost impossible to detect."

"Leave those to me," said Rhys. "I'll take care of the trip-wires if you make sure we don't walk into any wards."

"They do not have the skill to set a ward I cannot detect," declared the big mage. "Do not worry, assassin."

Towaal flitted along beside Ben. Ben caught her shaking her head at the older mage's confidence. He was skilled, no doubt, but he wasn't the only one who had access to ancient secrets. There was no telling what the Purple knew or what surprises they'd been able to develop over the centuries.

They were headed toward a thick stand of trees that circled a wide mesa. Atop the rock formation sat the Purple's fortress. It wasn't intimidating, as fortresses go, Ben thought, except for the two hundred paces of rock one would have to climb to get to the front door.

Their plan was to scale the ragged backside of the mesa. Towaal had scouted the structure through far-seeing and discovered a crumbled section of wall they could slip through. There didn't appear to be many guards on the walls, and at night, the lights were few in the open areas.

They assumed the Purple relied on secrecy and a net of magical wards to keep their fortress safe. Given the difficulty Ben and his companions had finding the place, it seemed the strategy was effective. At least, it had been.

A thick wall of trees rose higher as they approached. A quarter league deep, it surrounded the mountain. On the far side of the fortress, a road cut through the growth, but they were certain that would be watched. Instead, they'd go in the back.

"That isn't natural," said Corinne.

No one responded. They all knew.

Up close, Ben saw underneath the trees lay a black lake of slimy-looking water. The trees grew out of it with tall, twisted roots that stood higher than Ben's head. The roots created a maze-like barrier at ground level. He saw they'd have to climb over or duck under the roots at nearly every step.

Verdant green fronds sprouted near ground level as well, forming a visual obstruction that prevented them from seeing more than ten paces into the thick forest.

"It's a jungle in the desert," mused Rhys.

Twenty paces from the vegetation, Gunther held up a hand, and they slowed to a stop. The big mage paced forward and waved Towaal to come beside him. They stared down at something lying on the ground. Ben and the rest of the companions cautiously approached.

A thick ribbon of copper was set into the rocky ground. On one side, dry red desert rock extended for leagues behind them. On the other side, it was a wall of lush vegetation.

"They've built their own ecosystem," muttered Towaal, kneeling near the copper strip.

"It won't keep us out," surmised Gunther. "The wards are designed to keep moisture in."

The big mage waved a hand forward, passing through the invisible barrier of the ward. He turned and showed his hand to the party. Tiny beads of liquid sparkled on his skin, lit by the moon.

"That explains how they make such good use of the garden," responded Rhys.

"Let's go," said Gunther.

They hesitantly stepped over the copper ribbon and were instantly engulfed in hot, steamy air.

"Feels like home, doesn't it?" jested Ben to O'ecca.

"Except that we're about to steal some incredible weapon from a group of ancient mages who will want to burn us to cinders. Aside from that, just like a normal evening walk for me."

Ben's boot splashed down into the water and he slid his toe along the slick mud underneath.

"I suggest we try to work our way along the roots," said Rhys, grabbing one and hauling himself up. "There's no telling what is down in that water. Plus, it's just like climbing a tree when you were a child."

"You remember being a child?" Ben asked. He climbed up after Rhys.

The rogue had scampered across half a dozen roots and was gently tugging on one of the vines hanging above him.

"Pretty sturdy," he called back.

"Until you find one that isn't and take a bath," warned Corinne.

She'd moved ahead of the others, easily stepping from one

root to the next. O'ecca followed her, gracefully drifting through the trees like she really was on a simple evening stroll.

Ben worked his way deeper into the wood, testing every step and vine before he committed to it. It made for slow going, but it was better than plunging into the murky water.

Gunther brought up the rear. The big mage was clearly nervous and uncomfortable on the roots, and didn't trust the vines with his weight. He was just as clearly not interested in wading through the muck underneath them.

Ben grinned. At least there was one thing the big mage wasn't good at.

The deeper they moved, the less light they had. The moonlight barely penetrated the thick canopy above, and the relative brightness of the desert faded as they moved away from the edge of the woods.

"We're going to have to try a little light," declared Rhys.

"They'll have at least a few watchers," argued Towaal. "They may not see our movement under the canopy, but they could detect light."

"It's going to be pitch black in thirty more paces," responded Rhys. "We can't make it through here blind."

"How about this?" asked Gunther from behind them. "With such a steep angle, they'd have to be hanging over the wall and looking straight down to see anything."

A silver glow spread out below their feet, creeping through the black water. The moonlight, realized Ben. The mage was capturing the moonlight and reflecting it in the water. The effect was subtler than a single source of light, and hopefully not noticeable even if someone was looking straight down.

Ben moved to the next root and paused. Below him, two pinpoints reflected the silver light.

"What is that?" he wondered.

"Oh hell," exclaimed Rhys, quickly stepping to a higher root. "It looks like a crocodile."

Twenty paces to Ben's right, he heard a thrashing in the water as something big moved away.

"What is a crocodile?" asked Amelie nervously.

"Remember that big lizard Gunther killed?" asked Rhys. "Imagine it swimming. Under your feet. In the dark."

O'ecca came back to the group, easily hopping root to root. "Crocodiles? They are common in some parts of Ooswam. I'm told they cannot climb, so do not worry."

"What happens if we fall?" asked Ben.

"Then you should worry."

Ben groaned and cautiously took the next step. The thought of moving made him nervous, but standing still wasn't any better with the unblinking eyes lurking five paces below him.

For the next two bells, they struggled through the thick jungle. Any slips could be fatal, but they had to press on. Walking down the road to the front gate would ruin any chance of stealth. This was the only way they could get in unseen.

"I see why they don't bother with guards," panted Corinne.

In the silver light from below, Ben could see rivulets of sweat streaking her brow. Under the trees, it was sweltering hot. The air was still and thick with moisture. It smelled putrid from the muck below them.

Ben's legs were aching from the stress of maintaining his balance as he stepped root to root. They were nearing the end. Just another hundred paces and he could see glimpses of the rock wall ahead of them. He swallowed. The rock wall.

Through a break in the canopy, he looked up. Two hundred paces of rugged rock soared above his head. Two hundred paces of climbing that had to be done before dawn.

"We'd better get moving," muttered Rhys.

"At least there won't be any ice on it this time," said Ben.

"Didn't you fall off last time we were climbing something like this?" asked Corinne innocently.

Ben didn't respond.

They finally reached the base of the mountain and he winced. The swamp ran directly up to it. There was no beach, no ledge, nowhere to rest.

"Drink up," suggested Rhys, slinging his water skin off his belt. "Halfway up, there may not be a convenient place to pause. After what we just sweated out, we need to stay hydrated."

"Put your weapons on your backs," added Corinne. "You want your weight to be evenly distributed. Test each hand or toe hold before you trust your weight to it. This rock is exposed to some brutal weather and may not be stable."

Ben drew a deep breath.

"We can't use magic, either," said Gunther. "It's possible some members of the Purple are sensitive enough to feel if we alter the energies of this place. We don't know what kind of wards we could trip."

"It will be daylight when we reach the top," warned Milo.

"We'll have to climb quickly," responded Rhys. "From far-seeing, it appeared there were only a few people moving around up there. It's a large keep, so I'm hopeful we can stay out of sight as long as we get there before daybreak."

"Let's start climbing then," said Ben.

He tried to sound confident, but it came out as more of a squeak. Corinne was right. The last time they climbed something like this, he fell into a snowbank. This time, it was rocks and crocodiles beneath them.

"You'll be fine," assured Amelie.

O'ecca wasted no time and slapped a hand against the wall. Like a spider, she ascended with no apparent effort. Hands and feet found natural cracks and crevices, and she gained ten paces before Rhys latched onto the wall below her.

"That little girl weighs about as much as one of my arms," complained Gunther.

Ben looked at the ancient mage and saw him taking deep,

steadying breaths. Ben resolved to climb up ahead of Gunther. If the big man fell, he'd take everyone else with him.

Fingers gripping the rock, Ben pulled himself up.

The mountain was made from sandstone and worn from ages in the open air. The rough surface dug into his palm but gave him confidence he wouldn't easily slip, at least until his hands started to get sweaty.

He refused to look down, only straight in front of his face or up to where his friends were climbing. In the moonlight, he could see O'ecca moving like a wraith. She would make the top before Ben was a quarter way up.

Rhys and Corinne moved behind her, climbing confidently, but without the speed O'ecca exhibited. Milo was next, steady but cautious. Then came Ben, Amelie, Towaal, and Gunther.

Fifty paces above the water, Ben realized that having the mages come last may turn out to be a terrible idea. If one the Purple's mages spotted them, Towaal and Gunther would have to battle while climbing. That kind of split concentration could end in all of their deaths.

He looked to the sides and grimaced. They were climbing up through a shallow chimney in the rock. It allowed for extra hand-holds, but there wasn't room for him to edge to the side and let the mages pass. Even if he could make room, he would have to cling to the rock waiting for them. He didn't trust he'd have the arm and leg strength to last.

"You can do it," encouraged Amelie from below him.

He gritted his teeth and reached up again, slipping his fingers into a narrow crack and then drawing his leg up to wedge his boot in the corner of the chimney.

Three bells later, his eyes stung from sweat dripping into them. The skin on his hands and arms was bleeding and torn. He couldn't feel his toes, but they still held when he shoved them into a crack or pressed them against a nub of rock. His arms and legs quivered like the string of a recently fired bow. Twenty paces above him was the base of a half-tumbled wall.

Rhys was sitting on it, nervously glancing at the horizon where a soft glow was emanating.

Ben struggled to hurry, but his leaden limbs couldn't move any faster.

Milo had just disappeared ahead of him, and he could hear Amelie moving below. He didn't dare look down to see how close the others were.

He gritted his teeth and hauled himself higher, ignoring the pain as rough sandstone ground against his torn skin. One hand, one boot, the next hand, the next boot, he hauled himself higher.

When Ben reached the top, Rhys placed a finger against his lips and nodded in the direction of Corinne. She stood a dozen paces away. Ben saw the broken section of wall they were climbing over was only a curtain wall. Across a narrow, grass-covered bailey stood the main wall. It rose two man-heights. Ben watched Milo sling a leg over the top of it and disappear inside.

Corinne gestured for Ben to hurry. When he got close, she whispered in his ear. "O'ecca is on the other side. She'll direct you to an abandoned shed where we will spend the day. It's visible from the gardens, so we have to hurry."

Ben groaned inwardly at the thought of scaling another wall, but this was one was built of poorly mortared blocks of stone. It was closer to climbing a ladder than a mountain. He flexed his hands, trying to regain some feeling, then scampered up. He ignored the bloody fingerprints he was leaving on the rock. At the top, he finally turned and looked out.

On the far horizon, an orange glow crept into view. It barely lit a few jagged shards of rock that stabbed out of the desert. The rest of the landscape was still in shadow. They were too far away to see Frisay or any other towns. All that Ben could see was empty rock and sand. No one would have any reason to come within days of this mountain. Perfect for hiding the Purple.

Unfortunately, the empty terrain would be nearly impossible to hide in once the mages realized their weapon was stolen. Speed was the only thing that would keep Ben and his companions out of reach. Of course, it would only be a problem if they actually made it in and stole the weapon.

He looked again at the faint orange glow and estimated they had a quarter bell until true dawn. In the heat of the desert, he knew that whatever work was done in the garden would be done then. No one would be crazy enough to be outside in the afternoon if they didn't have to be.

Below him, Amelie was stumbling across the bailey to Corinne. She looked drained and lifeless. Rhys was bending across the curtain wall to reach a hand down, Ben assumed to Towaal. He hoped Gunther was not far behind, but he wouldn't wait to see. He crawled across the top of the main wall and half-climbed, half-fell into the garden below.

There was a decrepit shed beside him with O'ecca standing in the doorway. In front of him was row after row of fruit trees. Between the trunks, he could see rows of beans, corn, lettuces, and other vegetables in the distance. Hopefully, it wasn't orchard day for the workers.

Ben waited at the base of the wall for Amelie to come down and helped her land on her feet as she staggered away from the rock surface. Her face was a mixture of exhaustion and relief.

They walked to the shed and ducked inside while O'ecca worriedly kept watch.

Wheelbarrows, bags of seeds, pruning shears, ropes, and saws filled the space. It looked like it hadn't been disturbed in at least a season. Ben sighed in relief then moved to help Milo rearrange the items to clear space on the floor. They wouldn't have hot food or a bed, but at least they could make room to stretch out.

Time ticked by and Ben and his friends glanced at each other apprehensively. Through the open door of the shed, they could clearly see the grey trunks of the trees and the small green fruits hanging from the branches. Anytime now, workers would pour into the gardens.

Ben took a step toward the door, anxious to see if he could help, but Amelie caught his arm. Either Gunther would make it over the wall before the keep awoke, or he wouldn't. Ben couldn't climb down the side of the mountain and haul the big mage up.

Finally, Ben let out of burst of held breath as he saw the others start to drop from the wall. There was a heavy thump when Gunther's huge body crashed down into the grass. Rhys helped the big man up. Glancing around nervously, they scurried into the shed. O'ecca closed the door, and they all stood there, looking at each other.

A smile curled on Ben's lips. They'd made it undetected into the fortress. There was still a lot to do, but step one was a success.

They rummaged through their bags, pulling out food and water. They'd eat quickly then rest. They'd take turns keeping watch, but until darkness fell again, they wouldn't speak or leave the shed.

BEN WOKE to sweat rolling down his forehead. The shed was stifling hot. He rolled onto his side and saw Rhys near the door, listlessly waving a hand in front of his face to try and stir the still air. It was silent. Ben couldn't hear anything outside, but from the rogue's look, he knew to stay quiet. He crawled over to his friend, who had the door barely cracked open.

Rhys gestured to it, and Ben peered out.

Nearby, there was nothing but the fruit trees. In the distance, Ben could see flashes of movement. People were tending to the rows of vegetables. He watched for a few moments until he heard a sharp call. The movement all changed to be in the same direction. Ben realized a foreman or someone had called the workers in. They may be going for a meal or may be done for the day. He wasn't sure what time it was.

Rhys cupped his hand and poured it full of water. He wiped it on his face and head, trying to stay cool. He offered the water skin to Ben, but Ben shook his head.

Ben mimicked the sun passing overhead and rose an eyebrow at Rhys.

The rogue held up five fingers then closed his fist. Five more bells until dark.

Ben crawled back to his space on the floor and closed his eyes. He may not get much more sleep due to the heat, but he would rest. They were in for a long night.

WHEN BEN WOKE AGAIN, half the party was up. They were eating, drinking, and preparing for the night. He saw Rhys had taken his turban and wrapped it around his body, securing his longsword and long knives so they wouldn't move as they stalked through the fortress.

Corinne was sharpening her hand axes, drawing a whetstone across them slowly to keep the sound to a minimum. Amelie had emptied out the contents of her belt pouch. She was sorting through the items, evidently deciding which would make a valuable catalyst for magic if she needed it. O'ecca was holding her naginata and stretching, bending down until her head nearly touched the floor before straightening up. She tilted to one side and then the other. Ben wasn't sure how the girl could get more limber, but he saw the wisdom in what she was doing. If they needed to climb, fight, or flee, it made sense to be loose.

He stood and started the Ohms, moving slow like Thyr had shown them. Ben felt his muscles protest at the activity, and he was glad he decided to do it. He was tight from the climb the night before and couldn't risk a cramp when they entered the keep.

Two bells later, everyone was awake and ready.

Unlike the assault on the keep in Irrefort, they had no information about what the interior of the Purple's fortress looked like. They could only count on the fact that there would be fewer people inside and likely none of the maids who roamed the halls at night in a public castle.

They waited three bells after full dark then slunk into the garden. The silver glow of the moon painted the orchard around them. On the far wall of the main keep, Ben saw sporadic points of light from windows. There were no lights on the exterior. Either the Purple kept it dark to increase secrecy, or they didn't want to waste coin to light the outside of such an isolated fortress.

Rhys stalked through the trees, his head constantly turning, scanning the walls, eyeing the doors, and any other opening a person could be lurking in.

He pointed, only his silhouette visible to them. Ben followed the angle and saw a flickering orange light in a tower near the front gate. At least one guard was on duty. Ben was certain now they'd see more of them.

Below the guardhouse, the gate was sturdy wood construction. Not as secure as the other keeps Ben had seen, but he surmised it was likely because the Purple didn't need protection from mundane attacks. If anything, they were worried about other mages.

The tweets of night birds and the howl of the wind across the high fortress were the only sounds as they passed out of the orchard. They hugged the main wall and moved toward the central building. In the dark garden, as long as they avoided being backlit, they stood a good chance of remaining invisible to anyone who glanced out the windows.

Ben tried counting the lit windows, eyeing which ones were

close together and estimating those parts of the keep may still be active.

Rhys was evidently doing the same because as they drew close, he steered them up a narrow flight of stairs to the outside wall. There, he crouched down below the level of the battlements and scuttled forward.

They moved one hundred paces that way, all of them crouched low, until they got to a bend in the wall. It was just two hundred paces further, then they would meet the side of the main building. Ben guessed there must be a door there. Where it led, they would have to hope was somewhere they wanted to be.

At the bend, Rhys held up a hand and stopped them. He crawled forward and was gone a brief moment. When he returned, he gestured for them to huddle close.

"I see two guards further down," he whispered. "They're not paying much attention, as you might expect, since they are guarding a wall that stands two hundred paces above the desert. There's no way we can all slip by them on this wall, though. Entering the fortress at ground level is also something I wouldn't advise. A building this big is almost certain to have someone awake on the main level."

"What do you suggest?" asked Ben.

Rhys drew one of his long knives and spun it slowly in his hand.

"It's your decision," said the rogue.

Ben frowned and looked at Amelie. She met his gaze but didn't speak up.

Ben turned to Gunther. "You are certain we cannot negotiate with the Purple?"

The big man shifted, clearly uncomfortable from having to stoop to stay below the battlement.

"These mages have spent literally a thousand years trying to figure out how to use the staff. They won't let go of it easily."

"Their original plan was to develop a weapon to stand against the demons, right?" asked Ben. He looked between Milo and Gunther. The former librarian's apprentice should know the Purple's intentions better than anyone.

Gunther merely shrugged.

Milo offered, "If they wanted to fight the demons, wouldn't they have done it already? The rift is destroyed, and the demon threat is rising. If the Purple in this land retained any intention of fulfilling their original purpose, they would have acted. I find it hard to believe a group like them wouldn't be aware of what is happening in the world. Remember, my master had serious doubts about them. That's why he wrote to Irrefort, the Sanctuary, even Gunther."

"We saw a caravan of slaves being brought in here earlier today," Rhys reminded them. "These are not altruistic people. I don't think we can bargain with them. There is nothing they will want that we'd be willing to give."

Ben breathed deep then exhaled slowly. "Do it, Rhys."

The rogue slipped away into the darkness.

Ben waited nervously until he returned. There had been no sound, no indication a razor-sharp blade was being slid into two living beings.

The rogue pointed to his belt where a set of iron keys hung and then gestured for them to move ahead. They all fell in line behind the rogue, staying low to avoid a tell-tale silhouette.

As they snuck along the wall, Ben expected to see the slumped over bodies of the guards. He never did. He realized Rhys must have pushed them over the edge either into the bailey or into the garden. In the darkness, even if a fresh set of guards came out on patrol, they'd have trouble finding where their fellows went. By daybreak, it would be obvious.

When they reached the end of the wall where it met the side of the keep, the party regrouped. A wooden door led into the building. Rhys tried to push it open, but it was locked. He slung the keys off his belt and glanced around the group.

Ben shrugged and gestured to the door. No sense in stealing the keys from the guards if they weren't going to use them.

Gunther approached the door, staring hard at it and the walls around it. He looked to Rhys and shook his head. Nothing magical to worry about.

The rogue tried a few keys until he found one that worked. With a sharp click, he unlocked it and pushed the door open. Inside, they found a spiral staircase and a sparsely lit hallway. Before they entered the tower, Rhys examined the doorway. He knelt and pointed to two stones set in the floor. He shook his head.

Ben understood. Don't step on those stones. He couldn't see what worried the rogue, but he trusted his friend's instincts when it came to sneaking into dark buildings.

Rhys stepped carefully over the stones then headed down the hallway. One by one, they filed after him. Ears were perked and eyes strained for any sign that they weren't the only ones moving about. They didn't know the interior of the place, but they'd made some logical assumptions about what to look for.

The Purple wasn't going to keep what was potentially the most powerful weapon in existence out in the open. The weapon wasn't going to be near the front door, and it wasn't going to be where the slaves or menial staff would stumble into it. They needed to find a locked laboratory or a treasure room. Somewhere that was likely to be guarded and warded with layers of magical barriers.

They were counting on that last bit. Gunther claimed he'd be able to sense even the subtlest wards if he was close enough. Their plan was to let the ancient mage follow his nose, so to speak, and lead them to the greatest concentration of magic in the fortress. There, they hoped to find the staff, and whatever else the Purple had been working on.

They moved deeper into the keep, selecting turns on Gunther's advice and finding sparsely populated hallways.

Down one dusty hall, Rhys stopped them at another trap.

A thin wire stretched across the hall at mid-calf. Ben followed it with his eyes and saw the wire led into the wall. Above it, the stone was perforated with tiny holes. He swallowed and tried not to imagine what would come out of those holes if they tripped the wire.

Ben breathed a sigh of relief when at the next turn they found the floor was worn from centuries of foot traffic. People used this path, so traps were less likely. Gunther glanced both ways down the hall, then started to the left, deeper into the keep.

Closed doors were the only breaks in the bare stone corridor. A lone torch hung in a sconce at the far end, sparsely illuminating the hallway. Cautiously, they proceeded down the corridor, looking at each door as they passed. None of them were remarkable, and none of them were warded.

At the end of the hall, Gunther stopped them again. He slowly waved his hand in a circle. Elegant blue script appeared on the floor, walls, and ceiling.

Towaal let out a low whistle. Ben saw surprise plastered across her face. Evidently, she hadn't detected the snare the Purple set.

Gunther motioned them forward, and Ben cautiously stepped across the glowing blue runes. Nothing happened.

The big mage waited until they were all by. Then he stepped through as well and lowered his hand. The runes faded into the stone of the walls and floor. Ben had to blink, not sure if he'd imagined them.

They were at a fork in the hallway. Gunther stood, staring first one way and then the other, apparently trying to sense in both directions. Finally, he pointed to the left, and they set off again, heading ever deeper into the fortress.

Rhys shadowed the big mage, watching in front of him for mundane traps.

Ahead of them, Ben detected a low noise. It was rhythmic, but he couldn't place it. It didn't sound like music.

They slowed, stepping carefully, eyes darting wildly.

Ben frowned. The sound was familiar, but its source eluded him. He was certain he'd heard it before.

He looked at Amelie and she shrugged. She couldn't place it either.

Rhys glanced over his shoulder and caught the exchange. He pumped his hips twice in quick succession. He winked at Ben and Amelie, turned, and led them closer to the noise.

Ben blushed slightly as they continued.

The rhythmic grunting grew louder and louder. Twenty paces down the hall, Ben could see a single open door with light spilling out of it. The sound of flesh slapping flesh was obvious now that he knew what he was listening to. Ben tried to focus on moving silently and keeping his imagination in check.

He caught the rogue's arm and whispered to Rhys, "Depending on who is in there, they may be able to tell us where the staff is. I think it's worth risking a little noise to capture them. They obviously aren't concerned with being found in this hallway. My guess is that all of these rooms are unoccupied."

Rhys nodded curtly and motioned to Corinne and O'ecca.

The three stealthiest members of the party padded to the door.

Amelie gripped her belt pouch where Ben knew she kept the little mirror she used to far-see, but here, in the heart of the Purple's fortress, they couldn't risk any magical activity. Any disruption to stasis might be sensed by the ancient mages.

At the doorway, Rhys paused and silently communicated to Corinne and O'ecca.

The grunts were coming faster and faster. Perfect timing for a surprise.

Rhys slipped out his long knives and dashed into the room.

Ben heard a strangled cry, which was quickly cut off, and then a heavy thump.

A thick-voiced female drowsily rasped, "Who are you?"

The rest of the companions ducked into the room and Towaal pulled the door shut behind them. It was a plain stone room, unadorned except for a single torch on the wall and a filthy wooden bed. The end of the bed was sprayed with bright crimson blood. On the floor lay a naked man. A knife protruded from his throat.

On the bed, poised on her hands and knees, with a simple dress hiked above her hips, was a thin, young girl. She stared at them open-mouthed, too shocked to scream or to attempt to flee. Her big eyes were glazed over.

Ben spied an empty jug of wine, a small bowl, a cylindrical pipe, and a pile of ashes on the floor.

"Durhang," muttered Rhys.

"You can cover yourself, girl," suggested Towaal gently.

The girl blinked at her then finally shifted to a sitting position, though she didn't bother to pull her dress down.

"Who are you?" asked the girl again, no more urgency or fear in her voice than the first time.

"Friends," replied O'ecca. "You are from Ooswam?"

The girl nodded.

O'ecca glanced at the rest of the group. It was clear they were all thinking the same thing. They'd found one of the slaves.

"What's your name?" asked Towaal.

"Innel," answered the girl. She was looking at the end of the bed in confusion, perhaps wondering where her partner went or why the bed was suddenly covered in blood.

"Innel," said Towaal, moving slowly to kneel in front of the girl. "I'd like to ask for your help."

Rhys bent to retrieve his long knife. He sorted through the dead man's possessions while Towaal quizzed the girl.

Ben saw the man was a guard. Dark leather armor, a plain

tunic, britches, a utilitarian scimitar, and a short spear were stacked against the wall. There was nothing of value to them, except the spear, which Milo picked up.

He patted the iron sickle-shaped blade that hung off his belt and remarked, "I think I'm more comfortable with the spear. I like to keep some space between me and my opponent."

Ben nodded. There was no harm in selecting a better weapon when one was available. He turned his attention back to Towaal and Innel. The mage was still questioning her quietly.

"She's starting to get nervous with so many men in here," remarked Towaal.

The men streamed into the hallway with Corinne in tow.

The hallway was silent, unchanged from when they'd entered the room. Ben guessed that the guard had taken the slave girl into a little-used section of the keep for their rendezvous. Durhang likely wasn't an approved substance for the guards.

They waited until Towaal appeared with the rest of the girls.

"I gave her more of the durhang," said the mage. "She'll sleep until morning."

"What did you learn?" asked Rhys.

"She's a slave, though, she doesn't know who she belongs to," answered Towaal. "She works in the laundry. The other slaves and guards are the only people she ever sees. She sleeps with the officers in the guard to get extra favors like alcohol, durhang, and a better bed. She goes along with it because the officers protect her from the other men. If they didn't, she says the other guards and slaves would rape her. She..."

Towaal trailed off. Her face was tight with anger. She drew a deep breath to steady herself.

Corinne gripped the hafts of her hand axes.

Towaal collected herself and continued, "She didn't know much, but she told me the slaves are confined to the first and second floors of this place. There's a third and fourth floor she knows nothing about. Only the officers and special slaves are allowed up there. Occasionally, she sees other men, but she doesn't know who they are."

"Do you think she'll talk when she wakes up?" asked Milo. He toyed with the tip of his newfound spear. "She saw our faces."

Towaal shook her head. "I can't imagine she wants to explain this to the other guards. Drunk, on durhang, and she made no move to stop or question us. No, I think she'll stay silent."

"So, we need to go up," remarked Rhys.

"I figured their secret laboratory would be hidden in the tunnels Gunther mentioned below here," murmured Amelie. "If I was an evil mage, that's where I'd hide."

"Even bad guys like sunlight and fresh air," responded Rhys.

They stalked through the hallways, following directions the slave girl had given to a stairwell that was forbidden for her. The closer they got, the more wards they encountered. Most of them were similar glowing blue runes, but the last was pulsating red. Even without being able to read the archaic script, Ben understood the threat. That ward was not meant to warn of an intruder. It was meant to kill.

"How are we getting by without Gunther draining the power from these?" wondered Ben. He was thinking back to Irrefort when Towaal defaced the wards before they passed. Gunther simply gestured for them to move ahead.

"These are designed to recognize friends," whispered Towaal. "The guard, the slave girl, they will have had a tattoo somewhere on their bodies. Gunther is mimicking that on our bodies while we pass."

Even whispering, Ben could hear the awe in her voice.

Before they found the stairs, they had to stop again. They entered a wide-open room that was filled with tables and chairs. There were games scattered throughout and a huge wine barrel in one corner. It looked to be a common room, thought Ben, probably a place where the guards relaxed when they weren't on shift. That late at night, no one was there.

They started moving across the room and heard a shriek from a far hallway.

They all dove for cover, scrambling under tables, hiding behind couches. Panicked heartbeats passed, but whoever was coming hadn't heard Ben and his friends over their own noise. Shrieks, laughs, and a sharp slap followed by more screams.

Ben peered out and saw a half-naked girl being dragged across the room by two guards. A third guard followed close behind.

"Shut your mouth, bitch," snarled one of the guards.

The girl responded by screaming again.

"Damnit," snapped the second guard. He pounded his fist into the girl's face.

She slumped in their arms, unconscious.

The first guard turned on his companion. "What was that for? You broke her nose!"

"If she kept screaming, the others would hear, and they'd come and take their turns. I want her to myself," he paused. "To ourselves."

"We make a deal with that ass Raim to steal the prettiest new girl and you break her damn nose," growled the first man. "What's the point of keeping her to ourselves if she don't look any better than the others?"

The third man was shifting around nervously, looking over his shoulder and fingering the sword he had at his side.

"What's your problem?" demanded the first man.

The third guard's voice cracked when he answered. He appeared three or four years younger than Ben. "You sure the masters won't be angry about this?"

The first guard dropped the girl and defensively put his hands on his hips. "Well, they won't know about it unless you go blabbing to someone. Besides, the masters don't give a damn what happens to the slaves. They don't come down here and, except for the really pretty ones, don't even see the girls. As long as their robes are clean and food is on the table, they couldn't care less about what happens in this place. You best remember that. Your seniors in the guard is what you need to worry about. Right now, your senior is telling you to pick up this girl and help drag her to the room before she wakes up. Busted nose on the girl or not, I ain't going to bed without having a little fun."

The first guard looked on, pleased as the other two gathered up the unconscious girl.

"I'll take my turn first," he declared.

"You said I'd go first," argued the second man. "I took your shift two days ago so you could go get drunk with Jonas. You owe me!"

"That was before you messed up her face," growled the first guard.

The girl stirred, lifting her head, blinking blearily. Blood dripped steadily from her nose.

"Good," cackled the first man. "It's better when they're awake. They got a little fight in 'em."

The second guard grunted and gestured to the third. They started dragging the girl away. Her heels slid limply across the stone floor, her head hung between her shoulders. They took half a dozen steps then stopped, stunned.

Corinne stood in front of them, hand axes held low around her hips, eyes blazing.

"Oh shit," muttered Ben.

He tried to scramble out from under the table he'd hidden behind, but Corinne was already moving. She flashed forward, axes raised.

The first two guards were too shocked to react. Before they could even drop the unconscious slave girl, an axe was buried in one man's forehead, and the other staggered back, clutching at his torn open throat.

The third guard had more time and was quicker. He drew his sword and yelled, "Attack! Assemble on me!"

He didn't have time for anything else.

Corinne caught the edge of his sword with the hook of her axe and yanked it to the side. The man was wide open. Her second axe swung forward and thunked into his face.

"We have to run," growled Towaal.

The mage charged past Corinne and headed down a hallway toward the stairs they hoped would lead to the Purple's chambers.

"Good work," mumbled Gunther appreciatively as he passed the huntress.

The slave girl lay on the floor, staring open-mouthed at Corinne.

"You're free. If you want to stay that way, you'd better run," called Ben as he rushed past.

Pick your battles. Fight the necessary fights. Well, now they were in for a fight.

THEY POUNDED down the hallway toward the four startled guards who stood in front of the stairwell. These men had never faced an actual threat to the fortress, guessed Ben. He and his companions were only a dozen steps away when the men thought to draw swords. It was too late.

"What the…" began one of the men. He was cut short when Rhys rushed by, slashing his sword horizontally and severing the man's head.

Ben raced up and skewered another through his tough leather armor, just as the man was drawing his sword. It clanged down to the stone floor. Ben yanked his sword clear. The Venmoor steel didn't punch through armor as neatly as his mage-wrought blade, but it felt comfortable in his hands.

Beside him, O'ecca spun her naginata in front of her, catching a guard's sword with the butt of the weapon and then whipping around the blade to bury it in his neck.

Gunther simply smashed his fist into the face of the fourth guard. The man went flying back and crashed against the stone wall. Ben winced at the spine-tingling crunch. The guard fell down, dead or unconscious, Ben couldn't tell.

The stairs flared with a rainbow of blue, red, purple, and green runes.

Gunther muttered, "They've got something up there they don't want anyone getting to."

"We need to hide that we're going up the stairs," suggested Rhys.

Gunther frowned then grabbed one of the dead guard's arms. He set a foot against the man's torso. With bulging muscles, he tore the man's arm off.

Ben stared, open mouthed.

Gunther offered him the arm. "Run this down the hall and shake some blood at a convenient turn. Bring it back and leave it by the body so they can't tell what you did."

Ben swallowed uncomfortably and then accepted the arm.

Gunther rumbled, "We aren't disturbing these wards as we pass, and we haven't displayed any of the talent. Hopefully, the mages upstairs assume that means we're still down below and that this is a mundane threat." He gestured to the stairs. "After you."

Rhys nodded and, without waiting further, trotted up the wide stone steps.

Corinne flanked him. Ben saw her reach out a hand to Rhys. The rogue caught it and squeezed before they disappeared out of Ben's line of sight.

Ben grumbled and dashed down the hall, flinging blood from the severed arm. He came back and deposited the arm by the bodies before racing up the stairs. Gunther followed close behind.

At the top, they met their first true opposition. A moment after they made it to the landing, a man just a few years younger than Ben stepped out of a doorway.

"Are you the ones who've raised the alarm below?" he asked curiously. His eyebrows knitted, and he wondered, "How did you get up the stairs?"

Gunther raised a hand and the air seemed to twist around the young man. It drew toward him, quickly closing on his body. The man's eyes snapped wide open. He raised his hands to fend off Gunther's attack, but he was too late. The inward rush of pressure crushed him. Blood and fluids squirted out of his body as he imploded. He collapsed like a used washrag.

"Don't wait for me next time," advised Gunther calmly. "Mundane blades will be quieter than a full-scale mage battle. In another heartbeat or two, that boy would have unleashed on us. You'd better center yourselves and hold stasis. I may not be able to protect all of you, and now the Purple knows we have practitioners."

"We've hardened our will against magical attacks before," declared Ben.

O'ecca called out, "I keep hearing you talk about hardening your will. What does that mean? Do the Ohms do it? I learned the first three."

"You'll be fine," encouraged Amelie, placing a hand on O'ecca's shoulder. Amelie shot Ben a concerned look.

"Stay behind Gunther or Towaal," suggested Ben.

Shouts and the stomp of boots rose from below, but the upstairs remained quiet. Ben hoped that Gunther was wrong. If the Purple mages detected magic, they may assume it was one of their compatriots. Since the wards hadn't been tripped, Ben and his friends could still be moving undetected.

Ben looked down at the crushed body of the mage on the floor. Blood and bodily floods spread out from him in a wide pool. No hiding that, he realized.

"I don't think we can cover that up," muttered Amelie, echoing Ben's thoughts.

He glanced around and observed their surroundings for the first time. Tapestries that could have been hundreds of years old graced the walls. The floors were plain stone, and simple oil-filled lamps lit the landing. Unvarnished wooden tables were set against the walls and held sun-bleached animal skulls.

Ben frowned and looked closer. They weren't animals. They were demons. Small ones and large ones. Row after row of demon skulls greeted everyone who ascended the stairs. In the corner of the room, a huge figure stood. It was draped in the preserved skin of a demon. An arch-demon, judging by the size. Ben swallowed nervously. The Purple had the body of a stuffed arch-demon decorating their foyer.

He caught Amelie's look.

"Did you expect fresh flowers?" she asked.

"We need to move," barked Rhys. "There are over three hundred people in this fortress. I don't know how many are slaves, guards, or mages, but let's not wait and find out."

Gunther led the way and they trotted down a dark hallway. There were no windows and no torches to light their path. Runes flared to life as they moved, layer after layer of them. The glowing colors painted the hallway in a vibrant rainbow of hues. Even Ben could sense the lurking power emanating from the bright script.

Hollow alcoves lined the hallway, man-size statues standing within them. In the dim light, Ben couldn't see any details, but he guessed they represented the Purple throughout the years. He couldn't explain why every fifth statue had the head of some beast. Lions, bears, or demons. All of their mouths, even the men, stood open in silent screams.

Ben scampered faster and walked close behind Gunther. He hoped the big mage was capable of keeping track of all of them as they passed through each wave of runes. Ben didn't know what the colors signified or what any of the script meant, but he was certain that some of them would raise alarms and some of them would strike him dead. The Purple had ages to prepare their keep to hold off a magical assault. It appeared they'd been thorough.

The slap of their booted feet echoed down the hall, announcing their presence. There was no use moving slowly to maintain silence anymore. The alarm had been raised. Speed was their only ally.

The creak of leather raised Ben's hackles. Out of the corner of his eye, he saw rune light flicker on metal.

"Corinne, duck!" he shouted.

The huntress dropped to a knee and a short spear flashed above her head.

Its owner followed, leaping out from behind one of the statues in an alcove. More men burst out of hiding and swarmed over Ben and his friends.

Ben hammered the pommel of his sword into a man's face and heard the crunch of broken bone. The sharp tip of the man's spear gouged the side of Ben's head, slicing a neat cut in his ear.

Another body crashed into them, forcing Ben to stumble back against the wall. He gripped the first guard's leather jerkin and yanked him close, hoping the man wouldn't have room to maneuver his spear. In the scintillating rainbow light of the runes, Ben saw a second guard yanking a short sword out of the back of the first. The man had missed Ben by a hands-length and accidentally stabbed his fellow guard in the process.

Ben thrust his longsword over the shoulder of the dead man and caught the second attacker under his arm, sliding behind his tough leather armor. Ben felt the tip of his blade bounce off bone and punch deep into the man's torso.

Another body crashed into them and Ben tripped. He lost his sword as he went down, flailing. The newcomer went down on top of him, struggling to maneuver his spear into a position where he could stab Ben.

Ben didn't give him the chance. He pulled out his hunting knife and slammed it into the man's neck, twisted it, and jerked it free. A fountain of blood poured out onto Ben. He wiggled out from under the body of the dead man and saw another guard pressing Amelie and Towaal back.

Amelie had dropped her rapier and was clutching the man's sword arm, holding on for dear life as he tried to twist the blade against her.

Towaal had her belt knife out and struck at the man, but the short blade scrapped off his armor and left him unharmed.

Ben rolled over and snagged the man's ankle, yanking hard.

Surprised, the guard staggered to the side and spun around, looking for the new assailant.

Towaal wrapped her arm around his neck and sawed her knife across his exposed flesh. This time, the little belt knife was effective.

Ben lurched to his feet but the fight was already finished. His companions were standing, panting. A dozen dead bodies lay at their feet.

"Everyone all right?" rasped Rhys.

Ben touched the side of his head and winced at the sting from the spear wound.

"Ben," exclaimed Amelie, "you're covered in blood!"

"Almost all of it is theirs," he assured her. "One of them got me, but it's just a shallow cut."

"We need to keep moving," said Corinne through gritted teeth. "The sound of fighting will draw more of them."

Ben saw the huntress had a hand pressed against her ribcage. Blue light from a series of nearby runes made the blood covering her hand look black.

"How badly are you hurt?" worried Rhys, moving to stand beside her.

"Bad." She coughed wetly. "But it doesn't matter. We can't stop."

Gunther shuffled over and placed a hand on her shoulder.

"Let me do what I can. You'll still be tender, and if you push it, the wound will break open," he advised. "The runes will cover a small expense of energy. Any more and the mages may be able to detect us."

"Thank you," said Rhys, breathing a sigh of relief.

"Anyone else wounded to the point you're incapacitated?" asked the big mage.

Milo stepped forward and Ben saw one of his arms was hanging limply by his side.

Gunther placed a hand on him.

"You could learn to do this yourself," suggested the big mage. "You have the strength of will."

"I've barely been trained," responded the former apprentice nervously.

"Really?" asked Gunther, sounding surprised. "Your body is well aligned. I sense you are close to attaining long-life. You're either a natural, or someone must have trained you very well."

"Maybe I am a natural like you say," mumbled Milo. "I only had a few years of training."

"Let's go," said Rhys, staring nervously behind them.

Stepping over dead bodies, they headed deeper into the fortress. Ahead of Ben, Corinne was moving tentatively. He could tell her injury was bothering her. Rhys strode by her side, head rotating constantly. He was watching the alcoves for any more ambushes.

They reached the end of the hall. The space in front of them was filled with twinkling silver lights. Runes sprawled across the wall and ceiling, shimmering with energy. Between the runes, silvery threads like spider webs stretched across the hall.

Gunther stopped.

"I can get us through safely, but I won't be able to mask our presence when we pass these," he admitted. "Someone is actively maintaining this barrier. I can feel an immense potential on the other side. It could be the staff. I believe this is the room we're looking for."

"I can feel it as well," remarked Towaal. "It's like a whirlpool drawing me in."

Ben looked behind them at the dark hallway. Past the runes that were activated near them, there were no sounds and no lights. He knew it wouldn't be long before someone found the crushed body of the mage at the top of the stairs. When followed to the pile of dead guards in the hallway, their route couldn't be more obvious. The Purple was certain to know they were on the floor and where they were going. Even if they turned around and tried a different route, it was only a matter of time before the Purple began sealing off different parts of the floor. Wandering around blindly and hoping to find another route to the staff was foolish.

"We either go in, or we try to escape now," stated Ben. "Those are the only choices."

"We've made it all the way here," said Amelie.

Ben nodded. "Let's go get this staff."

Gunther lifted his huge black-iron hammer and rolled his head back and forth, cracking his neck.

"When we get through these doors," he instructed, "Amelie, grab the staff and prepare to flee. We're going to have to fight our way out, and I want to be ready for anything. Karina, you back me up. We can discuss what to do with the staff after we're safe."

"Fair enough," agreed Amelie. "It's yours when you ask for it."

Lady Towaal nodded tersely.

Gunther turned to the ward. The pulsing silver tendrils that stretched across the hallway suddenly snapped back, and the runes crackled with energy.

Gunther shouted, "Go, now!"

In a rush, they all poured across the barrier. Ben felt a tingle crawl down his spine as he did but no pain, no sudden death.

Through the barrier, they found a tall double door. Twice the height of a man, it was built of thick pieces of ancient wood. In the center of each door hung a copper face, an ancient man and ancient woman. Their faces were twisted into a rictus of rage.

"I don't think we should…" started Milo.

Gunther strode by him and raised his hammer. Colors swirled, causing the black iron to appear transparent. The mage swung the hammer with incredible force. It smashed into the door.

Ben felt a thump in his chest as energy burst out from the impact. Lightning crackled. Smashed pieces of wood flew into a black void beyond the door.

The two copper faces hung motionless in the air.

Ben gaped at them. Nothing supported them that he could see.

"Damn, they were real," muttered Gunther under his breath.

He drew back his hammer again. He brought it down on each of the copper faces. The metal crumpled and was blown back into the room. Silent screams rang in Ben's head with each blow of Gunther's hammer. It reminded him of the way Eldred spoke to them.

Behind them, all of the runes in the hallway blazed alight. It washed the companions in a blast of vibrant light. By the multi-hued glow, Ben could see a wide balcony through the shattered doors.

"We'd better hurry," advised Gunther.

The big mage stepped confidently through the doorway and gestured for the others to follow. Amelie darted ahead, staying in his shadow, prepared to grab the staff and flee with it. The rest of them came close behind.

A stone railing encircled the balcony, and two staircases led down from either end. Beyond the railing, it was pitch black.

Towaal entered last and placed her hand on a smooth stone on the wall.

Hundreds of stones flared to light, illuminating a cavernous chamber. The balcony they were standing on overlooked an open area the size of a small village. In the center of the chamber stood two huge stone archways. They were inscribed with arcane glyphs and stood eight or nine stories tall.

"Damn!" exclaimed Rhys.

"How are we supposed to get those out of here?" wondered O'ecca.

"This isn't what we came to find," stated Towaal flatly. "Those are rifts."

Ben let out a low whistle.

Gunther grunted. The big mage was staring uncertainly at the huge stone structures, evidently as surprised as the rest of the party.

"They have to be twice the size of the one in the Wilds," exclaimed Amelie. "What do they need two of them for?"

"What did you expect to find here?" asked a calm voice from behind them.

They spun and saw an elderly man flanked by five other men. They wore loose purple robes and held no weapons. Behind them, two dozen guards poured onto the balcony.

No one answered the man.

"I found the body of Simon," continued the man, unperturbed by their silence. "He was new among us and not strong, but I am still impressed you overcame him." The man's gaze turned to Towaal. "You are from the Sanctuary. We have been preparing a long time for your leader to locate us. I knew she would want to recover what was taken so long ago. Now that you found us, I'm almost ashamed about how worried we were. It's impressive you made it to this room, but what do you think you can do against us by yourself? I have been alive for over a thousand years. You are like a child to me. I thought I'd be facing dozens of you when this day came."

Towaal stared back at the man. Ben guessed she was trying to process what the man said.

"Master," muttered one of the younger men.

The elderly man, clearly enjoying his moment, spared an irritated glance at his underling.

The younger man simply pointed to Gunther.

The older man turned and Ben saw his eyes go wide in surprise. The man's gaze locked onto Gunther's hammer.

"Who are you?" he demanded. "Where did you get that?"

"You spent all those years preparing for Sanctuary mages," rumbled Gunther. "You should have gotten ready for me."

Gunther stepped forward and one of the younger Purple rushed to meet him. The man's hands were raised, the sleeves of his robes falling back to reveal swirling energies clutched in his fists.

The giant head of the black-iron hammer swung forward. The young man skidded to a stop, apparently surprised at a physical attack, and crossed his arms in front of his body. He must have intended to stop the blow with his will alone.

Light sparkled like shattered glass. The young man barely had time to grunt in shock before the hammer smashed into him. His body was pulped instantaneously. A shower of gore was flung back across the balcony and splashed against hastily raised shields of the other Purple.

"You're him," exclaimed the elder Purple. "The hammer mage. I know of you."

Gunther glared at the man. "Why did you build these rifts?"

The guards were fanning around the edge of the balcony, ready to engage Ben's companions, but obviously not interested in going anywhere near Gunther and his hammer.

The elder Purple didn't answer.

"Do you think you'll be able to tap the energies outside of our world using this?" growled Gunther. "I've sensed you trying. It will be futile. Rifts do not work like that. The tunnel you create will bypass the power you seek."

The bearded Purple mage frowned. "You've been monitoring us. Why did you not intercede?"

"You would not have been able to control the power which you sought. You are not strong enough, and it would have destroyed you." Gunther gestured to the rifts behind him. "It appears you not only are missing the will, you are missing the knowledge."

The Purple mage stood straight, stretching his ancient body to its full height. "You are right. We realized we do not have the strength to control the power flowing between our worlds. I spent five hundred years learning that. Even the staff we took from the Sanctuary is beyond our control."

"Are you trying to replicate what your peers in the north did?" pressed Gunther. "Are you attempting to meet the demon threat with this?"

"No," answered the mage sharply. "Those fools abdicated their power when they built the first rift. They didn't see what was sitting in front of them. We didn't either, I must admit, not until recently."

Ben glanced between Gunther and Towaal. Both looked unsure.

"And what was that?" asked Gunther slowly.

The elderly mage smiled. "The rift in the Wilds was a portal between our world and the demon realm. That's not all it has to be. The fabric of space and time can be bent, twisted, and manipulated in many ways. Our ancestors discovered this, but they never made use of it. They opened the door a crack. We wondered what would happen if we threw it wide open."

"You built these rifts to somewhere else," guessed Towaal suddenly. "You're using them for transportation. You could send yourself anywhere, but why?"

The Purple smirked. "Rifts cannot be used to transport people. The surge in energy they expel is deadly to any lifeform from this world, but demons are uniquely suited to absorb that surge in power. They seek it and feed off it."

Ben looked at the two rifts. They sat facing each other. Both of them would go somewhere. Demons could pass through one and then immediately go through the other.

"Demons are the weapon!" exclaimed Ben.

The elderly mage cackled. "An army of demons appearing anywhere I choose. We finished the construction on the second rift four years ago. We've been testing it slowly. Sending demons to places they would be expected like the Wilds. Other places they wouldn't like the mountains above Whitehall. The stupid lords never figured out what hit them. We could have sent four times as many of the creatures, but we didn't need to. We've proven that no army can stand against us. Soon, it will be time to show the world."

The elderly mage had removed a rune-covered copper disc from his robes and was toying with it while he spoke. It was a rift key, Ben saw.

"Don't let him activate that!" shouted Ben.

"Drop it," snarled Gunther, his hammer rising menacingly.

The old man smiled grimly. "If you are able, you will destroy me no matter what I do with this."

"I am able," snapped Gunther.

"I believe you," conceded the Purple. "I knew it as soon as I realized who you were. I wanted to explain what we created so you know what you're up against. I hope you understand now that it's not me you need to worry about."

A flicker of blue-white light burst out behind them. Ben's heart sank. A rift had been activated.

He glanced over his shoulder. Arcs of lightning danced around the edge of one of the rifts. In its center, thick black smoke billowed out, obscuring the hot red glow of magma. The same heat that destroyed the rift in the Wilds coursed through the home of the demons. Ben could see it behind the roiling clouds of soot. He could see shapes moving there too, squat, black, and coming closer. They began to fill the space on the other side of the rift.

The Purple tossed the rift key into the air. It levitated in front of him, and he watched as scorching green fire engulfed it, melting the disc into a glowing ball of molten copper.

Gunther stared at the ruined rift key in dismay.

"I can fashion another, I suppose," the elderly mage remarked coolly. "If I don't, then that rift will remain open. Demons will pour into this world unabated. If you kill me, you will never close the rift. You will have to destroy it. When you do, it will obliterate you and anyone within several leagues of here."

Gunther took a step closer to the mage.

An enraged shriek sounded from the rift then another and another. Ben raced to the railing and looked down. He saw demons pouring through the open gate.

A short spear came flying across the room, thrown by one of the Purple's guards, streaking toward Gunther. The big mage spun his hammer and crashed it against the spear, bursting it into a thousand splinters.

One of the younger mages charged, brilliant whips of bright orange fire streaming from his wrists. He lashed one at Gunther. Gunther raised his hammer and let the whip wrap around the black iron. Blue fire burst from the hammer and streaked back down the whip. The Purple mage released the whip, and it flew into the air, burning into nothing.

A screaming guard hurtled across the stone floor at Ben. He barely got his sword up in time to parry the man's spear thrust. The man's strike went wide and his body crashed against Ben's shoulder. Ben drew his longsword across the guard's throat.

Amelie pulled back the sleeve of her tunic, revealing the vambrace they'd collected in Irrefort from the dead Thin Blade. She held up her arm and her eyebrows knit in concentration. A flurry of fist-sized fireballs blasted out and showered one of the younger mages. He shrieked as his body was immolated in the unnatural fire.

A crackle of electricity split the air. Luminous bolts of lightning blasted across the balcony. Ben wasn't sure which mage was directing them, but the surging charges burned iridescent streaks into his eyes.

A pack of the spear-toting guards stormed toward Ben. He dropped into a fighting stance and waited. He could no longer pay attention to the mage battle.

Corinne took his side. They ducked and spun under the first wave of men, longsword and hand axes striking legs as the guards ran past. Ben felt his sword slice into a guard's thigh-bone and the blade lodged, stuck.

A second wave of spearmen was on him. Razor-sharp tips of the weapons thrust at him. He had to drop his sword then roll across the stone floor to avoid being skewered. One of the thrusts still caught him on the arm. He felt the point of the spear stab painfully into his flesh.

O'ecca flew over him, and the heavy blade of her naginata swept into Ben's attacker, lifting the man off his feet and flinging him back.

Ben scrambled to his sword and tore it free from the injured guard. He ignored the man's scream as the steel was wrenched out of his body. The man thrashed helplessly on the blood-slick stone floor.

Ben turned and saw O'ecca and Corinne were holding off half a dozen of the spear-wielding guards. The men were clearly used to training instead of actual combat, but six, sharp-tipped spears were enough to keep the girls at bay.

As Ben watched, one man swept his spear around Corinne's axe and nicked her leg. The huntress grunted and stumbled back. Another spearman punched his weapon into her shoulder.

O'ecca's naginata swept down and took the man's hand off, but the damage was already done. Corinne tucked her left arm to her side and grimaced in pain. She still held her hand axe in her right hand, but the reach advantage of the spears was nearly insurmountable. She was bleeding from the earlier wound in her side, her leg, and now her shoulder.

Ben charged into the fray, smashing his longsword down on a spear then changing course and whipping his steel into the man's face.

More guards stormed after the first waves, evidently preferring to engage with sword and spear instead of fire and lightning.

Ben risked a look over his shoulder and saw only two of the younger Purple mages remained. Gunther was stalking them across the balcony with his hammer.

Both of the robed men were clutching devices, pouring a dark cloud of ominous smoke toward Gunther, but Ben didn't take time to study it closely. The panicked look on their faces told him all he needed to know about how effective they would be at stopping the big mage.

Rhys and Milo slammed into the backs of the bunched guards and wreaked havoc amongst them. Rhys slashed his mage-wrought blade through them with surgical precision. Milo stabbed his borrowed spear into the backs of the men while they were reeling away from the rogue's glowing blade. There were still a dozen of the spearmen standing, but Ben was gaining hope, until, behind him, he heard an ear-shattering howl.

Three chest-high demons scrambled up the stairs to his right and plunged into the battle.

One of the creatures charged directly at Ben but found a spearman first. The unfortunate man stepped back, escaping a blow from O'ecca's naginata. The demon pounced on his back, slamming him into the stone floor. Jaws snapped down on the man's skull, crushing it with a powerful bite. The man's terrified wail lapsed into a wet gurgle.

Ben thrust his blade into the demon's spine before it looked up from its feast.

A thunderous boom rattled the entire chamber and Ben stumbled to his knees. Across the balcony, Gunther and the two Purple mages were lying on their backs. All three were stunned. Acrid smoke filled the space between them.

The elder Purple mage was the only one still on his feet, but instead of attacking Gunther, he turned and fled.

Corinne raced after him, limping on her injured leg, wounded arm against her side. Blood flowed freely down her leathers.

"Don't bother," shouted Towaal from the stairs. "We have too much to deal with here. We can find him later."

Corinne ignored the mage and picked up her pace.

The Purple mage turned in the shattered doorway of the balcony. His frazzled beard stuck out wildly. His eyes locked onto the huntress.

Rhys ran after Corinne, his longsword boiling sparkling silver smoke.

Corinne flung her axe at the bearded Purple mage. The man raised an arm in defense and cried out when the axe head thumped into his forearm. Half the head of the axe disappeared into his flesh.

He glared at the huntress. In his other hand, crackling energy snapped around his closed fist.

Rhys screamed but was only halfway there when a snap of brilliant white electricity shot out of the mage's palm. The line of crackling power arced toward Corinne, sizzling as it flashed into her chest. The huntress was thrown backward and skidded across the smooth stone floor. She thudded into the stone railing.

Wordless anger burst from Rhys' throat. He raised his longsword, closing on the elderly mage.

The man directed his lightning at the rogue, but the bolt fizzled against Rhys' hardened will.

The mage's eyes bulged wide and he spluttered a panicked cry. The old man fell to his knees, futilely trying to raise his wounded arm in defense.

The rogue's longsword swept down and cleaved through the Purple's arm and then his neck. His head spun through the air. His body, gushing blood, fell to the side.

Ben heard a sickening crunch. He tore his eyes away from Rhys and saw the last of the Purple mages get flattened beneath Gunther's hammer. Ben looked in shock at Corinne, who lay motionless against the stone balustrade.

Jolting him out of his stupor, a spearman vaulted the body of the dead demon in front of him, the sharp tip of his weapon aimed for Ben's heart. Ben parried the spear away and slammed his shoulder into the spearman, knocking him back. The man flopped to the floor, and heartbeats after he landed, a demon scrambled on top of him.

Ben backed away, O'ecca and Milo flanking him.

The remaining spearmen were locked in a battle with four demons, both sides taking grievous injuries.

"We have to close the rift!" shouted Towaal from across the balcony.

The mage was standing atop the far stairwell, raining fire down where Ben assumed a mass of demons was trying to make their way up.

"We have to flee!" argued Gunther. "We can't hold this room indefinitely. We can figure out a way to destroy the gate when we're safe."

"I have another rift key," declared Towaal, holding up the copper disc she'd been carrying since Northport. "If we wait until we're a safe distance away to destroy this thing, thousands of those demons could come through. My key is not attuned to these structures, though. I need to get closer to use it."

Gunther strode to her side, his massive hammer ready.

"Save your anima," he suggested. Then he charged down the stairs.

Ben, Milo, and O'ecca joined Towaal. They followed the big mage. He was swinging his hammer indiscriminately, coruscating waves of color thrumming through the massed bodies of demons below him. Black iron met black flesh and crushed it beneath the powerful blows.

Before they disappeared down the stairwell, Ben saw Rhys fly into the massed demons and spearmen left on the balcony. His sword was blazing white, painting his face in an eerie and unnatural glow. Ben thought he could see tears streaming down the rogue's cheeks.

Amelie was kneeling beside Corinne. She met Ben's gaze and shook her head.

At the entrance to the balcony, three young, purple-robed men burst out and then skidded to a stop. Mouths dropped open as they took in the scene in front of them.

"I've got this," asserted Amelie to Ben. "Help Towaal and Gunther. We have to get that gate closed." She rose to her feet, vambrace held ready. Facing the three new arrivals, she shouted, "Rhys, we've got company."

Ben turned and rushed down the stairs. It was five flights to the bottom. A surging river of angry teeth and claws was flooding in from the open gate and up the stairs, blocking their way down. He saw several giant shapes looming over the crowd on the floor of the room. Arch-demons.

Gunther hammered his way down the stairs, arms churning like a blacksmith at the forge. With each strike, spikes of color flew off his hammer, scything through demons, shattering masonry, and filling the air with a sticky purple mist.

Ben slid and tripped down to stand with Milo and O'ecca. Towaal was ahead of them, cautiously following the path Gunther was clearing. None of them wanted to get too close to the mage's hammer. A careless back-swing could easily crush them.

Howls of rage welled up from the floor of the room as the demons watched their peers get annihilated by Gunther.

Ben grimaced when he saw the taller shapes wading through their minions, converging on the base of the stairs.

"Gunther!" he called. "Arch-demons."

The big mage didn't respond. He kept pounding his way through the throng of creatures in front of him.

An enormous roar shattered the air in the room. Even Gunther paused. A black mass blotted out the light of the rift as an incredible arch-demon stepped through the opening. It stood three stories tall. Its wings brushed the edges of the stone archway as it entered the room. The smaller demons cowered away from it, squealing in fear.

Gunther, who'd made it to a landing one story above the base of the floor, placed a hand on the balustrade and called back, "Watch my back."

He easily vaulted over and plunged down into the writhing mass of creatures below.

"Oh damn," mumbled Ben.

He and O'ecca raced past Towaal and leapt onto the railing.

Below them, Gunther whipped his hammer in a circle, smashing demons and clearing a space around him a dozen paces wide.

"You ready?" Ben asked O'ecca.

"You owe me for this," she snapped.

Together, they jumped down after Gunther, landing in the space he'd cleared.

Demons immediately surged forward, eager for lifeblood that wasn't behind Gunther's hammer.

O'ecca's naginata shot forward and caught one of the beasts in the face. Ben jumped after it, slashing his longsword in a defensive pattern, trying to keep the creatures back. In the press of bodies, it was a waste of time to aim his strikes. Any swing would hit something.

Bestial cries echoed throughout the chamber, some in pain,

most in rage. Purple blood flew off the tip of Ben's blade as it churned through meat.

The swarm of demons swirled around them, and Ben and O'ecca backed toward Gunther. They retreated from the press of creatures in front of them, but were reluctant to get too close to the mage as he swung his hammer.

Ben could feel the surge of energy behind them. He briefly reached out with his senses then quickly pulled back. He was rocked by the waves of power radiating from the big man. Like clockwork, Gunther lashed out and blasted the demons with physical might and magical fury. They were flung away from him as easily as a child would kick away his toys.

Ben and O'ecca fell back into the space he created, keeping the throng away from Gunther as he powered ahead toward the rift.

A burst of energy sang around them, and flickers of lightning leapt from demon to demon. They were packed so close together Ben could barely see the flashes of light as they danced through the crowd. Screams overpowered the sizzling sound of burning flesh.

Between the stairs and Ben, a road was blazed of fallen demons. Racing forward, Towaal and Milo ran across the twitching corpses to join them on the floor of the chamber. Lady Towaal's hands burned with energy.

The demons shied away, giving Ben and O'ecca opportunity to dart forward and cut gaping wounds in them. Ben slid his blade into one of the creatures and twisted it free. A clawed hand swung into his periphery vision and smacked the side of his longsword. The blow knocked him off balance. He stumbled, exposed.

The demon lurched at him, sensing an opportunity, but Milo skipped forward and jabbed his spear into its eye before dancing back behind Ben.

The normally timid young man was like a viper, darting

around Ben and O'ecca, thrusting and stabbing fatal injuries into the demons, then retreating back. Creatures dropped from his blows, fouling the legs of others and providing chances for Ben and O'ecca to make use of the space and confusion to keep a deadly wall of steel in front of them.

Shrieks of terror and rage washed over Ben, not quite covering the sound of the thumps as Gunther swung his hammer and released his magic. Ben glanced over his shoulder and saw the creatures were still streaming in from the rift. For every demon they killed, two more came in. At this rate, they would never catch up.

"Gunther," yelled Towaal. "This isn't working. I have to get closer."

"Hold onto something," shouted the big mage.

Ben looked around wildly. They were in the middle of an open stone floor and surrounded by demons. Hold onto what?

He settled for dropping to the ground as soon as he saw Gunther twirling his hammer over his head. The heavy iron whistled with a fury that overwhelmed the cacophony of the demons. The creatures in front of Ben staggered back, clutching their heads, wailing in agony at what Gunther was doing to them.

"Oh my," mumbled Towaal, slumping down.

She lay next to Ben, gripping the body of a dead demon beneath her. Her eyes were squeezed tightly shut.

"What's he doing?" called Ben.

"He's ripping the energy from them somehow," responded Towaal. "I don't understand how it's possible."

"Why do we need to duck?" wondered Ben aloud.

"What is he going to do with the energy of hundreds of demons once he has it?" answered Towaal. "He can't hold it forever."

Ben cowered lower.

A heavy body fell on him, and a thick-set demon weakly bashed a claw against his head. It crawled forward, mouth open, eager to sink its teeth into his neck and taste his lifeblood. Stars filled his vision, but he retained enough wits to draw his hunting knife and slide it into the demon's eye. He shoved it hard to reach the creature's brain.

The blow had struck him at the same spot the spear did earlier. Ben felt a fresh river of blood running down his face. Ignoring it, he looked for more demon attackers, but the ones in the immediate area were collapsing, falling to their knees or flopping over, senseless and weak.

An arch-demon towered above them, but even it was effected. The big monster stumbled drunkenly, its hate-filled glare focused on Gunther. It evidently didn't have the coordination to reach him.

A lone, piercing howl filled the room. Ben rolled over to see Gunther standing in front of the giant arch-demon. The thing rose five times the height of the big mage. Around them, smaller demons lay like carpet, flopping impotently on the stone floor. Near Gunther, the air twisted and thickened, churning with the roiling energy.

"We have to close the rift!" shouted Towaal. In her hand, she clutched the rift key, but the huge arch-demon was standing between them and the gate.

Gunther stopped spinning his hammer and held it straight in front of him, pointed at the massive creature. Its wings opened, obscuring the rift, blocking out half the light in the room. A roar burst out of Gunther's throat and raw energy blazed from him, rays of light, wind, and sound.

The arch-demon stood tall, prepared to absorb the blast. Wave after wave of energy smashed into its body. The tips of its wings burst into flame and smoke boiled off its skin. It staggered backward, and flesh sloughed off its leg. It was being roasted by the might of Gunther's attack. He took a step forward, his hammer steadily pointed at the enormous beast, the air in front of him undulating with raw power.

The arch-demon stumbled into the rift and Gunther's power crashed against the stone of the gate. Rock cracked, lightning flickered, and white-blue lights strobed into the room, turning it as bright as day then as dark as the blackest night. The huge arch-demon's skin fissured and sizzled, its wings incinerating around it. It stumbled through the rift, knocking scores of smaller demons back out of its path as it retreated.

Gunther kept up his attack, pouring energy into the rift gate, training his might on the demons crowded on the other side of the opening. They scattered, terrified of the power that was chasing them into their world.

"Close the gate," Gunther called to Towaal.

The mage gripped the copper rift key and scrambled across the weakened demons to the smoking gate. She stood and held the rift key in front of her, but nothing happened.

"It's not working!" she exclaimed.

"Now!" shouted Gunther. "There are countless demons on the other side of this thing. I can't hold them forever."

"The gate is damaged," yelled Milo. "Look. The runes are shattered."

He was right, Ben saw. The entire face of the stone archway was melted and cracked. None of the runes were intact.

"Finish it, Gunther," demanded Towaal, clutching the key in frustration. "That arch-demon is badly wounded, but there will be more like it. Who knows how many of those things exist on the other side. If we can't close the rift, we must destroy it."

"If I destroy this," snarled Gunther. "We all die. We're too close. The blowback will pulp your mind like mushy potatoes. Everyone in this mountain will be decimated. Us, the Purple, the slaves."

One of the arch-demons recovered enough to take advantage of the break in Gunther's attack. It charged him, but the big mage simply turned and slammed the haft of his hammer into its groin. The huge beast was thrown across the room and smashed against the far stone wall. Bones shattered and purple blood sprayed out the creature's nose and mouth before it slid to the floor.

The black iron of the hammer was outshone by shimmering, iridescent colors that pulsed from deep within the metal. Ben could feel the hammer as Gunther moved it like a tiny sun was being held by the big man.

"We can't leave the rift open," declared Towaal.

"Give me the key," instructed Gunther.

Towaal handed it to him. "The runes are destroyed. They cannot respond to the key. What will you do? Do you know how to repair them?"

"They're damaged on this side," remarked Gunther grimly. "There are two sides to any door."

Towaal's eyes grew wide. "You'll be trapped. You can't do this!"

Gunther strode toward the rift gate, kicking dying demons out of his way as he walked.

"You're too valuable," exclaimed Towaal. "We need you here. Let me do it."

Over his shoulder, the big mage responded, "You couldn't survive passing through the rift. That Purple mage was right. Your life-force would be snuffed out in an instant."

"Won't yours?" argued Towaal.

"I'm stronger," answered Gunther resolutely. "It will be painful, but I believe I can make it."

The demons started to stir around them.

"What if you can't?" challenged Towaal.

"Then you know what to do. There is no time to discuss this," stated Gunther. "Only I can pass through. You are needed here."

The big mage brought his hammer down, squishing the skull of a demon crawling at his feet.

"I know how to draw power from these creatures much the same way they feed off us. It may be enough to sustain me until I can find a way back. Tell Jasper what happened here. He'll understand what to do."

Gunther raised his hammer, preparing for battle on the other side, and stepped through the rift.

Ben watched as manifest terror converged on the big man. Smoke, demons, and fire surged toward him. He spun his hammer in one hand and raised the copper disc in the other. The scene flickered then vanished.

Through the open archway, Ben saw only the stone wall of the room they were in.

10

A STAB TO THE BACK

Around them, a hundred demons struggled weakly on the floor.

"What do we do with these things?" asked O'ecca nervously.

"Kill them before they get up," declared Towaal.

Ben plunged his sword down, stabbing one of the creatures in the head. O'ecca's naginata swept down next to him and decapitated another. Purple blood spurted out of the stump of its neck, splashing across Ben's boots.

"Sorry," mumbled O'ecca.

Ben sighed and set to work, stabbing and hacking his way methodically across the floor.

High above them, Amelie peered over the balustrade.

"What happened?" she called.

"Gunther went through and closed the rift," Ben yelled back.

"What do you mean he went through?" questioned Amelie. She saw their expressions and mumbled, "Oh."

"Where is Rhys?" asked Ben.

"He went looking for more Purple," responded Amelie. "I tried to follow, but I think he's better off on his own. I wouldn't want to be a Purple mage right now."

Ben opened his mouth to ask about Corinne, but he closed it.

He knew the answer to his question. Grimly, he went back to work.

Across the room, a large arch-demon rose unsteadily. The lights flickered in the room, and a thin spear of fire flew from Towaal's hands, striking the creature square in the forehead.

"I can't believe we lost Gunther's hammer," complained Milo.

Ben glanced at the former apprentice. He was efficiently plunging his spear into demons, working his way closer to Ben.

"If Gunther didn't take it with him, he'd have no chance," replied Ben.

"A chance at what?" scoffed Milo. "That was a suicide mission, no matter how strong he was. We lost the most powerful weapon we were likely to get our hands on. We've done nothing here except sacrifice lives."

"We stopped this," remarked Ben, gesturing to the ruined rift. "If we hadn't come, the Purple could send demons anywhere they pleased. I saw what happened at Northport, and so did you. They could have demolished anyone who stood against them."

Milo grunted. "The Purple can't send demons around the world, but there are still thousands of them loose in Alcott. The rift in the Wilds is still destroyed, and they'll continue to cross naturally, showing up in unexpected places where no one is prepared to hunt them. You may have fixed something you didn't know was broken, but the original problem still exists. That hammer was the solution, and it's gone now."

Ben kept hacking at the demons.

SEVERAL MORE ARCH-DEMONS attempted to rise, but Towaal cut them down before they could regain their strength. The smaller demons thrashed around hopelessly, unable to defend themselves against Ben and his friends. It was tiring, brutal work. By the end of it, Ben's arms ached, and he was covered in foul purple blood halfway up his thighs.

"Better than chopping down the live ones," quipped O'ecca.

Ben grunted. She was right about that.

When they finished the clean up, they ascended the stairs and found Amelie and Rhys. The rogue had returned from his own clean up endeavor. He was kneeling by Corinne's body, holding her head in his lap. His tears had dried, but cold rage still painted his face.

Ben knelt beside him and placed a hand on the rogue's shoulder.

"I found more of the bastards," Rhys rasped. "I killed a couple of them, but there's one more pocket I couldn't get to. They're at the end of a narrow hallway behind a solid metal door. I couldn't find a way to circle behind them." The rogue looked around the group. "I have a favor to ask."

Ben looked at Corinne's body and gripped his longsword. "She was our friend too. You don't need to ask."

"Do you need time?" Amelie asked Rhys.

Rhys gently laid Corinne on the floor and stood. She was pale in the dim light of the room. "There will be time to mourn later. Now, we have business to finish."

"When this is done," suggested Ben, "we can take her with us. Find somewhere peaceful to lay her to rest."

Rhys shook his head. "There is nothing but sand and rock for days around here. If we bury her, the scavengers will be at her in no time. I won't let that happen to her, and she wouldn't want us to fret over her body. It's not her anymore. She's gone."

Amelie wrapped her arms around Rhys. After a brief moment, they looked one last time around the rift room then departed. They followed Rhys to the stairs.

Ben felt a tingle along his spine as they passed through the wards, but Towaal assured them they weren't lethal.

"The deadly variety have to be actively charged. Whoever was doing it must be dead. The rest will be ringing bells for any Purple mages that remain, but if they didn't come running for what just happened, then they won't come because a simple ward went off."

"I've already been through and back," mentioned Rhys. "None of the ones in this hallway will hurt you. If you see a red glow though, stop. That will do more than warn someone."

Ben swallowed. Without Towaal's presence, the wards were invisible to him.

"We also need to keep an eye out for mundane guards," cautioned Towaal. "A spear will kill you just as quick as a fireball."

Ben adjusted his grip on his longsword and peered around them. They were passing through the hallway lined with alcoves and statues, the one they'd been ambushed in a bell earlier.

They made it to the stairs without incident, and Rhys led them down. They kept going, flight after flight, deeper into the mountain. Bodies littered the path, showing where Rhys had already been.

"Leave any for us?" muttered Ben as he stepped over another fallen guard.

"Not all of these are mine," replied Rhys. "Some of the slaves have gotten loose. It's not going well for the guards."

Ben smiled. The Purple and their minions deserved everything they got.

Six flights down, a hallway branched off from the main stairwell. It was unmarked, but the hallway was wide and clear of dust. The way was well-trafficked.

"This corridor is heavily warded," said Towaal. "I haven't sensed anything like it except for outside of the rift room. The mages wanted to know if someone came this way."

Rhys grunted. "I came this way earlier following one of them. Little bastard was faster than he looked. A younger one. Not yet strong enough to do anything to me. After I caught him, I ventured a little further to see where he was going. There's a barred door there with guards inside. As you say, they're protecting something."

"Their leader said they stole something from the Sanctuary," reminded Towaal. "It certainly wasn't the rifts. There's something else he thought we came for."

"The staff Gunther spoke about," said Ben. "Maybe it is down here."

"Let's see how bad they want to keep it," Rhys growled ominously.

They passed a body dressed in purple robes. There was a hole and a dark stain on his back.

"How many of these Purple were there?" wondered Amelie.

"Including the ones in the rift room, about fifteen that I've found so far," offered Rhys. "There could be more hiding deeper within the mountain."

"A miniature Sanctuary for men," remarked Ben.

"It seems like it, doesn't it?" murmured Towaal. "They must have not been very confident because they kept well hidden. The Sanctuary's mages wouldn't come near here because they fear the Dirhadji. No one from Ooswam would be interested because they think it's empty desert. Even the Dirhadji likely don't venture here when they come out of the deep desert. There are no established towns within days of this place. No reason for anyone to come within sight of it."

"Unless they're trading slaves," growled Ben.

"Do you think they were just hiding here until they were strong enough to challenge the Sanctuary?" asked Amelie.

"I think the answer may lie behind that door," suggested Rhys.

They turned a corner. Ahead of them, a massive iron door barred the hallway. Torches bracketed it, casting an eerie light across its bands and rivets.

Suddenly, a small window slid open. A crossbow bolt came flying out, speeding toward them.

Ben yelped and jumped back around the corner just in time.

The bolt breezed a hands-length away from his face. It crashed against the far wall and fell down next to two like it.

"Sorry," apologized Rhys. "I should have mentioned that. They have a crossbow."

"Thanks," responded Ben dryly.

"There are wards in the hall," mentioned Towaal.

"There are wards everywhere in this damn fortress," groused Ben.

"They sensed us when we drew close," explained Towaal. "That means someone is monitoring the wards. There's at least one mage behind that door."

Ben frowned.

"I'm weak," continued Towaal. "I used nearly everything I had on those demons. Unless it is a rank initiate, I don't trust myself to face another mage."

"I'm spent as well," said Amelie with a sigh. She lifted her arm with the fireball-launching vambrace attached. "I was able to magnify my strength, but I don't think I could manage more than a spark right now. Even if I could hold it long enough to hit someone, it would only annoy them."

The party turned toward Ben.

He met their looks. O'ecca was leaning on her naginata, clearly worn out from swinging the heavy weapon. Rhys still seemed eager, but Ben knew he was running on rage. His anger at the Purple for what they did to Corinne would keep him going, but he wasn't the same man he used to be. His strength wouldn't last forever. Amelie had her rapier, but it wouldn't do more than scratch the heavy iron door and would do even less against a mage. Milo had wandered back down the hall and was leaning against the stone wall with his eyes shut. It was difficult to judge what he was thinking.

Ben looked down the hall behind them. Faintly, sounds of fighting drifted to him. Mundane combat he guessed, likely the slaves attacking the guards. The safe bet was to flee. Even exhausted, he'd stake their party against untested guards. They could get out, make it to the coast, and head for Alcott.

He sighed. "We can't leave yet. We've come too far. Sacrificed too much to let this go. I don't know what it is, but the Purple has something behind that door they don't want anyone to see, something they thought we'd be more interested in than their rifts. If it's that important, we can't go. We have to get in there."

"How do we do that?" asked Amelie. "That door is solid iron, and we have no energy for magic."

"Was there a key hole?" queried Milo.

Ben glanced at the timid young man. He was still leaning against the wall of the hall with his eyes closed. Muttering to himself, Ben risked a quick peek around the corner. Immediately, the window in the door slid open again, and Ben saw the business end of a crossbow held up to it. He ducked back before the bolt was fired.

"There's a safer way," suggested Amelie, pulling out the small mirror she used for far-seeing. "I think I have strength for this."

The scene in the hallway flickered in the mirror. Two torches, iron door, and an empty hallway.

Milo sauntered over and studied the image.

"No key hole. No way to pick the lock from outside," he mused.

Ben studied the door, searching for a way in, but the thing looked impenetrable.

Milo glanced at Amelie. "Can I see your vambrace?"

She frowned and unstrapped it.

"I thought you didn't have the skill to use it?" she asked.

He shrugged. "I didn't expel any anima in the battle with the demons. I still have some strength left. Maybe I can figure it out."

"You think we can get them to open the window then lob some fireballs through it?" wondered Ben.

Milo shook his head. "We'd still be facing a locked door that can only be opened from the inside. If we kill all the people in there, we may actually make our problem worse."

"What are you thinking then?" asked Towaal. She was eyeing the former apprentice skeptically.

"I'll let you know if this works," replied Milo with a grin. He brushed a loose strand of curly hair out of his face and stepped around the corner.

Ben gasped as the former apprentice raised his arm and a thin stream of fire burst from the vambrace. Unlike the fist-sized fireballs that Amelie launched with the thing, this was a steady blast no wider than Ben's finger. Even from six paces away, he felt the heat of the flame.

"How are you doing that!" exclaimed Towaal, mouth open in shock.

Milo didn't answer. Instead, he stepped forward, aiming the beam of fire down the hall.

Ben and his friends followed the former apprentice as he moved closer to the door. Already, the iron was glowing red, hot from where the concentrated beam of flame touched it.

The small window slid open. Milo flicked his wrist and trained the fire through the gap.

A man screeched in agony and the window was slammed shut.

Milo went back to pointing the flame at the door. Ben stared in wonder, realizing that the heat was searing a hole through the thick iron. Milo was directing it to one side, where the lock would be located. In moments, he was going to burn a hole through the thing!

"Get ready," grunted Milo through gritted teeth. "As soon as it burns through, they'll have no reason to hide behind the door. It's going to be a fight."

Ben, Rhys, and O'ecca formed up behind Milo. The former apprentice was right. The heartbeat the lock was destroyed, it was going to be a battle. Towaal and Amelie stayed behind, prepared to counter any magical attacks that were launched. Ben silently hoped they still had the strength to do so.

"Take advantage of the narrow hallway," advised Rhys. "These guards are poorly trained, but there may be a lot of them. As long as we don't foul each other's blades, we can hold this spot and prevent them from surrounding us. I doubt they have anyone who can meet us one on one."

Ben nodded and gripped his longsword. O'ecca shifted to the middle of the group. Her naginata would be most effective with ample space.

A third of the iron door glowed angry red. The spot where Milo directed his fire blazed orange and white. The steady stream of heat erupted from Milo in a constant blaze. The metal creaked with the stress. Suddenly, a scream rang out from behind the door.

"I think you're through," said Rhys dryly.

Milo dropped back behind them, rivulets of sweat pouring down the side of his face. His mop of hair was plastered to his scalp. He tore the vambrace off and tossed it to the floor where it shattered like a brittle plate. Smoke drifted off Milo's arm. His sleeve was singed black where the piece of armor had been strapped.

"Are you okay?" asked Amelie.

"I need a minute," gasped Milo. The young man was gently clutching his arm.

Ben ignored him. Milo was alive, and they could see to healing him later. Ben stayed focused on the door, ready for whatever was going to come out of it.

They waited. Moments passed, and the red glow receded. They heard people shuffling about behind the door. No one spoke, and no one came out.

"Do you think they're waiting for it to cool down?" asked O'ecca hesitantly.

They heard a loud scrape. Like furniture behind dragged across a stone floor.

"Damnit," exclaimed Rhys. "They're not going to open the thing."

"Then we go in," growled Ben. "You ready?"

"Let's finish these bastards off," snarled Rhys.

"If you get the motion started, we can help," called Amelie.

Ben charged. The heavy iron door stood shut in front of him, but he knew the lock was burned through. Hopefully, the thing was well constructed with sturdy hinges.

He made it to the door. At the same moment, the window slid open.

A guard stared into his eyes.

"Hello," called Ben. "Mind if I come in?"

He kicked the door with all of his might and felt a jolt of energy in his leg. Towaal or Amelie was giving him a boost. It wasn't much, but it was enough. His leg was jarred with the impact, and the iron door flew open.

Ben grinned at the startled face of the man on the other side as the huge slab of metal smashed into him. The man was flung clear, but half a dozen other guards stood in his place.

They surged forward, and Ben yelped and leapt back. Six spears all thrust at him at the same time. He backpedaled, half a pace separating him from the razor-sharp points.

Rhys had drifted along the wall. As the spears flashed by him, the runes of his longsword blazed silver. He chopped an overhand swing and caught all six spears, hacking through the wooden shafts. The tips of the spears clattered harmlessly to the stone floor.

O'ecca stepped past Ben, twirling her naginata. The heavy blade of her spear swept forward and sliced holes in the startled guards. They scrambled back through the door, waving pacelong sticks in a fruitless attempt to defend themselves. Crimson blood flew from where O'ecca had injured them. The tiny lady followed them into the room, her weapon lashing out and inflicting grievous wounds wherever it landed.

Ben chased after her and found himself in the middle of a wide open circular room. Including the one he came through, four doors broke the wall, but Ben didn't have time to look at them. The room was filled with men carrying crossbows.

"Duck!" yelled Ben.

Bolts sprang from the weapons while he and O'ecca dove to the floor.

A long knife flew over his shoulder and caught one of the crossbowmen in the chest, but several others got off clean shots.

A strangled cry from behind alerted Ben that Rhys had been hit. He looked back and saw his friend stumble into the hallway to get cover. Ben and O'ecca were alone and exposed in the room.

Several of the men had fired, but a dozen more were now taking aim.

Ben crouched, looking wildly for help. The doorway was ten paces away. There was nothing between him and the crossbowmen but open, stone floor.

O'ecca stood and readied her naginata to try and block the bolts. Ben knew it was useless. There were too many of the men, and it was an easy shot. He prepared to charge, thinking he might force the crossbowmen to fire on him, allowing his friends to come in and meet them blade-to-blade. They could meet swords, but that many crossbow bolts would be impossible to dodge.

A yell burst out from one of the other doors and a score men and women charged out. They were wearing plain linen smocks and nothing else. That didn't stop them from swarming over the crossbowmen. Fists and feet flew as they attacked.

They had the numbers and surprise, but the guards were still armed. They discharged their remaining crossbow bolts into the new arrivals and drew scimitars.

"Who are these people?" cried O'ecca.

"I don't know," yelled Ben, "but let's help them."

They rushed forward and plowed into the guards. The Purple's men were trained to watch empty desert and handle slaves. They weren't prepared for brutal, up close, to the death combat. They weren't prepared for Ben and O'ecca. Where their blades landed, guards fell.

Out of the corner of his eye, Ben saw a lone purple-robed man struggling with a set of keys. He was standing by a doorway barred with a massive metal gate.

"Someone get him!" yelled Ben.

He was too late. The man slid a key into the lock. With a twist, he slid a thick bar out of its hasp and yanked open the gate. He fled inside.

One of the smocked men raced after him. Ben tried to follow but had to drop to his belly when a scimitar came swinging out of the press of fighting bodies. He barely made it down as the sharp steel whistled above him.

Ben twisted on the floor, lashing out with his foot. He caught his assailant's leg and that of one of the smocked men. Both came crashing down. The guard lay on top of Ben and bashed the hilt of his weapon into the head of the other man over and over again. The blows were glancing, though, and the smocked man fought back, digging his thumbs into the face of the guard, trying to rip out his eyes.

Ben growled in frustration and attempted to roll the two men off, struggling to get free to chase after the robed man. He knew it must be one of the Purple's mages. Ben was certain that wherever he was going, they didn't want him to get there.

The two combatants were locked onto each other and thrashing. Ben couldn't get himself out from under them.

Suddenly, Rhys appeared above and calmly slid his long knife along the guard's throat.

"This isn't time for a nap," he jested.

Ben watched as his friend stood and plunged into the battle

with half of a crossbow bolt stuck out of his shoulder. He must have snapped off the end of it.

Ben kicked and shoved his way out from under the two men and scrambled to his feet.

The fight in the room looked to be in hand. Rhys and O'ecca were delivering punishing blows to any of the Purple's guards who made their way out of the melee with the smocked attackers.

Towaal and Amelie had arrived, but they were edging around the side of the room to stay away from the battle. Amelie held her rapier out and ready.

Ben ran after the Purple and the smocked man, ducking through the gated entrance to a dark hallway. A set of plain stone stairs led deeper into the mountain. Ben started running down them, taking the steps two at a time. Three flights down and he still didn't see the Purple mage or the smocked man. A single torch lit each flight of stairs. The flickering flames cast spooky shadows as Ben charged deeper.

He heard a terrifying screech, and his blood ran cold. He knew that sound. There were more cries, dozens of them. Screams of rage, screams of hunger. He lost count of how many. He stopped by a torch, peering into the darkness below.

Suddenly, the smocked man came flying around the corner, his bare feet sliding on the stone.

"Run!" he screamed.

Ben blinked as the man pelted up the stairs and flew past him.

Another chorus of shrieks broke out and he heard a man's wailing cry that was quickly cut off. The Purple, he realized.

"Oh damn," Ben muttered under his breath.

He turned and started to run back up the stairs.

The sounds of claws on stone chased him as he raced higher. Demons were coming after him. Dozens, scores, he couldn't tell. He didn't want to know.

As he reached the metal gate that led into the circular room, he risked a glanced behind him. Two of the creatures had caught

AC COBBLE

up and were within eyesight. Thin, with delicate wings on their backs, they'd be the fastest of the bunch. The stronger demons would be coming behind.

Ben flew in to the room of the battle, spun, and slammed shut the metal gate. He found the bar on the outside and rammed it into place heartbeats before the two demons crashed against it. Ben stumbled back as claws struggled to reach through the bars of the gate.

"There have to be over a hundred of them down there," the smocked man was stammering. He'd fallen to his knees and was spitting out words between ragged gasps for air.

Ben glanced around and saw that all of the Purple's guards were fallen. A dozen of the smocked men and women and his friends remained standing.

Rhys ran to him, staring at the two demons behind the gate. A dozen were already up the stairs behind the first two. They heard more coming.

"We need to leave, now!" shouted Rhys to everyone in the room.

Towaal and Amelie ran in from the opposite door and slid to a stop.

"What the..." began Towaal. She didn't bother to finish.

More of the demons were coming and pounding against the metal gate. As they watched, a muscled arm squeezed through a pair of bent bars. Sharp claws grasped as the demon tried to reach them. Without discussion, everyone turned and fled.

As they raced down the hallway, Ben realized the other group were slaves. They'd somehow gotten loose and taken advantage of the opportunity to break out.

He also saw that Towaal was grasping a carved wooden staff. It must be the staff Gunther had spoken of, the Purple's weapon, but he didn't have breath to ask about it. They had another five flights of stairs to ascend before they would make it to the main floor. Then they would need to get off the mountain. After what

248

they saw, Ben didn't think anyone intended to stop until they were far away.

Other groups of slaves started to venture out into the halls, and Ben's party shouted at them to run. Some did, but some just stared in confusion.

"We don't have time to stop and convince them," growled Rhys.

Ben kept running and didn't respond. He knew anyone who didn't flee would have no chance once the demons broke through the gate, but Rhys was right. They'd be dead too if they stopped.

They charged through the corridors until they saw a set of massive, wooden doors down an elegant foyer.

"That has to be the front door," panted Ben. He was gasping for air after running at full speed up so many flights of stairs. "Let's catch our breath. There are likely to be guards at the gate."

One of the smocked men, the one who had chased the Purple down to the demon pit, limped over to them. Ben was surprised the man had kept up.

"What was that?" asked the stranger through deep, ragged breaths.

"Demons," Ben replied.

"There were hundreds of them down there," the man said with a shudder. "That man I was chasing opened a door at the bottom of the stairs. There was a brilliant flash of light, and I saw weird writing on the wall, but it quickly faded. I didn't know what was happening, and I didn't realize what the man was setting loose. I came up behind him and smashed his head against the wall. He was stunned for a moment. I looked down and saw a nightmare coming toward the open door. A roiling mass of those creatures. There were only a few lights in there, but I couldn't see an end to them."

Ben grimaced.

"They were going to feed us to them," the man added. "I'm

sure of it. That's why they brought us to this place. Who are these people?"

"No one, anymore," said Rhys. He paused, then added, "If there are hundreds of demons down there, we have to move. They'll consume everyone in this fortress."

The smocked man swallowed.

"You said you saw a light and fading script," interjected Towaal. "Tell me about it."

Just then, the front doors swung open. A score of the Purple's guards poured in.

Ben's heart sank. His friends were worn out and injured.

The guards fanned out across the room. One man wearing a badge of rank stepped forward. He opened his mouth to speak, but a roar of rage interrupted him, echoing from far down the hallways. The man turned white.

"Sir," called one of his soldiers. "What was that?"

Ben guessed the captain knew exactly what it was. Clearly, his men didn't. Only the most trusted guards would know what lay in the caverns below the fortress.

"The door downstairs is open," advised Ben. "We're leaving unless you want to spend time fighting us."

"Gather everyone from outside on the walls and go to the central stairwell," barked the captain harshly to his men. "Guard the hall from anyone, or anything, trying to come up."

"Sir, these are intruders!" protested his man. "They must have set off the alarms. We should capture them."

"Go now!" screamed the captain. "I'll handle these people."

Ben, his friends, and the escaped slaves watched nervously as the Purple's guards streamed by. The men eyed their captain suspiciously, but they followed his orders.

When they were out of earshot, the captain spoke. "During an alarm, there will be over a hundred men positioned on the walls. They should buy us a few moments."

The man spun on his heel and ran out the door.

"I have to find my sister," said the slave they had been speaking to.

"Find her quickly," responded Towaal. "As soon as you hear screams on the stairs, you must leave."

The man nodded and started directing the other slaves to gather food and find missing companions. Then he gave stern instructions to quickly assemble at the front gate. He had the bearing of a leader, a military man, thought Ben.

The man glanced at Ben's friends. "You gave us a chance, and that is all we can ask. Go now. We'll be right behind you."

Ben nodded and turned to leave.

"Can I see it?" asked Milo.

They'd been running all day and finally stopped as the sun set. Ben's legs felt like lead weights, and he knew that no matter the threat, they simply didn't have the strength to continue.

Milo wanted to see the staff that Towaal found in the Purple's chambers. In the mad dash out of the fortress, no one had taken time to examine it.

Towaal eyed the young man suspiciously, then wordlessly passed him the staff.

Ben saw it was fashioned in the shape of a serpent with sharp spikes along its back and a wide-open maw.

Milo walked to the edge of their camp and sat on a broken rock. He turned the staff in his hands, studying the subtle carvings.

Ben strolled over to join him, curious about what they'd found. Miniscule runes were etched in tiny, overlapping patterns, creating serpent's scales. Milo looked into the open mouth but didn't turn it to face him. Instead, he eyed it from the side. He traced his fingers along the intricate etchings, thousands of them, painstakingly worked into the pale wood.

"Wyvern fire," he breathed softly.

"Wyvern fire. What is that?" asked Ben.

Milo jumped and shot Ben a glance. "Something I heard a long time ago. This staff looks like a wyvern, doesn't it?"

Ben shrugged. Wyverns were mythical beasts as far as he knew. Even Gunther said he didn't know about them. If that ancient mage didn't know, Ben assumed no one did.

"It looks like a lizard to me," suggested Ben.

"What do you know about wyvern fire?" asked Towaal from across the camp.

Milo jumped again.

"Nothing. It's just something I've heard," he answered quickly. "I think I saw a drawing of a wyvern once in Northport's library. It was fantastical, probably a children's story. It looked like this, I think. They spit fire, don't they, in the stories?"

Towaal walked over and held out her hand.

Milo reluctantly passed the staff back.

"First Mages, wyvern fire. There seem to be a lot of ancient secrets that spill out of your mouth that you just happened across in Northport's library."

Milo shrugged. "Lord Rhymer has an extensive collection of old books. I'd thumb through them when the Librarian was busy with his own studies."

"What is wyvern fire?" asked Ben.

"A legend," answered Lady Towaal. "A legend from before my time."

She looked over the staff the same way Milo had. A look of wonder and fear passed across her face.

"Each one of these scales has glyphs carved to form them," she marveled. "There have to be thousands of them. Tens of thousands. The detail is exquisite. It's like nothing I have seen before. This would have taken a lifetime to carve. Multiple lifetimes, maybe."

"What do the glyphs do?" asked Amelie.

"I'd have to study it further, but I believe they gather and concentrate heat," murmured Towaal, peering closely at a section of the staff. "With this many of them, the fire released from this device would be unworldly. I believe it could burn through doors, walls, melt steel like it was butter. Like what Milo did with the vambrace, but at a scale the size of a town. With this, an attacker could blow a hole through any fortification in Alcott. Even Whitehall's walls would be like putting a torch to a paper screen. A demon horde would be nothing against this."

"Should we test it?" suggested Milo hopefully.

Towaal shook her head and frowned at the former apprentice. "I'm afraid we wouldn't be able to gather sufficient energy to activate it. Even if we could do that, I'm not sure we could control it. It's too risky. Anyone nearby would be in grave danger if I tried. No, I think we should bring this to Jasper. He's an expert on devices. He can advise how we can make the best use of this."

Towaal turned to Ben. "This is what we needed, the reason we came to this continent. If we can make use of this, no swarm of demons can stand in our way. We can't cover the entire continent, but where we go, demons will fall. In time, I think that will be enough."

Ben smiled, then lost it when he saw Rhys. The rogue was sitting quietly, ignoring their discussion. He was staring in the direction of the Purple's fortress. They may have found what they needed, but they'd lost a lot along the way.

THE NEXT MORNING, they woke sore and exhausted. They needed rest, but the brutal terrain of the desert wasn't the place to do it. They all knew it wouldn't be long before the demons feasted on everyone left in the Purple's fortress. Then, they would come looking for more lifeblood. They had to move.

The rest of the day they walked across broken rocks and shifting red sands. They were heading north to Ooswam and the city of Shamiil, the emperor's city. They would alert him of the threat and then gain passage to Alcott. The track they followed was barely a road, but it wound around the jagged ridges and spines of rock that dotted the desert. It was faster than trying to move cross country.

They plodded slowly. Both Amelie and Towaal were barely able to lift their feet. The two mages had burned their reserves dangerously low in the battle.

Behind them, Ben spied a thin column of dust.

"There's someone else out here," he called to his friends.

They kept walking, eyeing the dust cloud.

"They're moving the same direction we are," surmised Rhys. "They're coming from the Purple's fortress."

"It could be the slaves," speculated Ben.

"Or the guards," remarked Rhys.

"It's one of the two," agreed Ben with a sigh.

For a bell, they kept moving, watching the cloud of dust draw closer.

"If they were guards," said Ben, "then they are no longer employed by the Purple. They may not be our enemies."

"All of the mages are dead," added O'ecca. "Whoever it is, if they left after us, they may have valuable information."

Ben glanced at Amelie, and she nodded. Her head bobbed loosely. He didn't think she could go much longer. Strong will only took you so far if your body didn't have the strength to continue.

"Let's wait for them," Ben declared.

They settled onto a group of tumbled rocks at the base of a jagged hill. In a bell or two, the spot would be shaded. Ben hoped they didn't have to wait that long in the heat. The rock was uncomfortably warm through his pants, but it was worth it to be off his feet.

Slowly, the dust cloud drew closer.

Ben could make out figures marching toward them. They were caked in the red dust of the desert. They could be guards, slaves, even his neighbors from back in Farview. He'd never be able to tell under the caked filth. He looked at himself and his companions and grinned. They were coated in the stuff too. Red dust monsters waiting on more red dust monsters.

A shrill whistle sounded from the approaching group and a single voice called out. "Hold."

A lone figure broke out from the party and approached.

Ben didn't realize it until the man was standing ten faces in front of them, but it was the same man who had followed the Purple into the demon pit and spoken to them before they left. Ben nodded, and the man smiled back.

"My sister says you saved her back at the fortress," he said. "A couple of guards took her and banged her up. She says they would have had her virtue too if you hadn't interfered. I have to thank you for that."

"Who are you?" asked Rhys. He dropped off his rock and walked toward the man, staring behind him at the group he'd been leading.

"My name is Crai. I was a captain in Lord Syvann's guard until the Red Lord razed most of the villages in our prefecture. I ran, along with a lot of others. We tried to make it to one of the fringe cities along the border between Ooswam and Qooten. We thought we could find shelter there. Instead, we found Dirhadji. Bastards took our camp at night. By morning, we were stuffed in a filthy cage and carted across the desert to that awful fortress. They sorted us out when we arrived. Took the pretty girls first, then the ugly ones. Some of the men were sent outside. Fighting men like me got sent deep into the mountain. I overheard them call us 'fresh meat'. I didn't know what that meant, until I saw what else was down there. You saved us."

Ben grunted. "I won't lie. That's not why we were there, but I'm glad you got out."

"Doesn't matter. We owe you," insisted Crai.

Ben wasn't prepared to argue with the man about it.

"Looks like we're going in the same direction," remarked Crai.

From behind him, a slim girl emerged from his group. Even under the dust, Ben could see the ugly purple bruise that spread from her nose to underneath her eyes. Both her cheeks were puffy and swollen. It was the girl Corinne had rescued.

"Where is the other girl?" she asked, glancing around Ben's companions.

"She didn't make it," replied Amelie quietly.

"I wish I could have thanked her," stated the girl. She drew herself up, standing tall and proud. "My life would be one thing, but what they intended for me..." The girl shuddered and closed her eyes. "That would have been worse than death. Your friend saved me. I wish I could have spoken to her."

Amelie stepped forward and pulled Corinne's axes off her belt.

"These were hers," she said, offering the girl the weapons. "Use them well. Use them the way she would have."

The girl accepted the gift and gave a short bow.

"We're headed for Shamiil," stated the man. "We need to tell the people there what happened."

Amelie glanced at Ben.

Ben nodded. "Very well. We'll join you on the road."

THAT EVENING, they camped three dozen paces from Crai and his party. Along with the leader and his sister, about eighty slaves had escaped. Many of them had just arrived at the Purple's fortress the day before, but they'd been hauled across the desert in suffocating boxes before they got there. They weren't in much better shape than Ben's party.

Crai and his sister came to join them after the camps were settled.

Towaal tucked the staff they had recovered under her bedroll. Crai seemed trustworthy, but the staff was far too dangerous to pass around. The smaller the group who knew about it, the smaller the chance it would fall into the wrong hands.

Ben gestured for Crai and his sister to take a seat. They had no fire and nothing else to offer them.

"When the Dirhadji came on us," started Crai, "I expected them to immediately slit my throat. I thought they'd take my sister into the deep desert to join one of their harems. It is what they have done for ages, and a risk we thought we could avoid. The desert warriors trade with the fringe cities and rarely cause disruption near them."

The man shifted on the sand, slinging a rock away that he'd been sitting on.

"Instead, we were brought to that place. My sister was to be raped, and I was to be fed to those monsters. I have to know. Who were those people? What was that place?"

Towaal nodded to Ben, giving him the lead on how much to tell the siblings.

The man caught the look.

"I owe you my life and more." He gripped his sister's hand. "We will not betray whatever you tell us."

"We are foreigners here," started Ben. "We came to this continent looking for a way to combat demons, those creatures you saw. They are threatening our homes in Alcott. We thought there was a solution here."

Crai frowned but didn't comment.

"That fortress was home to an ancient cabal of mages," continued Ben. "Mages we hoped had developed a weapon that could be used against the demons. Instead, we found they had built a weapon that could be used against men. We stopped them and destroyed the weapon they created, but you saw what was released. Those demons will be a threat here just like they are to our home. There are thousands of the creatures loose in Alcott."

"Mages and demons. It sounds like make believe," mumbled Crai. "These things are stories here. I know what we saw in that fortress, though, and I know what we heard."

Ben nodded. "The threat is real, but until you have seen it, I understand how it is difficult to believe. In Alcott, no one has the choice anymore. The demons have overrun dozens of towns, maybe worse since we've been gone."

"The girl who saved me," asked Crai's sister, "she fought the demons too?"

Ben's lips twisted into a bittersweet smile.

"All of her life," he said. "She lived in a city called Northport. From there, she ranged into the Wilds and hunted the foul creatures. There was a huge battle there, which is when we started our quest. She never hesitated about coming with us. She'd seen what horror the demons brought to her home. She was an important person there, but she felt this quest was even more important. She knew what was right and did it no matter the consequences to herself."

"I know," whispered the girl. She looked at her brother then back at Ben's friends. "I want to help. What can I do?"

Ben paused before responding. "You can tell people. At least one town has already fallen in Ooswam, and it will only get worse. If people are not prepared for what is coming, they will die."

"It will not be easy to convince people this is real," suggested Crai grimly.

"We have to convince them," said Ben.

"We want to help, but the petty squabbles of the lords are consuming Ooswam," remarked the girl. "It will take the emperor to stop them and force the Houses to focus on the combined threat. We are common people. Now that House Syvann is gone, we wouldn't even get to the front stairs of the emperor's palace."

"I can," suggested O'ecca.

"Who are you?" asked Crai with an eyebrow raised.

"Lady O'ecca Iyrron. I've seen the ruins of Ayd. The demons slaughtered everyone in the village. I battled that swarm, and it was only twenty of the creatures. What we saw at the fortress…"

They all understood, they'd been there.

"I will make the emperor believe," O'ecca finished emphatically.

"We will help however we can," assured Crai.

"There is one other thing," requested Towaal. "Tell me about the white light and the script you saw when the man opened the door to the demon cavern."

Crai scratched his head, thinking.

"If the Purple had a way to seal the demons inside," murmured the mage, "that could be as important as anything else we've discovered."

A bell later, Crai and his sister returned to their camp and Ben and his companions turned in for the night. In the morning, they'd leave the others behind and make haste to Shamiil. Ben and his friends wanted to hurry back to Alcott with the staff and the information Towaal had gotten from the siblings. O'ecca was desperate to tell the emperor what was coming from the desert. She was certain he'd put a stop to the Red Lord and other factions warring within Ooswam once he knew a real enemy was out there.

Ben laid down next to Amelie and squeezed her hand.

"Did you talk to Rhys?" she whispered.

"I don't think he wants to talk," responded Ben.

"I'm sure he doesn't," responded Amelie. "That doesn't mean he shouldn't. You know him. At the next town we find, he's going to drown himself in ale. You should talk to him, Ben, while he's still sober enough to hold a conversation."

AC COBBLE

"You're right," acknowledged Ben. "I'll talk to him first thing in the morning."

∽

BEN ROSE EARLY, unable to find a comfortable spot on the hard desert floor. Rhys was up already. The rogue was resting on his haunches, staring at the eastern horizon. Ben settled next to the rogue.

"Waiting for sunrise?" he asked.

"I am," agreed Rhys. "For a long time now."

"I'm sorry about Corinne," acknowledged Ben.

Rhys ran a hand through his hair, brushing the salt and pepper strands behind his ear. Ben looked at his friend's weathered skin. Veins stood out above the bone and muscle. The creases of the rogue's face had deepened since Ben first met the man. Rhys was aging.

"I'm sorry about her too," the rogue replied.

Ben wasn't sure what else to say, so he sat with his friend quietly.

"I can't keep track of the people I've lost," whispered Rhys, still looking out at the empty horizon. "There have been so many. Friends I drank with, warriors I fought with, criminals I worked with, partners in mostly unsuccessful business ventures, lovers both long term and short. Even a few women I was all but married to. Ben, I've forgotten more of them than I can remember. It's like they're gone."

Ben frowned. "I've always heard that when you lose someone and find someone else, you aren't replacing the first person. Your heart grows larger to accommodate more."

Rhys snorted. "Bull shit."

"It's not," argued Ben. "Edward Crust in Farview is a double widower. I can tell you for certain he loved both of his wives equally. He would have died for either one of them."

260

"I'm sure," replied Rhys. He sighed. "Ben, I can remember the faces of some women I've been with but not their names. I can recall the names of others but not their faces. I can only guess at how many I've forgotten entirely. Before the Blood Bay war, I lived in Fabrizo for nearly forty years. I can't remember a single person from that place. I don't want to forget these people. It just happens. I don't want to forget Corinne, but that will happen too."

"You won't," assured Ben, placing a hand on his friend's shoulder.

"You don't understand," hissed Rhys. "I've been alive for over two thousand years. My memory is gone. My mind is like a murky pool. Sometimes, things float up, and I can recall them clearly, but there is so much under the surface I can't see. I know it's there, but it's lost to me. I can already feel the memory of her slipping away. There is nothing I can do about it."

"I'll help you remember," assured Ben.

"Maybe you can help me remember Corinne," said Rhys, "but what about the others? I'm stretched too thin. I can feel it now. In my bones and my soul. It's been long enough for me in this world. It's time to let go."

"What are you saying, Rhys!" exclaimed Ben.

Rhys looked at him, and Ben saw the certainty in his eyes.

"I won't abandon you," declared Rhys. "I'll see this through as best I'm able, but I can feel the end coming. I can feel the weight of time pulling on me like it never has before. You should know. An end is coming for me, and when it does, I'll be at peace."

Ben opened his mouth to speak but was cut off when Towaal cried out behind them.

"Where is Milo?" she demanded.

Ben turned and saw the mage looking frantically around the campsite. Amelie and O'ecca were sitting up on their bedrolls, peering at Towaal sleepily, not understanding her concern.

"Relieving himself, probably," suggested Ben.

"Where is his bedroll then?" screeched Towaal.

Ben blinked and stood. She was right. Milo's bedroll was missing.

The mage dove toward her pack and threw it to the side. Only bare rock and sand was underneath it.

"Damnit!" screamed Towaal.

Rhys jumped to his feet and started circling the camp.

"What's going on?" asked O'ecca, covering a yawn with her fist.

"The staff," exclaimed Towaal. "He took the wyvern fire staff!"

Amelie sprang to her feet as well, looking around wildly. Ben rushed to Towaal's side and stared at where her pack was. He clenched his hands into fists.

Rhys knelt on the northern side of the camp, studying the red sand. Squatting, he moved forward, eyes on the ground.

"Someone feel where his bedroll was," instructed the rogue. "See if it's warmer than the ground around it and then pack up. We'll eat on the move."

They sprang into action, glad for something to do.

O'ecca knelt where Milo had placed his bedroll the night before and shook her head.

They packed quickly and started off in the direction Rhys went. He'd only made it two hundred paces past a low ridge of rock they'd camped in the shade of. His face was twisted into a sour grimace.

"There are too many rocks," admitted the rogue. "I can see the occasional scuff that might be from a boot, but it might not be. There's no way we'll be able to follow a trail across this ground. We've already lost him."

"Ho there!" called a voice.

They turned and saw Crai trotting toward them.

"I didn't expect you to leave so early. Are you worried about the demons catching up?"

"We didn't expect to leave so early either," responded Rhys. "It's not the demons."

"We decided we need to get moving," added Ben. "We've been gone from home a long time. We need to return there, but we must inform the emperor of what is coming before we go."

Crai nodded in understanding. "My man saw your companion leave a couple of bells back. He tried to hail him, but the boy kept going. He was in a hurry, my man said."

"You saw Milo leave?" questioned Towaal, interest burning in her eyes.

"Is that his name?" wondered Crai. "Yes, after what happened last time we camped in this desert, we set a watch. One of my men mentioned seeing the curly-haired boy heading out before dawn. Is he going to Shamiil to prepare the way for you with the emperor? He didn't strike me as someone who could get an audience at the imperial palace."

"Shamiil," demanded Towaal. "Your man is sure he is going to Shamiil?"

Crai shrugged. "They didn't speak, but the boy was headed due north. Where else would he be going?"

"Thank you," mumbled Ben, shocked at their good fortune.

"I will tell the emperor about you when we see him," said O'ecca to Crai. "You are a good man, and Ooswam needs all of the good men it can find. I am certain he will find a place for you. If he doesn't, I will."

Crai bowed at the waist. "I appreciate that. I spoke to my sister, and we would like to fight the demons, no matter how dangerous it is. Foul creatures like that have no place in this land."

Ben slapped his hand on the former captain's shoulder. "I'm sure the emperor will be grateful to have your sword. Stay vigilant, and be ready."

Crai offered a quick bow then returned to his camp.

Ben looked to Rhys and the rogue broke into a quick trot.

They would move fast while the sun was low in the horizon. By midday, the heat of the desert would be brutal, and they would have to slow. They wanted to cover as much ground as possible before then.

The former apprentice would know that at first light, they would be coming for him. He was alone and fit. He wouldn't rest for bells. Ben knew they couldn't catch him in a day, but with grim determination, Ben decided they would catch him.

Weapons jingled, and packs were tightened while they ran. Shamiil was a week away, and it was the largest port on the South Continent. If they didn't catch Milo before he got there, he could disappear into the city or find a vessel sailing to nearly anywhere in the world.

11

SHAMIIL

From leagues away, giant white stone lions dotted the road to Shamiil. Every five hundred paces, a pair of the creatures reared out of the rolling green hills. They stood on waist-high pedestals, towering above Ben's head. O'ecca explained that they represented the emperor's influence, and with each new emperor, another row of lions would be added, always expanding out from Shamiil.

Traffic was heavy on the road, since the city was both the imperial heart of Ooswami government and the largest commercial center. Streams of wagons passed along both sides of the track until armored columns of men passed through. Everyone would scramble to the side to make way. Highborn led many of the columns, and they were liable to lash out at anyone who caused them to slow their stride.

Ben and his friends kept a sharp lookout for Milo, but they didn't expect to find the former apprentice in the crowd headed to Shamiil. Milo had stayed ahead of them for a week now, and Ben was certain he was already inside the city.

He was also certain that the young man had always been more than he seemed. His appearance in councilman Rettor's cham-

bers in Irrefort, his attitude toward Eldred in Hamruhg, the way
he'd fought in Indo, his ability with Amelie's fireball-shooting
vambrace, and a dozen other times he'd displayed surprising skill
or knowledge. Milo wasn't some simple apprentice who
happened to be in the right places at the right time. That still left
the question, though, what was he?

"Let's spread out across the docks first," suggested Rhys,
holding a hand above his eyes to try and catch a glimpse of
the city.

"I could ask the emperor to task his guards with finding
Milo," offered O'ecca.

"No," responded Towaal. "We do not know Milo's true ability,
and we don't know the full capabilities of the staff either. I
suspect he may know more about it than we do. If he is able to
use it, the damage to Shamiil could be catastrophic. We must
surprise him or face him away from a large population center.
We cannot put so many lives at risk."

"You think the Librarian taught more than Milo let on?"
inquired Ben.

"I'm not sure it was the Librarian who taught him," replied
Towaal grimly.

Ben frowned, ready to press further, but his attention was
drawn away by angry shouts behind them.

A horn blared, and a deep voice boomed, "Clear out of the
way for the Red Lord."

O'ecca spun, dropping into a fighting stance.

Amelie grabbed her arm and dragged the girl toward the side
of the road, whispering frantically into her ear.

"Over there," muttered Rhys, directing them into the knee-
high grass at the base of one of the lion statues.

Around them, other travelers were doing the same. The Red
Lord was evidently well known.

Ben watched as black armored soldiers strode down the wide,
dirt road. They wore full armor, but their helmets hung at their

sides. Top-knotted heads turned and stared with disdain at the people clustered on the side of the road. Ben saw the haughty superiority in their looks and wanted to remind them how many of their brethren he'd cut down in Indo. These were hard men, child killers, and he would have no qualms about chopping down a few more of them.

In the center, the Red Lord rode a jet-black steed. His bright red, lacquered armor stood in stark contrast to the black-armored men around him. He didn't mind standing out on the road or on the battlefield. Ben couldn't help but notice the man wore his helmet, though. Worried about an ambush, maybe.

Behind him, Ben could hear Amelie fiercely admonishing O'ecca. The diminutive lady was prepared to attack, but with three hundred of the Red Lord's men around him, it would be suicide.

Rhys stepped next to Ben, his hand gripping his longsword.

"Now isn't the time," hissed Ben.

Rhys smirked and released his grip. "I know. It's hard to stand still while those butchers march by. I'm surprised we can't see the blood of Indo staining their boots."

"We can't right every wrong, settle every score in the world," chided Ben.

"You sound like me," admonished Rhys.

Ben sighed. "It's a fight worth fighting, but it's not ours. We have a larger mission to consider."

Rhys cocked an eyebrow at Ben.

"Fine," conceded Ben. "I do sound like you. I'll give you this. If there's an opportunity, we'll do something about that murderer."

Rhys nodded curtly. "Fair enough."

The Red Lord's men passed without incident.

"They'll be at the emperor's palace," stated O'ecca, her voice tight with anger. "That place is filled with lackeys and gossips. Anything I say to the emperor will find its way to the Red Lord."

"Does that matter?" challenged Ben. "The Red Lord has no

reason to object to facing the demons. He has as much incentive as the rest of Ooswam to want them stopped."

"He has reason to oppose anything I do," warned O'ecca. "Anything that brings my House closer to the emperor is a threat to him. He will not be a friendly voice in the emperor's ear."

"Maybe that opportunity will come up after all," said Rhys darkly.

~

THEY MADE it to the city gates and stared at two massive white stone lions. These creatures were larger than a building and towered over the low walls that surrounded the city. For a city the size of Shamiil, the walls looked tiny to Ben.

"No one challenges the emperor," explained O'ecca when Ben asked about it. "Shamiil hasn't been attacked in millennia. Why would it need tall walls and battlements?"

Ben shrugged. From what he'd seen, the emperor would be wise to assume less about loyalty.

The gates stood wide open and looked to have been left that way for generations. Around them clustered a dozen soldiers wearing bulky, lacquered armor. At first, Ben thought they were the Red Lord's men, but as they walked closer, he saw that instead of a red stripe on their chests, they had gold. And instead of helmets formed like insects, theirs were formed like lions.

Ben glanced up at the two huge lion statues and then back at the guards. For leagues, they'd been seeing lion statues. The emperors of Ooswam had an unhealthy obsession with the animals, he decided.

"Let's enter with no fanfare," recommended Rhys, speaking directly to O'ecca. "I think we should get caught up on the latest court politics before we go barging into the emperor's throne room and demanding assistance. Remember, the Red Lord is here. If he is able to strike at you to harm your father, he will."

"You're right," conceded O'ecca. "I don't like it, but it isn't time to face that monster. Yet."

The guards made no move to stop or question them, and they easily entered the city as part of a constant river of people flowing in. The streets were teeming with people, all rushing about the normal tasks that made up city life. Merchants were calling out their wares, and vendors sold food out of tiny kiosks on the side of the street. Women bustled about carrying goods from the market, and men poured into taverns or carted around deliveries. Young people clustered on the corners of major streets, gossiping and joking. It was all so normal. It seemed strange after the trip through the desert and the battle with the Purple. The contrast was jarring to Ben.

"Let's find a tavern," grumbled Rhys.

"Let's find an inn and then go look around the docks," suggested Ben, thinking that once Rhys sat in front of an ale barrel, it'd be impossible to get him going again.

Rhys didn't argue.

"There's a nice inn about a block away from the palace," advised O'ecca. "I've stayed there before."

"We need to go somewhere you haven't been," said Towaal. "Somewhere no one would expect you to stay."

"I know a place," mentioned Rhys. "It's been a long time, but I bet it's still there."

"Of course you know a place," Amelie responded with an eye roll.

The place Rhys led them to was a squat building two blocks from the docks. It smelled of fish and men who hadn't bathed in weeks. Before they could enter the front door, two sailors burst out brawling with each other, fists, teeth, and blood flashing in the afternoon sun.

"I know of another place if you don't like this one," Rhys offered O'ecca. "It's similar to that establishment you took us to in Vard. What was it called, the Goat Keeper's Daughter?"

AC COBBLE

A flush crept into her face and O'ecca scurried into the inn.

It was as Ben expected. Dirty floor, dirty tables, questionable-looking plates of food, and drunken men shoveling it down in between mouthfuls of ale.

"No one will expect to find me here," choked O'ecca, narrowly avoiding stepping on a man who had slumped over on the floor.

The party steered around the man and moved deeper in the room, looking for an innkeeper in the mess of harried serving women. When they finally found the proprietor, they hired rooms and stowed their gear. Then Ben and Rhys slipped out to scour the docks.

The tavern was rough, but the women could handle themselves in that place. No inebriated sailor was going to cause problems for any of those three ladies. The fewer of their party on the docks, the more difficult it would be for Milo to spot them.

"Shouldn't we have at least brought Towaal?" asked Ben.

Rhys shook his head before pulling up his hood. "We want to avoid a battle, remember? This is about stealth. We can figure out how to deal with him once we actually find him. An open confrontation in the middle of a city is definitely not the answer."

Ben still thought the mage could have been useful, but there was no point in arguing. Instead, he pulled his hood over his head as well and started looking around.

The docks were crowded with porters carrying goods, stacked piles of merchandise coming on or off ships, ropes, animals, and the cacophony of commerce. The harbor and huge merchant vessels sat on one side, rows of expansive warehouses on the other. The space extended along the waterfront as far as Ben could see.

"These docks have to go for half a league in either direction," complained Ben.

"Maybe we'll get lucky," offered Rhys.

Ben didn't think the rogue had any more hope than he did about how lucky they would get.

They picked a direction at random and started walking, skirting close to the ships where they suspected Milo might be. Wherever he intended to go with the staff, they figured it wasn't Shamiil. No, he'd only be in the city long enough to find passage to Alcott.

Every time a shaggy-haired head popped into view, Ben's heart skipped a beat. Time after time, it was a false alarm. There were a surprisingly large number of them until Ben started thinking about how many sailors were just arriving after a month at sea. Those men wouldn't bother shoring their locks while on the ocean.

Ben began to notice a number of serious men clutching notebooks bulging with bundles of paper. They were always flanked by pairs of bored guards. The men would be poking into goods as they were unloaded from ships and directly questioning captains and crews.

As they passed one of the conversations, Ben overheard an officious-sounding man confronting what appeared to be the captain of the ship.

"You give me permission to inspect these goods, or I'll do it without your permission!" demanded the official.

"What is this?" retorted the captain. "I've been doing business here for years. Why are you singling me out?"

"You aren't being singled out," claimed the official, "but I must inspect your wares. It is not up for debate sir, and if you refuse, I will have my companions here gather a legion of their peers. We'll seize this ship and inspect your merchandise at my leisure."

The captain crossed his arms, looking put out. He eyed the guards who were suddenly becoming interested in the conversation. "Why all of this scrutiny?"

"Smugglers," growled the official. He spat.

"I'm not a smuggler," insisted the captain.

"Then we shouldn't have a problem, should we?" pressed the

official. He set his hands on his hips. It was clear he was done discussing.

The captain sighed and gestured for the official to examine the tightly sealed crates his crew were hauling down the gangplank.

"Must be getting pretty bad for this kind of turnout," remarked Rhys, glancing down the docks where they could see half a dozen other customs officials bustling about cargoes.

"The emperor doesn't like losing the tax revenue, I guess," responded Ben.

"There are smugglers in every port," declared Rhys. "You can't avoid that."

Ben grabbed the rogue's arm and pointed at a shaggy-haired figure unwinding a thick rope from around a bollard.

"The build is right," muttered Rhys, stepping behind a stack of crates and peering around to observe the figure. "It could be him."

Moments later, the man turned. Ben sighed. It wasn't Milo.

"Ben!" exclaimed a startled voice.

Ben turned and saw a familiar face staring back at him. The man was shirtless and wearing loose, salt-stained pants. A knit cap kept his hair off his face, and he had a black rat tattooed on his chest.

"Ben," continued the man. "It's me, Martin."

Ben blinked, then slowly replied, "You worked for me at the brewery in the City."

"Aye, I did," responded the man with a laugh. "I hated hauling those heavy barrels around all day, but every evening made it worthwhile when we sat down and had a mug of your ale. Best ale I've ever wet my lips with, honest truth." The man paused and glanced around nervously. "We all thought you were killed with Lord Reinhold's men. At least, when the news first hit, we did. Afterward, we started wondering if the commotion at the Sanctuary had something to do with you. That fancy lady you ran around with was claimed to be dead, but a lot of people didn't believe it. A bunch of crazy lights went off at the Sanctuary, and some ships were burned on the water. The mages didn't say a word, but everyone in the City knew who was responsible. Some of us hoped you somehow survived the ambush and whatever else happened, but the boss didn't want us to go looking. He said if you'd made it, you would have come back to see us. Some of us who knew you always held onto a little hope. Things got a bit dark after you left."

"I, uh, yeah, I made it," mumbled Ben. "What do you mean dark? Is everyone okay?"

"You haven't been back at all, have you?" guessed Martin.

Ben shook his head.

"Come find me at the Fish Head. We'll be berthed a couple of more days. I'm usually over there around nightfall. I'll catch you up over a couple of pints. The Fish Head's lager doesn't hold a candle to your stuff, but it's cheap."

A man leaned over the gunwale of a nearby ship and yelled, "Martin, you want us to bring the rest of the barrels down now or what? The boys are eager to get into town."

"We have to wait on customs," shouted Martin. "Soon as they're done, we'll finish up, and the boys'll get their fun. Don't worry. Customs don't wanna be out here any longer than we do."

"Still carrying heavy loads I see," jested Ben.

"Nah," replied Martin with a wink. "I'm the captain of this merry little crew. I just don't dress like it because the girls charge captains three times what they do crew."

"The captain," said Ben. He whistled in appreciation as he eyed the ship again. "Moving up in the world, Martin. Well, we'd better let you get to it."

"Remember, the Fish Head after dark," said Martin. "A lot happened in the City after you left. I think you'll want to hear about it."

"We'll be there if we can," agreed Ben.

Martin turned and started barking instructions to the crew. He directed where they'd unload the goods and instructed they leave some of the supplies on the ship. The men jumped when he pointed, and all deferred to his commands. Ben was impressed. His former porter really was the captain of the vessel. A big promotion in such a short time.

"Watch," suggested Rhys, nodding toward some of the men.

Ben followed the rogue's gaze and saw Martin's men get to work. They were rolling big barrels down the gangplank and stacking them in front of the ship. He assumed the customs officials would inspect the cargo, then locals would cart it off to where it was going. He was amused to see that, even as captain, Martin was still handling ale kegs.

"What are we watching?" asked Ben.

"How strong do you think that man is?" asked Rhys, gesturing to a sailor who was backing down the gangplank, using his hands to roll a barrel as big as he was.

Ben opened his mouth to speak then closed it. The barrel was at least the size of the man and should be filled to the brim with ale. A keg that size would weigh three times as much as the sailor who was moving it. Ben had moved plenty of ale kegs, but never one that large by himself.

Martin came bustling up and pushed the sailor to one side, helping him move the barrel down. Ben's former employee glanced around then scolded the sailor as soon as they got off the gangplank. Together, the two of them rolled the barrel to stack it with the others.

"I don't understand," muttered Ben.

"Those kegs aren't full of ale," guessed Rhys. "It's an old smuggler's trick. They put a tube in the center of the barrel and fill the rest of it up with ale, or wine, or whatever they can buy cheap. The liquid is distributed evenly, so it rolls and stacks like a normal full keg would. In the hollow tube, they put their real cargo. If customs wants to inspect it, you can tap a few kegs and pour them a nice, frothy ale. If it's an aggressive agent, you pour 'em a few more ales. You keep tapping kegs and pouring ales until they leave you alone or pass out drunk. There's not a customs agent in the world who will try lifting a heavy barrel instead of drinking a free ale."

"What do you think they're smuggling?" wondered Ben.

Rhys shrugged. "No telling. I wasn't even sure that is what they were doing until I saw that lone man managing the ale barrel. These guys are organized and good."

"He spoke about his boss like it was someone I knew," mentioned Ben.

"You know any smugglers in the City?" asked Rhys.

"No, I…" Ben trailed off. "Maybe I do."

THEY SPENT the rest of daylight searching the docks in vain. They were counting on random chance, Ben knew, but that was all they had. Shamiil was filled with hundreds of thousands of people, and Milo could be anywhere amongst them. The soft-spoken apprentice didn't stand out in a crowd, and Ben had already seen upward of fifty people who could match a rough description of him.

They guessed Milo would be departing on a ship, but they didn't know for sure. If he had a specific destination in mind, they might have a few days. If he was willing to hop on the first ship out of port, he was already gone.

As the sun fell below the horizon, painting the clouds above them brilliant shades of pink, gold, and orange, Ben and Rhys decided to stop for the day. The docks would be poorly lit at night, and there was nothing they could achieve there.

Back at the inn, the companions clustered around a filthy table and planned.

"Searching the city is a fool's errand," admitted Ben. "It wasn't going to work in Irrefort, and it won't work here. We have to be smarter than that."

"What do you suggest?" asked Amelie.

"Let's think about where he could be going with the staff," suggested Ben. "Maybe that will give us a clue of where to start looking. We agree he's taking it somewhere, right? Or, more specifically, he's taking it to someone."

"Yes, but to where?" questioned Amelie. "We found him in Irrefort with councilman Rettor. Before that, he was in Northport with the Librarian. They're both dead. He can't be going to either of them."

Ben sipped his ale, thinking it over, and then sat forward. "He said he was in Northport for what, two or three years? Where was he before that?"

Amelie blinked. "I'm not sure. I don't know if he ever said."

Ben leaned his elbows on the table. "He said he was in the guard in Northport, I think."

"That's what he told us," confirmed Towaal. "He said he was the last of several sons, and his parents couldn't afford an apprenticeship, so he joined the guard. He claimed he was picked out of that bunch to assist the Librarian. We have to assume that was a fabrication."

"There's no way he was in the guard," agreed Rhys. "He was a wonder with that trident and spear, but Northport's men use swords, axes, bows, and pikes. They didn't train him to use a short polearm like that. Someone else must have."

"Someone trained him how to use his will also," muttered Amelie. "He was able to manipulate the fire from the vambrace like he was born to it. Gunther said he was close to being long-lived, didn't he?"

Rhys scrubbed a hand across his face. "I should have seen it. Obviously, he wasn't who he said he was. There were so many signs. I can't believe we missed them."

"We had no reason to think he was lying," responded Ben.

"It seems clear he wasn't in the guard, but then, where did he come from?" wondered Amelie.

"Whoever he is working for knew about the Librarian," said Ben. "They placed him there with a purpose in mind. There are only so many people who could have known about the Librarian."

"Rhymer knew about him," said Amelie, "but he would have no reason to place a spy inside his own library. Who else?"

Ben frowned. "Remember, the Librarian wrote a letter. That is how the Coalition Council found out about the Purple in Irrefort. That would have been a little bit before Milo joined him, assuming he wasn't lying about that timeline. Who else did the Librarian write to?"

Towaal, her voice low with dread, listed the recipients. "Gunther, the Coalition Council, the Sanctuary, and Lady Avril. Those are the people the Librarian wrote to."

"It wasn't Gunther," said Amelie, "and Rettor is dead."

"Lady Avril is dead too, and has been for several centuries. At least, that's what we were told in the Sanctuary," added Towaal. "I don't know if we can assume that is true any longer either."

"Milo could be working for her, I guess," said Amelie, "if she's still alive. Though, I don't understand what her motivation would be."

"The correct answer is usually the simplest one," declared Rhys.

They sat quietly, no one wanting to state the obvious.

"That bitch," Towaal finally hissed. "The Veil has been slow playing this, playing everyone."

Rhys slammed a fist down on the table. "She infiltrated the Purple in Northport and almost got someone inside the Purple in Irrefort."

"That's why Eldred didn't attack our vessel when we fled Hamruhg," said Ben, a sickening feeling growing in the pit of his stomach. "She saw Milo standing on the deck."

"Eldred has no reason to hold back, now," muttered Amelie. "If she is in league with Milo, then she could be here in Shamiil."

"Is this Eldred really that dangerous?" asked O'ecca.

Towaal nodded grimly.

"I don't think she's here," said Ben.

Towaal raised an eyebrow at him. "Why not?"

"Milo is in league with the Veil and Eldred, right?" he asked rhetorically. "That makes the most sense. If Eldred is able to track us, then it's likely she could track him as well. Or maybe he can even communicate with her from a distance through a thought meld or however she speaks in our minds. If they are in cahoots, he would go straight to her. If she was on the South Continent, he would find her."

Ben paused. "Even if none of that is true, we know she would have sensed the conflagration at the Purple's fortress. She'd know it was us and come running. Now that Milo has the staff, she'd have no reason to avoid a confrontation. No, I think if she was here, we would have already seen her."

Rhys finished his ale and added, "That makes sense. Shamiil is the obvious location to find us, and we walked right in the front gate. She would have had watchers there if nowhere else."

"What do we do?" asked Amelie.

"We have time," stated Ben. "If she isn't here in Shamiil, then she is in Alcott. Maybe she's waiting for Milo. Maybe she's waiting for us. We'll have to deal with her sooner or later, but not today. We have time to plan. One thing we know, if Eldred and the Veil have the wyvern fire staff, they aren't likely to use it for benevolent purposes. We need to stop the demons and stop them. To do that, we need more resources."

"What resources are you thinking about?" wondered Towaal.

"We're in Shamiil," responded Ben. "Let's start here. Let's go talk to the emperor."

"I spoke to my father's representative," O'ecca told them the next morning. "He can get us in without raising suspicion. The Red Lord is there, but he is also waiting for an audience with the emperor. Apparently, The Red Lord is to be censured for his attack on Indo and other atrocities. He pushed it far enough that the emperor has been forced to act."

"That is good for us, isn't it?" asked Ben.

O'ecca nodded.

"If the emperor is already turned against the Red Lord," suggested Amelie, "we can use that. The Red Lord is weakening Ooswam by instigating internal strife. Strength will be needed for the battle to come. We just have to convince the emperor of that."

"He prefers to stay out of the squabbles between Ooswam's lords," said O'ecca, "but the traditional role of the emperor is to protect the realm from outside threats. It doesn't get more outside or threatening than the demons. I believe he will agree to face them."

"He has to," said Ben. "If he doesn't, they'll come to him. Those things aren't going to stay in the desert for long."

"I am certain we can convince him of the danger," agreed O'ecca. "It's all falling together. In three bells, my father's man will come get us and bring us to the emperor. I must prepare myself, and I suggest you do as well."

"Prepare how?" asked Rhys.

O'ecca looked him up and down. "Put on some clean clothes for starters."

Lord Iyrron's man arrived promptly on time. He was a thin man, draped in finely stitched robes that were cinched tight with a broad belt. His robes were dyed bright green, matching the colors of House of Iyrron. His belt was black with a silver medallion affixed to the front. It designated his rank, Ben assumed.

The man bowed deeply to O'ecca and largely ignored the rest of the party. By their dress, he must have thought they were peasants, which, Ben admitted ruefully, wasn't far from the truth. He had few coins, no home, and no occupation.

"Lady Iyrron, I'm afraid I have just received horrible news," stated the man in a quivering voice.

She looked at him, waiting patiently.

The man drew a deep breath then let it out slowly. "Your father and brothers faced the Red Lord just six days past."

The color drained from O'ecca's face.

The man shifted uncomfortably. "They did not survive, my lady. You are the head of the House now. You are Lady Iyrron."

Ben pulled out a chair and O'ecca sat heavily on it, her face a mask of sorrow.

Amelie knelt next to the diminutive lady and wrapped her arms around her. Amelie knew what this feeling was like.

"Tell me the details," instructed O'ecca, her voice taut with pain.

The functionary grimaced. "The Red Lord was spotted moving around the outskirts of Seawatch, our last operable port. Your father and brothers chased after him and were ambushed. I am no military man, but from what I heard, I believe it was a trap. Nearly all of the men with them were lost. The might of the house is seriously weakened, my lady."

"Will the emperor act?" asked Amelie.

The man shrugged hopelessly. "I'm told The Red Lord is to be censured, but he is gaining power, and the emperor has always been hesitant to interfere between lords. Will he merely chide the Red Lord, or will he severely punish him? I do not know. The emperor is not the strong leader his grandfather was."

"We have to make him strong," asserted Amelie, gripping O'ecca's hand.

The slim girl didn't respond. She sat, shocked, visibly unable to process what happened.

Amelie stood, still holding O'ecca's hand. "O'ecca, I know what you are feeling right now. My father was killed too. He was caught up in the swirl of politics of more aggressive lords. I wanted nothing more than to take revenge, and I couldn't. I've poured myself into this quest to battle the demons. Sometimes, I can convince myself that I've forgotten what happened. If I had a chance, though, I would go back and be with my people. I would lead them, protect them, and right the wrongs that were committed against us."

O'ecca looked up and met Amelie's eyes.

"We have a lot to discuss with the emperor," said Ben. "The Red Lord, the demons. We can tie all of it together and get justice for your family."

"We do have a lot to discuss with him," agreed O'ecca firmly.

She stood, brushing out her green silk dress. She wiped a finger under her eyes, removing the tears and black kohl that had started to run down her face. She looked down at her dress.

"I think I will go change."

A quarter bell later, O'ecca rejoined them in the common room of the inn. She wore light leather armor, her hair was tied up in a warrior's bun, and her naginata rested on her shoulder. The look on her face sent other patrons of the tavern scrambling out of her way.

"M-My lady," stammered her representative. "Are you certain that is appropriate dress to see the emperor?"

"It is appropriate for what I want to accomplish," she said. "Let's go."

They followed O'ecca and her man out into the street, heading to the emperor's compound.

12

FAMILY, HOME, EMPIRE

As THEY WALKED through the streets of Shamiil, Ben tried to process the horror of what O'ecca faced. Her father, her brothers, all of them had been killed in battle with the Red Lord. She had responsibility for her House now, and if she wasn't able to convince the emperor to assist her, she'd be hard pressed to defend her people. If he wasn't severely censured, the Red Lord was certain to go back to the Iyrron prefecture and finish the job he'd started. Her House's army was seriously weakened, and with her in Shamiil, it would be a disorganized shamble.

On top of that, there were hundreds of demons that would be escaping the Purple's fortress. There was no telling how the emperor would react to that, but if he didn't do something, then the Red Lord might be the least of everyone's worries.

Ben was startled out of his reverie when the former guard captain Crai shouted, "Ho there! I thought you'd be gone by now. Did you find what you were looking for?"

The man was standing on the side of the street. He had acquired lacquered armor and a sword. He now looked like the former captain he claimed to be instead of a recently freed slave.

"Not yet," responded Ben. He paused. "You should know the Red Lord is here."

Crai grimaced.

"We must hurry," stated O'ecca's representative.

"Come with us," Ben said to Crai. "We go to see the emperor. Your testimony about what happened in Lord Syvann's prefecture and the Purple's fortress could add weight to our claims."

The former captain fell in beside them as they marched through the crowded streets of Shamiil. The city was sprinkled with low hills but was otherwise flat. Atop the hills sat the palaces of the wealthy. Above the throng of the city, they got a better breeze off the sea and didn't have to deal with the smell and refuse of their neighbors. The palaces were behind tall walls studded with sharp spikes. They clearly did not welcome visitors.

The rest of the city contained remarkably similar architecture to Indo, white stucco buildings with black trim. The profusion of vegetation and colorful flowers wasn't as dramatic in the city, but many of the windows held planters that sprouted herbs or vegetables.

The palace of the emperor stood above it all. A sprawling compound of white, pink-veined marble structures, it sat atop the highest hill in the city. At the top of the towers, all of Shamiil would be visible, from the port to the southern gates.

The hill below the compound's walls was covered in a forest of sharpened stakes. They sprouted like a hedgehog's quills. From a distance, Ben could see that men patrolled the walls with long wooden bows. Every hundred paces, towers rose even higher. Ben guessed a sharp-eyed lookout could see for leagues up there.

"I wouldn't want to attack that place," murmured Ben.

"In Ooswam, the emperor is the supreme power," said O'ecca. "It is imperative that he shows that power to the world. If the other lords or foreigners see him as weak, they may be tempted to strike."

"Having power is frequently about projecting power," agreed

Amelie. "If the people and the other lords perceive that the emperor is unassailable, then they won't try."

"Has anyone ever attacked the compound?" wondered Ben.

"Not with an army," answered Towaal. "Many an assassin has tried. A few have been successful. The emperor shows his might because he needs to. The other Houses are almost as powerful as the imperial line, and they chafe under that yoke."

"What happens when an emperor is assassinated?" asked Ben.

He was mildly curious about the answer, but he was more interested in distracting himself from their mission. Convincing the emperor to meet the demon threat to the south, to confront the Red Lord, and then to lend them a ship was going to be near impossible.

"His son will inherit, the same as any House. If there is no son, then a daughter, a cousin, and so on," replied O'ecca. "The emperor has only one legitimate son, so the succession will be clear and is expected to be bloodless."

"Do you know the son?" asked Amelie.

O'ecca nodded, her face tightening.

"You don't like him?" guessed Ben.

"Chesson is not yet ready for rule," she responded. "He also does not yet have a wife, and he believes that every girl in Ooswam should want the position. There have been some scandals as you can imagine."

O'ecca fell silent, but her face grew darker and darker as they walked.

Amelie surmised the reason. "With the news about your family, you are now the Lady of your House."

O'ecca nodded. "Chesson has already made advances toward me. My unexpected inheritance will only entice him more. He lives in his father's shadow with no formal authority. By marrying me, he'd take control of a significant prefecture. The problems we have with the Red Lord would vanish as soon as a betrothal is announced. Merchants would come flocking to do business with us at generous terms, and lords would trip over themselves to ally with us. Chesson is, after all, the future emperor. Gaining his favor now would pay dividends for a lifetime."

"Can you say no to him?" asked Amelie.

"We shall see," responded O'ecca quietly. "He would be a powerful ally, and my people need help."

Ben shuddered.

THEY MARCHED up the twisting walkway to the gates of the emperor's compound. An approaching army would be exposed the entire way. Ben mentioned as much to Rhys.

"That's true," agreed the rogue. "Of course, by the time an army got here, they would have already pillaged the entire city. Notice how the emperor's walls are twice as high as the city's? He's not worried about foreign invaders. He's worried about an attack from within."

At the gates, a dozen men wearing the black and gold armor of the emperor stood watch.

"Back again so soon?" one of them asked O'ecca's representative. "House of Iyrron must need even more assistance than is rumored."

O'ecca's official offered a curt bow of the head. "I'm back as often as required."

The guard rolled his eyes and waved them through, apparently trusting O'ecca's man wouldn't bring in anyone who didn't belong.

Inside, the top of the hill was covered in extensive manicured gardens and squat, pink-veined white marble buildings. Ringing the hill were heavily manned walls. They didn't have the soaring intimidation of Whitehall's massive barriers or even the thick utility of Frisay's, but the emperor didn't need that. As Rhys said, he wasn't worried about siege weapons. He was worried about assassins. He was well protected against those. Scores of his men were visible, patrolling the walls, walking the grounds, and standing guard at every door. Ben estimated they'd seen a full company of the men by the time they made it to a two-story side building.

"Not the throne room?" asked O'ecca.

"You didn't want to be noticed, did you?" asked her man. "The emperor will meet us in his library. I'm told he spends many afternoons reading, so no one will suspect he's seeing us."

More guards were stationed outside of the library, but they appeared to know the party was coming. They didn't speak when Ben and his friends followed O'ecca inside.

The building was a single open room. In the center were plush rugs, couches, stuffed chairs, and polished wooden tables holding oil-filled lamps. The space was surrounded by thousands of finely bound leather volumes. Each of the four walls were covered in bookshelves. There were only two doors on either end of the building and no windows, but the room was brightly lit by skylights above them.

"What do you think the emperor of Ooswam reads?" wondered Rhys, meandering over to view some of the titles.

Ben drifted toward a table in the center of the room. It was painted with a magnificent map. It detailed much of the South Continent, though the desert of Qooten appeared to be underrepresented. Out of curiosity, he looked for the Purple's fortress or Frisay, but both were missing.

O'eccca, noticing where he was studying, remarked, "The emperor's mandate is to protect Ooswam from external forces, but as long as those areas outside of the border and are not sending armies, I don't think he cares about them."

"And why should he?" asked a high-pitched tenor.

Ben looked to the opposite end of the room and saw a young man standing there. He was clothed in a bright white robe and had his long hair slicked back with some type of oil. A sharp nose and receding hairline dominated his face. He waved behind him, and two soldiers exited out the door.

"Chesson," said O'ecca, sketching a quick curtsy to the newcomer.

"My father told me you were here," said Chesson. "I'm disappointed you didn't write to let me know. After the Spring Gala last year, I thought I made it clear I'd like to see you when you were in Shamiil."

Ben wasn't sure whether he should consider the emperor's son a man or a boy. He must have intended his haughty demeanor to add years and gravitas to his appearance, but he came off as immature and petulant to Ben.

"Where is he?" asked O'ecca.

"He'll be here," assured Chesson. "I wanted to see you first."

O'ecca waited.

"Your family is dead," declared Chesson abruptly. "I've informed my father to support your claim for the House seat. It is the least I could do."

"Yes," agreed O'ecca. "That is the least you could do."

A slight frown marred the fop's face, but he pressed on. "You knew already, didn't you?"

O'ecca nodded.

"Good," said Chesson, stepping closer to O'ecca. "After you are done speaking to my father, I suggest you stay and dine with me this evening. It has been a long time, and I believe there is much we should discuss."

"I'll see how the conversation goes with your father," replied O'ecca slowly. "You are right. There is much to discuss."

Chesson opened his mouth to respond, but a relentless clanging sounded from outside. An irritated glare fell across Chesson's face, and his mouth snapped shut. He shot a look to the door where his guards were stationed, but none of them were coming inside or shouting alarm. After several moments, the clanging stopped.

"This is not good," muttered Rhys.

"It may have nothing to do with us," protested Amelie quietly. Gesturing at Chesson, she added, "It's not like we snuck in, this time."

"If not us, then what does it have to do with?" worried the rogue.

"That sequence is an alarm," explained the former guard captain Crai. "It signifies an attack."

Chesson waved a hand to quiet them, fighting to wipe the perturbed pout off his lips and appear regal.

"Some fool must have accidentally struck one of the gongs," he claimed. He moved toward O'ecca. "Do not be alarmed, my lady. You are with me."

Ben glanced at Rhys and could tell the rogue was thinking the same thing he was. No one accidentally hits an alarm gong over and over again for that long.

Chesson reached out to take O'ecca's hand but was interrupted when one of his guards burst inside.

"I told you to wait outside," snapped the young lord.

"Sir," quivered the guard, "something is wrong."

"Go fix it," insisted Chesson. "Do not bother me again!"

Chesson turned to O'ecca and a false smile slid onto his face. "Do not worry yourself about this disruption. Maybe we can go somewhere..."

"Sir!" shouted the guard from the door.

Chesson spun to the man but didn't get the chance to admonish him.

The guard grunted and staggered into the room. His face registered shock. He stumbled into a table, knocking it over, and fell face down on the floor. A red-feathered arrow stood from his back.

The blood drained from Chesson's face.

"This is not good," said Rhys.

"Go see what is happening," instructed Towaal.

She bustled over to the fallen guard and fingered the feathers of the arrow.

Rhys ducked his head out of the door then immediately pulled back in, cursing.

"We need to go," he said.

A scream sounded from the open door, and Ben saw black-armored men rushing by with swords drawn.

"Out the other way," clarified Rhys needlessly.

Ben drew his longsword and trotted to the door they'd come in. Luckily, the gate was out that door. Whatever was happening, Ben was certain they'd be better off away from the palace.

Outside, he saw men rushing toward the main building. To the emperor's quarters, he guessed. He nodded to himself. They certainly had no reason to go that direction. He gestured to friends that the route was clear.

"O'ecca!" called Chesson. The young lord was standing in the center of the library, wringing his hands. "Stay here with me. This place is defensible. My men are outside. They'll quickly sort out whatever is happening. It's best we stay in the building."

Another of Chesson's guards ran inside. "Sir, we have to leave."

A scream sounded behind the man.

"That door," he added, gesturing to the one Ben was peering out.

"Looks like we're together for now," muttered O'ecca.

They dashed into the bright sunlight. Around the grounds, the emperor's guards were swarming toward the palace. It wasn't clear who was attacking.

A shout drew Ben's attention and he saw another one of the guards fall to an arrow.

"There," he said, pointing to one of the towers that dotted the walls.

Under the shade of the tower, it was impossible to see who was inside, but arrows flew out. The shafts struck the guards as they raced across the lawn below. Outside of the tower, guards were pounding on a wooden door, trying to get inside.

"Another one there," called Rhys, looking to the other side of the compound.

"Stay low," growled Chesson's guard.

The man was eyeing the open space between them and the palace. They'd be exposed to arrows for two hundred paces. He glanced to the main gate. The way seemed clear.

"We'll follow the exterior wall and meet up with the gate guards," instructed Chesson's man. "There's a dozen of them. They can hold the guardhouse if needed."

Ben noticed a tiny golden stamp on the man's shoulder, an insignia of rank, he assumed.

Rhys looked to Ben and Ben nodded acknowledgement. If the guard was headed to the gate, they may as well go with him. Ben had no interest in staying inside the compound while a war broke out.

They dashed across the open space. Ben kept his head low and tried to ignore the tickle in his back at the thought of an arrow plunging into him. The arrows had enough force to punch through the thick lacquer armor of the emperor's troops. The heavy barbs would have no problem piercing Ben's skin.

Amelie jogged beside him, scanning the walls above. So far, none of the towers near them were raining arrows.

They made the wall and tracked along it, staying in the shadows and hopefully out of sight for the archers. Shouts drifted across from the palace, but Ben still couldn't see any of the attackers. Twenty paces ahead of them, he saw the gate to the compound stood open. Good, he thought. He had worried the guards had a protocol to close it anytime there was an alarm. With it open, they could easily walk out and let the mess sort itself out.

He thought that until they made it to the gate. Bodies of the emperor's guards lay scattered underneath the portcullis. The dozen men who stood guard earlier were all dead.

"They must have been ambushed," guessed Rhys.

"Doesn't matter," stated Ben. "The way is open. Let's get out of here."

"It's not open," remarked Towaal. She had walked out the gate and was looking down the path. Ben heard the stomps of booted feet. The mage turned. "We need to find shelter inside."

Chesson's guard looked around wildly then pointed to the palace. "The north tower. It has a side entrance, and the stairs at the top are easily defensible. There are men stationed there and weapons stored. If we can link up with those men, we could hold the tower stairs against a much larger force. You will help fight if needed?"

Ben nodded. "I don't know who is attacking, but they are no friends of ours."

"Good," answered the man. "Follow me."

Chesson tried to hold O'ecca's hand, but she slapped him away.

She gripped her naginata and instructed the fop, "Be ready to fight."

Chesson gripped his hands together nervously and shuffled to be near his arms man.

Ben got the impression that Chesson rarely did his own fighting.

They started to follow Chesson's man across the lawn, but Ben snagged Crai's arm, stopping him.

"Wait behind the guard house," he whispered. "When it's safe, sneak out the front gate. Alert the city watch and the barracks. Whatever is happening here, I'm sure the emperor will need those men."

Crai nodded then ducked into the shadows behind the guard house.

Ben hurried to catch up with his companions. They were moving quickly, but suddenly picked up the pace when an arrow plunged into the turf beside them.

"Do they know who I am!" barked Chesson.

"You're lucky they don't," muttered Rhys.

The young lord was huffing and puffing halfway across the lawn. The arrows started to come faster. They may not realize Chesson was the son of the emperor, but they were one of the few groups still brave enough to dash across the open space.

A shout rang out behind them. Ben glanced over his shoulder to see a line of men pouring through the gate. He didn't take time to see how many were coming. There were enough.

Twenty paces away from the entry to the north tower, a squad of black armored men burst out of the door.

"We're under attack!" shouted Chesson's guard. "I have the emperor's son. Hold this door while we get to safety."

"The emperor's son?" chortled the squad leader. "My lucky day."

"Oh damn," grumbled Rhys. The rogue drew his longsword.

Chesson's man stepped forward, admonishing the new arrivals, "Yes, hold this door with your lives. I'll see you're…"

He didn't get to finish his sentence. The squad leader yanked out a short blade and rammed it into the gut of Chesson's man.

"What is this!" exclaimed the young lord.

Ben and his friends didn't waste time talking. Rhys sprang into action, shearing through armor with his mage-wrought blade. Ben ran after him, surprising their opponents with the ferocity of his attack. O'ecca flanked Ben and twirled her naginata with lethal effectiveness. In the open space of the lawn, none of the men could withstand the speed and power of her blows. In heartbeats, the eight men in the squad were down.

"Good work," said Amelie.

Ben grinned at her. She held her rapier ready but hadn't joined the fight.

"Save it for when you need it," Towaal advised Amelie. "You're growing in knowledge and will. Go there first. Use the blade only when you have the advantage or when you are forced to."

"Let's go," snapped Rhys, grabbing the stunned Chesson and dragging the young lord to the north tower door.

An arrow shattered on the wall beside them, spraying them with slivers of wood as they ducked inside.

Chesson touched his face where a thin trickle of blood was leaking down his cheek.

"I'm bleeding," he quaked. "They fired at me. They could have killed me."

The pounding of booted feet drew Ben's attention and he looked out the door. Halfway across the lawn were two dozen black-armored men. On their chests, they had bright red stripes.

Ben slammed the heavy wooden tower door shut and exhaled in relief when he saw the thick iron bolt that locked it. He slid the bolt home then turned to his friends.

"The Red Lord is the one attacking."

"You're sure?" asked O'ecca.

"Impossible!" argued Chesson.

Ben nodded tersely. "Those men who poured in through the gate are all wearing his armor. Either they are his men, or someone wants the emperor to think they are."

"They are his men," declared O'ecca. "I see what is happening now. The Red Lord didn't come here to accept chastisement from the emperor. He came as an excuse to bring his men into the city. The assault on my father's towns, everything else we've heard, it was part of a plan. He's been staging this for years. It's a coup."

"He was in Saala's band, didn't you say?" asked Amelie. "It's the same plan Saala was accused of plotting that the emperor foiled with the Red Lord's help."

A heavy body slammed into the door and the iron bolt rattled.

"Can we discuss this later?" suggested Ben.

There was a staircase that spiraled up into the tower and a broad hallway that led deeper into the palace. Neither one offered an obvious advantage.

"Where to?" Rhys asked Chesson.

"I-I, uh, if we go down the hall we can reach my father's throne room," stammered the fop. "That's where he and his guards will be."

"Up the stairs then," stated Rhys.

"But—" Chesson started to object.

Rhys grabbed him by the scruff of the neck and propelled him up the stairs. "Your father's throne room is also where the Red Lord's men will be headed. Some of them may already be there, and more are coming from behind. We'd be trapped between them."

The young man held his tongue as they jogged up the stairs.

For three flights, they found hallways leading deeper into the palace and rooms on the exterior of the tower. The rooms were wide open and designed for entertaining large parties of guests. They offered little defensive advantage.

On the fourth floor, Rhys paused. The tower room was like the others, and a similar hallway led into the palace. The stairs above them narrowed considerably. The decorative touches vanished as well.

"What's on this floor?" Rhys asked Chesson, glancing down the hallway.

"Guest apartments," mumbled the emperor's son. "They're set high to catch the sea breeze. My father…"

Rhys cut him off. "The Red Lord's men will be focused on the first floor, but if he's guesting here, we run a high chance of encountering his men or his allies. Also, they could be looking to secure any valuable guests for ransom."

The rogue looked up the stairs.

"What is up there?" he asked. "Your man thought we should hide in the tower."

Chesson shrugged. "I've never been that way."

Rhys snorted then started up the stairs. Whatever was up there, they would have to hope the Red Lord's men didn't think it was important either.

They passed one floor which looked to be storage for linens, clothing, and chamber pots. The next floor held a simple kitchen. Water was boiling on a wood-burning stove, but no one was visible.

Beyond the kitchen, they found a thick door that spanned the stairwell. It hung open, so they filed through.

On the other side, Rhys and Ben both tugged to pull it shut. The hinges screeched with disuse. When they finally got it shut, Ben slid a bolt thicker than his wrist through a hasp in the door and into the stone wall.

"Chesson's man was right," admitted Rhys. "We could hold this thing for days."

"We don't have any food on this side," mentioned Amelie.

"I wasn't saying we should, just that we could," replied Rhys.

They passed another floor which held an empty guard room. There were racks of weapons on the wall, tables where men could spend their time playing cards or bones, and narrow windows they could fire arrows from. The place was prepared to stage a defense, but like the kitchen below, it was abandoned.

They headed higher, Rhys in the lead. Then they paused.

"Karina, you'd better come see this," Rhys called from around a bend in the stairwell.

The mage had been bringing up the rear of the party. She slipped around the rest of them to join Rhys at the front.

"What is it?" called Ben. "We should keep going."

He was listening to the sounds of armed men moving around somewhere below them.

"It's warded," hissed Amelie.

"That doesn't make any sense," protested Ben. "There aren't any mages in Ooswam."

Rhys whispered back, "Let's go quickly but silently as you can manage. Something above these stairs is not meant to be found."

They trotted quietly up the stairs. They rounded one bend, and Ben saw the fading glow of runes on the wall. Shimmering silver faded into the dark stone. Ben swallowed. Amelie was right. He grimaced and kept going. Around the next turn, he found a solid stone wall spanning the stairwell. Rhys and Towaal had vanished.

He glanced down at Amelie and saw her looking at him wide-eyed.

"Come on," hissed Rhys.

Ben jumped. The rogue was nowhere to be seen.

A boot slid out of the stone wall and settled on the top step.

"It's a light shield," muttered Amelie.

"Like we used on the ship!" exclaimed Ben.

The rogue's head slid through the barrier. His body seemed to be leaning out of solid stone. He growled, "We don't have time for this. Get up here."

Swallowing, Ben raised a hand and watched as it passed into the stone. He felt nothing but air. He walked through and found himself on a stairwell just like the one below.

"The skill it would take to form a barrier like that which holds up under close scrutiny is unprecedented," declared Towaal. "Be ready for anything."

They continued up two more flights, Rhys edging around them to retake the lead. Towaal followed close behind, clearly prepared to launch an attack at whatever they found.

At the top of the stairs, they stopped again. Ben peered between Towaal and Rhys at another door. This one was fashioned of pale wood. In the center was the copper face of an old woman. The face was friendly, but the eyes held a mischievous look, like it had been waiting for them.

The door opened and a young girl looked down at them.

"Hello, Rhys. It's been a long time." She paused. "You've gotten older. Have you been getting yourself into trouble?"

Ben watched his friend's back. The rogue was tense, like he was prepared to attack. The tip of his sword raised, then it dropped. His shoulders slumped.

"Hello, Lady Avril."

The girl rolled her eyes. "No one calls me a lady anymore, not that I ever was one. You know that, Rhys. Now, I am being rude. Bring your friends and come inside."

The girl turned and disappeared through the door.

Ben met Amelie's eyes and saw the fear reflected in her look. Lady Avril, the former Veil. Supposedly dead for over three hundred years. Not anymore.

Nervously, the companions followed her through the door.

They found themselves in a small, elegant chamber. A curtain obscured a bed on one side of the room, and a small table with a single chair rested against the other. In the middle, the stone floor was covered in a plush rug and comfortable-looking chairs. Books and an odd assortment of devices sat scattered across every flat surface. Near one window, Ben spied an onyx table like a smaller version of the one they'd found in the Wilds for far-seeing. Even to a layman's eye, the room was filled with a wealth of magical devices.

"Who are you?" demanded Chesson, drawing up to his full height.

Avril looked at the young lord. "I am an advisor to your father."

Chesson snorted. "I know all of my father's advisors, and you are not one. His concubine, perhaps. Did he give you all of this? If you're not in the quarters with the rest of his harem, then you must be quite the roll."

Avril smirked and turned to the rest of the group. "We'll have to kill him."

Ben blinked. Lady Avril looked to be no more than sixteen or seventeen summers. Blond hair, blue eyes, red lips, a simple white tunic with blue skirts. As she declared Chesson's death sentence, she looked as innocent as any girl from Farview discussing whether they should bake cookies or a cake.

The former Veil looked at O'ecca. "Her too."

O'ecca dropped into a fighting stance, her naginata held ready in front of her.

Avril flicked her wrist. A tight burst of air smacked O'ecca across the room. Her weapon went spinning and she crashed into the wall, slumping to the ground. Another blast of air whipped Chesson's head around. A sharp crack filled the room, and Chesson fell lifelessly to the floor.

Towaal and Amelie both raised their hands, prepared to attack, but Rhys held up a hand.

"Wait."

Lady Avril raised an eyebrow at him.

He glared at her. "You could flee instead of killing them."

She smiled sweetly. "I do not see how that is advantageous for me."

"I need this girl," stated Rhys.

"I am sure you do, but I do not," responded Avril. She placed her hands on her hips and tilted her head. "Even when we worked together, we were never friends. I wouldn't have helped you then. Why do you think I will now?"

"I don't need your help. I'm only asking you to refrain from killing this girl."

Avril started tapping one of her fingers on her hip. "And?"

"We have a common cause," suggested Rhys. "You need us."

"I do?" asked Avril, her lips forming an oval of mock surprise.

"You need us to defeat the Veil," pressed Rhys.

Avril studied them, her fingers tapping a quick rhythm. "Where is Gunther? He is the one I need, along with the staff you took. I watched you leave the Purple's fortress. You had the staff, but not the mage. Now you have neither. Where is it, and where is he?"

"He took the staff on a mission for us," lied Rhys. "Without our help, you will never find him."

Avril snorted and crossed her arms.

"You know that is the truth, or you would have already found him. He slipped by you, and he will continue to do so. We can help," pleaded Rhys. "You've been plotting against the Veil for a long time. She is still there, and you are still in hiding. You were outmaneuvered all of those years ago, and from what I see in this room, nothing has changed. You need the staff, you need Gunther, and you need us to get them."

"You have no idea what I have been doing these years," declared Avril. "I've been busy."

"You need her too if you want to stay in Ooswam," said Ben, pointing to the unconscious O'ecca. "She is the answer to the Red Lord and the demons. When the Red Lord is defeated, she can convince the emperor to raise his army and stand against the demons. If he doesn't, your tower will be overrun just like the rest of Shamiil. Unless you have another plan for the demons that is."

Ben watched the former Veil. Since they arrived, her face had been expressive like a canvas she painted her thoughts on. Now, it was blank. He'd surprised her.

"You don't know about the demons, do you?" asked Ben.

Avril pursed her lips. She sighed dramatically. "Very well. Tell me about the demons."

"Hundreds of them," responded Ben. "Maybe thousands. The Purple was building an army of them. They kept them in the tunnels below the fortress. We destroyed the Purple, but the demons were released. They'll come here next."

Avril took a step toward her far-seeing table then paused. She looked to Rhys, frowning.

He nodded confirmation.

"Maybe you can survive an attack by several hundred demons," continued Ben, "but Shamiil cannot if the city is unprepared. To stop them, if you even have the ability, you would have to use enough power that even the mages in Alcott would feel it."

"She doesn't have the strength to stand against hundreds of demons alone," declared Rhys.

"Are you sure about that?" snapped Avril.

He stared at her. "I am."

Lady Avril set her hands on her hips and frowned around the room.

Finally, she admitted, "You are right. I cannot stand against so many of those creatures. Where is Gunther? If he is still in the fortress, why is he not stopping them? He could stand against a hundred demons with that hammer of his."

"I told you, he's on other business," responded Rhys.

Avril's frown turned into a glare.

"We plan to confront the Veil," said Ben. "Will you help us?"

"I will not." She paused. Her full red lips pressed together. "I will not hinder you though, either."

"Can you heal her?" Ben asked, kneeling beside O'ecca. "Let's call it a sign of good faith."

Lady Avril knelt beside O'ecca. "Haven't you heard? Mages don't help out of good faith, we always get our due. What will you offer me, young man?"

"When the time comes, we'll help you against the Veil," said Ben. "You have my word."

"Your word," smirked Avril. "What kind of currency is that? Tell me where Gunther is, and I will heal the girl."

Ben stared back at her impassively.

"He has a task that is too important to be thwarted by your meddling, no matter the consequences for us," claimed Rhys. "We will not tell you where he is now, or ever, if we cannot remain friendly."

Finally, Lady Avril acquiesced. "I will heal the girl. The boy was dead the instant I struck him. Not even I can do anything about that."

"What are we supposed to tell his father?" muttered Ben, glancing at Chesson's dead body. "He was meeting with us right before the attack. It will be well known within the palace."

"It won't matter if you don't do something about the Red Lord," advised Avril, standing from where she'd been working on O'ecca. "I suggest you deal with that situation quickly if that is your intention. I will let you go, but when the time comes, I will hold you to your word. You will not have to wait long, but I warn you, do not cross me, boy."

Ben nodded uncomfortably.

O'ecca blinked and groaned.

"You should be regaining energy quickly," the mage told the girl. "I boosted your natural reserves. Within a day or two, it will dissipate. You will feel very weak. During that time, do not overextend yourself."

Ben reached down and helped O'ecca to her feet. She stared at Chesson's prone body.

"He didn't deserve that," she accused Lady Avril.

Avril smiled coldly. "There is only one person who I care gets what they deserve."

O'ecca scooped up her naginata and glared murderously at the former Veil.

"Care to try your luck again, girl?" asked Avril.

O'ecca shook her head.

"The emperor is aware I am here," continued Avril, "but he does not know my nature. He thinks I am a scholar of sorts. I did not lie when I said I am his advisor. I would like it to stay that way. I'm willing to let you go as long as it remains beneficial to me. If I feel you are becoming too talkative or becoming a risk, I will kill you as easily as I did that fool Chesson. Understand you cannot harm me. You could only die trying. Depending on how spectacular your death is, it may inconvenience me."

301

O'ecca turned from the mage, refusing to make eye contact with her.

Turning to Rhys, Avril instructed, "Make sure she understands, or we've wasted our time discussing her fate."

"I will," agreed Rhys.

"Go now," said Avril. "The Red Lord's men converged on the emperor's throne room, but he was not there. The Red Lord is now trying to find him in the harem quarters. The emperor is not there either, so the Red Lord will not stay long. The hallways are clear, but I cannot promise they will remain so."

Rhys nodded to Avril and turned to go, waving the rest of the party after him.

Ben heard Avril make one last comment as he followed Rhys down the stairs.

"Do not think I didn't recognize you, Karina Towaal. I remember you as a brash, undisciplined initiate. Nothing seems to have changed."

"I remember you as an arrogant woman who constantly thought too much of herself and underestimated those around her," rejoined Towaal. "I guess that's two of us who haven't changed."

Avril laughed a delicate, tinkling titter. "Maybe you are right, or maybe I have changed. I cannot defeat the Veil alone. I have realized that. I've set the stage for her downfall, though, and many people will have a role to play. Be ready when it is your turn."

Towaal didn't respond. Ben heard her coming down the steps behind them.

"That was weird," remarked Ben.

Rhys grunted.

"What if she finds out where Gunther is?" asked Amelie.

"Assume that woman can hear every word we say until we're out of this compound," instructed Rhys.

They fell silent after that.

"What happened up there?" asked O'ecca finally. "All I can remember is that one moment the woman was threatening my life. Then, the next I wake up, and she's kneeling next to me. I saw Chesson. She killed him after she attacked me, didn't she? Who is that woman?"

"She's a bad memory," answered Rhys.

"She acted like she knew you," mentioned Ben.

"She used to," acknowledged the rogue.

Before he could elaborate, they made it to the palace levels of the tower and found a man standing near the foot of the stairs. He had black armor with the red stripe of the Red Lord's men painted on his chest.

"Who are you?" he demanded.

Rhys responded by pounding his fist into the unsuspecting man's face.

The guard collapsed on the stone floor.

Rhys grimaced and shook his hand before drawing his long knives. He winked at Ben. "It's easier with these. If that man's head was any harder, I could have broken a knuckle."

"This place is swarming with the Red Lord's men," said Ben, ignoring his friend's attempt at humor. "How are we supposed to protect the emperor from them?"

"You kill a snake by cutting off the head," declared O'ecca. "We don't need to battle every one of his men. We just need to find the head of the snake."

"Let's head to the harem quarters then," suggested Amelie. "If we're quick, we should find the Red Lord there."

"Let's do it," agreed Rhys.

The rogue set off down the hallway, following the directions Lady Avril had given, and the rest of the party followed.

The doors were shut, and no staff was visible. Ben assumed they'd all hidden when the attack started. The guest wing of the emperor's palace was extravagant. It reminded Ben of King Argren's keep in Whitehall. Ostentatious wealth displayed liberally. The emperor was making a point to his guests. Just like the spike-covered hilltop the palace sat on, the entire design was to give the impression of power. Apparently, the Red Lord wasn't buying it.

At a few doors, they found armored guards nervously standing watch, soldiers of visitors who had no dog in the fight. Their leaders would remain out of sight until the conflict was all but settled. Then, Ben was sure, they'd emerge and help the victors finish off whatever was left of the losers. The arms men stared at them as they jogged by but made no move to interfere. A handful of bodies marked the rooms where someone did try to interfere.

They slowed as they approached the center section of the palace. There, four wings came together to meet in a barrel-shaped core. According to O'ecca, the center was open throughout all four floors of the palace. Down the hallway, they could hear the sounds of clashing steel, shouts, and the familiar clamor of battle.

"Pass through quickly. Engage only as needed," advised Rhys.

"Where have I heard that before?" retorted Amelie.

They saw a circular balcony in front of them that overlooked the atrium. The noise of battle was coming from below.

"Maybe we'll get lucky," offered Ben. "It sounds like they're all down on the bottom floor."

Just then, half a dozen of the emperor's men backed into view, furiously defending against a group of the Red Lord's soldiers.

O'ecca charged.

"Damnit," snarled Rhys. "Follow her!"

Ben and Rhys ran after the lithe girl, spreading out on her flanks.

She smashed into the Red Lord's men with fury. They were entirely focused on the emperor's men in front of them and were completely taken by surprise. Leaping into the air and spinning, O'ecca whirled her naginata around and chopped through two men before they saw her. The first man's head flew off, and the second caught the blade of the spear on the side of his skull. A third man stumbled away from her but wasn't quick enough to avoid the long reach of the thrusting spear. It punched through the armor covering his chest and found vital organs. O'ecca twisted her wrist and yanked the weapon loose. The man slumped down.

Ben and Rhys joined the fight.

Ben swung a brutal overhand attack at one man. The blade slashed through a raised arm and buried in the man's shoulder. Ben kicked him and jerked his blade free.

The man flailed back, not yet dead, but with a severed arm and gaping wound in his shoulder, he wouldn't survive much longer.

One of the Red Lord's men charged, looping powerful swipes with his short sword. A foolish choice of weapon, thought Ben, as he used the extra reach of his longsword and rammed it into the man's eye.

Another of the Red Lord's soldiers advanced, but one of the emperor's men recovered and wrapped an arm around the soldier's head. He plunged his short sword into the soldier's side and rode the body to the floor. He then leapt up, backing slowly away from Ben.

The skirmish was already over. A squad of the Red Lord's men lay dead on the floor.

"We have no fight with you," Ben told the emperor's man.

The man glanced around at the fallen Red Lord's men and nodded. "Thank you for your help."

He and his party turned and dashed off around the balcony.

"Let's go find the Red Lord," said Rhys, shaking sticky blood off his blade.

Four floors below them, the battle raged on. Ben spared a moment and looked down. Several hundred men, wearing the thick armor common in Ooswam, surged back and forth across the marble floor. It was slick with blood, and the men scrambled and slipped. Neither side appeared to have an advantage in the ugly fight.

"Evenly matched," muttered Ben. "That could go down to the last man."

Beside him, O'ecca advised, "If one of the sides loses their leader, they'll stop fighting. That's why we have to hurry."

"Won't the emperor execute them for treason or whatever you call it here?"

O'ecca started to make her way around the balcony and Ben followed.

"They'll be taken as prisoners of the emperor," she explained. "He'll sell them as indentured servants to another lord or use them himself. They'll be paid a little, and after a few years, they'll be allowed to return to their families. It's common in Ooswam to prevent internal skirmishes from turning into full-scale battles. Let the men have a chance at a normal life, and they no longer fight after their lord falls."

Ben grunted. It sounded reasonable.

The next hall was barred by an iron gate with silver filigree work. It would have been beautiful if it wasn't smashed open. Scores of dead men, both the emperor's and the Red Lord's, lay strewn like refuse on the floor. Ben's companions stepped over them and entered.

Open spaces for pleasure lined the main walkway. Thin, silk curtains hung between different areas, separating the space and diffusing the light from the windows. Water pipes for smoking, countless decanters of wine, low couches, soft tapestries, plush carpets, and overstuffed pillows decorated the room. The place smelled like perfumed oils, sex, and the sharp tang of blood.

"He must have quite the harem," muttered Rhys appreciatively.

"I'm told it is hundreds of women," responded O'ecca.

"If Chesson had survived, you could have ruled this place one day," jested Ben.

O'ecca didn't smile at his joke.

Amelie punched him in the shoulder and he dropped his grin. Too early, he thought. Maybe they'd appreciate it later.

The kept moving deeper into the room and passed the body of one of the concubines. She was dressed in a flimsy robe and little else. Her skull was caved in. A dozen paces past her lay one of the Red Lord's men, a delicate silver knife was buried in his back. The concubine had been a loyal one.

A shout drew their attention and they hurried across the room to where the bright light of day shone through an open door. As they approached, they could hear a man raging at someone.

"You said you'd be with him!" boomed the man's voice. "You said you were his favorite and that he was wrapped around your finger."

"I am his favorite," snapped a young woman's voice. "You were supposed to attack this evening. You're three bells early. I was going to bring him to you, but his men took him when the alarm bells went off. It doesn't matter how good my plan is if you can't stick to it."

They heard the smack of flesh striking flesh. Ben winced. He was certain the girl had just tasted the back of the man's hand.

"Look," whispered Amelie.

In her grip was the small mirror Jasper had given her. It displayed a patio with a score of men on it and one woman who'd fallen to the tile floor. A huge man in bulky red lacquered armor dominated the scene. He was standing over the girl. Through the door, Ben heard him admonishing her.

"I didn't pay you to make a plan. I paid you to have the emperor in the throne room today."

The Red Lord drew his huge two-handed sword and towered over the frightened girl.

"I think your usefulness to me is at an end."

"He's distracted," hissed Rhys. "Now is the time."

Ben and his friends padded to the door and rushed out into the sunlight.

The Red Lord had his sword raised above his head and was about to bring it down on the girl. He looked up in surprise as they charged him. His men spun and barely drew steel before Ben's companions arrived.

Ben singled a man out and drew back his sword. The man responded, raising his blade in defense, but Ben ducked low and rammed a shoulder into the man's midsection, sending him flying back.

A second man jumped at Ben, evidently thinking Ben's longsword would be fouled by the first. Instead, he found himself furiously parrying Ben's attack as it whipped toward his face.

The butt of O'ecca's naginata crunched into one man's nose. Then she dropped to a knee, spinning the spear to sweep the legs out from another of the Red Lord's men.

Amelie jumped on him, stabbing down with her rapier at the gap in his armor between his breastplate and leggings.

Rhys danced between two men, lashing his longsword like a whip, slicing through their lacquer armor as if it was paper.

"That one!" shouted the Red Lord, holding his two-handed sword in one hand and pointing at Rhys with the other.

His soldiers converged on Rhys. Ben sprinted across the patio to his friend's aid. Amelie and O'ecca were left facing the Red Lord.

"Let me do this," said O'ecca.

Amelie nodded and backed away, her rapier held ready, but even if she wanted to attack, the thin blade was no match for the Red Lord's massive two-handed sword.

Ben tore his eyes away from Amelie and O'ecca as he fell onto the backs of the Red Lord's men. Three of them turned to face him, but a crackle of energy snapped in front of his eyes. All three men fell back, dancing like marionettes. The men around Rhys dropped as well, but Ben heard the Red Lord laughing. He turned and saw the man was still upright and unharmed by Towaal's lightning attack.

"He's hardened his will," the mage explained calmly.

"I thought that was useless, a fairy tale," cackled the Red Lord. "I learned it anyway, though. The Dirhadji are good for something other than smuggling slaves. I've never been so glad I disregarded my own instincts. I'm immune to you, mage."

The big man hefted his sword.

"Tell me, can your will protect you from steel?"

"You have to worry about me first," declared O'ecca, moving to confront the red-armored man.

"And us," said Ben.

"No, Ben," instructed O'ecca. "Let me do this."

Ben frowned and moved to help her, but Amelie blocked him.

"I know what she went through. That man killed her family. Let her do this."

The Red Lord stomped toward O'ecca, a smile splitting his face, clearly unconcerned about a slim girl who couldn't be more than a third his mass.

She was ready for him. Her naginata twirled in front of her, and she jumped at him, stabbing with the heavy blade of her spear.

The Red Lord stumbled back in surprise, the tip of the spear striking his armor but not with enough force to penetrate and damage him. He slashed a powerful blow in response, but O'ecca easily ducked under it, wisely avoiding parrying his huge weapon.

"You're quick, girl. I'll give you that," he acknowledged. "Doesn't do you any good if you don't have the power to get through a man's armor. Your brothers were quick too."

O'ecca didn't respond with words. She leapt at him again, feinting at his face and then stabbing at his leg. He shuffled out of the way. Her spear missed him by a finger-length. The Red Lord's face swelled with rage and he stormed at her, slashing rapid downward blows. She danced back, letting his blade swing by, catching nothing but air.

Ben gripped his longsword tightly. The Red Lord was relying on his size, the length of his sword, and his heavy armor, but he was fast too. He moved the two-handed blade with the ease a lesser man would swing a short sword. When O'ecca attacked him, he was quick to step out of reach or turn his blade to defense. The two-hander was long enough to limit O'ecca's normal reach advantage.

"We have to stop this," muttered Ben. "She needs our help."

"She needs to do it on her own," responded Amelie. "He might be bigger and stronger, but she's faster. Look."

As Amelie spoke, O'ecca jabbed with her naginata and caught the Red Lord on the side of the head. It dazed him but wasn't a strong enough blow to break his skull.

He blinked his eyes and raised his sword. Blood flowed down his face and his lips twisted into a bestial snarl. He swung at her and she scurried back. Anger painting his face, he attacked again and again. She didn't meet his blows. She didn't attempt to strike him either. She kept retreating and letting his swings sail by.

The concubine he'd been about to kill when they arrived started to scoot away toward the door.

Amelie saw her and walked over. She kicked the toe of her boot into the woman's stomach. The soft-bodied concubine flipped over onto her side and groaned.

"You're not going anywhere," Amelie snapped at her.

The Red Lord stopped, glared at O'ecca, and howled a battle cry. He charged, clearly ready to end the fight.

O'ecca didn't run. Instead, a heartbeat before he reached her, she crouched and dropped the butt of her naginata to the stone floor, setting it against her foot. The arms-length blade was pointed directly at the Red Lord's chest.

He tried to knock it aside with his sword, but he was coming too fast, and the tip was already past his guard. The blade of O'ecca's naginata slammed into the Red Lord's chest. He was skewered by the force of his own charge.

Her feet slid back across the tiles, pushed by the big man's momentum, but two hand-lengths of steel disappeared into his armor before he stopped. His sword clattered to the tiles and he staggered back, gripping the haft of the naginata in his hands. Blood dripped from the man's mouth, and he stared disbelieving at O'ecca.

Like a tall tree, the big man swayed, then fell.

O'ecca strode to his body and grabbed her spear. She tore it from the Red Lord's corpse and spit on him.

"Well done," said Amelie. "You can't fill the hole in your heart left by your family, but at least you have closure now. At least they have justice."

O'ecca nodded, tears filling her eyes. "They have justice."

"Let's go," said Rhys quietly. "We need to let the men fighting below know the Red Lord is dead, and we still have much to discuss with the emperor if we can find him."

"You think they'll just believe us?" asked Ben. "We need a symbol to show he's dead."

"We could bring his head," suggested Rhys. "Want to cut it off?"

Ben stared at him.

The rogue sighed. "Why do I have to do everything myself?"

Ben looked away as Rhys chopped down with his longsword, severing the Red Lord's head.

Amelie grabbed the traitorous concubine and dragged her to her feet. "You're coming with us too."

They ran back through the harem and to the circular chamber where the fiercest fighting was taking place.

"The Red Lord is dead!" bellowed Rhys, leaning over the balustrade, brandishing the Red Lord's severed head.

The men continued to fight below. There were half as many as before, but as Ben watched, fresh soldiers poured in. Without knowing where the emperor or the Red Lord was, the men must be converging where the fighting was most intense. The blood-slick marble floor below them was turning into a charnel house.

"Towaal, can you help?" asked Rhys.

She nodded.

"The Red Lord is dead!" called Rhys again. This time, the sound seemed to shake the palace. Rhys slung the head down from the balcony to the thickest contingent of the Red Lord's men.

13

JUST REWARDS

THEY SAT IN A QUIET STUDY, waiting to meet the emperor. They'd seen him, briefly, after the battle for the compound. He was an older man with a long, white mustache and a slow, measured gait. His shoulders had been slumped, evidently feeling the weight of the death of his only son and the traitorous attack by the Red Lord.

News of how the fight stopped and their role in procuring the Red Lord's head had spread quickly throughout the palace. So far, there had been no discussion about their role in Chesson's death. Ben hoped they would be gone by the time the emperor began putting that timeline together.

They'd been told that the emperor was eager to meet them to thank them for stopping the coup. Ben was glad. It should make convincing the man to help them that much easier. He hoped to use the opportunity to warn him about the demons and also ask for his assistance in Alcott.

"How many men do you think we can request?" asked Ben. "If we play on his gratitude, we might be able to acquire a decent number of them. I know he'll want to keep plenty here, but a few companies could make a big difference."

"I'm not sure he'll be open to that, Ben," replied Amelie.

"We deserve some reward," argued Ben. "Surely, he'll want to thank us for saving his realm. His men were surprised and losing the battle. I heard only a tiny fraction of his forces are stationed near the palace. If it hadn't been for us, his guard wouldn't have been enough. We stopped the Red Lord, and with our help, Crai roused the emperor's men from their barracks around the city."

"The gratitude of powerful lords isn't always the same as small-town farmers and brewers," cautioned Towaal. "Be careful when asking for his resources. Do not assume he'll readily assist us."

"Even Lord Jason agreed to help us a little," protested Ben. "The emperor is not a strong ruler if he can't acknowledge our assistance."

"Start with a boat," advised Rhys. "See how he reacts to that request. After that, maybe we can ask for more. Towaal and Amelie are right. It's never wise to make assumptions about how a powerful man will assist a weaker."

Ben sat back on a comfortable couch and frowned.

Time passed and he began to fidget. He was sure the emperor had a lot to do after fending off a coup. The man also had to prepare for the demons if O'ecca had already warned him, but they didn't need much of his time. They'd been sitting there for bells. Ben stood and began to pace back and forth across the room.

Rhys acted bored as well and started rooting around in cabinets and drawers in the room, probably looking for booze. Towaal and Amelie watched the both of them.

Lady Towaal had been quiet ever since they'd found Lady Avril. When Ben tried to ask her about the former Veil, she simply shook her head and declared it a conversation for another time.

"There's nothing we can do, Ben, except wait for him," remarked Amelie. "You can't hurry an emperor."

"I know," acknowledged Ben. "That's what is so frustrating."

There was a sharp rap on the door, but before anyone could call out, it opened.

O'ecca slipped inside, glancing over her shoulder as she did. She was dressed in traditional attire and was unarmed. After traveling through the desert with her, it was strange seeing her in the wide silk dresses and pale makeup typical of Ooswam's noble houses. Her hair was gathered in an intricate bun, and her lips were painted into a bright red pout.

Or a frown, thought Ben.

"You need to leave," she stated without preamble.

"What?" asked Ben.

O'ecca sighed. "I tried to convince him otherwise, but the emperor is determined that you should stay and help battle the demons. He just finished questioning his concubine, the one who betrayed him, and he's already spoken to Crai. He knows what you are capable of. He wants to use you. With the coup and the demons, he is scared. I don't think there's anything you can say to change his mind."

"He should be helping us," exclaimed Ben, "not kidnapping us!"

"I'm sure he doesn't see it that way," remarked Amelie calmly. "O'ecca, how do we get out?"

"Wait," said Ben. "This isn't right."

"I am sorry," assured O'ecca. "It isn't fair, but the emperor does as he wills. Having a group of heroes under his banner who defeated the Red Lord and a cabal of powerful mages will go a long way toward cowing any lords who feel the coup gives them cover to act out. He'd compensate you richly, I am sure. If you wanted, you could likely establish your own Houses here in Ooswam just like the Red Lord did when he stopped a coup."

"That's not what we want," grumbled Ben.

"I know," said O'ecca. "That is why I came to warn you. You must leave now, or you may lose your chance. The emperor is changing his clothing after questioning that woman, and when he is done, he will come here."

Ben stalked around the room in frustration. Finally, he turned to O'ecca. "Will you come with us? You know what we are up against in Alcott. We could use your spear."

A bittersweet smile crossed O'ecca's face. "The emperor requested I join his court. What's left of my family, my people, they will be protected and cared for if I acquiesce. I am not able to leave."

Amelie crossed the room and hugged O'ecca.

"It's better than marrying Chesson," Amelie said, trying to insert some levity into the dark mood.

O'ecca guffawed. "That is true. Now, you cannot delay further. Take the window and circle to the front gate. It's unlikely the guards will have been told to keep you here, yet. Once the emperor finds out you are gone, word will spread. The entire city will be dangerous for you. Having you under his banner would be a boon for him, but anyone finding out you fled his service would be terrible in his eyes. You cannot stop in Shamiil. You must keep going."

"You are certain you cannot leave?" asked Ben. "There must be another way to help your people."

O'ecca shook her head. "You have your battles ahead, and I have mine."

Rhys pushed open the window and ducked his head out.

"A two-story drop," he reported.

Ben groaned. He watched as the rogue wasted no time and disappeared through the opening. Towaal followed quickly. After one last hug for O'ecca, Amelie went out as well.

"Thank you for going with us to Qooten," said Ben. "We couldn't have made it as far as we did without you."

"You fought the Red Lord in Indo. You prevented a coup by him. You defeated the demon swarm overrunning Ayd and defeated the Purple. Ben, Ooswam owes you and your friends our thanks. I am sorry the emperor does not see it that way, but know you have my support. When the emperor has forgotten about this, I will do what I can to assist you. Ooswam is behind you. You have my loyalty."

Ben nodded then squeezed out the window after his friends. As Rhys said, it was a two-story drop to the lush lawn below. He dropped down and landed softly.

Yet again, they were fleeing a fortress with only their weapons and the cloaks on their backs. Yet again, they had an uncertain path toward a dangerous horizon.

14

INTO THE BARREL

THEY PASSED through the palace gates without incident and rushed down the winding walkway into the city. The people in the streets were on edge, aware that a coup had been attempted, that the emperor had survived, and little else.

Ben guessed they feared an inquisition. Some of the people in Shamiil must have assisted the Red Lord, and the emperor would come looking for them. After their own experience, Ben guessed the emperor wasn't the type to worry about sticking a few innocent fish in the barrel as long as he got the traitors.

"Where should we go?" asked Amelie.

"We can be out the south gate long before the emperor realizes we've left," offered Towaal. "Four of us traveling light, they're not going to be able to catch up to us. We can follow the coast until we get to a port and find passage there."

"If we don't find a vessel waiting," argued Amelie, "we could be stuck for days. We have no idea if the emperor will simply let us go or if he'll pursue us. This is the biggest port on the continent and there are plenty of ships here. Let's take one."

"The port here is too risky," challenged Rhys. "Even if we're not pursued out of Shamiil, they'll check the harbor. We may have only a few bells before soldiers are scouring the docks. It's too tight a timeline to guarantee we weigh anchor before they find us."

"We're going to Alcott. We have to find a ship somewhere," remarked Towaal.

"We know of one vessel we could catch a ride on," suggested Ben.

Rhys raised an eyebrow at him.

"Martin," added Ben.

Rhys grinned. "To the Fish Head, then."

"Let me guess," grumbled Amelie. "It's a tavern?"

Rhys winked at her.

THREE BELLS LATER, they sat in a small, grimy room. A single, hanging lamp lit the circular table in the middle of the space and not much else. Ben was glad it didn't illuminate the corners of the room as he was almost certain he'd heard the squeak of rodents.

"You sure that's safe to drink?" asked Amelie, gesturing at the ale Ben clutched in his hands.

He shrugged. "The liquid is boiled when making ale. It's probably safer than any water served in this place."

Amelie winced and pushed her tankard away.

Rhys refilled his ale and offered the pitcher to Amelie. "If things go according to plan, we'll be stuck on a boat for the next four weeks. There's no telling how they'll be stocked. I suggest drinking now while you can."

Amelie turned up her nose. "If that's what's available, I think I'll pass."

"How about you?" Ben asked Lady Towaal.

She shook her head.

"Is everything okay?" he asked her.

She paused, rubbed a hand over her face, then answered. "Seeing Lady Avril again was deeply disturbing. I've been wracking my brain trying to figure out what she has been doing here, what it portends that we saw her."

"She looks like a girl," remarked Amelie. "A few years younger than I am."

"She's not young by anyone's standard," responded Rhys.

"You knew her before?" inquired Towaal.

Rhys grimaced then gulped down his ale. "Aye."

"Why didn't you tell me?"

Rhys refilled his ale mug and sat back before answering. "Avril was the fourth woman to wear the Veil and the longest to hold the seat. I knew them all. Every one of them needed people with my particular skill set from time to time. That's how you and I first met, remember, right after the Blood Bay?"

Towaal nodded curtly.

Rhys continued, "Sometimes, I'd be contacted by an intermediary. Sometimes, when it was a sensitive target, I'd work with the individual mages. I worked with Avril more than I care to admit."

"A sensitive target?" wondered Amelie.

"Through five Veils, the transition of power in the Sanctuary has never been bloodless. These are ambitious women who live forever. When someone new is ready to take the seat…" Rhys shrugged and left the rest unsaid.

"You helped those transitions?" asked Towaal.

"I didn't help remove Avril, but I helped her get there," responded Rhys. "I don't know what happened when she fell from power. After seeing the woman alive today, I'm second guessing everything I thought I knew about it."

"But you worked with her before then," accused Towaal. "You were her blade in the night."

Rhys nodded and turned up his tankard, draining the ale in three big gulps. He refilled it and looked at Towaal.

"When the Sanctuary rose to power, the world was chaotic," explained Rhys. "It was dark times. The world had nearly been overrun by demons, and the various factions of mages dealt with it in their own ways. The First Mages no longer held sway, and the younger generation were exploring the depths of their power, sometimes in awful ways. You all know of the Society of the Burning Hand, Eldred's death magic?"

They nodded.

"Groups like them were growing in power. They'd started to use that power to gain territory and control cities and people. The Sanctuary at the time was a stabilizing force. They opposed the worst of the mages. They offered free healing to anyone who came across them and advice to the leaders. They were good, as much as any group of mages at the time."

Ben sipped his ale, barely noticing the sour undernotes. He listened intently to Rhys.

"Back then, the concept of highborn was just beginning. There were no families with long lineages to brag on, no wealth and fortresses passed down generation to generation. Leadership was passed from the most capable person to the next, usually because the first died either a natural or a violent death. It was that way for a long time. The Sanctuary was no different except the mages didn't die natural deaths. I helped them out. It was a small evil, I thought, to conduct a greater good."

"Is that really why you did it?" challenged Amelie.

Rhys smirked. "They offered the usual incentives as well. Gold, women, and drink." He shrugged. "I helped Avril with a number of smaller tasks while she rose through the ranks. When she came to me with a request to remove her predecessor, I welcomed the challenge. After that, we continued to work together from time to time. I really did believe she was dead, though. That was the word all over Alcott."

"I remember," murmured Towaal. "We were told assassins snuck in and killed her in her garden. They hanged several unsavory-looking men because of it. They even had a funeral for Lady Avril with a body. There were rumors, but Coatney, the Veil, was my friend. I didn't believe she had anything to do with it."

"Maybe she didn't," said Rhys quietly. "I assumed she thought I was loyal to Avril and paid someone else to stick the knife. With Avril still alive... I'm not sure what to think."

Ben blinked.

"So, she's been in hiding for hundreds of years?" wondered Amelie.

"She must have known Lady Coatney was ready to move on her and assume power," guessed Rhys. "She left before she ended up like all of the other Veils before her."

"Then Coatney must know Lady Avril still lives," pondered Amelie.

"And she'd know that Avril wasn't going to quietly accept an early retirement," added Rhys. "I think we can assume these two women have been plotting against each other for centuries. They are powerful and devious. It makes me wonder how many of the current difficulties in the world can be laid at their feet."

"We have to do something about it," declared Amelie.

Rhys grinned. "Not enough on your plate already?"

"Amelie's right," said Ben, "but so is Rhys. We have to prioritize. We'll deal with the mages when we can. First, we've got to get to Alcott and find Milo and the wyvern fire staff. It's too dangerous for that to fall into the wrong hands." Ben paused. "Well, it already is in the wrong hands. You know what I mean."

"Don't forget about Eldred," mentioned Rhys. "We're going to have to confront her sooner or later."

"Ben is right. First things first," interrupted Towaal. "We have to get out of Shamiil."

A knock sounded on the door. Ben moved to open it.

Martin slunk in and immediately went to the ale pitcher. He filled a mug and slurped it noisily. When he sat it down, he glanced around the room. "This isn't going to be as easy as we anticipated."

Amelie groaned.

"What do you mean?" questioned Ben.

Martin scrubbed a hand over his face and leaned forward.

"Word's gotten out that some people escaped from the emperor's compound, people who look suspiciously like you. You should have told me who you were running from," chided the man. "The emperor's own guards have been patrolling the docks. I'm told no one is getting out the gates without a thorough search of their wagons. I was going to walk you straight down to the ship. We'd both be locked in some dungeon!"

"Who did you think we were running from?" asked Ben.

Martin shrugged. "The usual. Customs officials or the thieves' guild."

"We're not thieves," muttered Amelie, acting offended. "We don't interact with them, and we certainly don't run from them."

"Well," conceded Ben, "there was that one time in Fabrizo. Also in Irrefort, now that I'm thinking about it."

"And the City," mentioned Martin.

Ben glanced at the man. "I must have missed that one."

"What?" said Martin with a snort. "You think your old partner was dealing honestly that whole time? Sure, he kept it a little clean while you were around, but he's a thief through and through."

"Renfro," muttered Ben.

Martin nodded. "He's loyal, though. I don't think he'd mind if we borrow the ship for a bit to get you out of here. Long as you don't get us caught by hiding things from me."

Ben sighed. "You're right. We should have told you. It is the emperor we're running from. It's not like you think, though. We did a favor for him. He wants us to stay, but we need to leave. I suspect he'll forget about it in a few days. Until then, we can't be in the city."

"I can get you out," assured Martin. "It's what I do, but it's not going to be a pleasant evening stroll anymore. We've got to smuggle you."

"Smuggle us?" queried Amelie.

Martin grinned. "That's my job, honey. You won't get caught, but it could be a bit of a bumpy ride."

~

BEN GRUMBLED as he climbed into the filthy barrel. It was damp and smelled of the sour ale from the Fish Head. He wedged himself deeper, pulling his knees against his chest and shifting, trying to force himself lower so Martin could affix the cap to cover him.

In a barrel beside him, Rhys complained, "I've had dreams where I dove into an ale barrel, but it never went like this."

"You can try walking past the emperor's soldiers," responded Martin dryly.

Ben sighed. "Can you push me down? I don't have the leverage to get in here."

Martin put his hands on Ben's shoulders. Apologetically, he offered, "Sorry about this."

"I don't like small spaces," admitted Ben, wiggling in a vain attempt to get comfortable.

"I said I was sorry."

Martin pushed down, shoving Ben deeper into the barrel. The slimy, ale-damp wood slid across his skin. Ben felt a finger-sized splinter break off into his arm. He winced in pain from the splinter and from the pressure of the barrel against his knees and chest.

"Should be good enough," muttered Martin.

One of his crew came over and set the cap over Ben's head.

Ben closed his eyes in the darkness and tried to ignore the four quick hammer blows that nailed the barrel shut. He supposed he should be thankful the story was that they were sneaking out empty barrels, or else Martin would have insisted on pouring ale in there with them. As it was, the empty ale barrel was unpleasant enough. He grunted when someone tipped the container over. Then his stomach lurched as the barrel started to roll.

He tried not to think about the tiny space, smaller than the cell in Fabrizo, the tight bunks on a ship, and anywhere else he'd ever found himself. He shifted his focus to where they were going, trying to block out the sense of creeping dread in the small, dark barrel.

Martin and his crew would roll the four of Ben's companions down to the docks, along with half a dozen other empty barrels, and then load them onto their ship. They'd sail with the midnight tide, but until then, Ben was stuck inside the foul-smelling container. It didn't make it better when he realized he'd been drinking ale out of a very similar barrel just half a bell before.

The ale sloshed in his stomach as he was turned over and over on the long journey down to the docks. He squeezed his eyes shut and tried not to think about getting sick, which only made it worse. After an interminable time, they stopped, though his head continued to spin.

He heard muffled voices outside. Someone tapped on the wood with hard knuckles. He heard more taps and then a screeching sound as one of the barrels must have been pried opened. Customs or soldiers, he guessed, ensuring the barrels were empty of smuggled goods. The problem was the barrels weren't all empty. If someone opened one of the ones his friends were hiding in, they couldn't help but discover them. And he was stuck, unable to get himself out, and unarmed even if he could. Martin's men were carrying the weapons.

More muffled voices then finally, a clink of a coin purse and the barrel started to roll again.

Ben was bounced and jostled for another quarter bell, his

forehead banging against the damp wood and his legs cramping from the awkward position they were forced into. His stomach churned. Belatedly, he realized his bowels were full. By his count, he had five ales back at the Fish Head, and he'd forgotten to pee before climbing into the barrel. He groaned, thinking of the bells still left before the ship set sail and it was safe for them to climb out.

His barrel slammed against another one and he heard a muted squeal. Amelie, he thought. The world tilted, and suddenly, he was upside down. He slid down and banged his head on the cap of the barrel, which was now below him. Moments passed, and the blood rushed to his head.

Without warning, he felt the barrel lifted up and it swung through the air. It crashed down hard onto the deck of the ship and his face was smashed into the wood again. His neck was twisted awkwardly, and the entire weight of his body rested on his cheek and nose.

The barrel was dragged into position, jostling him further. Then, mercifully, the movement ceased. He thanked whatever lucky stars that had stopped the jostling, until he realized that the barrel was in place. It wouldn't be touched again, and he was lying upside down.

The bells passed.

Ben listened to the shouts and calls from the sailors, trying to guess when they were finally ready to sail. Over and over, he guessed wrong.

He passed out, either from boredom, or the blood pounding in his head.

He woke suddenly when his barrel was toppled over. A sharp crack and the cap was pried off. Strong hands reached in and grabbed Ben's tunic, hauling him out of the tiny space.

He lay on the deck of the ship, panting like a dying fish. His entire body tingled as blood rushed to his extremities.

Beside him, Rhys was sprawled on his back, staring up at the midnight sky.

Amelie was kneeling, a pool of vomit lay below her. She fingered slimy strands of hair and flopped onto her side.

"You didn't have any barrels that were used for lavender oil or cotton maybe?" she griped.

Martin, who had assisted them out, snorted. "We sell ale, lady. That's all the barrels we got."

Towaal was standing, stretching her back and shaking her arms to loosen her shoulders.

"I don't think I'll ever drink ale again," complained Rhys.

Ben snorted and the rogue laughed.

"You're right," admitted Rhys.

"As long as you don't mind sea water, you can wash up at the back of the ship," suggested Martin. "Though, I'd wait until we're out of the harbor. There are rags and soap behind the forecastle. We saved a bunk for you, and we've got some spare clothes you might want to change into. You four smell terrible."

Ben grunted and rolled onto his stomach. Slowly and painfully, he stood. His muscles protested, and his joints cracked. He shook his arms and stomped his feet, slowly feeling his blood begin to circulate again. Once he got moving, the sharp tingling sensation felt good.

"You two go first," suggested Rhys, still not moving off his back.

Ben looked at Amelie and she winked at him. They moved to the back of the ship and saw a couple of buckets with ropes tied to them. They waited a few moments until the vessel cleared the harbor and then Ben dropped two of the buckets over the side and filled them in the water below. He hauled them back up and turned to find Amelie had stripped off her shirt.

A silly grin stretched across his face as Ben brought her the buckets.

"Need some help?" he asked, looking around to see if anyone could see them. "I could wash your back."

"Yes, that would be nice," she murmured. "When I'm done with my hair, you can start on my back. There's a lot of me that needs to get clean."

She ducked down and Ben helped pour the bucket over her head. She scrubbed at it with soap and rinsed it with sea water. Finally satisfied, she stood and turned her back to him.

Ben's grin grew wider. He sloshed water across her smooth skin, watching the tiny rivulets that formed when he brought the wet rag over her shoulders. He stripped off his own shirt and began soaping her back. He ran his hands over her, feeling the small raised scars she'd accumulated in their time together, and marveled at the hard muscle lying beneath her silky skin.

Amelie leaned back against his bare chest, and his hands slid around to her front. He squeezed the rag, covering her chest with soapy water. Then, he felt her breasts. Her nipples stiffened underneath his touch. After a few moments, Amelie caught his hand and pushed it lower, over her ribcage, past her flat belly and navel, and down to her belt.

"It's dirty down there, too," she whispered, turning her face to bury it in his neck. "Do you think you can help?"

She undid her belt and slipped her britches down over her hips.

Ben felt his excitement rising.

Amelie must have too. She wiggled against him, pressing her body against his. He heard a small moan as his hand dipped between her legs.

"Hey!" yelled Rhys. "You weren't the only ones stuck in those ale barrels. Are you getting clean back there or just wasting time?"

Amelie yelped, scrambling to cover herself, but Ben saw Rhys hadn't come around the side of the forecastle. Or maybe he had and then ducked back out of sight.

"J-Just finding the soap," stammered Ben loudly. "Give us a few moments."

He and Amelie quickly rinsed off and changed into the clothing Martin's men had provided.

Amelie grabbed Ben and pulled him close, grasping his head and pulling it to hers. Her lips parted and her tongue darted into his mouth.

"We'll find time later and pick back up where we left off," she whispered.

"I can't wait," responded Ben.

He thought he really couldn't wait.

He briefly considered tossing Rhys off the back of the ship, but he felt bad when they came around and he saw the sour ale still clinging to the man. Even Lady Towaal looked perturbed. She held her arms away from her sides as if she was disgusted to touch herself.

Rhys, Ben couldn't help but notice, already had an ale mug in hand.

Martin nodded at it. "The men get restless if we unload everything. I always keep a few kegs held back for the return trip. Fancy a mug?"

Ben glanced at Amelie and she smiled at him, evidently pleased he would seek her opinion.

"Sure," responded Ben. He didn't have anything else to do for the next four weeks.

BY THE NEXT MORNING, Ben realized they did have something to do. Something they needed to do. They needed to plan. He called Amelie, Towaal, and Rhys together. They met in the cargo hold of the ship where they'd have privacy from the crew.

"We've been following leads and relying on hope," stated Ben.

"More often than not, it's backfired on us. I think we are worse off than before we went to the South Continent."

"We stopped the Purple from using demons as a weapon, and we gained an ally in O'ecca," reminded Rhys. "The emperor isn't our friend, but we have someone close to him now. We know we can't do this alone, which means we need to enlist others. In that sense, the mission wasn't a total failure."

Ben stared at him.

Rhys sighed. "You're right. In all other respects, it was a failure."

Amelie touched the rogue's shoulder, evidently thinking about Corinne.

"The demons won't wait for us," responded Ben. "The Alliance and the Coalition won't either. We don't even need to get into Lady Avril, the Veil, and whatever is planned for the staff Milo took. No, we don't have time for another wild chase around the world. We have to settle down, agree on what we can do, and do it."

"We're listening," said Towaal, a sly smile forming on her lips.

"I was hoping you might have an idea," suggested Ben.

"As Rhys said," replied Towaal, "we need people to join us. We can't do it alone."

"How do we get more people to help?" pressed Ben.

"We need a leader," answered Towaal, "someone who can inspire them. Someone who can give them a reason for hope amongst the threat of darkness. If people realize there is another option between the Alliance and the Coalition, they'll take it. If they realize there is someone standing up to the demons, they'll follow. The Veil, Lady Avril, neither one of those women will ever gain followers through anything other than fear."

Ben sat back, glancing between Towaal, Amelie, and Rhys.

"It's too bad we lost Gunther," he said. "He was the kind of man people would follow."

Towaal leaned forward. "Ben, don't you see? Gunther

followed you. Amelie followed you. Corinne followed you. O'ecca followed you. Rhys and I decided to follow you."

Ben blinked.

"You are our leader, Ben."

"I'm no lord," he protested. "No mage. Not even a blademaster."

"She's right, Ben," stated Amelie. "You aren't a lord, a mage, or a blademaster, but you're a good man. A better man than any other I have met. Nearly everyone we come across agrees to help you. They sense the same thing I do, that you can be something special. Something Alcott needs right now."

"Some of the people I ask for help agree," said Ben, "but some of them try to capture or kill us. Remember why we fled Shamiil?"

"You can't please everyone," quipped Rhys.

"I don't know what to do!" complained Ben. "I don't have the strength or the knowledge to do this, to be a leader against these forces."

"You're not alone, Ben," assured Towaal. "A leader of people doesn't have to be the strongest, or the wisest, or even have the best ideas. The leader has to be the one who inspires people, who takes what they have to offer, and molds it into something more. You make us greater than we are as individuals."

"I don't even know where to start," muttered Ben.

"Step by step," advised Towaal. "What can we do that will have the biggest impact, and what can we address that is most urgent? That is where you should start."

Ben frowned.

"If we can find Milo and the wyvern fire staff, that would be a big impact," stated Rhys. "We need that weapon to face the hordes of demons loose in Alcott."

"Eldred is urgent," responded Amelie. "We have to assume she'll still be hunting us. One way or the other, we're going to have to face her. I don't see any way around it. We can do it on our terms, or we can wait until she surprises us."

"There are thousands of demons loose in the north. They'll continue to cross unrestrained," said Towaal. "The Alliance and Coalition are still gearing for war. Those are big problems. We can't solve them today, but we can start to plan. We can put things into motion."

"I agree Eldred is the most urgent concern, but we can't do anything about her while we're on this ship," challenged Ben. "We don't even know where she is."

"She's going to come for us," said Amelie, talking her way through an idea. "After what I did to her face in the Sanctuary and then when I stabbed her in Hamruhg, she won't rest until she kills me. If we make ourselves known facing any of these other threats, she'll find us. What if we made it easy for her?"

"What do you mean?" asked Ben.

"I doubt she knows exactly where we are or where we are going. She can't track us by our blood. She likely couldn't track our journey in the barrels through far-seeing, but there is one other way she could find us. We could use the thought meld and indiscriminately give out our location."

Towaal laughed out loud, startling Ben.

"That's a bold idea," acknowledged Rhys.

They fell silent.

"It could work," said Ben finally. "If we allowed her to know where we are and do it a few times, she'd know our course. She'd know exactly where we are headed."

Amelie nodded, determination on her face.

"It's risky," advised Ben. "We've faced her before, and we had to flee. Are we sure we can beat her? Maybe we should find Jasper first, and see if he can face her."

"We can beat her," said Rhys. He drew his longsword. "I've been thinking about it. Eldred uses dark magic. She feeds on death. She draws in power every time something is killed near her. It makes her stronger. Her magic is a void, always seeking to be filled. My longsword feeds on life. That is why I aged in Northport. The sword drew heavily from me when I faced the arch-demons. If I can fill the void inside her, her power would be greatly diminished, and I think we could beat her."

"Would using that much power with your sword be any different from what happened in Northport?" worried Ben.

Rhys looked at him silently.

"Rhys," cried Ben. "We can find another way."

The rogue shook his head. "I told you after Corinne passed that I felt the end. Maybe this is it. Maybe it isn't. One thing we know, we have to stop Eldred. We have to reclaim the wyvern fire staff. We won't accomplish everything we want to do without sacrifice, Ben."

"We need allies," argued Ben. "I can't think of anyone else I'd rather have by my side."

"I may not suffer the same effects I did in Northport," responded Rhys. "I'd never used the sword like that, and I didn't know what would happen. Maybe now that I do know, I can contain it and be more efficient. It's a huge risk, I admit, but it's a necessary gamble. We have to face her sooner or later. Let's do it now when we can pick the time and place. Besides, if you keep saying I'm the only one you want by your side, Amelie may get a little jealous."

Amelie rolled her eyes.

Ben looked to Towaal, hoping the mage would have another solution.

"You are the leader, Ben," she reminded him. "The decision is yours. If it helps, I think this is our best chance to stop Eldred, and hopefully Milo, before they return to the City. Once they're behind the Sanctuary's walls, I don't know how we can get to them. We can't make a direct assault on the Veil. She has too many mages under her command. We can't win an open battle against all of them."

"Ben," said Amelie. "We can't avoid a confrontation with Eldred forever. We're going to have to fight her. If we have a plan, we have a chance. If she finds us when we're not ready, it will be over before it starts."

Ben grimaced. Finally, he responded, "Do you have the thought meld with you?"

She drew the disc from her pouch. "I have this, my rapier, and hardly anything else."

"Good," Ben said with a sigh. "Let's tell Jasper where we are headed and cross our fingers that Eldred is listening."

AFTER CONNECTING with Jasper through the thought meld, Rhys and Towaal stood.

"I'll tell Martin to change course," she said.

"Do you need me to talk to him?" asked Ben.

"He remembers me from the City," replied Towaal. "Being a mage has its uses. He'll do as I ask."

"I'm going to find a sunny spot on deck," said Rhys. "I want some fresh air, and I need to explore what I can do with the sword. I've had this thing for centuries. Whenever I needed it, I was able to draw from the ambient life around me. Northport was the first time I drew from myself in such a high amount. Of course, that was also the first time I'd faced a dozen arch-demons at once. I don't think Eldred will be any easier. I want to test how quickly I can gather energy."

The mage and the rogue made their way up the narrow ladder out of the cargo hold.

Ben looked at Amelie.

"I believe there was something you are supposed to be doing for me," said Amelie, a coy smile crawling across her lips.

Ben raised an eyebrow and grinned as she leaned back against the curved hull of the ship. He crawled over to her and hovered above. His lips met hers. Her lips parted and she wrapped her arms around him. He kissed her, deep and long, and then moved to her neck, tasting her skin. It was salty from the water and the sea air. He moved down to her collarbone.

She stripped off her shirt and britches, giving him access to her body, grabbing him and pushing him where she wanted him to go.

He took his time, touching her, kissing her, working his way down below her waist. He grinned to himself as she writhed beneath him. He used his lips and tongue, alternating fast and slow rhythms, flicking across her sensitive skin until she wouldn't be teased anymore. She moved to her knees and shoved him down where she'd been lying.

"You going to return the favor and tease me?" he asked, a grin splitting his face.

"I don't tease," she declared.

She yanked off his pants, straddled him, and plunged down on top of him.

Ben's eyes rolled back in his head and he let out a groan of pleasure.

They stayed down in the cargo hold for another three bells before finally, exhausted and completely spent, they climbed up to the deck of the ship.

Rhys was walking across it and saw them.

"Hey, I was looking for you in our bunk," he called. "We'll need to be ready when we get off this thing, so I was thinking we could do the Ohms. Get a little exercise, a stretch, and explore on how it can help harden our wills."

"I-I, uh…" Ben stammered.

Blushing furiously, Amelie admitted, "We already got in a bit of a stretch. I think we could use a little rest now. Maybe later?"

"You, uh, stretched that long with Ben?" wondered Rhys. "I would've thought that'd be over quickly."

Ben rolled his eyes at his friend.

Rhys winked at him. "I'm going to check if Martin has more of that ale. Let me know when you've recuperated enough to do something productive."

Ben watched his friend walk away. He knew the rogue was still in pain over Corinne, but he was glad that some of the man's humor had returned. They had a long road, and if Rhys gave up now, he wouldn't make it to the end.

15

AKEW WOODS

"It's sparsely populated, which could save some lives, and it's far enough from the Sanctuary she can't get help from them. Shamiil is one of its few trading partners, so it will make sense that we are on a vessel headed there," stated Rhys.

"Why does it sound so familiar?" wondered Ben.

"Akew Woods is where Saala and Seneschal Tomas went before we fled the Sanctuary," explained Amelie. "Remember? Tomas said they were sent on a diplomatic mission. We later found it was to get them away from the City so Lord Jason could snatch me from the Sanctuary."

"What kind of mission would your father have in Akew Woods?" wondered Towaal.

Amelie shook her head. "None that make sense to me, but I wonder now if Tomas did have some reason to go there? Or he may have simply been looking for a way to get Saala out of the City. Regardless, he had other immediate plans for me. I don't think anything he did in Akew Woods will impact us."

"We can hope," said Towaal.

Ben could tell the mage was worried about any unknown

factor, and he didn't blame her. They were counting on everything falling into place perfectly, and if it didn't, they could be dead before they had a chance to react.

When using the thought meld to contact Jasper, they asked Martin to steer close to other ships that were following the same trade route. Eldred would know where they were and where they were going, but she didn't know which ship they were on. They hoped that she wouldn't simply torch anything that came within sight of land. Instead, they expected she would be watching the town, waiting for them to disembark.

Based on her past behavior, they believed the dark mage would want to confront them. She would try to toy with them before delivering a fatal blow. They needed that, so they could get close enough for Rhys to take her on. The plan had risk, but Ben was confident they'd assessed the woman's personality accurately. She liked getting her hands dirty. She would want to see their blood when she spilled it.

The trick was that they had to surprise her and not the other way around. In preparation, Ben found one of the sailors who'd been to Akew Woods and quizzed the man about the town.

"Not much to see there," the scrawny sea faring man declared. "It's a small place, much smaller than the City, and you can't go inland. They got uncivilized people living outside of town in the woods. The town itself is a trading hub, so there's a lot of visitors coming and going. It's got a few decent taverns, but the girls are a bit spoiled for my taste. Charge you far more'n they are worth. I recommend the One-Eyed Badger though, and a girl named—"

Ben cut the man off. "That's not really what I was interested in. Can you talk to me about the layout of the place? What we should expect, anything we should watch out for?"

"You should watch out for getting overcharged by one of the uppity whores," grumbled the man.

Amelie cleared her throat.

"Sorry," sulked the sailor. "To understand Akew Woods, you gotta understand that it's just about the only real town west of the Venmoor River. Everything else is wilderness and hill people. The hill people live in little dirt villages, I'm told. Like anyone though, they gotta trade. They come to Akew Woods for stuff they can't make in a mud shack or the forest. Merchants come up from Shamiil with foodstuffs, ale, wine, and the like. Lotta ships from the west berth there too, bringing luxury goods and weird spices. They trade with the merchants from Shamiil."

"The west?" wondered Amelie.

The sailor looked at her. "Yeah, the west. It's where the sun sets."

"I thought Akew Woods was the west," she said, struggling futilely to keep the exasperation out of her voice.

"It's the western tip of Alcott," explained the sailor, speaking slow like he was telling a child about numbers. "It ain't the western end of the world. It's not like the sea just falls off into the air beyond there."

"What is to the west then?" queried Ben. He'd never heard tale about any lands other than Alcott and the Southern Continent.

The sailor shrugged. "Don't know. Never been there."

"Tell us more about the town then," suggested Amelie.

"It's on the tip of a peninsula, which kinda curls around the harbor," said the sailor, hooking his hand to demonstrate. "The backside of the town sits on a steep cliff. Then, the front slopes down to the docks. Just like anywhere, the rich folk live above and the poor down below. Shit runs downhill, you know?"

Ben nodded. He knew.

"There aren't any walls or conventional defenses like you'd see in a lot of places," continued the man, "but they do have some pretty big ballistae they could fire at approaching ships. Keeps the pirates in line, I was told. Most of the foreigners stay down near the docks. You load, unload, then get out of there without seeing much of the place. It can be a dangerous town if you're not careful."

"Pirates?" quizzed Ben.

The sailor nodded. "Aye, I told you ships from the west berthed there. They're pirates for the most part. Deadly men, the type you don't want to run afoul of in the tavern. That's why I think the One-Eyed Badger is where you should go. It's safe, and the proprietor sells the ale and the girls cheap. You can get two girls for the price you'd pay at some of the other—"

"Akew Woods is a pirate port?" demanded Amelie, interrupting the man and trying to ignore his insistence on describing the town's working girls.

"Aye," said the sailor, "of course it is. Isn't that why you want to go? Martin said you used to be partners with the boss. What else would a person like you be doing in a place like that?"

Ben coughed.

They had the sailor draw a map of what he recalled of the town, which focused heavily on the location of taverns. Then, they met with Rhys and Towaal to discuss strategy.

"A town full of pirates and a dark mage seeking our blood," said Rhys. "I'm feeling better and better about this plan of yours, Ben."

"Hold on," objected Ben.

"He's kidding with you," said Amelie.

Rhys winked at him and Ben bent back over the map, grumbling under his breath.

"We're taking a bit of a gamble," said Ben, turning the conversation to business, "but we don't think Eldred can detect us unless she gets lucky far-seeing or we manipulate enough energy she could sense it from afar. With that in mind, I'm pretty confident we can sneak into town."

"What are you thinking?" inquired Rhys.

"We wait until nightfall. Then we slip over the side of the

ship," said Ben. "We'll swim to shore in the harbor. In the dark water, I doubt she'll be able to see us. There are too many vessels for her to be far-seeing all of them at the same time, and she has to sleep."

"I'm not sure about that last bit," remarked Rhys, "but I agree she can't watch every ship all the time. At night, far-seeing a dark harbor will be almost useless. What do you think, Karina?"

Lady Towaal nodded. "It's a sound plan."

"We still have to find her once we get on shore," reminded Amelie. "If she's there and waiting, then she'll be in position to spring a trap for us."

Ben grinned. "Exactly. That's why we need to set a trap of our own."

Amelie raised an eyebrow.

"If giving away our position with the thought meld worked to draw her to Akew Woods, then giving it away again will bring her right where we want her."

"Where do we want her?" asked Rhys.

"I'm thinking here," said Ben, stabbing a finger onto the map.

Outside of town, there was a deep bowl of rock. The sailor told them it was used for festivals, games, and events. The way he described it, it sounded like it was originally a rock quarry. It was away from the people in town, a place they could take their time preparing as best they were able for Eldred. They should have good range of vision to see when she approached.

"I wish Jasper was here," mumbled Amelie.

"He has another mission," said Ben. "If all goes well, we'll see him soon enough."

Towaal and Rhys shared a look, and the rogue shrugged.

"Let's get ready then," suggested Towaal.

THEY SAILED INTO AKEW WOODS' harbor in broad daylight. Ben, Amelie, Towaal, and Rhys clustered below deck, taking turns peering out of a narrow portal. It was a safe assumption that Eldred couldn't spot them, and Ben hesitated to admit it, but they weren't even sure she'd be there. Depending on where she was in Alcott, it could mean significant travel to Akew Woods. Still, all of them were worried that they'd miscalculated, and a sizzling bolt of energy would fall upon them at any moment.

They slowly drifted by other ships in the harbor, and Ben studied them closely.

"After they unload, they move away from the docks so they don't have to pay the warfage fees any longer than necessary," explained Rhys. "A merchant vessel comes and goes as quickly as possible. Time is money after all. But a pirate captain likely wants to give his men time to rest, heal, and prepare. Maybe he needs to recruit a few more men if the last raid went poorly. They've got to plan and find an optimal time to strike."

"Is anyone on those ships then?" asked Amelie.

"I'd guess the most junior cabin boy is left behind to keep an eye on things," said Rhys. "The fighting men will be in town, getting drunk, and spending time with the women. Most of those taverns will be set up to cater to a man's every need while he's in port. When it's done right, the sailors won't even leave a place. They'll stay, getting drunk and laid until the captain comes and collects them for the next voyage."

Amelie tsked in disapproval.

Rhys grinned and waved his finger back and forth between Ben and Amelie. "Try spending a few months at sea without someone to give you a roll. A smart captain always makes sure his men have enough coin in their purses to have a bit of fun when they make port."

"Look at that," said Ben, interrupting the banter.

They all looked out the portal and saw three corpses hanging from the yardarm of a vessel. They were shirtless and bootless, only wearing dirty trousers. From what Ben could tell, they were freshly hung and had been beaten before getting strung up.

"Betrayed their crew, maybe," suggested Rhys. "Pirates aren't known for loyalty. Remember that when we move through the place. Don't trust anyone, and watch your backs."

Ben watched the other ships as they drifted by. Compact catapults and ballistae sat on several of the decks. The vessels sprouted sails and had slots for oars. They floated low in the water, lean and fast. There was minimal room for crew quarters or even cargo. In those boats, the pirates could close on another vessel fast, foul their rigging, grapple the other ship, and pull it close. Once they boarded, it was a matter of time and how much blood would be spilled before the victims surrendered. No merchant sailed with enough arms men to fight off a boat full of pirates.

Judging by the lack of cargo holds, these ships didn't go out to rob wheat or beans. They would be interested in valuables. Carpets, precious metals, fine wines, oils and perfumes, or magical devices, the type of stuff that would be easy to transport and would fetch a good price even if its providence was suspect.

They felt their vessel slow and heard the shouts of a pilot guiding them to the docks. They'd stay below deck until midnight and then slip into the water away from the town. They hoped anyone watching for them would be focused on the gangplanks and traffic on the dock instead of the water.

"Let's get some rest," suggested Rhys. "We have a long night ahead of us."

~

THE SHIP CREAKED as the waves gently rocked it against the dock. Wood rubbed on bumpers, and ropes stretched and relaxed. Outside of the comfortable sounds of a boat at dock, it was quiet.

Martin hadn't originally intended to travel to Akew Woods,

so they had little cargo to unload there. He and the crew had taken the day off and were out carousing in the taverns. Only the cabin boys remained on ship, sleeping on deck, watching for intruders. Ben supposed that when the port was full of pirates, you couldn't be too careful.

One of the boy's eyes flicked open as Ben and his party passed. In the moonlight, Ben could see the boy tracking them. Other than that, he didn't move. The cabin boys had been instructed to ignore what they were doing. As crew on a smuggler's ship, Ben suspected it wasn't the first time they'd witnessed shady activities.

On the far side of the vessel, two empty barrels had been dropped over the side and were floating in the water. A hemp rope hung down to them.

"Don't slip," advised Rhys. "A big splash will give us away."

"Thanks for always reminding me of the worst-case scenario," muttered Ben.

"Any time that Benjamin Ashwood is climbing something," retorted Rhys, "is the worst-case scenario."

Grumbling under his breath, Ben slung a leg over the gunwale and rappelled down the side of the ship. He didn't fall, and when he got to the bottom of the rope, he slipped noiselessly into the water. He began untying the empty ale barrels. By the time his friends joined him, they were able to paddle out from the boat using the barrels for flotation and cover if they needed it. Barrels floating in the harbor shouldn't be a remarkable sight in a busy port.

For a bell, they kicked slowly, swimming to the far corner of the docks where they hoped Eldred's watchers wouldn't be waiting. It was dark there with no ships on berth, and none of the warehouses showed any signs of activity.

Finally, they made it and clambered onto a rocky beach that marked the end of the commercial docks. There were small fishing skiffs and personal crafts dragged up on the beach, but no one appeared to be watching them. Pirates had no interest in stealing those.

They opened one of the barrels and pulled out neatly tied bundles of clothing and their weapons. After changing quickly into the dry clothes, they stuffed the wet ones back into one of the barrels. Rhys yanked the tap out of it then shoved the barrel back into the water. With any luck, it would sink to the bottom of the harbor before daylight. They didn't want to leave any trace that someone came ashore, and they definitely didn't want to slink through town with an armful of wet clothing.

They skirted the dark warehouses and moved closer to the light and sounds of Akew Woods. Even at midnight, the taverns blazed with activity. Boisterous singing floated on the night air, giving the place a sense of frantic revelry. The occasional clash of metal or scream added a dash of danger.

Halfway to the first well-lit street, Rhys held up a fist. He pointed ahead of them and Ben saw a spark of light in the shadows. A man was sitting on a crate and puffing on a pipe.

"Thieves guild, maybe?" wondered Ben. "Thieves are common in most of the ports I've seen. Potentially unguarded ships and drunk sailors who aren't paying attention to their purses. That's how Renfro made his bread before we met him."

Rhys shook his head and whispered, "That looks to be a full-grown man. Local thieves would use children for this kind of work. It may be confirmation Eldred is in the city." Rhys paused. "Want me to go find out for sure if he's working for the dark mage?"

"No," Ben answered. "If that is her man and he goes missing, it will alert her that something is going on. We need her overconfident when she walks into our trap."

Rhys grunted. "I hate to leave an enemy alive when we'll have to deal with him later, but I see your point."

"You're just looking for an excuse to use those long knives," chided Amelie.

"What good is sneaking into a place at night if you don't stab someone?" complained Rhys.

"Let's move," said Towaal. "We still have a long way to go to clear Akew Woods before daybreak."

They set off again, veering into the dark alleys between warehouses to avoid the man sitting on the crate. Their pace was slow, and several more times they stopped and circled around people on the streets. They didn't think they were all Eldred's men, but any of them could be. They didn't want to risk being seen by anyone.

Rhys stopped them again. Ahead, a five-man brawl spilled out of a brightly lit tavern into the dark street. Punches were thrown, and kicks were launched. Then one man went down. Another pounced on top of him, plunging a knife into the fallen man's body. Suddenly, all of them drew weapons, and the fight continued. No one called out. No one yelled for help. They fell on each other wordlessly. The only vocalization was when one of the men took a blade to the gut and died slowly.

In heartbeats, only two men remained standing. One limped to the other and threw an arm over his shoulder. They both stumbled back into the tavern. Three bodies lay motionless behind them.

Another party came down the street, singing drinking songs loudly in the night. They stepped over the bodies and entered the bright door of the tavern. No one came out to look. No one alerted the watch.

"Ruthless killers," muttered Rhys. "Don't get in a tavern fight in this town."

They moved on, steering clear of the taverns and bawdy houses, sticking to the dark alleys and commercial streets that were shuttered for the night.

"What would your father's seneschal Tomas be doing in a place like this?" wondered Ben.

"I don't know," replied Amelie, "but I see why he would have wanted Saala with him."

Near the edge of town, they found a pair of watchers pacing back and forth in front of a row of dark buildings. Ben guessed the men were moving to stay awake through the night. They were standing just half a block from the end of town.

The men were watching the hard-packed road that led into the forest. Ben was sure of it.

For a quarter league, the road outside of town was barren and lifeless. The spit of land that housed Akew Woods jutted out from the mainland and was only five-hundred paces wide outside of the city. It was all rock and thick moss. Nothing that would hide a party of four on a moonlit night. Anything even resembling a tree had been cut down and used in construction or burned.

The companions watched the men for several moments.

Finally, Ben whispered, "Is there something magical you can do?"

Towaal shook her head. "We're too close to Eldred. She might sense any disruption I cause."

Ben sighed. "There's no way around these two, and I don't see any other choices. We can't wait here all night. Rhys?"

"I'll take care of it," the rogue said.

"Wait," hissed Amelie.

She pointed and Ben saw a group of men coming down the moonlit road. There could have been ten of them, but it was difficult to tell in the dark.

The watchers perked up but didn't act alarmed. As the new arrivals drew closer, the watchers stepped out into the center of the street and waved. Both groups met and held a quick discussion.

Ben's party slid deeper into the shadows of a nearby alley and crouched against the wall.

Eventually, the two groups on the road separated, and the ten men marched into town. They jingled as they walked, and broadswords hung at their sides.

When they passed, Ben whispered, "Sanctuary men. They look just like the ones in Hamruhg."

"It doesn't change what we have to do," said Amelie. "We still have to get out of this town, and those men are still in our way."

"Rhys," said Ben, "the lady is right. It's your turn."

He looked back, but the rogue wasn't there. He wasn't anywhere in the alley with them.

"Where did he go!" exclaimed Ben.

"He was just here, right beside me," claimed Amelie.

"Wait," advised Towaal.

Her sense of calm gave Ben some relief, but their friend had vanished into thin air.

Moments passed, and Ben grew more and more anxious. Then, deep in the town, a bell started ringing.

Ben stood and peeked out of the alley. Down the street, he saw an orange glow. A building was on fire. A town like Akew Woods was made up of mostly wooden structures, a fire could devastate the entire place. All hands would be expected to respond with whatever buckets or blankets they could bring. They'd work together to douse and smother the flames.

At the edge of town, the pair of soldiers shifted nervously.

"What are you two doing!" shouted a voice. "There's a fire. Come on!"

The men looked at each other and then called back, "We're on duty. We can't leave here."

"You ain't the city watch," growled the first man.

He was hooded and hunched over, to all appearances, an old man with back problems. A really old man, thought Ben. Older than dirt.

"If you don't get moving, I'll tell the authorities and you boys are gonna get hung. We need every able body we can get. Hurry!"

Reluctantly, the guards started down the street.

"Run, you lazy bastards!" screamed Rhys.

"Okay, okay, old man," said one of the guards. They broke into a jingling trot, passing Rhys and heading toward the fire.

As soon as they were by him, Rhys shuffled down the street, waving for Ben and his friends to follow.

"We've got a few moments at best before they realize there isn't much threat and come back here," said Rhys.

"What did you set fire to?" asked Ben, worried his friend sacrificed a great deal of lives for them to escape.

"Don't worry," said Rhys with a grin. "I followed those soldiers and saw where they were bunking. A score more men were in the common room. All Sanctuary. Behind their inn, I found a completely empty stable. Set up for merchant's horses or oxen, but the soldiers are taking up the entire inn. I set fire to the hay. The stable is away from other structures, and it was made of stone. The hay went up fast, though. Should be a hot enough blaze to keep them busy, but there were enough of them to put out the flames before anything else burns."

"Eldred may suspect something," worried Amelie.

"It wasn't a direct attack on her men," said Rhys. "None of them should be harmed. No reason to think it's anything other than a simple accident. At the very least, it's better than leaving the two watchers with their throats slit."

Amelie evidently decided she couldn't argue with that, and she stayed quiet as they raced down the road. They had to make it far enough to disappear into the rocks before the watchers came back. If they were caught running from town, Eldred and her men would be on them before they had a chance to prepare.

Six hundred paces of mad dashing and they made it behind the first rocky outcropping that could hide all four of them. They ducked down, and when they caught their breath, Ben peeked over the lichen covered rock at the town. The alarm bells had died down and the glow from the fire seemed to have disappeared. Lights sparkled in several more windows than they had before, but there didn't appear to be any pursuit.

"I think we made it," he said.

"Now for the hard part," responded Towaal.

THE FIRST SHARDS of daylight were breaking over the rim of the abandoned quarry when they finally reached it. It was a league outside of town, tucked down under a sharp ridge of rock, and formed like a shallow bowl. Trees lined the rim of the bowl, broken only by the road that led into it. Shattered pieces of equipment and seating sat scattered around the edges, giving it an ominous, abandoned look.

"It doesn't look like anyone has been here in a season," said Amelie.

Ben nodded. "Perfect."

"We should rest this morning and then get to work in the afternoon. We'll get a good night sleep after we've prepared and then send out the signal. Within a bell of us showing ourselves, I expect Eldred and her men will be here."

They slept fitfully that morning then spent the afternoon preparing as best they were able for Eldred. The dark mage was stronger than them, she had an unknown number of soldiers, and they'd already been unsuccessful facing her. On the surface, it seemed like a suicide mission. Underneath, Ben thought they had a decent chance if they could maintain surprise.

"We still have time to back out of this," remarked Rhys. "We've slipped by her. We could be in the City in a month. She'd never know what happened."

They were sitting around a sheltered fire, hidden behind a pile of debris. It was late summer, and they didn't need the warmth, but something about the flickering flames gave them all comfort.

Ben shook his head.

"We have to deal with her sooner or later," he said. "Besides, if we can't defeat Eldred, what are we going to do against the Veil and the demons? This road won't get any easier."

"No," agreed Rhys. "It won't."

"I hope we're doing the right thing," worried Amelie.

"We're doing the best we can," assured Ben. "Regardless of the situation, that's all you can ever do."

"You are doing the right thing," said Towaal. "It may work. It may not. There are unknowns, but there are always unknowns. Managing that, and still being able to make a decision, is the hallmark of a leader. Even if you don't want to, you're stepping into those shoes, Ben. Continue to stand up for what is right, continue to make the correct choices, and people will follow you. That's what we need, and that's how we must face these next challenges."

"You keep pushing leadership on me," mumbled Ben, picking up a broken spoke from a long-abandoned wagon wheel. He stirred the fire with it, watching the sun-bleached wood blacken in the flame. "I'm not sure I'm ready."

"No one is ever ready," responded Rhys. "You said it yourself. You do the best you can, and that's all you can do."

"If we don't survive this tomorrow," remarked Amelie, "I'm glad I've been through it with the three of you. When you collected me in Issen, I never could have imagined this journey. Each step along the way, we tried to do the right thing. I can rest peacefully knowing that."

"I'm glad we've been on this journey together as well," replied Towaal. "It took me a long time, but I finally fought the right fight. Win or lose, that is worth something."

"We drank some good ales, didn't we?" quipped Rhys.

"I doubt there is anyone who's had as many good ales as you," chortled Ben.

Rhys grinned. "If you're going to go down, you might as well go down doing what you love."

Amelie scooted close to Ben and leaned her head against his shoulder.

"You may as well take it out," Towaal said to Rhys.

He raised an eyebrow at her.

"We all know you and how you think. You've got something stashed away, ready for the right moment. That moment is now."

Rhys sighed dramatically, then fished a silver flask out of his cloak.

"I hope this survived the journey," he said. "I snitched it from the emperor's library. It's his private stash, the best stuff coin can buy. There's nothing like a cold ale, but this should do."

"Let me give it a try," offered Amelie, straightening up and taking the flask from Rhys.

She opened the top and sniffed at the liquid inside. Smiling, she turned it up and sipped a mouthful. She passed the flask to Ben, who sampled it as well. The liquor was smooth as silk and slid down his throat with a mellow, smoky heat. He passed it to Towaal.

"Hey now," complained Rhys.

"Don't worry," assured the mage. "We'll save a little for you."

When Rhys lowered the flask, he eyed it appreciatively.

"We may have to write O'ecca and figure out where they get this stuff," remarked the rogue.

He passed the flask back around the circle.

Amelie snuggled up to Ben again, and he leaned back on his elbows, glancing at the twinkling stars in the sky.

"The further away from civilization, the brighter the stars," claimed Rhys.

"Really?" asked Ben.

"It's true," acknowledged Towaal. "The ambient light from cities drowns out the light from the sky. In the right circumstances, even the smallest lights shine brightly."

"That's poetic," murmured Rhys.

"It's physics," Towaal informed him.

They quieted down and slowly finished the emperor's liquor. A beautiful evening, fine drink, good friends, and a pretty girl sitting beside him. Despite the looming threat of the next day, Ben had never been so content in his life.

On the ground next to them, the rogue's longsword sat in its battered leather sheath. A soft white glow emanated from where the mage-wrought steel poked out. Inside, the runes were pulsing brightly, absorbing the energy from the friends.

16

DARK MAGIC

A SUBTLE VIBRATION thrummed in Ben's head.

"I'm here," said a familiar voice.

"We've made it past Akew Woods," responded Amelie. "The Sanctuary's men were in the city, but we slipped by with no problems. We'll camp in an abandoned quarry outside of town for a few days, then we'll leave for the City."

"Be careful," replied Jasper, speaking directly into their thoughts.

The four companions were seated in a tight circle, everyone with a finger on the thought meld. They were calling out, loudly and clearly, where their location was. Hopefully, they were giving Eldred the opportunity to sense them or even overhear the conversation.

Amelie left the line of communication open for several more moments and then shut it off.

"Time to get ready," she declared.

They stood and started moving into position. They figured they'd have close to a bell before anyone came, but there was no reason to tarry. Eldred could be closer than expected, or she may have men patrolling the roads who could arrive sooner.

The sun was high above them, shining down bright and warm. As Ben scrambled into position, he started to sweat. Nerves and the heat had his heart pumping furiously. He piled wet pieces of wood onto their fire and stoked it, building the flames and sending a column of thick grey smoke into the sky. He hoped they had enough fuel to keep it going until Eldred's forces drew close.

He glanced one last time at their supplies scattered around the fire and adjusted one of the bedrolls, rumpling it so it looked slept in and natural. Then, he wiggled under a pile of debris, burrowing into the weathered wood and faded fabric they'd scavenged.

Around the quarry, his friends were hiding in similar piles they'd arranged. All of them were trying to stay calm. It was critical they maintain stasis. They expected Eldred to immediately attempt some sort of attack on the area. If they could harden their wills enough to survive it, they had a chance.

The fire burned, and their supplies lay staged in an obvious camp. With any luck, Eldred would head straight to it to investigate. They needed her close.

Ben lay still and silent. He felt beads of sweat dripping down his forehead and back. After a quarter bell, he started to cramp from the awkward position he was in. Slowly, so as not to disturb the debris he was under, he shifted. He couldn't risk jumping up with a limp when the action started.

The sun hung above them, pounding them with late summer intensity. It wasn't as hot as the desert, Ben told himself, but at least then they'd been able to walk around and catch a breeze. Buried and hiding, he couldn't risk the movement.

He glanced about the seemingly empty bowl of rock and marked the piles of debris his friends were hiding under. They hoped Eldred's men would walk down the road and straight into their trap, but it was foolish to assume they wouldn't be tactically minded enough to send men to surround the area. If anyone came from behind and spotted them, they'd have no chance. So, they hid, buried deep.

Despite his pounding heart, Ben felt himself getting drowsy in the midday heat. It'd been over a bell, he was sure of it. No reason Eldred and her men shouldn't be there yet. Maybe Eldred wasn't really in Akew Woods. Maybe she couldn't really track them. Had she trailed them to Hamruhg, or had she just gotten lucky? Were those really her men in Akew Woods? He was growing less sure.

Ben waited. He estimated another bell had gone by. He thought about coming out and conferring with his friends. They were wasting time if the mage couldn't locate them through the thought meld. Maybe Amelie should try it again and ensure Eldred would have their location. Maybe they should just leave for the City now and try to catch Milo. Ben needed to talk to his friends.

He glanced around the quarry at the other debris piles. No one was moving. He thought about calling out. Anyone from the road would have difficulty hearing him if he pitched it right. None of his friends were stirring, though, so he stayed still. Another bell passed.

It was madness, decided Ben. Their plan had no chance of working to begin with. The idea Eldred could track them through the thought meld was based on Jasper's assumptions and guesses. The ancient mage hadn't been sure it would work, had he? Ben tried to remember what exactly the man had told them. He was struggling to remain still and in hiding.

Suddenly, an unexpected, jagged shard of pain ripped through his body.

It felt like a big man was slowly sawing him in half with a rusty lumber saw. Every muscle clenched uncontrollably. Only the vicious spasm that rocked his chest kept him from screaming. He quivered, imagining each tooth of a saw as it ground through the fibers of his muscles and into bone.

He closed his eyes, struggling to fight through the pain and to breathe. With stupendous effort, he forced his jaw open and was able to suck in a quick breath. The fresh air gave him hope, and with hope, he began to reassert his will. He focused on his breathing first, taking another ragged breath, feeling the air fill his lungs, then letting it out. From his chest, and back, he concentrated on stasis. They weren't being torn apart. It just felt like it. It was psychological. It was imposed on his mind, and he could fight it. Bit by bit, he hardened his will and extended it through his body, pushing the sensation of terrific pain down to his extremities, then out.

He started to push further then paused. Somewhere, Eldred was directing the attack. Given he was able to fight it off, he guessed she didn't know where they were and was simply directing her will at the entire area. He concentrated on himself and let her will flow freely around him. She could do her worst to the broken wood and rocks nearby. Let her exhaust her power on nothing.

As the moments passed, Ben found it easier to maintain stasis. Either the strength of the attack was dissipating, or he was getting better holding it off with practice. He stayed alert, though, in case the dark mage modified her assault. He was fully awake and focused now. He wouldn't be caught off-guard again.

Half a bell passed and nothing else happened. Ben could still feel the tension of Eldred's will pulsing around him, occasionally spiking then receding. He suspected she was exerting her will in sweeping waves, lashing back and forth across the area. No one entered the quarry, though. There was no sign of the mage or her men.

Ben waited patiently, assured that what they planned was starting to work. Eldred was there, and they had an opportunity to draw her into the trap. None of his friends had cried out and given themselves away. If they'd been able to harden their will like he had, they would be ready for what came next.

Finally, he saw a soldier appear on the road into the quarry.

Tentatively, the man stepped into the rock bowl, edging one foot out first then following with the rest of his body.

Nothing happened.

The soldier took another score of steps forward, turned, and waved to someone back in the woods. Ten more soldiers appeared and walked out to join the first. They fanned out and started scouting the quarry, looking for traps, Ben guessed.

They kicked aside scattered bits of iron scrap and broken chunks of wood. Slowly, the men circled the camp and made their way closer. By now, the fire had died down to smoldering embers, but the rest of the camp was still intact. The men didn't touch anything. They just looked.

After a quarter bell of investigation, they waved again toward the woods, and more men streamed into the quarry. Ben swallowed uncomfortably. There were at least forty soldiers in the rock bowl now. Even without Eldred, it was a formidable force.

The original group of men waved broadly to someone behind Ben.

He slowly shifted his head to glance through a narrow gap in the rubbish, looking toward the back of the quarry. He saw movement on top of the rim of rock that surrounded the bowl. At least another score of men up there, he guessed. There was no way of being certain.

Ben returned his gaze to the men scouting the campsite. They toed some of the debris piles, but there were upward of a hundred of them scattered around the empty rock floor. Ben hoped they wouldn't check them all.

Movement caught his eye. Back at the road, a figure with a black cloak and deep hood joined the chain-mail armored soldiers. The figure paused, either waiting for something to happen or sensing for magical traps.

A shiver ran down Ben's spine as he saw the brilliant white porcelain mask peeking out from within the dark cowl. A nightmare like that shouldn't be possible in the bright light of afternoon, but there she was. Eldred.

The dark mage stepped into the quarry, moving cautiously. It was obvious she expected a trap, but they'd been careful to obscure the surprises they had planned.

Both Towaal and Amelie knew Eldred. Towaal had known her for centuries. They'd been initiates together and then full mages of the Sanctuary. Amelie first met the dark mage less than a year before, but she'd studied under Eldred during that time. They had interacted almost daily.

The dark mage had gained exceptional power through whatever the Veil did to her, but she could not have gained additional knowledge that quickly. They knew they couldn't beat her in a contest of strength, but they might be able to outsmart her. They would use their experience to lure her into a situation they could control.

Eldred's head swiveled, looking for an attack, but nothing came.

"I think they're gone," called one of the men. "Maybe they knew we were coming and fled."

The mage didn't respond. Instead, she strode toward the campsite.

"Who builds up a fire in the middle of the day?" argued another one of the men. "There is a purpose to this. It must be to draw us closer. It's a trap."

"They're not here," snapped the first soldier, "and we haven't been attacked. How do you explain that?"

Eldred ignored them. She walked around the campsite, stirring their equipment and bedding with her foot. She looked into the fire then glanced around the rest of the quarry, her white mask sparkling in the afternoon sun.

She raised a hand. A sizzling ball of orange flame sprung from her palm. She hurled it at a nearby pile of rubbish. The fireball impacted the pile and ignited it with a whoosh. Wood, rocks, and loose fabric exploded with the force of the blast.

Fortunately, it wasn't a pile that Ben and his friends were hiding under, but he saw another ball of fire forming in the dark mage's hand. It wasn't the signal they agreed on, but they couldn't wait for Eldred to torch all of their cover.

Around the quarry, pieces of iron scrap suddenly glowed bright red and exploded with sharp cracks. Hundreds of nails, wagon fittings, and leftover armaments from tournaments were blasted to bits. Hot shrapnel was flung like hail, slamming into the legs and feet of nearby soldiers, shredding their lower bodies like over-cooked meat from the pot. Men went down screaming all around them.

Ben and his friends burst out of hiding.

Eldred and the men directly around her hadn't been harmed in the attack. The dark mage had quickly erected an expanding circle of force around her. Scalding, jagged metal bounced off it and clattered down to the rock floor.

"I'm glad you didn't run," said the mage's voice calmly, directly in Ben's head.

Ben looked at Towaal and Amelie. They stood across from him, forming a triangle surrounding the dark mage and her men.

Bolts of lightning erupted from Eldred, striking out at Ben's friends.

Ben didn't try to harden his will and stand against the attack. He was certain he couldn't stop a direct assault from the dark mage. Instead, he threw dignity to the wind and dove out of the way. The pile of debris he'd been hiding under exploded, showering him with rocks and shattered wood.

Eldred wasn't facing him, though, and he wasn't the one who'd drawn her focus.

Lady Towaal was flung backward, smoke and the crackle of electricity following her as she was smacked into the rock floor of the quarry. She lay motionless.

All around them, men screamed in agony.

Eldred looked at her men. Three quarters of them were down. The men clutched ruined legs, grabbing at where the burning iron had stabbed into them. Their wails filled the quarry with an awful choir of pain.

"Effective, I admit," she hissed, her voice echoing through Ben's mind, "but did you think that would actually injure me? I'm disappointed, Karina."

"She didn't do that. I did," declared Amelie. She was standing defiantly, her hands balled into fists.

Eldred turned toward her, showing her back to Ben.

"I have plans for you, girl." Eldred's voice was like a rusty iron gate being forced open. Her words scraped across Ben's consciousness, cutting through the screams of her men.

Towaal stirred from where she'd fallen, but the mage didn't have the strength to rise.

Ben needed to buy time for her to recover. He stepped forward and raised his sword. Some of the guards saw him and moved into position to block his attack. Eldred ignored them. Regretting that he didn't have his mage-wrought blade, Ben dropped into a fighting stance and held his longsword ready.

Amelie threw one of her hands up, launching a ham-sized fireball at the dark mage.

The fire splashed harmlessly around Eldred. The dark mage didn't bother raising her hands in defense. Ben thought she would have laughed had she been able.

Amelie tossed her prism to the side. She'd been gathering heat all day with the thing. She'd crippled Eldred's soldiers using it and the iron scrap, but it had done nothing to the dark mage.

Ben's turn. While Eldred was distracted, he took two running steps and hurled his longsword. It spun in the afternoon sun, flying end over end.

Eldred's men called out in alarm, but the blade wasn't directed at them. They moved to block it, but they were too slow. It sailed between two of them and pierced the dark mage's back. The Venmoor steel of the longsword punched into her flesh, sinking deep. She stumbled forward, surprised at the mundane attack from behind.

She spun to face Ben. Her voice screeched inside his head. "You again."

Ben stared, wide-eyed. Half the length of his blade protruded from Eldred's chest. She had regained her balance and was standing straight, ignoring the steel stuck through her body. No blood pumped from the brutal wound, and the mage didn't appear injured by it.

"Oh shit," mumbled Ben under his breath.

He hardened his will a heartbeat before a concussion rocked his body. His vision went blurry, and two Eldreds seemed to dance out from each other, wavering wildly. Brilliant colors cascaded in front of his eyes and the ringing of a bell filled his ears. He flopped to the ground, stunned and defenseless against Eldred's attack. His mind wasn't functioning. He felt like he'd had two dozen ales. The world spun around him, and he could only lie on the stone, trying not to get sick. For some reason, he thought that was important.

"I'll enjoy dealing with you later," he heard through the confusion.

The two guards stepped toward him. He wasn't sure if they meant to deal with him before Eldred had the chance, or if they were simply moving to protect her from anything else he tried. Not that he could. His head swam, and his vision was blurred. His only thought was to keep from retching. He realized that even if he could gain his feet, he had no sword.

From the ground, he struggled to watch as the dark mage twisted an arm back and gripped the hilt of his longsword. She yanked it from her body and let the steel clatter to the ground by her feet.

Ben groaned and tried to corral his spinning thoughts, to maintain stasis, to fight what the mage was doing to his mind.

A guard moved behind the two who were facing Ben. Eldred paid him no more mind than the others.

She was focused on Amelie. "Now, girl, I have been waiting for a very long time to do this."

The guard suddenly surged toward the dark mage, whipping a longsword from his sheath and slashing at Eldred's head.

Sensing something, she ducked, but she wasn't as fast as her attacker.

Silver smoke trailed the blade and it smashed into the side of Eldred's head, spinning the dark mage like a top. Rhys, in the guise of one of her guards, stalked after her. Black robes floated out around Eldred as she spun from the impact, stumbling away from Rhys.

Ben saw her stark white porcelain mask fly free. The mask crashed to the rock and shattered. Eldred's body fell beside it, face down on the stone. His heart soared.

Then Eldred pushed herself up, to her knees and then to her feet. She faced Rhys. The rogue squared his stance, and held his longsword before him.

Ben's stomach lurched when he saw Eldred. Her hood had been thrown back, giving him his first view of her underneath the mask. She had the desiccated face of a rotted corpse. Her skin had the appearance of months' old jerky. Her forehead glowed with soul-sucking red runes. One side of her face was destroyed from where Rhys struck her. Her cheekbone was smashed in and half her jaw was missing. One eye dangled from a ruined socket. Rhys had damaged her, but not slowed her.

Her hands blazed with crackling energy. A bolt of lightning snapped out toward Rhys, but the rogue bore the brunt of it, hardening his will and letting the energy flash around him and his sword.

The blaze of power flickered out and Rhys stood tall. The

runes on his sword flared in the afternoon sun, the sparkling silver light shining like a beacon.

"You felt that, didn't you?" crowed Rhys. "Your power sheared away like your face. This blade will end you, witch."

The corpse didn't miss a beat. Another bolt of lightning shot out, but this time it didn't strike Ben or his companions. Eldred attacked her own men. Bodies twitched and screams were cut short as the bolt of lightning leapt from man to man. One by one, she killed a score of them.

The able soldiers turned to flee, but most were helpless, crippled by the exploding iron Amelie had set off when they sprung their trap. They'd given Eldred a supply of immobile life forces, and the mage was taking them one by one.

The remaining half of Eldred's jaw creaked open with silent laughter.

Rhys, realizing what was happening, charged. His longsword streamed silver smoke and the runes flared as the rogue unleashed the full power of his weapon. The corpse of Eldred spread her arms and black shadow billowed out from her robes. Rhys chopped down at the mage.

Ben expected the mage-wrought steel to shear through Eldred, but her shadows formed into a shield. An ear-shattering wail sounded when the silver smoke met the black shadow.

Eldred stumbled back, her jaw still wide in a silent cackle.

Rhys kept up his attack, furiously raining blow after blow, alternating positions, coming like a whirlwind.

Eldred blocked his attack over and over, but some of the strikes slipped through. The rogue's longsword tore chunks out of the dark mage. Sparks and smoke trailed away from each of the wounds, but as Ben watched, darkness flowed across and filled them. The mage was repairing herself as they fought.

Around them, the soldiers continued to die. Even the ones who ran were struck down mid-flight.

Ben felt the dark mage's energy pulse toward him, and he

hardened his will. The force of her attack battered him, but with Rhys striking at her, she had little concentration to spare.

Heartbeats later, an injured man a dozen paces away twitched and died. Ben looked on, unable to stop her from killing her own men and absorbing the energy from their deaths.

The two guards who stood between Ben and her didn't seem to realize their leader had turned on them. They stalked toward Ben, swords raised.

He grunted. It figured those would be the two she killed last. He rose to his feet, wavering with the aftereffects of Eldred's assault. Considering he lacked a weapon, the soldiers were as dangerous to him as the dark mage herself. Stout chainmail guarded their bodies. Their heavy broadswords were drawn and held steady.

Behind them, Ben could see Rhys tiring as he battered Eldred. The corpse mage still stood, but she was fighting a defensive battle, barely keeping the rogue's blade from carving out a fatal chunk of her. Shimmering silver flakes marked places the rogue had struck her that she could no longer repair. Everything she stole from her men went into holding Rhys back.

Ben hoped his friend had the stamina to keep pressing her, the strength to outlast the energy Eldred absorbed from the men she was killing. Ben didn't have time to worry about that, though, as the two guards broke into a charge. He had heartbeats to react, but it was enough time to see they were both right-handed. He sprinted forward and veered to his right, the guard's left. They turned together and kept coming.

The closest one had to scramble to avoid a pile of rubbish. Ben flew at him, trying to time the attack to arrive while the man was swerving around the debris. He came close.

The guard brought his sword up at the same time Ben rushed past the point of the blade. Ben felt the steel of the broadsword slap against his side. The heavy weapon wasn't as sharp as a smaller blade, but the edge still bit into Ben's skin, leaving a long laceration. Blood wet his ribcage, but Ben was inside the man's reach.

He gripped the man's neck and looped a foot behind his leg. Shifting his weight, Ben hurled them both to the ground, aiming the guard's head toward the debris pile and a large chunk of rock. With a crack, the man's head impacted the stone.

Ben saw the light flicker out of his eyes, then the second man was on them, thrusting down with his broadsword.

Ben rolled, yanking the body of the first guard over him. He had the air knocked out of him when the broadsword speared the body, pushing the heavy, armored guard down on Ben.

He kicked out, catching the standing man's knee with his foot, but the man stepped back out of reach. He raised his sword again, prepared to bring it down for a fatal strike this time.

Ben rolled the other way, shifting out from under the first man. The second stepped after him. Still on his back, Ben grabbed the bloody rock he'd brained the first guard with and raised it just in time to meet the descending broadsword.

Sparks and rock chips flew as steel met stone. The blade bounced to the side.

"Sorry about this," muttered Ben.

He kicked up with all of his might. Instead of at the man's legs, Ben aimed his foot directly in between them.

The soldier squealed a high-pitched whine and his eyes crossed. He dropped his broadsword with a clang. The soldier didn't have armor protecting that area from below.

Ben drew his hunting knife and buried it in the man's knee, twisting it as he yanked it back out. The soldier stumbled back and collapsed to the ground.

Ben started to crawl over to him and finish the job, but a blast of hot air reminded him Eldred was still standing. He'd let the man live for now. He stood and saw Rhys was now on the defensive, stumbling back, furiously slashing at dense tendrils of black shadow and flickering tongues of fire. The thick darkness streamed from Eldred and came at Rhys from half a dozen directions.

The rogue's clothing was torn and bright crimson slashes marred his skin. It looked like he'd been mauled by a beast. One of the tendrils latched onto the rogue's arm and Ben gasped. It appeared to be sucking the blood and flesh from him.

The glowing silver longsword whipped through and severed the streamer of blackness, but the injury didn't dissipate with the smoke. A fresh river of blood flowed down the rogue's arm.

Ben glanced around wildly and saw Towaal was still lying on her side, struggling to gain her feet. Her hair stood on end and smoke drifted away from her. Her eyes looked glazed over and dazed.

Ben cursed. They'd counted on the mage slowing Eldred enough for Rhys to get a fatal blow. Instead, Towaal and been knocked out for nearly the entire fight.

Amelie was moving, but she was gripping her leg. It was twisted unnaturally. While Ben had been fighting the soldiers, Eldred must have attacked Amelie and broken her leg.

Around them, every one of Eldred's men lay dead except the one Ben had maimed. She'd slaughtered and drained them all. Her own men.

Ben swallowed the bile in his throat and stepped toward the dark mage, unsure what he could do. He could see Rhys had moments left, at best. The rogue was slowing, and his body was covered in sticky blood.

Ben kept moving closer, his mind racing. He drew his hunting knife, but it would be worthless against an opponent like Eldred. They needed power. They needed magic. Will and knowledge. Anything in the world was possible with will and knowledge.

An arm-thick tendril of black smoke lashed out from Eldred and caught the side of Rhys' longsword, smacking it out of his grip. The silver runes started to fade as the weapon bounced across the rock floor of the quarry. Rhys followed it with his eyes, defeat clouding his gaze. The tendril snapped at Rhys again and he flew back, blood streaming behind him like the tail of a kite. The rogue crumpled to the ground. Corpse Eldred advanced on him.

Ben had to do something. He broke into a run.

"Ben," shouted Amelie. "Her power is stored in the runes on her face!"

The dark mage didn't spare Amelie a glance.

Suddenly, Towaal staggered to her feet and raised her arms. She looked frazzled, but the bewildered confusion had faded.

Sunlight streamed down, stabbing into Ben's eyes. He held up an arm to block the light and slowed his run, halfway to Eldred.

The black smoke around the dark mage contracted suddenly as if it was burned by the intensity of the light. Eldred hunched down, bowing before the brilliance from above.

"I learned one thing from Gunther," declared Towaal through gritted teeth. "Let me show you."

The sun blazed brighter. Ben squeezed his eyes shut, worried he'd go blind.

When Towaal had used the light of the sun against the demons, it had been one flash. This was constant. Ben felt the heat on his skin, burning it in moments worse than an entire day out on the sea.

Eldred cackled, the sound clawing at Ben's sanity. He smelled the musty scent of long-buried graves. He risked opening one eye and saw the dark mage facing Towaal. The light surrounded Towaal, but an evil wind was blowing against her, flapping her clothes, and forcing her to stagger back a step.

Eldred opened her mouth, and the sound of her laughter jabbed into Ben's conscious, forcing out every other thought. Towaal faltered and fell back again. The dark mage advanced on her, ignoring the rest of the party.

Amelie was propped up on one elbow, but Ben could tell from twenty paces away that she was entirely drained. She'd already expended everything she had. Rhys was lying on his back, blood forming a wide pool around him. Ben wasn't sure if he was still breathing.

Tears streamed down Towaal's face, and Ben could see anguish there. Eldred was moments away from crushing her.

He couldn't let that happen.

Ben started running again, unsure what he was going to do, but certain he couldn't stand by idly while his friends were slaughtered. He jumped over or swerved around the refuse that cluttered the floor of the quarry. He glanced at the hunting knife in his hand then threw it down, knowing it wouldn't be effective against the dark mage.

Eldred ignored him, solely focused on Towaal.

Then he reached her and leapt onto her back.

It was like tackling a skeleton, except the pile of bones and dried flesh didn't go down. Eldred stumbled then straightened underneath him, fueled with dark power and possessing unnatural strength.

She tried to flip him off, but Ben clung to her like his life depended on it. Which, he realized, it did. He suddenly regretted jumping on her.

Towaal fell to one knee and Ben met her eyes.

She was spent. She couldn't help him.

"Anything is possible," she said, her voice a feather on the wind.

Eldred spun, trying to buck him off.

He clung tighter, looping an arm around her neck and clamping it down. The tight hold would have strangled a person, but Eldred was no longer a living being.

She grasped his arm with her bony hand and Ben felt a terrible chill seep into him. The chill of the grave crept up his arm, threatening its way into the rest of his body. Instinctively, he knew that if that chill reached his heart, he'd be dead. He hardened his will, but it only slowed the intrusive cold.

He tightened his arm, refusing to give up.

Eldred spun around again. Ben saw Amelie. Her hand was on her leg, holding the broken bone. She was struggling, trying to drag herself closer with only one elbow. Tears streamed down her face. Rhys was near her, every one of his failing heartbeats pumping the last of his life-blood out onto the rock.

Ben wouldn't let Eldred win. He wouldn't let her take his friends.

Knowledge and will. Anything was possible with that.

Amelie had said the corpse mage's power was in the runes on her face. He had to destroy them, he knew that. He had to have the will to do it.

The dark mage's bony fingers dug into his flesh, but she was brittle and frail. Her body burned with unnatural strength, but the dry bones would shatter if she applied too much force. Ben grinned grimly. She wouldn't be able to rip him off of her. Instead, she spun again, trying to loosen his hold. He got one last look at all of his friends. Then, he wrapped his legs around the corpse's torso and locked them together with his feet. He put his other arm around the dark mage's head.

He felt her broken teeth sink into his arm, tearing at his flesh. Blood streamed freely, but he didn't stop. He gripped tighter, twisted, and pulled.

The mage's thrashing became panicked, and she slapped both hands on his arm, forcing the cold of death deeper into his body. He felt her will battering him, the unfathomable pain from earlier directed through her hands into his flesh.

He hardened his will, retreating deep inside himself. He was resolute and determined. There was nothing he wanted in the world more than stopping the evil witch.

The sound of her voice wailed inside his head, tearing at his consciousness, but he didn't bother to understand her. Her fingers clamped down on him. Both of his arms were numb.

From the cold, the blood loss, or both, he didn't know. He could no longer feel what he was doing.

He fought on.

He fought for Meredith, for Grunt, for Gunther, for Corinne. He fought for Amelie, Towaal and Rhys. He fought for Eldred's men, those she'd killed and any who may still survive in the woods. He fought for Farview and Northport. He fought for Shamiil and Irrefort. He fought for everyone the dark mage had killed and everyone she would slaughter in the future.

His mind began to shut down, unable to withstand the mental assault Eldred was throwing at him. His body didn't respond to the limited commands he was able to give it. He was a being of will and instinct, unable to do anything other than execute his function. He couldn't think about what was happening to him, the cold taking over his body, her teeth ripping his skin. He could only think about what he had to do.

Keeping his legs locked, he arched his back, pulling with every fiber of his being.

The dark mage wailed in his head, shattering his conscious, driving out all remaining thought.

He was pure will.

His world went black. He didn't see. He didn't hear. He didn't feel. He didn't know.

Outside of his awareness, he roared like an animal. He twisted his body, biceps bulging with the strain.

With a crack, and the sound of ripping parchment, he tore Eldred's head off.

The mage's body stumbled, refusing to acknowledge what happened. It staggered in a slow circle and then flopped over.

Ben fell with it. He landed hard on the rocky ground, unable to relax his arms or legs. Drawing a deep, ragged breath, he felt pain cascading through his body as awareness returned. He screamed, his body ravaged by agony. He screamed until he lost his breath. Then, he lay panting.

Slowly, ever so slowly, the world returned to focus. His body burned with cold. His heart hammered within his ribcage.

Ben looked down and saw the dark mage's head resting on top of him. He screamed again and threw the head away.

Queasily, he watched it bounce on the rock floor of the quarry, the glowing runes cut into her face fading into scars.

"Ben," called Amelie.

He grunted, unable to form speech.

"Can you make it to Rhys?"

Cold fear shot through Ben's body and spurred him to action.

He rolled to his stomach and forced himself up. Stumbling to Rhys, he looked down and winced when he saw his arm. His entire right forearm was white like it was frost bit. A chunk had been ripped out of it, but his flesh was numb and he couldn't feel the wound. He was covered in his own blood from his elbow to his fingertips. Bile welled up in his throat and he swallowed it.

He was still alive. His friend had a bigger problem.

Rhys wasn't moving. He wasn't breathing.

Ben knelt beside him. A score of punctures marred his friend's body, each steadily leaking blood. They weren't pumping blood any longer. The rogue's heart was stopped.

Ben started to push on the rogue's chest, something he'd seen Edward Crust do once before in Farview. He knew if he could get his friend's heart pumping again, there was a chance. Even as he thought it, he knew there wasn't really a chance. Any blood that the heart pumped would come spurting out of the open wounds.

If he couldn't bind the injuries, a beating heart would kill Rhys from loss of blood. Without a beating heart, his friend was already dead.

Ben had to try. He had to do something. He set his hands and compressed on the rogue's chest.

His arm gave out the moment he put his weight on it and Ben flopped down. He didn't have the strength in his right arm to push against anything. The cold numbed flesh was useless. Refusing to give up, Ben pushed again with his left hand. Over and over, he pressed on the rogue's chest. Nothing was happening.

"Something's happening," yelled Towaal.

She was standing, wavering like a punch-drunk fighter. Ben didn't know what she was talking about.

"We have to go," she demanded.

"We can't leave Rhys!" shouted Ben.

"Eldred was a repository," snarled Towaal, "a bigger one than I've ever seen. Ben, the energy that was housed inside her is boiling. It's going to release. It's going to explode."

Ben kept shoving on the rogue's chest. He couldn't leave his friend. He had to fight the right battles, and this was one he wouldn't give up. No matter the danger.

"All of this was for nothing if we don't get out of here!" exclaimed Towaal. "We have to go."

"You're a mage. Can't you heal him?" snapped Ben.

"I'm expended," admitted Towaal. "Surviving Eldred took everything I had. There's nothing, Ben, nothing I can do."

Ben looked to Amelie. She was still lying where she fell, unable to rise on her broken leg. Her look told him she was done too.

"Look at us," growled Ben. "We couldn't run if we wanted to."

"You can," insisted Towaal. "If you don't, you'll die." She fell to her knees, no longer strong enough to keep her balance. "Go now, while you can. Find Jasper. Keep doing what you need to do."

Ben shook his head. "This is what I need to do."

"Leave us," pleaded Towaal. "It's what Rhys would want."

"Eldred," interrupted Amelie. "You said Eldred was a repository of energy. Can we use it?"

Towaal blinked. "I'm not sure... I... If I tried to absorb her power, it'd be too much. It'd rip me apart."

"The healing disc!" exclaimed Ben. "The one Jasper gave us. Can we charge it with Eldred's energy?"

"I-I don't know," mumbled Towaal.

"We don't have anything else to try," declared Ben. "Do it."

He dug the disc out of his pouch and tossed it to Towaal. The disc bounced off her hands. She stooped and lifted it. Grimacing, she shuffled over to where Ben had thrown Eldred's head. She fell to her knees and placed a hand on the desiccated skull.

The runes flared to life, glowing blood red. The jaw snapped open, and Ben jumped, but Towaal remained calm.

"Ben," she whispered, "come here."

"Heal Rhys first," he demanded.

"He's dead, Ben, but I can help you."

Ben looked down at his friend. He wasn't breathing. The leaking blood had slowed to a trickle.

"Hurry, Ben," said Towaal, her voice quivering with strain, "I may be able to channel the energy through the disc, but if I hold it too long, it will destroy me. If I don't stop what she put inside you, you'll be dead before I am."

Ben shook his head.

"Seal his wounds first," he commanded.

Towaal met his eyes. Suddenly, a tingling warmth suffused Ben's body.

"I'll do what I can," promised the mage.

Trembling with strain, she poured energy into the disc and directed it back out at Ben. He felt it coursing through him. It pulsed along his veins, throbbing in time with his heart.

17

OUT OF THE WOODS

BEN LOOKED down at his scarred forearm.

"This will never heal," he grumbled.

Amelie, sitting next to him, snorted. "It's good to carry some scars in life. It reminds you of where you've been, what you've done, how you survived."

"She bit me," complained Ben. "The corpse of a dark mage using ancient death magic killed sixty of her own men and then bit me! Why do I want to remember that?"

"You did rip her head off," mentioned Amelie. "That's something you'll want to tell your children about one day."

Ben laughed. "That's true."

He paused.

"Children?"

Amelie shrugged but didn't look at him. "Maybe they'll think hearing you whine about your scar over and over again is attractive. I certainly don't."

Ben narrowed his eyes and stared at her.

"Healing energy can only boost your body's natural abilities," explained Towaal. "You can't heal something that is no longer there. That chunk of your body is gone, lost in the quarry or in her stomach I suppose."

Ben shuddered. "Do you think she ate real food and not just people's arms?"

Towaal shrugged. "I have no idea. I have no idea how they created her, either. As I said, healing magic can't bring back something that is gone. What the Veil did to her is dark, evil. They reanimated her and somehow brought her mind into that body, but it was twisted. I can't imagine how filthy her soul must have been inside of there, inside of that thing. It didn't survive on food. It survived on death. It makes me cringe to think about the number of people she murdered to sustain herself between here, Irrefort, and Hamruhg."

Ben set down the piece of sausage he'd been eating.

Amelie saw it and grinned.

"I don't think I'll ever be able to eat again with this arm without getting a queasy stomach." He sighed. "I need an ale."

"Me too," rasped a muffled voice.

Ben turned and saw Rhys peeking out from under his bedroll.

"You're supposed to be resting," chided Ben. "According to Lady Towaal, you were technically dead for a while there."

"I rest better after a few ales," groused the rogue. "Besides, if that witch couldn't kill me, a pint isn't going to do it either."

"We'll stop at the first tavern we find," assured Ben.

Rhys rolled over and the companions were quiet until soft snores rolled out from under the blanket.

"He'll need weeks to recover enough to travel," murmured Towaal.

"Should we move him to Akew Woods?" wondered Ben.

Towaal shook her head. "Maybe in a few days. For now, I think even that may be too much strain on him. We'll need to go back there to collect supplies, though. Now that Eldred is finished, it should be safe for us. Relatively safe, I mean."

Ben nodded. It was a pirate town. Safe compared to the dark mage wasn't saying much.

"I agree we need to get supplies," said Amelie. "We have a month of hard travel to reach the City. We've heard there are people in the forest, but I don't think we can count on them to provision us. We should be prepared to live on what we can bring or what we can forage for."

Towaal nodded. "There are tribes in the forest, but little is known of them even in the Sanctuary. They're said to be a people devoid of magic, but I find that hard to believe. I think that is more of an excuse for the mages to ignore them. Some have claimed they're all bandits, but there's not enough commerce through the region to support that. They trade in Akew Woods, according to the sailors on Martin's vessel, so perhaps we can learn more about them there."

"Tomorrow then," said Ben. "We'll venture into Akew Woods, gather supplies, and learn what we can about the forests. Maybe we can even pick up a skin of ale or two for Rhys. That'd be okay to give to him, wouldn't it?"

"He's right. If ale hasn't killed him yet, it never will."

THE NEXT MORNING, Ben and Amelie stood at the edge of the trees and looked down at Akew Woods. The town sparkled in the morning sun. The harbor was full of ships, and it was bustling with activity. Some vessels were rushing to make it out on the morning tide, and some were headed to the docks to load or unload. All along the wharf, workers bustled about between the ships and the warehouses. The heart of commerce beat strongly.

In other parts of the town, they could see small figures moving through the streets, likely doing the same kinds of errands they did in Farview or Issen. Housewives getting fresh baked bread, children running loose before they were sent off to school or to an apprenticeship, husbands working their trades. The routines of the morning were much the same in any town, Ben had found. Everything they could see was so normal, the people so ignorant of the conflict that had happened just a league away.

"These people are happy," remarked Ben.

"Blissfully unaware, I think they call it," responded Amelie.

"To think, this time two days ago, Eldred woke up under one of those roofs. Utter evil slept beside them and sat in their taverns, and they probably didn't know it. How could they not? How could they not sense it and want to fight it? Even if they simply ran, I would understand that."

"People don't see things until they are right in front of them, until they can't look away," answered Amelie. "Also, I think for some, it's easier to ignore what is happening. Surely, even here, some of them must suspect the demon threat is growing. Someone must have noticed all of Eldred's soldiers in town. It didn't affect them, though, not that day, so they ignored it."

Ben grunted.

"It's the nature of man," continued Amelie. "Ignore what you can. Only face what you have to."

"Are you suggesting we should ignore what's happening?" inquired Ben.

Amelie shook her head. "These people are ignorant, innocent. Even if they weren't, they don't have the skills to face what we did yesterday. Even if they wanted to, they would have caused more harm than good by getting themselves killed and feeding that awful thing. With guidance and leadership, people like this can stand up to a few demons and maybe even make a difference in a conflict like the Alliance and the Coalition, but they need people like us to protect them from the rest."

"Someone has to fight the monsters?"

"Someone has to fight the monsters," agreed Amelie, "and it might as well be us."

Ben hitched his belt, feeling his longsword bump against his leg. "Eldred's dead. That's one monster down."

"Don't forget the Purple," reminded Amelie. "No one knew the true threat they represented, but we stopped them as well."

"Monster fighters," smirked Ben. "Do you think that's what they'll call us? It's not very catchy."

Amelie smiled at him. "I think they'll call us heroes."

Ben stood beside Amelie, looking down the hill at Akew Woods. They stayed there for several long moments, basking in the normalcy of it.

"I hope they don't call us anything," said Ben, finally. "I hope they never know what happened in that quarry, and that they never have to worry about the darkness that exists in this world."

"I understand," responded Amelie quietly.

They watched as a group of children raced out of the town gates and scampered over the rocks and moss that lined the road. They were playing a game of tag or running for the simple joy of it.

"Those children are innocent," said Amelie, gesturing to them. "I wish we could keep them all that way."

"We'd better get to it then," replied Ben with a grin. "The Veil, the Alliance and the Coalition, and the demons. We have a lot to do."

"We do," agreed Amelie, "but first, breakfast."

They made their way down the hill and to the town of Akew Woods, watching the children play in the sun-drenched field.

18

REVIEWS, ACKNOWLEDGEMENTS, AND NEWSLETTER

I'M AN INDEPENDENT AUTHOR, and it's a tough world out there. If you enjoyed the book, please consider making it a little easier on me and leaving a review on Amazon and/or Goodreads. Then go tell your friends.

Special thanks for this book go to James Z for his beta reading services. I encourage everyone to hold him responsible for any logical inconsistencies that remain. I also have to thank my wife for allowing me to stay holed up in my office while she dealt with the kids – including a brand new baby! She let me sleep at night, battling the little guy alone. I can't overstate how important that was to getting this book finished.

I've had the same professional team involved in all of my books. My cover and social media package were designed by Milos from Deranged Doctor Design (www.derangeddoctordesign.com). Milos did a great job of creating covers that match the feel of the books. The cover for Empty Horizon is easily my favorite from the set of six covers Milos has done for me. Inside the cover, Nicole Zoltack yet again did great work proof-reading (www.nicolezoltack.com). She's proven that I know almost nothing about the English language. I met her in person for the first time at a writer's conference the day after I e-mailed the Empty Horizon draft. She refrained from sharing with our fellow authors just how bad those drafts are before she does her magic. I'm grateful for that as well. Tantor Media is my audiobook publisher. After reading this, I'm certain you'll want to give it a listen as well. The audiobooks can be found on all major online outlets. Eric Michael Summerer is the narrator and he did truly amazing work.

Thank you for reading my book,
AC

TO STAY UPDATED and find out when the next book is due, or to receive **FREE Benjamin Ashwood short stories**, I suggest signing up for my Newsletter. In addition to the short stories, I stick in author interviews, news & events, and whatever else I think may be of interest. One e-mail a month, no SPAM, that's a promise. Website and Newsletter Sign up: https://www.accobble.com/newsletter/

Of course I'm on **Facebook** too: https://www.facebook.com/ACCobble/

If you want the really exclusive, behind the scenes stuff, then **Patreon** is the place to be. There are a variety of ways you can support me, and corresponding rewards where I give back! Find me on **Patreon**: https://www.patreon.com/accobble

BURNING TOWER: Benjamin Ashwood Book 5 is available now! You can find it at nearly any online book retailer.